FOR
Jeffrio-Mio

PRAISE FOR *CLOSET CASE*

"A HILARIOUS FOLLOW-UP [to *Fag Hag*] . . . Rodi fans should rush out and buy this novel immediately."
—*Out*

"FUN TO READ . . . Grows comically with each turn of the page."
—*Library Journal*

"A WINNER ON ALL LEVELS . . . Robert Rodi will doubtless become one of the premier gay humorists."
—*Bay Windows*

"Here's a book for Gay and Lesbian Pride Month . . . Roars to its much awaited finale."
—*Advocate*

"CLEVER . . . RODI'S CARICATURE OF OFFICE POLITICS IS A HOOT."
—*Kirkus Reviews*

"UTTERLY HILARIOUS . . . Rodi writes in a breezy straightforward style . . . You'll experience anew what it's like to laugh with a book."
—*New City Chicago*

"CLEVERLY STRUCTURED AND CONSISTENTLY FUNNY."
—*Christopher Street*

"Gladdens the hearts of closeted homosexuals and hopeless romantics."
—*Publishers Weekly*

"A FAST AND FUNNY BOOK . . . entertains all the way through."
—*Dallas Voice*

ROBERT RODI, a former closet case, is an advertising copywriter who lives in Chicago with his partner, Jeffrey Smith. He is the author of two other novels, *Fag Hag* and *What They Did to Princess Paragon*.

closet case

case

A NOVEL BY **robert rodi**

A PLUME BOOK

PLUME
Published by the Penguin Group
Penguin Books USA Inc., 375 Hudson Street, New York, New York 10014, U.S.A.
Penguin Books Ltd, 27 Wrights Lane, London W8 5TZ, England
Penguin Books Australia Ltd, Ringwood, Victoria, Australia
Penguin Books Canada Ltd, 10 Alcorn Avenue, Toronto, Ontario, Canada M4V 3B2
Penguin Books (N.Z.) Ltd, 182–190 Wairau Road, Auckland 10, New Zealand

Penguin Books Ltd, Registered Offices: Harmondsworth, Middlesex, England

Published by Plume, an imprint of Dutton Signet, a division of Penguin Books USA Inc.
Previously published in a Dutton edition.

First Plume Printing, May, 1994
10 9

REGISTERED TRADEMARK—MARCA REGISTRADA

LIBRARY OF CONGRESS CATALOGING-IN-PUBLICATION DATA
Rodi, Robert.
    Closet case : a novel / by Robert Rodi.
        p.   cm.
    ISBN 0-452-27211-4
    1. Gay men—United States—Fiction.   2. Coming out (Sexual
orientation)—Fiction.   I. Title.
[PS3568.O34854C56   1994]
813'.54—dc20   93–47343
                                                        CIP

Printed in the United States of America
Designed by Leonard Telesca

PUBLISHER'S NOTE
This is a work of fiction. Names, characters, places, and incidents either are the
product of the author's imagination or are used fictitiously, and any resemblance
to actual persons, living or dead, events, or locales is entirely coincidental.

BOOKS ARE AVAILABLE AT QUANTITY DISCOUNTS WHEN USED TO PROMOTE PRODUCTS
OR SERVICES. FOR INFORMATION PLEASE WRITE TO PREMIUM MARKETING DIVISION,
PENGUIN BOOKS USA INC., 375 HUDSON STREET, NEW YORK, NEW YORK 10014.

prologue

It was coming.

Everyone *knew* it was coming.

The floodlights had just gone out with a sharp, electric snap and a brief, otherworldly echo. The set's high-contrast, construction-paper garishness receded at once into the more muted tones of everyday life. The air, too, rushed in cool and sweet the moment the floods stopped their blistering barrage. It was like a return to reality from a gaudy, one-dimensional fantasyland.

The actor, his task completed, donned his black leather jacket, shook Hackett Perlman's hand, and headed for the door.

And everyone knew it was coming. It was definitely, positively coming.

They'd known it as soon as the actor displayed his complete ignorance of how to operate an electric chainsaw, which was his sole responsibility in the commercial they were shooting. He didn't even have any lines; he was merely obliged to stride manfully onto the set, turn on that state-of-the-art hunk of hardware, and attack a cord of firewood like a pit bull mauling a ferret.

So when he'd had to be taught how to start the saw—and then appeared actually *frightened* of it once it was up and running—virtually every man on the set experienced a little thrill of superiority, a little reinforcing jolt of his own

unquestionable maleness. Every one of them took a figura-
tive step away from the actor, and where their manner
toward him had previously been informed by camaraderie,
now it was colored by the condescending, anti-male taint
of courtesy. Every one of them was thinking the same thing.
But who would be the first to come out and *say* it?

When the slab of metal door fell into place behind the
actor, shutting him out physically just as the crew had shut
him out socially, Hackett Perlman got a wicked glint in his
eye and scurried over to the spot where his client and two
colleagues were waiting. He lowered his excessively suntanned head and grinned. And it was he who finally said it—
that potent little word, that *oh*-so-hilarious slur, that instant
excommunication from the realm of the worthy:

"Fag."

Then Perlman, who was the creative director at Deming,
Stark & Williams Advertising, rolled back on his heels and
laughed, as though that single damning syllable had been a
witticism worthy of the Algonquin Round Table on one of
its most memorably epigrammatic days. And sure enough, a
little eruption of laughter filled the studio and lightened its
mood, and the director and crew felt suddenly free to go
about clearing away the debris from the shoot. The tension
had been released; the air had been cleared.

But Lionel Frank, who was an account executive at the
same advertising agency, seemed to have more to say on the
matter. He nodded his head in the direction of the discarded
chainsaw and said, "Should've told him we wanted him to
sit on the fucking thing. He'd've found a way to turn it on,
all right."

Lionel's three companions offered up only token chuck-
les. After all, Lionel was the junior member of the foursome;
the other three men here—Perlman, Julius Deming, the
agency president, and Babcock Magellan, their client—were
all, officially, his superiors. He might have to laugh at their
jokes, but they didn't have to laugh at his. Still, this was a
brotherhood, wasn't it? A fellowship. They were gathered
for the manly purpose of producing a television commercial,
and now stood together, awash in a sea of commingled tes-
tosterone, exchanging profanity and merry insults—*bond-
ing*, as the vernacular would have it. If Lionel's high spirits

led him to try to claim executive joke privileges ... well, they'd give him a little rope.

Babcock Magellan even went so far as to encourage him, by hitting him on the back and saying, "Saw him look at you, boy. Could be waiting for you out in the parking lot. My advice is, when you go to your car, for God's sake don't drop your keys!"

Lionel laughed far too loudly and too long, and Magellan rang in with his own basso profundo roar, obviously enjoying having his wit flattered so outrageously. As the founder, president, and towering embodiment of All-Pro Power Tools—as well as a millionaire, philanthropist, yachting enthusiast, and somebody or other's Businessman of the Year every year for the last seven—he was accustomed to being surrounded by sycophants and yes-men; but few debased themselves before him as enthusiastically and good-naturedly as these three he'd hired to do his company's advertising. He liked them for it; and they *had* done a good job with this chainsaw spot. Even the lanky, skittish, perfectly coiffed actor they'd hired hadn't been a disaster, once he'd gotten some direction from Magellan.

Julius Deming, his face white as a billiard ball and nearly as shiny, pushed his glasses up his nose and said, "I don't know, Babcock. Lionel's been dressing awfully *fancy* lately." He reached over and fingered his employee's expensive silk tie. "Could be he's *trying* to find Mr. Right." And at the sight of Lionel's face, which now fell into a silent-movie spasm of horror, he and the others laughed all the harder.

Deming slapped Lionel on the back to show him he hadn't meant it, and then Perlman slapped him on the back as well, and Babcock Magellan punched him in the arm and winked at him—an almost unprecedented sign of favor. And then all four men looked at their watches, congratulated themselves on a job well done, and filed out of the studio and into the parking lot, where they paused to congratulate themselves one last time before getting into their cars.

"Congratulations, assholes," Magellan said as he depressed the button on his keychain that deactivated the auto theft alarm in his Jaguar. "Didn't think you cocksuckers could pull it off."

"Well, now you know what a couple of real men can do

with one of your cheap-shit production budgets," said Deming with a cocky smile as he unlocked the door of his Saab.

"Kiss my ass," said Magellan as he slipped into the Jaguar's driver's seat.

"You'd *like* that," said Lionel from out the window of his Celica.

"Not as much as *you* would," countered Perlman from his Beemer, prompting a last spate of laughter.

They all agreed to meet again in the edit suite the next day, then started their engines, backed up one by one, and drove out of the fenced-in parking lot in single file (Magellan first, of course, and Lionel last).

And Deming drove home to his wife Peg, and Perlman drove home to his wife Becky, and Magellan drove home to his wife Dolores (but not before stopping to see his mistress Wilma).

And Lionel didn't drive home at all. He started out in that direction, but after fifteen minutes a storm of recrimination and self-loathing and fear and anxiety overwhelmed him, and he knew he needed immediate release or he'd do something desperate, like swing his car into oncoming traffic.

From the highway he could see a shopping mall, its parking lot empty at this late hour. He slipped down the next exit ramp and made his way there.

He drove to the farthest side of the lot, where the trees were most concealing and the light from the overhead lamps most indirect.

He rested his head on the steering wheel and tried to get a grip on himself, but every time he closed his eyes, one image conjured itself up before him—the image of the actor leaving the set, of those splendid buttocks tucked so beautifully into the faded workman's jeans he'd worn for the filming. It had seemed to Lionel that, at alternating steps, each cheek had waved a sad little farewell to him, their ardent admirer for so many hours that day.

Finally, he could stand it no longer. He unzipped, picked up his car phone, and spent two-and-a-half budget-smashing hours dialing the numbers he'd come to know by heart: 1-900-BOY-TOYZ, 1-900-HOT-GUYZ, 1-900-CUM-QUIK . . .

part

1

chapter

■ ■ ■ ■ ■ ■ ■ ■ ■ ■ ■ ■ ■ ■ ■ ■ ■ ■ ■

one

Hackett Perlman didn't so much step into Lionel's office as insinuate himself in; that was his way. He was a slippery man, reptilian, and whenever he sat in the chair that faced Lionel's desk and crossed his legs, Lionel couldn't help but think of a snake coiling its body before striking.

"Got some news," he said, staring Lionel in the face with a cold smile that said, I know all of your secrets and will not keep them. It was the look he gave everybody, and one of the chief reasons for his success—it put all his subordinates in a state of expectant terror of him, as though he were a vampire or a Kamikaze pilot or some other inscrutable, alien-brained villain. But Lionel was accustomed to Perlman's air of B-movie menace, and knew it amounted to nothing.

He closed his radio rate book and pushed it aside, then sat back in his chair and put his hands behind his head. Very heterosexual, he thought this made him look. He rocked the chair back and forth. "Good news or bad?" he asked Perlman.

The creative director arched an eyebrow and said "Good" in a way that sounded like he really meant "Dreadful." Another of his paradoxical character traits, and another reason for his success; no matter how he praised his staff for their work, they always nervously decided that they'd better do better next time.

He lifted his hands and studiously pushed back one of his cuticles. "Remember the chainsaw spot?" he said, his dark, wet eyes fixed on his fingernails. His sunned-to-leather face wore a secretive smirk.

"Sure," said Lionel, still rocking back and forth. "One with the fag in it, right?" It slipped out of his mouth before he could stop himself.

Perlman stopped in mid-cuticle and looked up, puzzled for a moment; then he said, "Right. That's the one." He knit his brow and resumed his mini-manicure.

Lionel cautioned himself to be more careful; he'd made a blunder with that remark. It hadn't impressed Perlman as a butch witticism, which, he supposed, had been its intent. To Perlman, all fags were nonentities; he was sure to have long forgotten the chainsaw-shy actor who'd afforded him such mirth during the filming four months before. That Lionel not only remembered him, but associated the entire project with him, was potentially revealing; it had certainly struck Perlman as odd.

Fortunately, the creative director was so eager to deliver his news that he let the peculiarity of Lionel's comment drop. "Been nominated for a Trippy," he continued, referring to a mildly prestigious Chicago advertising award. He finished one final cuticle, then dropped his hands into his lap and looked at Lionel again. "Best Regional Spot, Budget Under Thirty-Thou."

"No shit," said Lionel, thinking that profanity was the best way to restore his masculine credentials. "What fuckin' *great* news. Congratulations!"

"Thanks. Anyway, thought you'd want to call Magellan and let him know." He peered at Lionel as though accusing him of murder. "Already reserved a place for him and his wife at our table."

"What table?" asked Lionel, suddenly on alert.

"One at the banquet," Perlman replied, untwining his legs in preparation for his departure. "Figured on eight of us: me and Becky, Deming and Peg, you and your date, and

Magellan and his wife. If Magellan can't make it, we'll take that new art director, Donna—you know, the dyke with the hearing aid. After all, she did the storyboards." He chuckled. "Just won't let her bring a date, that's all. Magellan'd go ballistic if we put him at a table with a couple of rug-munchers."

Lionel suppressed a little shudder. He was grateful to have a lesbian art director at the agency, because she diverted attention from him, serving as a lightning rod for any anti-gay sentiments among the staff. But, paradoxically, every expression of those sentiments made him feel more and more fearful of exposure. (They were so *virulent.*) And now the idea of the Trippy banquet made his fears suddenly and terrifyingly concrete.

His foot started tapping on the acrylic pad beneath his swivel chair. "Uh—when's the banquet? What date, I mean." He was trying to hide his anxiety.

"Two weeks," said Perlman. His tone was perfectly conversational, but Lionel could see the light glinting off his incisors; they looked like fangs. "Sixteenth. A Thursday." He rose from his chair and took a sliding step toward the door.

Lionel scooted his chair up to his desk and yelped, "Hey, you know, I—I—I might be—I think I *am*—busy that night. I honestly don't think I can make it."

Perlman grimaced. It was one of the only unpleasant expressions in his repertoire to have a genuine feeling behind it. "If Magellan's there, you'd better be, too," he said. "You know that. Whatever you have planned, cancel it." He didn't say, but didn't have to, that Magellan brought the agency close to a million in billings each year. The agency's partners were in no mood to risk displeasing a million-dollar client, especially since they'd just lost the Romeo Springs sparkling water account, which had also, unfortunately, been Lionel's. (The loss hadn't been his fault—the company had gone under due to a consumer panic following the discovery of traces of ammonia in some of their Light 'n' Lemon bottles—but Lionel had taken their departure badly, and was now terrified of losing his sole remaining account.)

He sighed. "Right. Right. Course I'll be there."

Perlman pursed his lips. "You okay?" His tone made it

sound like he was asking if Lionel had any last requests before his lethal injection.

"Yeah, fine," said Lionel, trying to sound butch and nodding his head like a speed-freak jack-in-the-box. "Totally."

Perlman nodded at Lionel's phone. "Don't forget to call Magellan."

"No, I won't, of course I won't."

Perlman slithered out into the hallway and Lionel dropped his head into his hands. He had to come up with a female date for the Trippy Awards banquet! It was enough to make him sick with anxiety. The last time something like this had happened, at the '91 City Awards, he'd invited an aerobics instructor from his health club, having heard she was a lesbian, only to find out after the banquet, when he drove her home, that she wasn't a lesbian at all—just very masculine in her approach to things. Lionel had to pay the tuxedo rental store for the damage to his zipper, and the scratch-marks on his car's front seat refused to come out no matter how much he buffed them with the twelve-dollars-a-pint vinyl restorer. Even worse, however, was having to go in to work the next day and answer all sorts of jocular questions about how he had "made out" and what Lisa was "like." Fortunately, he'd been able to fake some fairly satisfactory replies. The truth—that he had screamed and flailed like Fay Wray when Lisa grabbed his crotch, sending her running into the plus-one of her four-plus-one, laughing hysterically—was of course not remotely hinted at. After all, it was inconceivable that Babcock Magellan would place All-Pro Power Tools' multimillion-dollar advertising budget in the hands of a pansy. And it was out of the question that the scrotum-scratching, belching-contest atmosphere of the Deming, Stark & Williams Advertising offices could ever accommodate a queer.

That was why it was so imperative that Lionel find a date for the Trippys. To keep his job, it wasn't only necessary to appear not gay; he had to appear actively straight, which, since his job involved maintaining that appearance from ten to sometimes twelve hours every workday, was tantamount to actually having to *be* straight.

And yet Lionel didn't consider himself repressed; he would've told you—if you could ever have gotten him to discuss it with you, which you couldn't—that he actually got a kind of charge out of being closeted, that he felt an illicit thrill at being in what amounted to the enemy's camp, making money off them and passing among them freely, unassailed. He might also have told you that he enjoyed the challenge—it kept him so nimble, so sharp, so *focused*— and that he enjoyed the opportunities to demonstrate (if only to himself) the vast powers of his wit and intellect, as they lifted him, invariably within seconds, safely out of every perilous situation into which he strayed (such as the time he was discovered alone in an absent secretary's office, staring at her Chippendale Dancers wall calendar; he'd immediately explained that he was just checking the date to see if it was Rosh Hashanah or something, because that would explain why Mindy wasn't at her desk). It was, in short, a joy to have so many opportunities to be so *clever.*

But his cleverness was failing him now. In his head, he ran through the list of single women he knew. They were few, and very far between. In fact, he didn't know many people, period. His life, being so bound up in his career, left him little time for friendships outside the office. With the exception of his hairdresser friend, Toné, he didn't even have any gay buddies. And he sometimes wondered how often he'd see Toné if he didn't need his hair cut once a month.

No, almost everyone with whom Lionel shared even a passing acquaintance was right here in this office.

That's when he thought of Tracy. She was Julius Deming's secretary, and the object of lust for at least three members of the account staff. She was a petite woman, with bobbed blond hair and a precious pug nose—a woman, in short, with the kind of kid-sister beauty that at first is easily dismissed, but which after repeated exposure proves irresistible.

Best of all, she and Lionel had been openly flirting for more than a year. It had started out as banter, playful exchanges about the weather, the clothes they were wearing, the gossip around the office. Lionel liked the fact that he could make her laugh, and that she laughed so easily and unabashedly. Soon they'd developed a kind of language of their own. They would pass each other in the hallways and sing a monotone "La-la-la-la-la" at each other, which was their way of saluting each other affectionately when they were too busy to stop and talk.

Things accelerated when someone gave Tracy a battery-operated monkey that when switched on repeatedly clapped together a pair of tiny cymbals. One day Lionel, being silly, named the monkey Abner, and over subsequent weeks he would stop by Tracy's office several times a day, chattering at length with her about Abner, telling her about his upbringing and early life, and how he'd left his native Nairobi wildlife preserve to pursue his dream of being a stunt double for the Prince of Wales, only to be jailed for the attempted rape of a penny arcade fortune-telling machine, and Tracy would invariably end up helpless with laughter. But whenever anyone came into Tracy's office to see what all the mirth was about, she and Lionel would immediately clam up; Abner was their secret reference, and they were unwilling to share him with anyone else. The erotic connotations of this were impossible to ignore.

Once, Lionel made the mistake of telling Toné about his weird office flirtation with this woman.

"Mon brave," Toné had said, yanking three finger-widths of Lionel's wet hair from his head and snipping off the ends with a scissors, "you are setting up that young girl for a disappointment *énorme."*

"Don't be ridiculous," he said. "She's got a boyfriend."

"Whom she would drop in an *instant* if you bade her come be with you." (Toné always talked like this.)

"Look," Lionel said testily—and as he said it a few of his clipped hairs fell onto his tongue, making him even more irritable—"you're always saying that straight people are screwing themselves up by not exploring their gay side. Well, I'm just exploring my *straight* side a little, okay? If I don't do this, maybe I'll screw *myself* up."

Toné sprayed his head with an atomizer, silencing him. "Just don't screw up that *jeune fille* while you're bounding happily toward self-realization," he cautioned. "No one's mental health is worth the broken heart of a poor, innocent *gamine.* Not even yours."

Lionel didn't give Toné's words a second thought, until some of the women in the office began making subtle remarks—in his presence!—about his and Tracy's future together. Then he panicked and, pleading busyness, began to drastically curtail his visits to Tracy's office. When the agency lost Romeo Springs, his workload temporarily lessened, but he didn't take the opportunity to renew his platonic courtship. He was too frightened to do so. It was a shame, really; he missed Tracy.

Well, this was the perfect opportunity to see more of her. She was still involved with her boyfriend, but he'd heard through the grapevine that they were feuding at present, so there was no barrier to her accepting Lionel's invitation. And she *would* accept, he was sure of that. They *liked* each other; they'd have fun, and she would know that.

Best of all, she was, well, not innocent, exactly, but kind of proper; a real *lady,* that rarest of beasts, almost extinct in the postwar prairie states—like the bison, only less intensely mourned. There would be no attempt at date-rape in his car if Tracy were his companion. And the day after the banquet, they could simply resume their friendship, just as it was before. Tracy might be a little mystified, but ... she still had a boyfriend, didn't she? She couldn't complain.

Thrilled with this brainstorm, he wasted no time but marched through the maze of corridors to Tracy's office. He poked his head around the doorframe and caught her typing a letter, one key at a time, as she read aloud from a stenopad: "A ..." Clack. "L ..." Clack. "S, E ..." Clack, clack.

"Show-off," he said.

She looked up and blushed crimson. He liked that about her. No one blushed as deeply, or as quickly, as she did—not even characters in cartoons. *"Pig,"* she said. "I can't *believe* you caught me doing that. It's this guy's name. It's got about twenty-six letters and I can never spell it from memory."

He strode in and sat before her desk. "Haven't checked in for a while. How's Abner?"

She leaned over and turned Abner's switch on and off a few times; nothing happened. She looked at Lionel and shook her head prettily. "Abner's on the roof and I can't get him down."

He laughed. "Get some batteries from Elsa."

"For an office toy? A *personal* item? Right. I can just see her deducting the cost of two triple As from my paycheck."

They smiled at each other, and there was a brief, rather unwieldy pause.

"Listen," Lionel said, looking down at his shoe, which he ground into the floor as if there were a palmetto bug beneath the heel. "I've been working like a sonofabitch, and—"

"I know, I know, I see your light on every night when I leave." She turned from her typewriter and folded her arms over her blotter. Her attention was completely his.

"I have no life, Tracy. I admit this." He ripped a page from her *Far Side* desk calendar and started to fold it into an accordion shape. "I have a parrot at home who doesn't recognize me. He's bonded with the mice in the apartment instead."

She didn't laugh; she wore a look of almost luminous expectation.

He cleared his throat and said, "Seriously, I have to go to the Trippy Awards banquet, and if I don't bring a date Magellan's going to start thinking I'm queer." He occasionally said things like this, to present the idea of him being gay as being so utterly ridiculous as to be funny. "And, well, I know you're still seeing Guy, but if he c—"

"Guy's a pig," she said. "Pig" was her all-purpose slur.

"Well, I was just going to say, if he can let you go for a night, maybe you'd like to come with me—to the Trippy banquet. It'd be a blast."

Her eyes actually flashed. Lionel always thought it a mere figure of speech.

And suddenly she looked incomparably lovelier than she had only a moment before. "Be your date, to the Trippy Awards?" she said, smiling brilliantly. "I assume there is a large fee involved."

He laughed, delighted and terrified by her acceptance, but mainly terrified.

chapter

■ ■

two

The dance bar called The Hague was a safe place for Lionel to visit, because its clientele wasn't exclusively gay—just predominantly. Male strippers might strut across its strategically placed platforms in G-strings and snakeskin boots, but on the dance floor itself, yuppies, dinks, japs, and other acronymed members of main-stream Chicago rubbed elbows with drag queens, hustlers, and lipstick lesbians. The music was the attraction; gay clubs were known for playing better dance tracks than their straight counterparts, and The Hague was arguably the best gay dance club in town.

Having successfully arranged a heterosexual, if platonic, liaison during office hours, Lionel felt he could allow himself a little side trip into the gay nightlife on the way home from work. He hadn't left the office till seven-thirty, so by the time he arrived at The Hague, it was just past eight. For a weeknight, that wasn't too early to see some excitement.

He walked in the door and loosened his tie. He liked appearing here in his workday garb; it was off-putting. It made him look not gay and available, but hip enough to be in a gay club even though obviously straight.

Heads turned briefly at his entrance—young heads, long

and angular, with manes of wavy hair and swooping sideburns—before turning away, unimpressed. Lionel knew he
was attractive but had deliberately made himself bland looking; he didn't want to appear too conscious of his appearance, lest someone at the office suspect that he was gay.
Still, he'd spent so many years playing down his attract-
iveness that now he wasn't sure he could remember how
to play it up again, and the absence of the kind of lingering
glances he'd expected caused him a little pang of regret.

But then, from the far side of the bar, he felt the unmis-
takable pressure of eyes upon him, and his spirits lifted; he
was being cruised. Careful not to meet the gaze of his admirer, he went to the bar and ordered an Amstel Light. (In
non-gay bars, he always ordered a Rolling Rock instead of
a light beer; wouldn't do to have anyone think he was
watching his weight, like some prissy queen.)

He slid a trio of dollar bills across the counter, then turned
away quickly, still acutely aware of the eyes across the bar
that were boring into him like All-Pro power drills. Growing
a little uncomfortable with this attention, he lifted the bottle
to his lips and took a long, cold swallow, then sauntered over
to the dance floor, where colored lights flashed in counter-
point to the heavy thump-thumpa-thump of the music video
being played on the various monitors around the perimeter
of the floor. Men were dancing with men by the dozens. It
was *really* gay in here tonight; there were almost no straight
people to be seen. Which of course increased the homoerotic
charge to the air, and made his predicament even worse. He
kept thinking, I'm being watched, I have to look hot, I have
to look attractive. But who's cruising me? And why can't I
bring myself to cruise back?

He started sweating at the idea of meeting someone in a
bar, someone he might even take home to bed. It had
been—God—more than a year since he'd done anything like
that. He'd never be able to go through with it tonight; he'd
lost the knack—he was terrified. He kept hoping that the
eyes would just leave him, melt away, or at least move on
to another, more responsive target. They'd followed him
more than long enough to gratify his ego; now it was just
plain awkward to be stared at this way.

Finally, he could bear it no longer. He had to confront

his admirer. Taking a big, straight-guy chug from his Amstel, he casually turned his head and let his glance fall, as if accidentally, on the man who had been eyeing him so insistently.

Jesus H. Christ on a *moped.*

It was *Toné*!

The hairdresser lifted his glass—it looked like he was drinking his usual Brandy Alexander—and nodded his head in salutation.

Lionel stormed over to him. "For Christ's *sake,* Toné, why were you *staring* at me like that? Almost gave me a fucking *heart* attack."

Toné swept back his jet-black, shoulder-length hair in indignation. *"Excusez-moi, mon brave,"* he trilled. "One didn't mean to cause discomfort. One simply recognized one of one's *intimes,* that is all."

"Then why didn't you just yell out a *hello,* for God's sake?"

Toné put one of his spectacularly manicured hands over his heart, as if appalled at the suggestion. "Because, *mon brave,* one does not *yell* in polite society. Aside from which, one suspected you might be, well, on the *prowl,* as it were. And one enjoyed the idea of watching you make a connection with some *garçon* of great beauty and loose morals."

Lionel blushed crimson. "I didn't come here for *that.*"

"Well, that makes one of us." He took another sip of his drink, apparently ready to dismiss the subject.

Lionel, however, wasn't quite so ready. True, he didn't want to have a sexual encounter with anyone tonight, but the possibility that he *could* excited him, and he wanted to hear Toné conjecture about it at greater length. "Anyway," he said, prompting his friend, "who would I pick up here? No one's my type."

Toné looked around the bar; Lionel hoped he would select a possible date for him just so he could protest that whoever it was would never go out with him, causing Toné to reassure him that that wasn't the case, and so on—all material Lionel could use to build a whale of a fantasy during his next jerk-off session.

But after a moment more, the hairdresser disappointed him by shaking his head. "You're right, *il n'y a personne* for you here tonight," he said in his irritating hybrid of English and fragmentary French. "But then, if none of the *beaux hommes* here is your type, one is less inclined to place blame on them than one is to place it on *you.*" He looked Lionel up and down, appraising him as if he were a prize heifer at a 4-H convention. "When one dresses in a blue suit from Capper and Capper, *cheri,* accented by a tie spangled with mallard ducks that one is certain must have a twin in Dan Quayle's closet—well, one mustn't expect to become the cause of much swooning at The Hague, any more than one would wear a red silk teddy and fishnet stockings to be interviewed by the Daughters of the American Revolution, and then expect to be invited to join." He chuckled, pleased with the analogy.

Lionel frowned. "I look fine." He angrily tried to take a swig of beer, but the bottle hit his tooth like a sledgehammer. He spat out the beer and clutched his mouth in agony.

"One might say that your *hair* looks fine," said Toné, who, being half Japanese and therefore well-versed in the sophisticated art of saving face for others, pretended not to notice the mishap. "One *might* say that, but one's modesty prevents one." He finished off his Brandy Alexander and handed the empty glass to a passing busboy, smiling coyly.

Lionel leaned against a pillar, holding his mouth. "I fing I broag my fugging toof," he moaned.

Toné, not about to let Lionel embarrass himself by admitting to self-inflicted pain, continued to ignore the little accident. He rolled up the sleeves of his linen jacket and said, "So, tell one, how is that *jeune fille* who slaves away in the salt mines with you? You know, the one whose heart you have so treacherously ensnared?"

"Oh, shud ub," said Lionel, testing his tooth with his thumb and forefinger. It felt whole, and didn't seem to have been loosened. Fear and pain subsiding, he removed his hand from his mouth and said, "How many times do we have to go through this? She's got a steady boyfriend."

Toné rolled his eyes. "Of course she does. Stupid of one to forget."

"Look, we're just *friends.* For God's *sake.*" He took another mouthful of beer, more carefully this time.

At that moment, the video screens went blank, and the

crowd on the dance floor gathered around a platform. It must be time for the first of the strippers to come on. Lionel shrank back into a shadow, not wanting to be seen ogling any nearly naked men. But his pulse thrummed with excitement; even from his scant few ventures to The Hague over the years, he'd become familiar with some of its regular strippers, and he had his favorites. Would it be Jerry the cowboy, tonight? García the construction worker? Bill the fireman?

"Ladies and gentlemen," said a voice over the speaker system, "The Hague is proud to present, for the very first time on our stage, 'Father' Todd!"

A new disco number started, and after several tantalizing beats, a tall, bearded man in priest drag gyrated onto the stage.

Lionel, who had spent his formative years sitting quietly at Sunday mass fantasizing that his church's handsome, young assistant pastor was wearing nothing at all under his cassock, felt something lurch forward and drop in his stomach. This was an irresistible, powerful fantasy figure for him: the horny, hairy, hot-tamale pastor; the priest who puts out; the father confessor with bikini tan lines. His throat went dry and his palms started to sweat. He really had to get out of here; by the same token, he really had to stay and watch. The warring imperatives clashed in his head and his loins, and made him itchy and fidgety and nervous.

When "Father" Todd teasingly began unbuttoning his cassock, revealing a blood-red rosary nestled in the crevice of an extraordinarily woolly chest, Lionel had to fight back faintness. Since he couldn't bear to watch, but couldn't bear to leave either, he decided to try to distract himself by continuing his conversation with Toné, who, after all, didn't like hairy men, and who was tapping his toes to the music rather dreamily, paying only the most obligatory attention to the show.

"As a matter of fact," Lionel said to him now, in as confidential a tone as the booming bass track would allow, "I *do* have sort of a platonic date coming up with her. The secretary, I mean. Tracy."

Toné turned his head slowly, like a crocodile. Then he raised an eyebrow and said, *"Oh?"*

"It's for a business function," he explained, trying not to stare at Father Todd's cassock, which was now gathered around his waist, catching the beads of sweat that fell from his naked chest and armpits as he writhed to the music. "The Trippy Awards," Lionel continued, his speech getting both faster and more halting. "We've won an award—for— a commercial we did—for one of our clients—we—" He finally had to turn away from the strip show entirely. He stepped around, his back to Father Todd and his face to Toné. "It's just platonic," he insisted. "She's from the office. It's a work function. She works there. So ..." His voice trailed off in defeat.

Toné raised his other eyebrow, and Lionel thought, Why the hell did I even bring this up? If I didn't get so god-damned weird at the sight of a male stripper ...

The hairdresser sighed and said, "Lionel, you *must* tell that *pauvre petite* that you're gay before she accompanies you to this event."

Lionel's jaw dropped. "Are you *crazy?*"

"*Pas du tout. Trust* one on this, *mon brave.* She has entirely different expectations from this *soirée* than you do. Business affair or not."

"You don't even know her."

"One doesn't *need* to know her, *cher ami.* One has heard all the stories you've told one. That girl is in love with you."

Lionel let his eyes fall shut and shook his head. "She's not, Toné. She's not, she's not, she's not."

"She is, she is, she is." He smiled and lowered his head. "Oh, dear, this *is* regressing into nonsense, *n'est-ce pas?*" He put his hand on Lionel's shoulder. "You'll be needing a trim before the *soirée,* of course."

Lionel shrugged. "Guess so."

"Then by all means, call one *à demain* and make an appointment. And in the meantime, consider what one has just told you." His eyes darted across the bar. "And now, if you'll excuse one, one thinks one might be about to meet the love of one's life." He leaned over and gave Lionel a gentle kiss on the lips, then trotted away.

Vaguely disturbed by the conversation, Lionel turned around in time to catch Father Todd tearing away his leather panties, revealing a purple satin G-string with a cru-cifix on the pouch. A moist patch of dirty-blond pubic hair crept out of the pouch and up his taut abdomen, collecting in a little furry circle around his navel.

Transfixed by the sight, Lionel stared in helpless lust as the stripper put his hands behind his head and commenced bumping and grinding, bumping and grinding, until his pelvis seemed to generate enough kinetic energy to fill the electricity needs of the better part of Chicago's lakefront. Lionel's mouth fell open.

A medium-size eternity later, he noticed someone waving at him. He managed to tear his gaze away from Father Todd and looked to see who it was.

There were two women, arm in arm, like lovers. And the one who was waving at him was Donna, the new art director at the agency.

All color seeped out of his face; his blood seemed to stand still in his veins. How long had she been watching him? How much had she seen of him staring, mesmerized, at the crotch of a male stripper? Had she witnessed the feline, effeminate Toné leaning over and kissing him?

An even worse possibility occurred to him: Donna, who was deaf, communicated with hearing people by reading their lips. Lionel had heard her, at the office, brag that if there was enough light, she could eavesdrop on private, intimate conversations that were taking place across a crowded bar or restaurant. Had she been reading his lips the entire time he'd been talking to Toné?

It was his worst nightmare come true: being nailed by someone from his office, for God's sake! For years, he'd been so careful, not letting any hint of his sexuality leak out to even the farthest removed acquaintances of his co-workers and clients, only to blow it now with someone who worked just down the hall from him!

He should've been more careful of her. He'd known Donna was gay from the day she started—*everyone* knew it. To *look* at her was to know it. (She wore a crew cut and had shoulders like a linebacker! She wore Doc Marten boots! She chewed tobacco!) And the relentless, increasingly filthy dyke jokes that had since been told behind her back (*literally* behind her back, as there was no danger of her overhearing them) had the effect of pushing Lionel farther and farther into his metaphorical closet, until he was trapped behind metaphorical tennis rackets and ski boots and piles of old, metaphorical magazines, utterly and hopelessly trapped.

Accordingly, he'd distanced himself from Donna, and had felt safe in doing so; after all, there was little enough chance of ever running into her on gay turf, since Lionel seldom ventured there; and even when he did, well, lesbians had their own exclusive stomping grounds from which they seldom strayed. But Lionel hadn't considered The Hague. *Everybody* came to The Hague.

Donna was still waving at him, her eyes wide and excited. He managed a trembling half-smile, then mouthed the words "See you tomorrow" and bolted from the bar.

In the cool night air, away from the press of bodies and the smell of sweat and the stinging aura of cigarette smoke, he felt as if he'd just awakened from a bad dream. I shouldn't be so silly about this, he scolded himself; Donna isn't going to say anything. It's *ridiculous* to worry about her tattling on me like some anal retentive second-grader.

Even so, as he walked to his car, he couldn't help dreaming up increasingly outlandish plots to *ensure* her silence. He could, for instance, try to get her fired; he could steal art supplies from the storeroom, then say he'd seen her take them. He could even hide them in her office, to be discovered by Elsa, the office manager (who was certainly the type to go and look). But didn't all art directors steal supplies all the time, anyway?

He could always plant cocaine in her desk. But hell, management would probably offer to *buy* it from her.

He could spread a rumor that she was mentally unstable and had been fired from her last job for irrational behavior, except that that came pretty close to describing the work history of about half the creatives in the advertising business.

By the time he caught himself thinking about ways to slip cyanide into her morning Diet Coke, he decided he'd better stop this deranged panicking and just face the problem like a man. If he couldn't bring himself to trust Donna, he'd just have to talk to her, tell her flat out that he'd appreciate her keeping mum about his unorthodox sexuality. It was his private business, after all. Wasn't it?

Well, *wasn't* it?

chapter

■ ■ ■ ■ ■ ■ ■ ■ ■ ■ ■ ■ ■ ■ ■ ■ ■

three

Lionel pulled up in front of the Victorian six-flat he called home. It was only nine-thirty but it felt like four in the morning. As he let himself in the front door and began his lonely trek up the stairs, he tried not to think about Tracy anymore, and certainly not about Donna. All he wanted was to settle into bed, dial a 1-900 number, and ask if they had any hot priests he could talk to. Would they think he was kinky? Might they laugh at him? Well, he'd risk it. As disturbed as he was about having been caught at The Hague by Donna, he didn't actually regret having been there, not with Father Todd still gyrating seductively in his head.

"Forgive me, Father, for I haven't sinned," he muttered to himself as he rounded the second-floor landing and continued climbing the stairs to his apartment. "At least, not nearly enough for someone my age."

He sighed mournfully as he put his key in the lock. To his surprise, the door swung open without his having raised the latch. He furrowed his brow, took a step inside, and set his briefcase on the floor of the hallway. The lights in the apartment were already lit. "Hello?" he called out, shutting the door behind him.

"Oh, Lionel, *hello,*" came a voice from the far end of the railroad apartment. Then Yolanda Reynoso darted out of the kitchen, dressed to kill. "I am sorry for being here so late," she said breathily, her stiletto heels tapping against the hardwood floors as she scurried down the hallway to greet him. "But I heard Spencer just screaming and screaming, so I came up to see if something was the matter with him." Spencer was Lionel's pet cockatoo; since Yolanda lived in the apartment directly below his, she couldn't help but hear the bird's blood-curdling shrieks.

Lionel untied his Dan Quayle tie and let it hang like a stole around his neck. "It's okay," he said. "Listen, I appreciate you coming up to look after him. You don't have to apologize." Yolanda worked most nights as a cashier in a science-fiction bookstore, so Lionel had given her keys to his apartment and invited her to come up during the day and play with Spencer anytime she wanted. "I mean, if it weren't for you, he'd get no companionship at all."

She smiled brilliantly, then leaned over, kissed him on the cheek, and headed back to the kitchen. Lionel followed her, appreciating—in a purely aesthetic sense—the gorgeous roundness of what Toné would call her *derriére,* which tonight was being hugged by an exquisitely clingy rose cocktail dress. She was also wearing dangly-jangly earrings, and had teased her hair into the kind of wild, Medusa-tendril state that drove straight men into a condition of sexual frenzy. *If only someone from the office could've come home with me tonight,* Lionel thought, *just to see me get greeted with a kiss by a woman who looks like this!*

"You look *terrific,*" he said, doffing his jacket and slipping it over the back of one of the cane chairs in his sparsely furnished kitchen. "Going out somewhere?"

"Yes, I am having a late dinner with Bob." She picked up Spencer from the floor, where she'd spread out Lionel's pots and pans for the bird to play with (he was entranced by his reflection and loved the sound he made when he banged his beak against the lids). "I am not used to eating so late; I may die of hunger before he gets here." She ran her hand over the cockatoo's back; the bird responded by making his pigeon-toed way up her arm and perching on her shoulder, where he snuggled against her ear and clucked in contentment. "What a good boy," she cooed at him. Then she turned to Lionel and said, "I think a firecracker must have gone off in the alley and scared him, but he is feeling better now."

"I should just give him to you," he said, kicking off his loafers and peeling off his socks. "He's crazy about you, and he can't stand me." He leaned against a wall and cracked one of his big toes with a little grunt of pleasure.

"Nonsense! He loves you in a different way, that is all." She opened her mouth and the bird stuck his tongue out, touching hers.

"Well, you better hand him over or he'll crap on your dress." He padded over to her, his arm outstretched, but as soon as he was within reach of Spencer, the bird lifted his crest in alarm, extended his wings, and hissed at him.

"Oh! Oh! Spencer!" cried Yolanda, holding his razor-sharp beak shut with her thumb and forefinger. (Jesus! thought Lionel. How does she *do* that?) "Bad boy! *Bad* boy! That is your daddy!" She let go of his beak and shook her finger at him, as though possessing nine others made this one expendable, then turned to face Lionel, an embarrassed grin on her face. "He is still a little scared, I guess. I will put him in his cage, okay?"

"Okay," Lionel said with a sigh. He hurled one last glowering look at Spencer, then turned his attention to his mail. He rifled through the envelopes—bill, bill, sweepstakes entry, bill. He tossed them on his butcher-block table, then noticed that once again Yolanda's *derriére* was protruding in his direction, as she balanced precariously on the footstool she needed to reach Spencer's cage (she was only five feet five). Lionel thought, if only I could *feel* something for that sight, something beyond a kind of abstract delight in the *symmetry* of it.

Yolanda made her wobbly backward descent from the footstool, while Spencer screamed at her in frustration at being locked up again. She pitched a little to the left when she reached the floor—balancing in those heels must have been like walking on stilts—then righted herself and, smiling at Lionel, began adjusting one of her earrings. "Spencer likes to try to pull the backs off these while he is on my shoulder," she explained. "He is a very talented cockatoo."

Oblivious to the compliment, the bird kept screaming,

and Lionel said, "Let's go to another room. I can't stand this noise." He started down the long corridor, Yolanda following him. "Get you a drink?" he offered.

"Oh, no, thank you. Bob will be picking me up at any moment now." At the darkest stretch of the hallway, a few feet beyond the point at which Lionel's track-lighting ended, she suddenly stopped, and said, "Oh, blessed mother. Now I have done it."

Lionel turned. "What?"

"The backing; I have dropped the backing. Oh, Lionel, my earring will not stay on without it." She fell to all fours and started running her hand across the floor. "I heard it land somewhere around here. Oh, Madonna, help me *find* it. I do not want to keep Bob waiting!"

"Jesus, calm *down*," he said, getting on his hands and knees and joining her in her search. He skimmed his fingers across the barely illuminated floorboards. "I'll never understand this big terror thing you have when it comes to Little Lord Fauntleroy."

"Oh, not now, *please*, Lionel. Can you not make it any brighter in here?"

"Hold on." He trotted into the bedroom, which was just a few feet away, and pulled a flashlight from his nightstand drawer. He switched it on to make sure it was working, then brought it back to the hallway.

"Here," he said, presenting it to Yolanda.

She snatched it from him—she was clearly too anxious to be polite—and dragged its syrupy yellow beam across the hallway, inch by inch. "You do not understand Bob," she said as she scoured the floor. "His scorn can be very wounding. He tries to teach me so much, but I am such a slow learner, and have far to go. I am so grateful for his *patience*, Lionel."

"*His* patience? What about *yours*?" He crouched down next to her again, and resumed the search. "I've watched you sit there, not saying a word, while he spends forty minutes telling you about a pair of shoes he almost bought."

She shook her head, and a snaky tentacle of hair fell into her face; she stuck out her lower lip and blew it away. She was, he recognized without feeling it, intoxicatingly sexual. "Lionel, please. Do not talk that way about Bob. It makes me feel disloyal to him just listening to you."

"Sorry, Yolanda. Really I am." And he was. Once, while totally plowed, sitting with her between cars in a restaurant parking lot during a tedious Bastille Day celebration they'd slipped away from, he'd been foolish enough to pour out his contempt for Bob in one vehement gush, knowing even as he did that it was the kind of contempt only a desperately closeted gay man can have for a brazenly effeminate straight one. "For God's sake, Yolanda," he said, "how can you waste your time on that trivial, shallow, self-obsessed piece of work? Can't you see he's just *using* you? I mean, the guy just got divorced from a *debutante*, for Christ's sake—he's *slumming*. He probably read in *Details* or *Interview* that it's hip to have a girlfriend who's ethnic. Well, I'm sorry, but you *are*. I'm just warning you, when push comes to shove, he's not going to be able to forgive you for not being a strawberry-blond giantess named Phoebe with a trust fund. All this guy wants out of a relationship is photo ops. When those run out, he'll be gone."

Yolanda had stared at him, her eyes full of tears and her face the exact shade of crimson it would've been had he hauled off and slapped her. Had she then told him that he was full of sour grapes, that he was just jealous because Bob Smartt had the confidence to do all the things that Lionel Frank was afraid to, like get adventurous haircuts and wear poofy clothes from Ultimo and gush fulsomely about Mabel Mercer records—had she told him that, Lionel would have had to admit defeat. But she wasn't sober enough to see that; she knew only that she had to choose between her lover and her friend, and accordingly fled the parking lot in tears, leaving Lionel with a forty-dollar bar tab that he couldn't move his legs to go and pay. (He eventually fell asleep with his face pressed against the tire of a Chevy Nova, whose owner was considerate enough not to awaken him before driving the car away. Lionel told his co-workers that the rubbery smudge across his forehead had been left by scuba gear; no one bothered to ask where he'd gone diving on a Tuesday night in Chicago.) Days later, he forced himself to apologize, and had made a point of being kind to Yolanda ever since. Everything about her—her barrio accent, the curious formality of her speech, the little-girl-in-a-woman's-body vulnerability she exuded so unconsciously—invited his kindness, made it almost imperative.

She let the flashlight lie limp in her hand for a moment, and turned to meet his eyes. "Things would perhaps be different if you were a different kind of man, Lionel," she said in a soft voice. "But you are not, so I am with Bob."

He smiled; she had her ways of being kind to him, as well. He certainly didn't think she *meant* what she'd just said. She'd never shown any romantic interest in him before. But then, she'd been long settled in her apartment by the time he moved in upstairs, so from Day One she would've been able to hear, through her ceiling, the all-out, all-male goings-on in his bedroom. If she ever had any illusions about him, they couldn't have been of more than a few hours' duration.

That all seemed so long ago now, before his career in advertising took off, forcing him—or so he saw it—to abandon his risky romantic life for the liability it was. Yolanda had reproached him for that once, upsetting him badly; she, too, apologized later. Ever since, as long as he forbore to deride her romance, she forbore to scold him for his cowardice.

Their moment of tenderness past, she started a new sweep with the flashlight. But half a minute later, they heard the doorbell to her apartment begin buzzing loudly. "Oh, Lionel," she cried, "that will be Bob! Oh, will you help me? Go and let him in, and tell him I will be there shortly!"

Taking his cue from the urgency in her voice, he dashed downstairs without protest. Yolanda's door was ajar, so he slipped in, buzzed Bob into the building, then waited on the landing just outside her apartment until Bob made his light-footed way up to him.

He appeared, all six-feet-three of him, in a daringly cut double-breasted wheat suit and burgundy slippers. His tie was a simple ribbon of royal purple silk with a jet-black outline around its edges and another black line bisecting its length. The moment he rounded the landing and saw Lionel waiting for him, he untucked the tie from his suitcoat and flapped it at him, a look of rapturous anticipation on his face. In his other hand, he carried a bouquet of tulips.

Lionel felt an explosion of hatred that nearly rattled his teeth.

Never one to waste time on pleasantries, Bob hopped up the remaining steps and got right down to business. "Isn't this tie the *best*?" he said. He extended his hand so that the tie stretched to its full length for Lionel to admire. "Cost a pretty penny, but have you ever seen anything like it? It really makes such a *statement.* I *had* to have it, *especially* for this suit." His voice, which sounded helium-drenched at the best of times, was now so shrill with excitement that it made the short hairs on Lionel's nape stand at attention.

I'm gay and he's straight, thought Lionel in amazement and frustration, as he always did when face to face with Bob. He shook his head and in his most sarcastic voice said, "I'm fine, thanks for asking. And you?"

Bob looked up obliviously, his little black eyes revealing no depth of comprehension whatsoever. "Hmm?" he said brightly. Then, a glimmer of realization. "Hey, where's Yolanda? Isn't she ready yet?"

Nice of him to finally think of his girlfriend, thought Lionel. "She's up at my place. She was looking after my bird and lost the back of her earring on my floor. She's trying to find it now."

"Not the Paloma Picasso earrings!" cried Bob, aghast.

He's straight and I'm gay, thought Lionel. "I don't know. Big, dangly things?"

"Oh, no. I didn't give her those." He looked relieved, as if the earrings must then be of no consequence. He swept a silky blond forelock away from his face, weaving it with his fingers into the body of his rich, pampered, set-in-gelatin hair.

Lionel glared at this unlikely Romeo. He wondered if Bob had ever been beaten up on his fifth-grade playground, as he had. He wondered if Bob had ever had the word "queer" spray-painted on his high-school locker, as he had. He wondered if Bob had ever been denied jobs he was qualified for because he wasn't able to reel off football scores in casual post-interview conversation, as he had. He wondered if Bob ever suffered for his effeminacy, or whether he was absolved from such suffering by having demonstrated his manhood not only beyond question, but beyond anyone's capacity to ignore—by marrying a fourth cousin of the Duchess of York, bringing her and her King's Road wardrobe to America, and siring two gorgeous children (names: Denzil and Felicity) through her before she left him for a middle-aged Zionist poet who converted her to Judaism and took her and the children to live on a West Bank kibbutz.

These were credentials Lionel could not begin to match. Even the bad ones were good. Because of them, Bob's heterosexuality wasn't just an accepted fact—it was juicy gossip. Despite his flaming effeminacy, no one doubted he was straight. After all, in order to be a father, one must have entered a woman. In order to be a cuckold, one must have claimed a woman. Was that enough? Lionel wondered. Despite Bob's braying and preening, did it come down to just that? Was it effeminacy that must be punished, or was it sleeping with men? The two didn't always go hand in hand, as he and Bob so ably proved. Was a nice, normal, plain-brown-wrapper gay man like himself preferable in the eyes of the world to a whiny, dandyish breeder like Bob—or was it the other way around? Was it fair to condemn either of them?

It was the same series of questions Lionel always asked himself when confronted with Bob. And the questions always boiled down to two, neither of which he could answer: Would he be Bob Smartt if he had the chance? Would he *kill* Bob Smartt if he had the chance?

For Lionel recognized in Bob his opposite number, a recognition made all the more frustrating by its not having been reciprocated by Bob, who appeared oblivious to anything to do with Lionel beyond his capacity to form an audience of one. Nor could Bob have appreciated the differences between them even if he *had* been willing to—he didn't know that Lionel was gay. Despite Yolanda's assurances that it would make no difference to him, Lionel insisted that she not tell him.

"We're going to this *camp* new restaurant," Bob continued, his enthusiasm bordering on rapture. "Everyone's been talking about it. It hasn't gotten a write-up in any of the papers yet, so it's still a really hip place. I heard Diana Ross was there last week!"

"I thought you said it was hip," said Lionel.

Bob didn't even hear the jibe; he was too busy barreling on. "It's called Café Krypton and all the waiters and waitresses dress like comic-book heroes. Vera and Tom Gunther went there last weekend and got waited on by a waitress dressed like Invisible Girl. They said she was perfect for the part because they didn't see her for half an hour after they were seated." He howled with laughter.

Come *down,* Yolanda, Lionel commanded telepathically as Bob, a touchy-feely type, leaned forward and clasped his shoulder, the better to share his glee. "What kind of food do they serve?" Lionel asked politely to disguise the fact that he was backing into Yolanda's door. It was no use; Bob took a step forward and was as close to him as ever. Lionel started fondling the brass doorknob.

"Oh, American," Bob said, wiping tears of mirth from his eyes. "I guess it's kind of *nouvelle,* but I'm not sure. It's gonna be a scream just to be able to say we've *been* there once everyone finally reads about it."

He's straight and I'm gay, thought Lionel.

"It's B.Y.O.B.," Bob continued. "They don't have their liquor license yet. So I picked up this great Pinot Noir with a picture of Queen Victoria on the label." He waited for a reaction and, getting none, he said, "Queen *Victoria,* on the label of a bottle of *wine.*" Still Lionel refused to react, but Bob was unfazed, and launched immediately into the explanation Lionel hadn't asked for. "Turns out it's a *New Zealand* vintner, a famous one that's about a hundred years old. I *knew* there were no English vineyards." He straightened his spine pridefully.

Lionel wondered how many people would have to hear this story tonight. Come *down,* Yolanda, he repeated in his mind—louder this time. He was now so worked up that he gave the doorknob a good yank, and a screw fell out of it onto the floor. *"Shit,"* he said, picking it up and trying to reinstall it. He was all thumbs; he dropped it and picked it up again.

Bob made no move to help him, but passed the tulips to his other hand, then shook his head and chuckled. "Invisible Girl," he repeated, giggling. "Didn't see her for a half-hour after they sat down!" And he started laughing again.

Lionel, who hadn't found it funny the first time, finished turning the screw and said, "Let me put those in water or something, while we're waiting." He took the tulips and ducked into Yolanda's kitchen, pulled a mason jar from a shelf and filled it at the sink. As it was filling, he could hear Bob still giggling in the hallway, and from upstairs, the sound of Spencer screeching like a condor with a bad case of throat polyps. The world seemed suddenly very irrational to him.

He plunked the jar onto the kitchen counter, resisted the urge to arrange the flowers more attractively, then went to rejoin Bob in the hallway, rolling his eyes in disgust as he went.

Fortunately, he had no sooner arrived at the door than Yolanda came bounding down the stairs, both hands behind her left ear, busily reattaching the earring. "Bob! Hello! I am finally ready!" Due to the dizzying height of her heels, she almost pitched forward, but managed to put out a hand to right herself and continued more carefully to the landing. "I am so sorry for making you wait so long. It could not be helped." She was actually panting by the time she came to a halt before him.

"That's okay," Bob said, not even bothering to hide the fact that he was appraising her outfit. "Cute," he said. "Told you that'd be a good color on you. It brings out your cinnamon undertones."

"Does it really?" she said, pleased, pulling the strap of her tiny purse over her shoulder.

"Oh, *yeah.* I brought tulips to match the color, but Lionel had to put them in water 'cause you were taking so long. You can see them when we get back."

She smiled and started for the door. "Oh, can I not just go and have a quick peek at them befo—"

"No." Bob suddenly became red-faced and petulant. "Listen, we're late enough as it is. I want to get some shots of us in front of the old Italian market before they close and turn the lights out."

"The . . . Italian market?" she said, puzzled.

"Yeah." He placed his hand over the small of her back and started to lead her down the next flight of stairs. "They have this great antique tin sign up with a picture of a cow on it, and I got this idea it'd be a *great* backdrop for a picture of us all dressed up for dinner. You know, a contrast kind of thing—sophisticated people in a squat little commercial setting, obviously on their way someplace terrific. I always get a heck of a charge out of that kind of thing. I have a whole scrapbook of ads like that at home."

"I know," said Yolanda, her voice now spiraling away from Lionel but its tone of worshipful awe still audible to him. "You have shown it to me many times."

I'm gay and he's straight, thought Lionel. He's straight and I'm gay.

He shut Yolanda's door behind him and had just started up the stairs to his own place when he heard Bob call out, "Oh, wait—*so long, Lionel*!" Yolanda's farewell followed immediately, almost like an echo except that her voice was deeper.

He sighed, knowing that they had almost forgotten him and, now that they were outside the building, had certainly done so. He entered his apartment, shut the door, and leaned against it. "That guy bugs the *fuck* out of me," he said, addressing his reflection in the mirror on the facing wall, knowing that it would share the sentiment.

Utterly dejected, he went to the bedroom, threw himself on the bed, and dialed the phone.

"Welcome to one-nine-hundred-HOT-GUYZ," said the congenial, rather lispy recorded voice at the other end of the line. "The charge for our service is two dollars a minute. If you'd like to speak to a leatherman, touch One. If you'd like to speak to a cowboy, touch Two. If you'd like to speak to a cop, touch Three. If you'd like to speak to a construction worker, touch Four. If your fantasy isn't any of these, touch Zero to ask a live operator for more options."

Lionel wasted no time in pressing 0, and within two rings, an operator picked up. "HOT GUYZ," he said chirpily. "How may I help you?"

"Well," said Lionel, burying half his face in his pillow; "I—this may sound kind of kinky—I don't even know if you—well, *do* you have any—uh—*priests*?"

Without missing a beat, the operator asked, "What denomination?"

Lionel's heart started pounding. "Roman Catholic?"

"Hold, please."

A few minutes later, he was asking "Father Lance" what he wore under his cassock. To Lionel's delight, the answer confirmed what he had always suspected.

chapter

■■■■■■■■■■■■■■■■■■■

four

In the elevator up to the office the next morning, Lionel was nearly overcome by anxiety. He'd intended to arrive early, so that he could lay in wait for Donna, ready to pounce on her the moment she walked through the door and demand that she tell no one of their meeting last night. But there had been a collision on the Kennedy Expressway that had brought traffic to a halt for twenty-five minutes while ambulances hurtled by on the shoulders, wailing like banshees. Lionel's own wails came close to matching these: he pounded on his steering wheel, punched the door, and rocked back and forth in his seat, wracked by frustration. After about four full minutes of this deranged behavior, he happened to turn his head while emitting a particularly violent shriek and saw that the woman in the next car was regarding him with an expression of no small alarm. Mortified, he slid down into his seat and waited for traffic to begin moving again, simmering all the while, like a vat of poison over a slow flame.

Now it was well past nine o'clock, and as he swung open the glass door to the Deming, Stark & Williams offices and took a faltering step in, he tried to decide how he should behave: should he hang his head and avert his eyes, thereby missing any smug, mocking glances that might come his way? No—if Donna *had* told anyone in the office that she'd seen him at a gay bar last night, any sign of embarrassment on his part would only serve as a confirmation. He'd be *acting* guilty. Better to brazen it out, head held high.

"Good *morning*, Alice," he chirped to the receptionist. He breezed past her with a smile and continued down the corridor. "Top o' the morning, Tomster! Lookin' fine and mellow, Maggie!" Actually, this was a little *too* confident and self-assured; better try to turn it down a notch. "What's the word, Angie-bird? Hey—Soo! Get off o' my cloud!" It was no use; everything he said this morning was going to sound like it came from a character on a bad sitcom. He might as well resign himself to it.

He felt some relief that no one had thus far looked at him with sly amusement or disgust. Everyone had been wrapped up in private thoughts or pursuing private errands, and had treated his greetings as negligible social exchanges, to be forgotten immediately. He wouldn't have been so easily ignored had he been the subject of a brand new office scandal. Donna must have kept her mouth shut so far. Well, he'd better make sure she continued to do so.

He reached his office and darted in, dropped his briefcase onto his desk, and slipped off his suit jacket, which he draped over the chair. Then, unbuttoning and rolling up his sleeves, he stepped into the hallway again and started a casual stroll over to the Creative Department. "Gimme five, Dave-monster!" he said, palm extended to the hairy keyline artist, who responded by grunting, "How 'bout I just give you one," and flipping him the bird.

His heart quivering like a glob of Jell-O, he stuck his head into Donna's office. She had her back to him, and was typing a message onto her TDD telephone line. He snuck up behind her and looked at the readout to determine whether this was a business or a personal call. On the screen were the words NEXT IN LINE AS OF TUESDAY, and Donna kept on typing in a similar obscure vein so that he couldn't tell if she was "talking" to a business contact or a friend. In either case, it would be rude to interrupt; plus, he'd have to touch her shoulder to call attention to himself, and he disliked the presumption of intimacy that entailed. He'd be better off waiting for a more opportune moment.

He was on his way back down the hall when Rosa, the tiny bookkeeper who had the office next to Tracy's, turned the corner and approached him, carrying a big blue ledger that looked like it might weigh a few pounds more than she did. He smiled, met her eyes, and prepared to toss a pleasantry at her, but noticed that her lips were pursed in an inscrutable grin, and as she passed she flicked her eyebrows up and down suggestively. "*Morn*ing, Lionel," she said, laughter in her voice.

He immediately flushed scarlet; his entire face felt like a newly burst blister. He dashed back to his office, threw himself into his chair, and sat there, terrified, not daring to leave his desk.

They knew! They knew! Donna had told them! It was spreading around the office even now—the delighted, delicious, malicious whispers, relating the tale third- and fourth-hand: Lionel at a gay bar. Lionel kissing another man. Lionel salivating over a naked male dancer.

"Oh, *God*," he croaked. "Oh, *Jesus.* Jesus Harry *Christ.*" He opened the drawers of his desk one by one, hoping that someone might have accidentally left a loaded pistol in one of them. Suicide was clearly the only answer. But not before he arranged to take Donna with him.

Time *crawled.* On an ordinary day, he'd have been prowling the corridors, haunting the media buyers, plaguing the creatives, exhorting everyone to do more, better, faster, for All-Pro Power Tools. Today, he couldn't bring himself to get out of his chair. He'd get that *look* again. That smirk Rosa had given him, as though she were imagining what he looked like with a cock in his mouth. It was beyond mortifying; it was paralyzing. He wished he could call someone for advice or consolation, but there was no one, no one at all.

Finally, at about seven minutes after eleven, Carlton Wenck stuck his head in Lionel's office and smiled surreptitiously. "Knock, knock," he said, a grin on his face that would have shamed the Cheshire Cat. Lionel's heart skipped a beat, then skipped another two, as though it were playing hopscotch. Of *all* the people to be the one to finally confront him! Well, it figured. Carlton was Lionel's chief rival at the agency. He had started the same week as Lionel, with the same number of accounts, but now, four years later, Lionel had only one account left, while Carlton had four—one of which he'd actually brought on board himself. Lionel consoled himself by remembering that All-Pro brought the agency more than the combined billings of all four of Carlton's clients (a radio station, a mail-order photo development service, a bridal magazine, and an accounting software package for universities). But Carlton was perceived as a golden boy, while Lionel was perceived as nothing more than a good, hard worker. The difference galled him.

And Carlton's appearance in Lionel's office now could only mean he meant to gloat; they were no longer rivals, and Carlton would know that. Lionel's career was over, and Carlton hadn't had to lift a finger; he was both victorious *and* innocent—what better reason to gloat than that? Oh, he'd disguise his gloating as camaraderie, but that wouldn't fool Lionel. He'd say, "Gosh, Lionel, why didn't you *tell* anyone you're gay? You don't think it makes any *difference,* do you? Hell, I've already talked to the partners about it, and we agreed: your personal life is none of our goddamn business. But, *hey,* pal, I'm a little *hurt* you didn't think you could confide in us. We're all on the same side, aren't we? This isn't going to make one *bit* of difference in how anyone thinks about you." And all the while there'd be that predatory look in his eyes, as he calculated just how long it'd be before Lionel was canned (for some invented failing, as in Chicago it was illegal to fire someone because of his sexual orientation), after which he, Carlton, would be awarded All-Pro Power Tools.

Now Carlton, grinning, entered Lionel's office and quietly shut the door behind him; that single action eliminated any small shred of doubt from Lionel's mind. This was definitely the encounter he'd been dreading for four years. He steeled himself in his chair. On his tongue he could taste a film of blood—or was it vomit? His right foot was flopping on the plastic mat beneath his desk, making a sound like hailstones on a window pane; he couldn't seem to stop it.

Carlton sat on the edge of Lionel's desk and leaned across

it. His tie fell onto Lionel's blotter and draped across Lionel's Cross pen. It was as if he were already claiming his rival's belongings.

Lionel tried to return his smile, but felt it must look more like he was biting a bullet. And then Carlton parted his lips ever so slightly, and whispered, barely audibly, *"So."*

Lionel flinched as if he'd been hit. *"So,"* he whispered back.

Carlton nodded and shifted his thigh so that it was closer to Lionel's arm. "Tracy, huh?" he said, still whispering.

Lionel blinked twice. His foot stopped flopping. He studied Carlton's face; the smile had turned to a leer. Lionel was confused. What did Tracy have to do with this?

"Tracy?" he whispered.

"It's all over the office, man," Carlton said, his voice thick with excitement. "You asked Tracy out on a date, and she actually said yes."

Lionel almost levitated out of his seat. He no longer felt the call of gravity. His relief was inexpressible. *That's* what this was all about! Not Donna and The Hague—Tracy and the Trippys!

"Not a date, really," he said, turning red with embarrassed pleasure. "Just the Trippy ceremony."

Carlton ignored this. "Man, I've been dyin' to bang that bitch ever since she started. Wouldn't give me the time of day. Don't know what you used to get through to her, pal. Whatever it is, you oughtta fuckin' *bottle* it."

Against his better judgment, Lionel laughed, as if acknowledging his studhood. Then, common sense reclaiming him, he said, "Listen. Like I said, I'm just taking her to the Trippys. Deming and Perlman are gonna be there, and *Magellan,* for Christ's sa—"

Carlton cut him off by extending his arm. "I just wanna shake your hand, is all I've got to say."

Lionel obliged. Then Carlton got up from the desk and went to the door. Just before he opened it, he cocked an eyebrow and said, "I want a *full report* the next morning, buddy."

"Full report?" repeated Lionel, confused.

"And it's not just for me. Couple other guys on the staff are *very* interested in hearing what Miss Tracy Pfaff is like when she's out of her business suit, if you know what I mean." He opened the door, and then said, almost as an afterthought, "Kinda relieved about you, too, guy. Gotta tell you. Got to the point we almost thought you were queer." And then he was gone.

Lionel felt the floor fall away, then come up again to meet him. Both accused and absolved in the space of a single sentence! He took a gulp of air, raised his eyes to heaven, and said thank you to whatever presence might be up there. Then he got up and slowly, shakily, began to integrate himself into the day.

But in fact he hadn't had the complete escape he'd thought; out of the frying pan was more like it. A secretary told him she thought it was great that he and Tracy were "finally getting together." Forty minutes after that, Julius Deming, Tracy's boss, buzzed him on the intercom and said, "Congratulations. Tracy just told me. Always thought you kids had something going on, if you'd only just sit up and notice it." And as he left for lunch, Alice the receptionist, without any explanation, blurted out, "Yellow roses are her favorite," then wore a beaming smile as if she'd just been of immeasurable help to him.

He darted into the elevator as it was closing, and just as the door slid shut he saw Tracy enter the reception area, purse in hand, and make her way toward the door. A narrow escape! He might've had to share an elevator with her. He heaved a sigh of relief, so heavy that it took him from the twenty-third to the nineteenth floor to complete it. He couldn't face Tracy, not today—not with so many people expecting so much from them, watching them for any little indicator of romantic passion.

Despite the rather dire nature of his personal predicament, he spent his lunch hour pondering the differences between gay relationships and straight ones. As he sat on a bench in the shady plaza outside the building, eating his take-out Szechuan and watching about two dozen angry Transylvanian demonstrators march in front of the building that housed the Romanian consulate, he remembered the single major love affair he'd had before getting his advertising job. It had been such a secret thing; everything from the initial introduction to the final breakup had been conducted behind closed doors. The few gay parties he'd gone to with his lover had been dark, secretive affairs as well, as though all the guests tacitly acknowledged this undercurrent of intrigue in their affairs; it was like being at a party for Soviet sleeper agents. During the entire length of the relationship, no one had known of it—not his family, certainly, and only one of his college friends, who was openly uncomfortable with the knowledge. And if he had difficulties with his lover, they had to solve them themselves. If they had problems over money, living arrangements, monogamy, or any other major issue, they had to work from scratch toward a solution. The toll of secrecy eventually began to drive them apart; and if they felt the desire to separate, what was to stop them? There was no earthly agency, no social institution, that compelled them to consider staying together.

But heterosexual relationships! Now, *there* was a different story. At the first sign of mutual interest, a couple experienced encouragement from all quarters. And if they succeeded in finally getting together, that encouragement turned to congratulation. Heterosexual relationships were as much a spectator sport as they were an adventure in intimacy; everyone connected with the couple was expected to shower them with approval, and even strangers in the street were taught to regard young hand-holding men and women with joyful goodwill. And if heterosexual partners ever experienced any difficulties in their relationship, they could turn anywhere for aid, from libraries lined with self-help books for straights to the storehouse of experience willingly shared by long-married relatives and friends. Even movies and television offered continual examples of ideal relationships from which straight couples could draw strength and inspiration.

Was it fair? No. Did it make him angry? Yes. If he and Kevin had received one one-hundredth of the encouragement and approval he'd gotten this morning alone just for asking a woman on a date, they might still be together. And that was a possibility to make even his beloved advertising career pale.

Well, spilled milk and the road not taken and all that. He couldn't change the world, he knew that well enough; but he *could* play by the world's rules. And that's what he was doing. He had a great job, made a good salary, had a decent home, and that was more than a lot of people had. He'd keep all of it, too; he'd get through this ordeal with Tracy somehow, and go on as before.

The only question now was—*how*?

chapter

■■■■■■■■■■■■■■■■■■■

five

On his way back to the office, Lionel crossed the street and found himself within a few yards of the Transylvanian demonstrators. He paused to take a closer look at them. Being fairly apolitical himself, he was always curious about overtly political behavior in others. And as these people also possessed that almost mystical Eastern European aura, so revered since the miraculous revolutions of 1989, he found them doubly fascinating—these creatures who, although many had undoubtedly lived in Chicago for years, had such close ties, of both blood and history, to a nation only now emerging from a latter-day dark age. They looked it, too; in spite of the occasional pair of Air Jordans or acid-washed jeans—or maybe because of them—there was a peasant air about them, an earthiness.

Lionel tried to dredge up all he knew about Transylvania, and all that came to mind was that it was where Dracula movies were set. For all he knew, then, it might be a mere storybook realm, not a real one. But judging by the placards (those that were legible) being hoisted aloft by these demonstrators, Transylvania was indeed a real place, and just as the Baltic republics had won their freedom from the Soviet Union, apparently Transylvania now wanted its freedom

from Romania. But why? What was their complaint against
that country? He tried hard to remember all that he could
about Romania, which was little enough. It had suffered a
bloody revolution not long ago, hadn't it? All those shocking, full-color photo spreads in the newsweeklies. He
seemed to recall a shamelessly self-aggrandizing dictator
with a name almost every American pronounced haltingly,
and an insane wife who got quite a lot of press (how the
media did *love* the insane wives of dictators). Then there
was a post-coup kangaroo court, a hasty execution by firing
squad—and that's all he could remember. He felt a little
flush of shame, just as he had felt at the time, watching
people crow over the fall of Romania's tyrant even though
they'd never heard of him six months before. He'd thought,
Americans have become a people who only like to read the
last chapter of a book, and then only if it has a happy ending.
And now, three years after the earth had rocked on its axis,
it was all no more than a Trivial Pursuit question—a Trivial
Pursuit question he couldn't even answer.

Instead of being so wrapped up in my own problems, he
thought, instead of gazing at my navel from dawn to dusk,
maybe I ought to *read* more. Maybe I ought to start following these movements, chart the ebb and flow of history,
look at the broad canvas of mankind's struggle on earth,
study th—

He was halted in mid-thought by the sight of a broad-
backed Transylvanian with a shaggy mane of hair and a big
black mustache. His heart quickened.

Babe-o-*rama*, he thought to himself, watching as this new
discovery, who was clad in a tattered jean jacket, khaki
pants, and a Bart Simpson T-shirt that read DON'T HAVE A
COW, MAN, passed before him, raising his fist and crying,
"Freedom!" at the top of his lungs. Lionel pretended to be
busy fumbling for something in his pocket while waiting for
the circle of marchers to turn again and bring this sizzling
Slavic number around for another up-close inspection.

And then another, and another, and another, until the
hunk, on his fourth go-round, met Lionel's eyes, and, boring
into them for one heart-stopping moment, shouted *"Freedom! Freedom for the people of Transylvania!"* before
marching angrily on.

Lionel, startled and disoriented by the unexpectedness of the confrontation, whirled around to escape and caught his foot on the leg of a mailbox. He lurched forward to free himself, but in doing so threw his left arm forward, knocking a carton of Chicken McNuggets out of a young girl's hand and sending it into an almost perfectly described aerial arc. By some miracle it landed square in the middle of a trash can, where a hungry bum who had been sifting through the garbage stared at it in delighted awe, as though it had been dropped there for his benefit by a benevolent Old Testament God.

Lionel blurted a "Sorry" to the girl whom he had so carelessly deprived of lunch, then brushed himself off and zoomed back to the office.

Back at his desk, he doffed his jacket and dropped himself into his chair, then heaved a little sigh of relief. Safe at last! And what a *disturbing* encounter that had been. He wasn't accustomed to having the objects of his lustful scrutiny turn and meet his gaze, much less fling a fiery political demand at him (as though he had any power to *do* something about it, for God's sake).

Well, he thought, good old Ivan sure embarrassed the *piss* out of me. Then he wondered, Is Ivan a name a Romanian would have? Well, why not? Hell . . .

Almost without realizing it, he had pulled a pair of binoculars out of his desk drawer and gone to the window. Lifting them to his eyes, he scanned the street fourteen floors down and a half-block north, until he zeroed in on the Transylvanian demonstrators. He deftly adjusted the focus, and within a moment he'd found Ivan again, still angry, still marching, still hairy.

"Oh, Ivan, Ivan," he muttered. "You goddamned fucking *tease*, you."

"What'cha lookin' at?" asked someone directly behind him.

Startled, he dropped the binoculars, then made a fumbling attempt to try and catch them; but they hit the window and glanced off it, slipping through his hands to the window ledge, where they knocked over the Bronze City Award the agency had won for the All-Pro E-Z Tire Pump spot that starred the weird celebrity ventriloquist and his even more celebrated dummy (who, in a highly theatrical flourish that had made the spot such a favorite, was the one who actually operated the pump). Both binoculars and award hit the carpet with a thud.

He whirled to face the intruder; it was Donna. Thank God, thank God, he thought. She can't have heard what I was mumbling!

"Donna," he said, "I was just—there's this billboard for rent on Grand I wanted to check out f—"

Before he could finish, Hackett Perlman leaned into his office and tapped Donna's shoulder. Donna turned to face him.

"I need to see you," Perlman told her, enunciating every syllable with annoying precision, as if Donna had only just learned to read lips that morning. Then he continued down the hall, having barely broken his stride.

Donna turned and winked at Lionel, then ducked down the hall herself.

As a reflex, Lionel called after her. "Hey, wait! Donna!" But of course she wasn't able to hear him.

He bent down, picked up the City Award and returned it to the window ledge, then retrieved the binoculars and stood upright again. He went to the hallway and looked after Donna, managing to catch her eye just as she slipped into her office. She winked at him again.

His heart was fluttering. That wink—*twice* now. What did it mean? He felt sure it was some kind of recognition of a bond between them. And what bond could that be, except the big *H*?

She probably hadn't yet picked up on the office gossip about the sudden flowering of his romance with Tracy. He got a cold feeling wondering how she'd react when she did. She'd demonstrated, just now, her gracious acceptance of his privacy—she hadn't gone and blabbed about his sexuality to anyone, and even face to face with him she conveyed her tacit understanding of that privacy with a wink. She would tell no one; he felt reasonably confident of that.

But even though she respected his privacy, would she respect his *hypocrisy*? Would she keep her mouth shut once she got wind of the latest gossip? He couldn't be sure; if she were enough of an activist, that might just be where she'd draw the line. Everyone was "outing" everybody else these days, and Lionel could easily envision it happening to him. Donna would do it for his own good; that's the way she'd see it.

He went back to his desk and put his hand over his forehead. His brain had started to hurt. It was *massively* irritating having to consider all these possibilities and counter-possibilities just because of a few *tiny* slip-ups he'd allowed to pass unchecked. Well, he wasn't going to allow them to ruin his life, but for the moment, he was just plain stumped as to what to do about them.

Finally, Gloria Gimbek from the media department buzzed his office intercom to ask if he was available to go over an All-Pro radio buy, and he was forced to abandon the dilemma before he had resolved it. He was relieved to do so, because after manipulating cold, hard numbers with Gloria, he could approach the murkier, more subjective problem of how to manipulate his fellow human beings armed with a fresher perspective.

At least, that's what he *hoped.*

chapter

■■■■■■■■■■■■■■■■■■■■

six

That night, Lionel drove to the suburb of Western Springs to dine with his family. He'd received the invitation—command, really—late in the day, when his father, Lieutenant Colonel Samson X. Frank (United States Army, retired), phoned him at the office.

"Lionel," he'd said, his voice crisp and authoritative and forestalling any opposition, "dinner will be served here at seven, and your presence is expected. I will tell you why. Your aunt has, predictably, made far too much lobster bisque for just the three of us in residence, and, as you know, I refuse to eat leftover seafood because the dangers outweigh any possible economic advantage. Therefore, we are forced to recruit additional diners from outside the house. I tell you this so that you know you may bring a date if you wish. You may bring the population of Pakistan if you wish. Your aunt has single-handedly placed Maine lobster on the World Wildlife Fund endangered species list."

Lionel sighed and said, "Okay, Pop." He had never refused one of his father's invitations. His older brother, Eugene, had done that once. Eugene now lived in Oregon. Lionel kept hoping that one day he'd sneak back into Illinois for a weekend or something.

Rush-hour traffic on the Eisenhower Expressway was appalling. "Gas-valves to grille-holes," as one radio announcer liked to put it. Lionel jumped around the radio dial, alighting on a succession of fudge-voiced classical music announcers reading overwritten advertisements for suburban restaurants, colorless news broadcasters reciting the litany of S&L bailout effluvia, and wearyingly smug disc jockeys chortling over their own sophomoric witticisms. Music, when he could find it, was no improvement, consisting largely of treacly piano concertos he couldn't hear over the white noise of traffic, base-heavy rap numbers exalting the punishment of women, and gooey rock songs about the hardships of a musician's life on the road (performed, inevitably, by twenty-year-old millionaires).

Eventually, he gave up, switching off the radio entirely, and concentrating instead on changing lanes to get ahead of traffic. This was only possible to a limited extent, and after swerving dangerously into and out of the congested lanes on either side of him for close to ten minutes, he found himself still roughly neck-and-neck with the bright orange Tastee Hen truck that had been right alongside him at the start.

Abandoning the effort, he curled his left leg under the seat and leaned his left shoulder up against the car door. He could keep up with the stop-and-go, snail's-paced flow of traffic by alternating his right foot between the brake and the accelerator—a tiny tap here, a short rest there, and so on. He sighed dejectedly, putting his mind on hold, and settled in for a long drive.

And he considered the problem of his family. There was his father, first of all, who had retired from the Army at the insistence of a young bride who had not liked the goings-on in Vietnam, not one bit (well, thought Lionel, opposites do attract), who then, only four years later, and just a few months after his wife had discovered a curious little lump on her breast, had found himself a widower. Having lost his commission *and* his spouse, he'd spent a brief spell brooding and wallowing in bitterness, until his sister came to help take care of his three young children. Aunt Lola was two years older than her brother, and even though he had been a Chinese prisoner of war during the Korean "conflict" (as he still insisted on calling it) and had a chestful of medals as mementos (or, more accurately, proof) of his valor under fire, she treated him like the most tiresome of adolescents and dismissed virtually every one of his opinions with a disappointed shake of her head and an, "Oh, Sonny, *Christ.*" (Lola was also the only human being alive who could call him "Sonny" with impunity.) Of course, she drove him mad. He responded to her looseness and irreverence by adopting the kind of manner he might have had had he never left the army at all—had he, in fact, gone on to make general.

And this was the mood of the house in which Lionel and his brother, Eugene, and sister, Greta, had grown up—in which Greta, in fact, still lived (she was a twenty-seven-year-old guitarist in an all-girl Christian heavy-metal band called Terrible Swift Sword; in other words, unemployable and broke). Lionel, who had had the added incentive of discovering himself gay, had fled the house at eighteen for college and never gone back for more than a visit. But each visit was as trying as a year in a Soviet gulag. His father and Aunt Lola seemed to exist now only to bedevil each other, and whenever Lionel went to see them, each clutched at his presence as if at a new weapon to wield against the other. He would often end up feeling quite battered about by the time he left them. And with his sister ever more pious and painted-faced, he found he had less and less to say to her, too. Even the family springer spaniel, Killer, whom Lionel had loved, had died the year before of extreme old age.

So it was an exercise in pain and futility, revealing the ultimate absurdity of the universe, Lionel thought, that he should go out of his way, undergo such agony as this traffic jam, to suffer a visit which he was certain would only make him utterly miserable.

The sudden flash of brake lights just a foot ahead of his front bumper startled him out of his dim reverie. He slammed on his own brakes and shouted a curse at the car ahead of him (a more vile curse than he would've dared utter outside). He looked around to get his bearings; the blocks of gray, grime-packed buildings on each side of the expressway had given way to tree-dotted neighborhoods. While lost in thought, he'd inched his way into the suburbs—and it had been relatively painless after all.

Still, the reminder that his fellow drivers were an unpredictable and dangerous lot left him less willing to put his mind on hold again, so he nosed his way into the right-hand lane, slipped down the nearest exit ramp, and drove the rest of the way to Western Springs on ordinary, sweet-smelling suburban thoroughfares.

By the time he reached his father's house—an undistinguished two-story colonial encircled by evergreen bushes that no one bothered to keep up (some were even dead, sitting brown amid the live ones like rotting teeth)—the skies, which had been cloudy for days, had finally broken, and a dull, drizzling rain had begun. Lionel parked on the street and hopped out of his car, then hunched his shoulders and trotted up the walk to the front door. It was seven-sixteen.

Before he could ring the bell, his father opened the door for him, wearing a white shirt and tie, as he always did. "You're twenty minutes late," he said flatly.

"Only sixteen," Lionel mumbled apologetically as he reached out and grasped his father's hand for a perfunctory shake.

"Still, I did say seven," the colonel insisted, accepting the shake coldly and then withdrawing his hand to shut the door behind his son.

"Sorry," Lionel offered, doffing his jacket and hanging it on the rack in the vestibule. "Traffic." He tried to change the subject. "How are the chinchillas?"

"Brave, as always." A few years back, the colonel had attempted to become an entrepreneur by raising chinchillas in the basement, whose pelts he had intended to sell at great profit. But once he realized he'd need a farm approximately twelve times the size of his basement to accommodate enough livestock to win the custom of even the smallest fur manufacturer, he'd given up and kept the beasts as pets, naming them all after famous generals and doting on them in his private moments.

Now he clasped his hands behind him, cradling them in the small of his back and standing with his legs wide apart, like a comic-book superhero. He didn't look remotely comfortable, but it gave him the desired aspect of military authority. "You didn't bring a date, I see."

Lionel shrugged and ambled into the house, hoping to entice his father into following him. "Course I didn't bring a date. I was at work, Pop. I don't take dates to the office with me."

The colonel stepped after his son briskly, hands still at his back. "Why didn't you call Lori?" Lori was a claims adjustor at Lionel's auto insurance company. He'd met her when he cracked up his Camry two summers before, and had somehow found the nerve to ask her to go with him to his cousin Marigold's wedding (he'd felt, at the time, that he'd need a "beard"). He hadn't seen her since, but the colonel had liked her, and, having seen his son with no other woman in the interim, had fixed on her as Lionel's "steady," despite Lionel's constant protests to the contrary.

"Pop," Lionel said, heading for the bathroom to wash his hands, "I haven't seen Lori in *ages.*"

"Would've been a good time to renew the acquaintance, then," Colonel Frank insisted. "I'm sure she wouldn't mind seeing your family again. We all got on, you know." He paused. "She did say she'd enjoy seeing the chinchillas. I recall her saying that. No prompting from me."

Lionel sighed and shut the bathroom door, as though requiring privacy for more personal functions than handwashing. The gambit worked; he could hear his father's footsteps, in apparent retreat.

He lathered his hands. The lavender-scented soap Aunt Lola always bought called up a flood of memories (chiefly of his father's protests that it was "no soap for a man," which only ensured Lola's loyalty to it till the crack of doom). He ran his filmy hands over his face, then splashed himself clean and toweled. He felt refreshed, almost invigorated.

He took a gulp of air, straightened his spine, then opened the door and headed for the kitchen, where the family ate on most nights (the dining room being reserved for holidays). Aunt Lola, tall and unwieldy and with a wall of irregular, multi-hued teeth that looked like the Chicago skyline at dusk, hopped up from her chair and gave him a big kiss. *"Honey,"* she cooed, "how wonderful, how *wonderful* of you to come." Aunt Lola had an annoying habit of starting a sentence over after only having gotten the first few words out; she'd always done so, but Lionel suspected she actually began cultivating it once she'd figured out how much it grated on the colonel.

"Wouldn't have missed it, Aunt Lola," he said, slipping

into the chair that had been designated his since his boyhood. Enveloped in this close, untidy, enervating environment again, he felt his old adolescent anxieties stir anew. He shook his head to quiet them, then reached for the soup tureen. "Lobster bisque—that's new for you, isn't it?"

"Uh-huh, uh-*huh*," Lola said brightly, lowering her big-hipped frame back into her own chair again. "Didn't do badly with it, if I do say so myself."

"It does have a taste to it," said Colonel Frank, looking into his spoon perplexedly as he lifted it again to his lips. He let a cooling puff of air issue from his lips, then tipped the spoon into his mouth. "Nothing like the taste of *lobster,* alas. Don't know how you managed to mask it, Lola, given the sheer number of the poor beasts you spent the day flinging into the pot."

Lionel turned to Greta and gave her a quick, private look, which she returned; it was their way of acknowledging that the colonel and Aunt Lola were at it again.

Greta herself was looking more like a Big Top attraction than ever. Her hair was wildly teased and was of a strangely unnatural hue—the kind of impossible blue-black Lionel had only ever seen fifteen years earlier, on the head of a Cher doll. He would've wondered if it were a wig, had he not been able to catch disturbing glimpses of scalp between the wildly spiraling, excessively teased fibers. Greta's dark purple makeup encircled her eyes like the Lone Ranger's mask, then stretched out to her temples, where it curled into little drawings of stars. From afar, it looked like she'd been smacked in each eye with a live cattle prod. And she was wearing a ratty old sweatshirt with the arms and most of the neck ripped away (the shirt's emblem, a crucifix made of flesh and dripping blood, was still intact, however). She also had on neon lime Lycra tights and black Reebok high-tops with neon orange laces. She reached for her glass of milk (she still drank milk with the fervor and frequency of a nine-year-old) and Lionel noticed a Cleopatra-like armband biting into her biceps.

He sighed in resignation and choked back any comment on Greta's haute couture. Instead, he flickered a smile at her and said, "Not the same around here without Killer." He stirred his bowl of bisque to cool it.

Greta shook her head and licked away her milk mustache. "Poor old Killer," she said with real emotion. It was the only point on which she and Lionel were still in complete agreement, and it was about the only thing they had left to talk about—the good old days with good old Killer.

But before Lionel could continue in that vein, his father jumped in. "How's business, son?"

"Good, good," said Lionel. He didn't know what else he could say; he knew that his father had only the faintest understanding of what his job entailed. Almost everything that Samson X. Frank knew about advertising agencies had come from watching old episodes of *Bewitched.* He still occasionally made the mistake of presuming that Lionel came up with all the ideas for his client's ads, and then wrote and drew them himself. That Lionel did none of this puzzled his father to no end. What, then, *did* he do? Lionel hadn't yet managed a satisfactory reply.

"I saw, I *saw* an All-Pro Power Tools commercial yesterday on *The Joan Rivers Show,*" said Aunt Lola as she swirled the ice cubes in her glass of tea (another of her annoying habits). "It was—I forgot what it was about—well, there was such, there was *such* a good-looking young man on it, I remember that much, he—"

"Chainsaw?" said Lionel at once, his spoon poised to enter his mouth.

"Yes, chainsaws, *that's* the one," said Aunt Lola brightly. "Clever of you, *clever* of you to remember. That one had some funny lines in it—" She stopped swirling the ice cubes and stared into space for a few moments. "Oh, dear—can't recall any of them . . ."

"Well, you're not the only one who got a kick out of it," said Lionel between gulps of bisque (which, contrary to his father's opinion, tasted quite wonderfully lobstery). "It just won an award. Matter of fact, we get to go to the awards banquet in a few weeks, and go up to the podium and accept it and everything."

Aunt Lola raised her eyebrows, and in a hushed, low voice, said, "Like the Academy, like the Academy *Awards*?"

"Kind of," Lionel admitted, blushing at the comparison.

She put down her soup spoon and placed her right hand over her chest. "Oh, my word. My *word.*"

"Should we watch for you on television, son?" the colonel asked, not even caring that he was demonstrating a shared enthusiasm with Lola, something he was usually loath to do.

"Course not," Lionel replied with a little laugh in his voice. He adjusted his napkin on his lap, embarrassed by the naiveté of the question. "These are just local awards—for the local advertising community."

"Oh, won't there be, *won't* there be any *stars* there?" Aunt Lola whimpered, moving closer to the edge of her seat.

"Well, no—I mean, unless you consider Franklin Potter a star. He used to be a copywriter at an agency here in town, so he's coming back to be master of ceremo—"

"Franklin *Potter,* Franklin *Potter,*" Aunt Lola gasped, clapping her hands to her face so forcefully that her left elbow almost upset the Eiffel Tower-shaped salt shaker.

Colonel Frank grimaced and wiped his lips with his napkin. "Who in God's holy name is Franklin Potter?"

Lola, who was bouncing up and down in her chair, blurted out the answer before Lionel could even open his mouth. "Franklin Potter plays Toby on *Breadside Manor,*" she squealed. "You know, that show about, that *show* about those three brothers who own a bakery, and one of them is divorced with a little nine-year-old daughter with a dirty mouth? Well, that's Toby, that's *Toby*—that's Franklin *Potter*! And besides which, *besides* which he's dating Helena Clement, who starred in that movie that got nominated for a People's Choice award with the name I can't remember—you know, the one about the girl C.E.O. with polio and cute clothes who marries the circus acrobat who doesn't believe in God? What was it *called*? I think it was, I *think* it was *The Wind at My Back.* Maybe he'll bring her to the awards ceremony! Oh, Lionel—oh, Lionel—hold on. Hold *on*!" And she heaved her bulk out of her chair and careened out of the kitchen, like a Velikovskian planet hurling through space.

"Stop shaking the floor!" the colonel called after her. "You'll disturb the chinchillas! And just when Eisenhower and MacArthur are busy mating!" He sighed in exasperation, picked up his spoon, and, before turning his attention back to his meal, cocked an eye at Lionel and said, with a barely perceptible smirk, "You appear to have impressed your aunt, son." Then, a beat later, "Please keep in mind how easily this is done." After a mouthful of bisque, he added, in a low voice, "Proud of you, boy."

Lionel must have beamed at this, for Greta pursed her lips and said, "Pride goeth before a fall," then angrily stuck her jet-black fingernails in a hunk of lobster to remove a little black speck of something-or-other. She examined it closely, then flicked it away and ate the remainder.

Lionel couldn't really expect congratulations on his success from the second guitarist in a thrash metal band that in two years had only managed to play Saturday afternoon church socials. But Greta's snarling admonition was a clear indication of jealousy, and Lionel, gratified, decided to take advantage of that.

"I know, I know," he said to her, "but who's proud? Man, I deal with celebrities every day of the week. It's not like there's anything *special* about them. It's not like it makes me any *better* than anyone else." He took his spoon and dipped back into his bisque, and from the corner of his eye he could see Greta turn his way. She was plainly dying to ask what celebrities he meant, but of course she wouldn't dare to, now.

Lola vaulted back into the kitchen carrying a cloth-bound book. She shoved it in Lionel's face, upsetting a spoonful of bisque that had been on its way to his mouth—a spoonful with a succulent chunk of pristine white lobster tail sticking out at him tantalizingly. Lionel almost groaned at the interruption.

He looked at the book, and despite its proximity to his face he could make out the word AUTOGRAPHS on the cover, rendered in a lovingly elaborate script. Aunt Lola flung the book open and revealed a random page.

"Charles Nelson Reilly," she said proudly, pointing to a signature that was too close to Lionel's face for him to focus on. He leaned back in his chair, but Lola just moved the book along with him. "He was in *The Ghost and Mrs. Muir* on TV, remember? He also played, he *also* played the major banana in that old Bic Banana commercial you used to laugh at when you were a boy. I got this from him, I *got* this from

him when he was at the mall judging the Miss Western Suburbs pageant. And here," she said, pointing to another stapled-in inscription. "Maria Ouspenskaya, who was a Best Supporting, a *Best* Supporting Actress winner sometime in the forties, and who was also in all those Wolfman movies I never let you watch. I got *her* when she was doing dinner theater in Evanston about forty years ago. She was Madame Arcati in *Blithe Spirit,* which closed after a three-day run because nobody went to dinner theater in Evanston in those days, and besides who could understand that accent? And here—"

"Lola!" the colonel barked. "Get that ridiculous artifact out of my son's face! You'll suffocate the boy!"

She clicked her tongue, shut the book, and put it under her arm. Then, hoisting a shoulder at her brother, she turned to her nephew and said, "Honey, would you *please* see if you can get Franklin Potter to sign this book? I'd be so, I'd be *so* grateful."

"Lola, sit *down,*" Colonel Frank commanded, tossing his napkin down before him in a tiny spate of fury. "Get a grip on yourself. You can't ask the boy to go running after film stars like a prepubescent *girl.* You shouldn't be acting that way yourself."

Greta picked at the hole in the knee of her Lycra tights and said, "Only the Lord Jesus Christ is worthy of worship, Aunt Lola."

Lola squinted and said, "Young Lady, no one said a word, no one said a *word* about worshipping them."

The girl pulled at a thread and watched it as it unraveled, leaving a web of neon Lycra just below her kneecap. "But the adoration you have for stars," she said, her voice as dispassionate as the HAL 2000 computer on Quaaludes, "is like the adoration you should have for your Savior." She belched.

"There are different ways, there are different *ways* of showing love for God," the older woman responded testily. She dropped back into her seat and placed the autograph book beside her on the table. "For instance, for *instance,* by keeping a clean and presentable appearance. Having good manners. Having respect for yourself. I don't need to be, I don't *need* to be lectured on loving God, dear, by you." She was red in the face now, the blood showing bright beneath her thin skin, like the juice of an overripe tomato. She picked up her spoon and started to sup again.

"The girl has a point, Lola," the colonel said with delighted smugness. "It's unbecoming in a woman of your advanced years to get so fanatical about these show-business prima donnas. Having a book like that one you've got there—that's bad enough. *Flaunting* it, though, that's beyond understanding. I'd have expected you to *hide* such a ludicrous habit, not display its accouterments to your family as though they were a Purple Heart or something."

Lola said nothing, but Lionel saw her artfully take her napkin, pass it lightly across her lips, and then drape it over the spine of the autograph book, where, just before it was obscured from view, Lionel could see written in black marker, VOLUME 8 N-R.

He grunted a laugh, then picked up his own napkin and applied it to his mouth, as if he'd only choked a little. Then, feeling somehow endeared toward Aunt Lola, and also feeling guilty for having had to refuse her, he decided to play up to her, to restore her confidence.

"So, anyway, Aunt Lola, how's business?" he asked brightly, balling up the napkin and reaching to the tureen for a bisque refill.

She pursed her lips and regarded him with a cocked eyebrow, as though she suspected him of having fired the opening salvo in a new barrage of mockery of her. But Lionel put on his most innocent, wide-eyed look, and she shifted in her chair, tossed back her mousy brown hair, and smiled. "Fine, honey, thank you," she said. "As a matter of fact, as a *matter* of fact, I'm expanding."

"Wonderful!" Lionel enthused, and his enthusiasm was genuine. Lola, after all, was not only an entrepreneur (something which galled her brother to no end) but something of a local celebrity as well. She had developed a line of greeting cards that she sold by mail; the cards were geared toward "nontraditional relationships." "Very nineties," she'd called the concept when she'd invented it, back in 1987. And indeed it had proven so; over the intervening years, more and more orders rolled in for Lola's dainty valentine drawings with typeset messages that said things like *Best*

Wishes on the Anniversary of Your Domestic Partnership and *Happy Birthday to Grandma's Special Friend.* The walls of her basement office were lined with newspaper profiles of her, and local magazine interviews. The press attention had peaked three years before, but it had caused Lola to adopt an imperial manner that hadn't, alas, declined along with it.

So the news that she was expanding her line was intriguing. Even Greta emerged from beneath her neon halo to take note of it. "You never told Pop or me this," she said accusingly.

"I only just today, I only just *today* confirmed it," Lola said, bringing a brimming ladle of bisque toward her bowl with her tongue wrapped firmly around her cheek. "I sent out a sample kit of the new cards to some specialized vendors to see how they did, and I got back some *very* interested inquiries." She spilled the bisque into her bowl, and a spattering of drops leaped onto her housedress. "Damn and, *damn* and blast," she muttered.

"So what's the gimmick here?" Lionel asked, sopping up the dregs of his bowl with a wad of doughy dinner roll. He popped it into his mouth and swiveled toward Lola, the better to watch her respond.

"It's a line," she said, returning the ladle to the tureen, "it's a line for *gays.*"

Lionel started to choke on his half-swallowed roll. It had been making its way effortlessly down his esophagus to his stomach, but when Lola had muttered The Word, it had seemed to swell to ten times its original size, stopping up his throat. He clutched his neck and doubled over, accidentally hitting his nose on the table, which only caused him to cough even more.

"No one make a move," commanded Colonel Frank, rising from his chair like the Angel Gabriel, his hands held out in a gesture of calm. "I've spent half my life dealing with emergencies. Leave this to *me.*" Rolling up his sleeves, he moved nimbly around the table to where Lionel was sitting choking; Aunt Lola and Greta stepped gratefully back as he passed them. Then he took Lionel, whose eyes were wide and watery and anxious, grabbed him around the stomach, and, with a grunt somewhat more frightening than that of

Conan the Barbarian in mid-battle, drew his massive arms to him, crushing his son's abdominal muscles in the process.

Lionel screamed, and a little burst of bread and butter and phlegm leaped from his mouth and onto the table. Greta curled her upper lip like an unhappy horse and said, "Guh-*ross.*"

Lionel, dangling now from his father's arms, somehow managed to find the voice to gasp, "Pop, for—Christ's sake, I'm—okay, let me *down*—"

The colonel released his grip, and Lionel dropped back into his seat like a load of wet laundry.

"You all right?" Greta asked meekly, her black fingernails curled around each cheek.

Lionel nodded, gasping.

"Oh, my word, my *word*," Aunt Lola exclaimed. "What a *relief*!"

"Just take it easy for a moment, son," said the Colonel, patting him on the back.

"God is merciful," said Greta in a hushed voice. Then she nodded at the table and said, "You wanna clean up your spit now? It's makin' me gag."

Lionel grabbed a paper napkin and wiped up the glob of bread he'd hacked up. As he did this, Aunt Lola scooted over to him and put her hand on his forehead. "Oh, *honey*," she cooed, "what *happened*? Was it something, was it something I *said*?"

Lionel balled up the napkin and dropped it on his place-mat, then looked up.

They were all staring at him, as though awaiting his reply. A chill ran up his spine.

Did they *suspect* it was something Lola had said? Or were they merely watching him to ensure that he wasn't going to have another seizure?

"I'm fine now," he said. "Really." Lola and the colonel returned reluctantly to their seats.

And then, before he could devise some more subtle way of squelching their suspicions, Lionel blurted, "Have I told you about this girl I'm seeing, Tracy? She's my date to the Trippy Awards banquet. I—I met her at the office, and—uh—"

He ground to a halt. But no matter. He looked up at his

father, and could see in the older man's eyes a glint of joy—
untrammeled, unhoped-for, undreamed-of joy. It was a look
that said, My name shall not die.

And Lionel thought, Oh, fine, now I'm in even *deeper.*
And he began to feel uneasy, as though he were standing
on the slippery edge of this great hole he was digging, and
he was losing his footing, and at any moment might fall in
and be swallowed up entirely.

As if she were reading his mind, Greta swallowed a gulp
of milk and gave forth a tiny burp.

chapter

■ ■

seven

The next day the world dared him to be frightened or unhappy. The chorus of car alarms that began at six o'clock each morning today sounded almost musical as they roused him from his sleep, the delirious *whoop-whoop-whoop* of one twining like a braid with the staccato *ri-ri-ri-ri-ri* of another—and the steady, shrill whine of yet a third providing an unearthly, strangely beautiful bass line. It sounded to Lionel like a record of bagpipes with a bad skip in it. And when he rose and threw open the curtains to see if one of the cars responsible for this glorious noise was his, the sun hit him smack in the face like a custard pie hurled by some heavenly devotee of Mack Sennett. He was so startled by the appearance of all this brightness that he stood for a moment gazing in dopey delight at the world outside his window, all garish and yellow and wonderful. And then his clock radio blared to life, right in the middle of an Elvis Costello tune. It was all too perfect to be coincidence. *God* was behind this.

He scrubbed himself clean, put on his best suit—daringly double-breasted—and drove down Lake Shore Drive with the radio cranked up high, loudly singing along with Todd Rundgren's "We Gotta Get You a Woman" even though he had the windows down. And as he glided into the Michigan Avenue exit lanes, he felt confidence and happiness bubble inside him as though he were a glass of Alka-Seltzer, and he said aloud, "I defy anything or anyone to spoil my mood today!" And just as he said it, the old Playboy Building reared its polished head and blotted out the sun, and the interior of Lionel's car fell into a chilly shadow. He looked at that unapologetically phallic structure looming above him, and wondered whether he'd made a mistake by tempting fate.

But he was a modern man, not given to taking signs and omens seriously. Within minutes he was flinging open the agency door and giving the receptionist his most dazzling smile. "*Good* morning, Alice," he said, sailing up to her. "*Great* color on you."

She looked down at the drab reddish-brown blouse she was wearing. "It is *not,*" she said incredulously.

"It is *so,*" he insisted, tossing his briefcase into the air and catching it as he passed her desk. "Brings out your cinnamon undertones."

Alice knitted her brow in bewilderment and opened her mouth to say something, but before she could do so, the phone buzzed. She grabbed the receiver and intoned, "Good *morning,* Deming, Stark and *Williams.*" Lionel turned and started into the corridor behind her. He was almost beyond her range of sight when he heard her say, "Oh, *hi,* Tracy."

His next step faltered, and then he stopped altogether. Alice had swung around in her chair and seen it, had watched him grind to a halt at the mention of Tracy's name. God*damn* it, he thought, cursing himself; why the *hell* did I do that?

She was mouthing Tracy's name to him now and pointing one of her manicured nails at the phone. He wanted to say, I *know* it's Tracy, you stupid mall vulture; I know it's Tracy, and I don't care. But he couldn't interrupt her to say that, nor could he just resume walking—he'd already rooted himself to the spot. His indecision had decided for him.

"Uh-*huh,*" Alice was saying, nodding her head. "Uh-*huh.* He *what?* Oh, my *God.* You're *kidding* . . . You're *sure* about it? But wouldn't he—" She spun her chair around again, showing Lionel her back. What was going on? "Okay, okay, hon," she cooed maternally. "You take it easy. I'll tell Julie you won't be in."

Then she hung up the phone, swung her chair toward Lionel yet again, crossed her legs elegantly, and gripped her exposed knees with her hands. She arched her back and gave him a luxurious smile; there was an almost feline kind of glee about her. Lionel began to sweat.

"That was Tracy," she said.

"I gathered that," he replied witheringly, suddenly wanting to tell her what he really thought of that color on her. "She out today?" he added, jiggling his briefcase, as if anxious to be on his way and not caring to spend too much time on so trivial a matter.

"Not *all* day," Alice said teasingly, her voice full of child-like merriment. "But she won't be in till after lunch because she had such an upsetting night last night. Said she broke up with her boyfriend, Guy. This time for good. Poor thing." She grinned at Lionel and rocked her chair back and forth. "Still, I bet I know *somme*-one who's happy to hear that bit of news," she trilled in an infuriating singsong. Then she actually had the audacity to wink at him! He had to turn quickly and leave before he lost control of himself and pulled her hair.

He mumbled inarticulate hellos to everyone he passed in the hall, and when he arrived at his office he found sunlight streaming into it, the same sunlight he'd so exalted only an hour before, only now it was a depressing thing. It flooded his desk, throwing into high relief all the millions of flecks of dust that covered his desktop like a carpet. It made the dust between the buttons on his telephone look deep and disgusting, like something might grow there. And it made his leather chair appear a mass of crisp, cracked platelets, pulling away from each other as in a textbook drawing of continental drift.

Cheap little office, he thought, resenting the sun for showing it to him; cheap little office, fit for a cheap little man with cheap little problems.

He put his briefcase on the desk, then went over to the windows and drew the blinds. The offending, revealing sunlight was cut off at once, and darkness eddied around him like a pool of cool, murky water. He went back to the doorway and flicked on his overhead light; a bluish-white phosphorescence immediately filled every corner evenly and neatly, giving it an impersonal, robotic feel, which was exactly what he wanted. "Just let me do my job today," he muttered, knowing even as he said it that his job required more from him than a set of objectively defined actions in which he might comfortably lose himself. He was an account executive; he had to schmooze with clients, cajole artists and writers, haggle with media sales people. But human interaction was beyond him right now; he wanted to spend the morning crunching numbers and forgetting about the mess his life was in, with his family and co-workers pushing him into a romance with Tracy that even Tracy's boyfriend was now agreeable enough to promote by allowing himself to become Tracy's *ex*-boyfriend.

For nearly an hour, nothing stirred in Lionel's office but the keypad of his calculator and the tail end of his ballpoint pen. He restructured Gloria Gimbek's proposed radio buy in a way that used All-Pro's diminished budget for the month to buy a level of exposure almost on par with one of their major holiday promotions, a feat he accomplished by cutting back on the usual stations and instead buying more drive-time on two smaller stations that had changed formats since the last ratings book. Gloria relied entirely too much on that damned ratings book. What, he wondered, would happen to this account if he left the radio buys up to her? He shuddered at the thought, then sat back and examined his handiwork. It was a masterpiece of efficiency and economy. He reflected with grim satisfaction that most artists create their masterworks while suffering.

He booted up his Macintosh and was getting ready to type an admonitory memo to Gloria when Carlton Wenck stuck his head in the door and said, "Knock, knock." (Carlton never actually knocked, he just verbally reproduced the sound effect, which was another thing about him that Lionel really, really hated.)

Lionel turned his head to face Carlton, but pointedly did not turn his chair, and he kept his hands poised over the keyboard; Carlton must be shown that he was interrupting him. "Hey, Carlton," he said in a dead voice. "Something I can do for you?"

Carlton took a few steps into the office. "Looks like one in the morning in here! You oughtta open some blinds. Beautiful day outside."

"I know it is. Need me for something?"

Carlton raised his eyebrows and cocked his head a little, as if taken aback by Lionel's abruptness. "Bad day, bud?"

"No, no," Lionel said, giving up and letting his hands drop into his lap. "Just busy, that's all." He still refused to turn his chair away from the Mac.

"Tracy's not in this morning," Carlton said, a little smirk sneaking onto his face. "Wouldn't have anything to do with your mood, would it?"

Lionel sighed, but decided to offer no other response.

Carlton grimaced and shrugged his shoulders, then said, "Okay. Listen. I'm putting together the company football pool this year, and—"

"Thanks, Carlton," he said, shaking his head. "But not this year."

"That's what you said *last* year." He laughed and scratched his nape.

"Well, I'm saying it again." He could hear how harsh he sounded, so he made an effort to soften his tone. "The thing is, I don't gamble."

"Well, it's hardly gambl—"

"I don't make exceptions, either, Carlton. Honest." He grimaced. "I mean—I used to have a problem with it, and now I—"

"*You?*" Carlton blurted. His jaw dropped.

Lionel finally gave up and swung his chair around to face him. He was a little stung by the incredulity implied by that *you.* "Yes, *me,*" he said heatedly. "In college. I lost a lot of money at poker. My dad had to bail me out. Not that it's any of your business." A total lie, but not, he thought, a bad one; anything to get him out of having to discuss football every morning.

Carlton looked at him a long time, as if reassessing him. Finally, he shrugged. "Well, if you change your mind."

"Right, right," Lionel agreed, and he turned back to his Mac.

Without another word, Carlton slipped out of Lionel's office. Almost as soon as he entered the hallway, he could be heard saying, "Hey, Donna, you up for the office football poo— Donna, wait a min— *Donna*! Hey, *DONNA*!" Then Lionel heard Titus, a production assistant, yell from down the hall, "She *deaf*, fool!" and then the sound of Carlton clomping down the hall after her.

His first impulse was to smile, but then he imagined what might happen when Carlton caught up with her. He'd invite her to participate in the pool, and she'd probably accept. (She had a poster of Mike Ditka on her office wall.) And then, in the course of discussing who else had signed up, Carlton would mention that Lionel was one of the few hold-outs, and Donna would say, Well, what do you expect? And Carlton would say, What do you mean, what do I expect? And Donna would say, How many faggots do you know who are interested in football?

Lionel shuddered, shook himself, and rolled his chair up to his desk, where he propped his elbows on his blotter and put his head in his hands. His pulse started thrumming. Donna wouldn't say that, would she? She wouldn't give him away. She'd already shown that. Hadn't she?

Ah, but what if Carlton happened to mention Lionel's romance with Tracy? Donna might not feel so protective of him then. And it *was* a subject Carlton couldn't seem to bring up often enough. Lionel could envision the scene that would follow. Donna would say, Not possible, Carlton; Lionel couldn't possibly have any interest in Tracy. After all, he's a . . .

He shuddered again, and stood bolt upright. This couldn't go on, this uncertainty, not knowing whether at any moment Donna might blow the cover behind which he'd spent so many years safely hiding. He *had* to talk with her.

He sat at his desk for a while, trying to figure out how best to approach her, how to handle her most successfully. He couldn't *forbid* her to say anything, and it probably wasn't wise to play on her sympathy—she might not have any. The best approach was probably simply to point out the sanctity of privacy, the right of the individual to deter-mine his or her own destiny. She'd probably respond to lofty ideological talk like that.

He steeled himself, then left his office and started down the corridor toward her. While en route, he ran into Perlman's secretary, Chelsea Monmoth, nicknamed "Chelsea Motormouth" by the staff at large due to her habit of relating long, excruciatingly detailed accounts of what happened to her the night before last, with the emphasis on how great she looked in what she was wearing and how what she'd said had put so-and-so in *her* place and wouldn't she think twice before being such a bitch again. Lionel noticed the look of expectation radiating from Chelsea's face, and he quickened his pace.

But she grabbed his arm as soon as he was within reach. "*Lionel!* I didn't even know you were *here* today. You been hiding away all morning?"

"Just busy, Chelsea," he said with a little laugh, and he gently extricated his arm.

"God, I know how *that* is," she said. "Last night I had to stay till seven-thirty printing out some ridiculous document for Perlman that ended up having about four more changes when I got in this morning, so I had to redo the whole thing anyway. *Plus,* you know that one command on the computer that's supposed to underscore a word? F-Seven, I think. Or F-Eight. One of those. Anyway, mine was broken and every time I tried it I ended up deleting a whole *line.* So I'm trying to figure out a way to do it manually, and meanwhile Perlman keeps bugging me, like, 'Chelsea, we need those printouts sometime this millennium,' and I have to eventually turn to the little Mussolini and go, '*Fine,* if you need them so bad, *you* can sit here and fix thi—' "

Lionel held up his hand, silencing her. "Listen, Chelsea, I'd love to hear the rest of this, but I was just on my way to see Donna. I've got to tell her something, like *pronto.*"

"Well, I hope it's not *that* urgent, 'cause she left for lunch about five minutes ago."

Lionel blanched. "No *way.*" He checked his watch. "It's ten minutes to noon! Why does she leave so early?"

Chelsea got her luminous look again, which could only mean more gossip. "Lionel, you wouldn't *believe* what that she-hulk gets up to in the plaza outside Illinois Center every day. She and a bunch of other dykes get together and make a complete *spectacle* of themselves. I didn't find out about it till last week, when Sandy and I went to lunch at this Mexican joint on State Street, what's the name of it, that one, you know, where the guy propositioned me around Christmas and I had to turn around to him and go, 'Buddy, if I were you I'd take a *long—*' "

"Illinois Center?" Lionel said, interrupting her. "Thanks, I'll look for her there." And then he dashed down the hall past Alice at the reception desk and into a fortuitously waiting elevator. Much as he wanted to hear what Chelsea had to say about Donna's scandalous activity, he had a feeling he could be witnessing it first-hand in the time it took her to spit it out.

chapter

∎∎∎∎∎∎∎∎∎∎∎∎∎∎∎∎∎∎∎

eight

The Illinois Center Plaza was filled with office workers sitting on benches and the rims of cement planters, eating hamburgers and French fries out of bags on their laps, their heads together, talking with great animation about whatever it was such people talked about. Lionel couldn't imagine falling into such easy intimacy with anyone he worked with. Some of the people he saw here— women, especially, in pressed woolen suits and high-collared blouses and Reeboks—were speaking in such hushed, frantic tones (you could occasionally hear one of them say, "You're *kidding*!") that he was sure they could only be gossiping, more likely than not about their co-workers. Lionel had noticed that about office drones: they seemed to have an insatiable curiosity about the most insignificant minutiae of each other's private lives. It was one of the things that most terrified him about them.

They looked now, however, a rather benign bunch, probably because of that beatifying sunlight, which was still in full force, beaming down on their heads and shoulders and giving each of them a kind of incandescent aura—a halo, if you will. He moved among them, his eyes peeled for Donna, who shouldn't, all thing considered, be very difficult to pick out in this crowd; there probably weren't many other women here wearing tank-tops that read ABORTIONS ON DEMAND.

He became aware of some kind of activity at the far north end of the plaza, barely visible behind a huge, typically hideous installation of scrap metal posing as "public art" (neither public nor art, as far as he was concerned). He moved around the monstrosity and found that the source of the movement he'd detected through the gaps in the metal was Donna and four other women, two of them fairly respectably dressed. They'd occupied a small clearing of the plaza, and were now engaged in a balletic series of movements, each woman perfectly in sync with all the others. First they extended their left arms to the side with great precision and elegance, then fanned them almost two-hundred and forty degrees, rotating at their hips as they did so; they then lifted their right legs, stepping forward carefully, bringing their torsos back into perfect alignment with their pelvises as they straightened their knees.

It was a mesmerizing sight, partially because of the fluidity of their movements, partially because of the glacial slowness of them, and partially because of their eerie synchronization. As Lionel paused to watch them, he noticed a number of other people doing the same, staring at them with a kind of bemused detachment—he imagined they were looking in vain for something to make fun of—before moving on and resuming their conversations.

He hesitated to interrupt this surreal performance by speaking to Donna, and wondered if he should just slip away and catch her some other time. But before he could make up his mind, she stretched her right arm in his direction, then turned her head to follow it, and in the process caught his eye—caught it and held it. Lionel grinned nervously and gave her a little wave, but no flicker of recognition crossed her face. Then she withdrew her gaze—and her arm—and was facing the opposite way again.

Lionel was quite aware that dozens of lunchers had seen him attempt to communicate with one of these bizarre women, only to be rebuffed. It made him angry; he hated looking foolish, and the only thing that would make it worse would be to slink away in shame. He took a deep breath, clenched his fists, and entered the little clearing the women had marked off for themselves.

He tapped Donna on the shoulder; she jumped at his touch, and when she saw who had interrupted her, her eyes flashed with irritation. "Lionel," she said. "What is it?"

He winced at her abruptness, but refused to give up. "I need to talk to you."

She shook her head. "I'm exercising right now," she replied flatly. She turned away from him and tried to catch up to where the other women had got to.

"What kind of exercise do you call this?" he asked, scooting around her to stay in her line of sight. But despite his efforts, she was watching her friends and not his face. It was going to be difficult, talking to a lip-reader who wouldn't consent to look at his lips. He tapped her shoulder again and repeated. "What kind of exercise do you call this?"

She shook her head, as if astonished by his gall. *"T'ai chi,"* she said. "It's the most popular form of exercise in China."

Well, that figures, thought Lionel; it'd have to have some socialist connection for Donna to espouse it. She was poised to continue now, but was watching him to make sure he'd finished with her and was going to go away.

The wind tossed his hair into his eyes, and he took a moment to brush it back over his head. Donna was waiting. It was now or never. She'd turn away in a second. Either bring it up now or just learn to live with the consequences.

"I want to talk to you about that night at The Hague," he said.

She took a deep breath and dropped her arms, and her body slumped a little. Behind her, the other women continued their course of movement. "What about it, Lionel? You want to apologize for being rude to me? I understand. It was a shock for you. No big deal."

"No, no," he said. "I want you to know—well, *why* I was there. I think you may have gotten the wrong impression."

She squinted at him, her head cocked just a bit. "Why do you care what impression I got?"

"Well," he said, a strain of nervous laughter in his voice that he was grateful she couldn't hear, "I wouldn't want you to think I was *gay* or anything." There. It was out. His heart was pounding. "Not that there's anything *wrong* with being gay. I mean, you—you're—you know—you're *fine.*" He was beginning to babble. He commanded himself to get a grip. "I just—*you* know. *You* know. I want to set it straight. The record, I mean. I want to set the record straight. You should excuse the expression." He blurted out a pathetic little laugh. He was *really* messing this up.

She was staring at his lips with a look of what he thought was increasing puzzlement. "Lionel, are you saying you're not gay?" She said it much louder than he would've liked.

"No," he said. "I mean, yes." He shook his head. "*No,* I'm not gay, *yes,* that's what I'm saying."

"But I saw you *kiss* another man."

Color seeped from his face like sand out of an hourglass. He *knew* she'd seen that, he just *knew* it. Fortunately, as a result, he had his defense ready. "I didn't kiss *him,* Donna, he kissed *me.* What was I supposed to do, recoil from him? He's an old friend. My hairdresser, actually. He was having some personal problems and he wanted to talk about them. I met him at The Hague because he feels comfortable there. I was just being a friend, Donna." His palms were sweating now.

The four women behind Donna were stretching their arms over their heads, flexing their biceps as they reached skyward. Donna said, "You were watching that stripper with your mouth open, Lionel. That stripper with the enormous schlong. I saw you staring at it like my dog, Artemis, stares at a hambone."

Lionel flinched. He didn't mind her being either crude or loud—but *both*? He'd better end this quickly. "I was just stupefied, that's all. I'd never seen a man strip before. I couldn't believe my eyes. It was—you know—*intellectual* curiosity. That's all." He stopped and took a deep breath, then barreled on. "That's why I got so embarrassed when you caught me watching. I *knew* what you'd think." A little bead of sweat slid down his nose like a skier off a ski-slope, and landed on his tie with a splat. He felt like he was being grilled by the CIA under a four-thousand-watt heat lamp.

Donna turned for a moment and looked toward her friends, who were likewise now turning their heads toward her every few seconds, wondering what had taken her out of the circuit. Lionel knew he was disrupting their entire routine, but couldn't help it; he was in waist-deep, now.

Donna looked him straight in the eye. "So what if that's what I think, Lionel? I still don't see why you give a shit."

"Because I'm beginning a new relationship—with Tracy," he forced himself to say. He'd straighten out *that* end of the problem later, but right now he needed to use it to his benefit. "I didn't want any weird rumors screwing that up."

She shook her head gently, almost imperceptibly, and let a little sigh escape her lips. "Fine, Lionel," she said. "You're not gay. Whatever you say." She turned back to her friends, nodded at them as if to say, Everything's okay, then stuck her right foot into the air and twisted it, pivoting on her hip away from him. He had been dismissed.

He was profoundly disturbed by the outcome of this confrontation. Donna had said "Fine, you're not gay," but she'd said it as though she were humoring him, as though she still believed otherwise but couldn't be bothered arguing about it. Well, there was nothing he could do about it now. At least he felt reasonably certain she wouldn't bring it up to anyone else. She'd shown a sliver of contempt for him, but that contempt would probably keep her from dishing him; no doubt she considered him beneath her notice.

He backed away, trying hard not to look at anyone who'd been sitting nearby who might've heard Donna's blaring accusations. But this entailed looking mostly at his shoes, instead of at where he was going, and within five feet of the *t'ai chi* circle he crashed into someone.

He was preparing his apology even as he looked up to meet his victim's face. The apology died on his lips. "Tracy!" he said. "Oh—Jesus! You startled me!"

"You should watch where you're going," she said with a Mae West inflection, as though it were a double entendre, which, Lionel decided after running it through his head quickly, it couldn't possibly be. "I was just coming over to say hi, not to slam-dance with you."

He looked over his shoulder and saw that Donna was now facing him, one arm pointed at him as though she were a French revolutionary preparing to denounce him to the crowd. He knew she couldn't help seeing anything he did now. So he turned back to Tracy, slipped his arm around her, placing his hand over the small of her back, and led her away.

Tracy looked surprised by this unprecedented and proprietary gesture, but he could see that she was also pleased and flattered. As they walked away, he took a swift glance back at the *t'ai chi* circle and saw that Donna had now swiveled her torso in the other direction. No matter. She couldn't possibly have missed his and Tracy's meeting.

Mission accomplished, he thought. But as he turned back to Tracy, who was wearing one of her most dazzling smiles and whose eyes had turned into little constellations of stars, he realized that his victory might be a case of out of the frying pan, into the blast furnace.

He cleared his throat and tried to steer them into shallower waters. "I was just watching Donna do this Chinese exercise thing when you found me. Pretty comical stuff."

"You think so?" she said, not a hint of reproach in her voice. "I think it looks kind of beautiful, myself. And it's impressive that she does it so well. A lot of deaf people, you know, have trouble balancing, because their inner ear is all screwed up. So watching Donna stand on one leg and stuff like that—that's a real achievement. I think she should be proud."

He lowered his head; as long as he'd known Tracy, she'd never mocked anyone. In fact, she'd always gone the other route, finding something to admire instead. It made him feel a little uneasy when she showed him up like that, especially since he knew it was never her intention to show him up at all.

"How was your morning?" he asked. They passed a middle-aged woman laden with shopping bags from various Magnificent Mile shops; the bags banged into Lionel's hip and thigh, and gave him an excuse to take his hand away from Tracy's back, drop back a bit, then rejoin her with a small but significant gap between them.

"Okay, I guess," she answered, and he noticed for the first time that her nose was pink, as if she'd been crying. "I just had some stuff to move out of Guy's place." She was taking it for granted that he'd know what had happened to her last night.

"Well, what's done is done," he said with ludicrous pomposity, as though he'd just imparted to her the wisdom of the ages. "Lots of life still ahead, you know."

"Oh, I *know*," she said, and she gave him a sly smile.

He swallowed hard, realizing he'd started a mechanism that was now running without him. The fiction of his long-simmering, now-stewing romance with Tracy had been taken out of his hands by an entire society of heterosexual handlers—his family, his co-workers, even his bosses.

Maybe it was time for him to remove himself from subversive outside influences, to take control and clear the air. Maybe it was time for him to simply say, Tracy, I know we like each other, and I know we have a good time together, but let's just take it slow, okay? And by slow he would mean, increasingly slow, a grinding slowness that would finally, down the road, end in a halt; but she wouldn't know that.

If he said this to her now, it might hurt her a little, but how much less so than later, after the Trippy Awards banquet, after the continued build-up of romantic expectations and exhortations that were being thrust on them almost hourly. It would practically be a *kindness* to speak now, to spare her that.

And so he turned and looked into her eyes, right there at a stoplight on Michigan Avenue, just across the street from the building in which they both worked, directly across the intersection from the parade of noisy Transylvanian demonstrators, smack up against a trash can, and mere steps away from a loudly muttering bum wearing a sandwich board filled with scrawled handwriting purporting to tell HOW THE POPE RUNS ABC, NBC, CBS AND CNN.

"Tracy," he said, and his voice sounded like a death rattle.

She looked up at him (which, considering that she was an inch taller than he, was something of an achievement), and said, "Yes, Lionel?"

The traffic light changed from DON'T WALK to WALK and a stream of pedestrians began filling the street and heading for the other side, but neither of them moved. "Tracy, I know we like each other," he said—and here his voice actually cracked, so that he had to drop it half an octave before continuing—"and I know we have a good time togeth—" He stopped short.

Impossible.

Impossible that this should be happening.

Impossible that he should be seeing *Toné,* of all people, coming down the street in his direction.

The look on his face began to resemble something from a Munch painting, and Tracy, suddenly concerned by his bulging eyes and quivering lips, placed her hand on his arm. "Lionel? Honey? Are you all right?"

No it wasn't *impossible,* because it was *happening.* There was Toné, his long black hair flowing behind him like a cape, breezing down Michigan Avenue with the regal bearing of a queen en route to a coronation, his eyes— thank God—skyward, as if contemplating the infinite. He hadn't yet seen Lionel.

"Lionel?" Tracy repeated. "Something the matter?"

That he should have to introduce Tracy to Toné—no, no, never, not in a million years would he allow such a volatile mixing of chemicals to occur. It would be just like Toné to *insist* on kissing him when they met, and Tracy was too sharp an observer not to read into that what was there to be read; and Toné would very likely be unable to resist making all kinds of veiled references that Tracy would spend an evening mulling over and from which she might draw awful conclusions.

No, no, *no.* But, if not, then what, what, *what?*

"Lionel," said Tracy sharply, "*tell* me. What *is* it?"

The end was near. Toné had just lowered his leonine head, seen Lionel, and waved.

Oh, God, I'm doomed, he thought. Hail, Mary, full of grace, may I please now be run over by the 146 bus.

Looking around frantically, like an animal seeking escape, he let his gaze fall on the Transylvanian protesters at the opposite corner of the intersection. They were in greater force than ever today, still yelping out their demands and brandishing placards, and by the way people were stepping into the street to get around them, Lionel guessed that their mood must be explosive. He pointed to them; his hand was shaking as he did so.

"Look, Tracy," he said. "Over there. Ever noticed them before?"

"What?" she said, squinting across traffic, not quite certain at first what he was pointing at. "Lionel, you're scaring me—I don't kn—"

"The Transylvanians! Over there!" He pointed them out to her again. As he did so, a couple of businessmen moved to enter the Romanian Consulate building, and several of the marchers deliberately blocked their way, then jostled and shoved them as they pressed through to the revolving door. Explosive, indeed.

"Transylvanians?" she said. "You mean, like where Dracula comes from?"

"I mean a people fighting for their freedom," he said, and his voice cracked again but this time he was past caring. Toné was almost close enough to call out to him. "The same way we Americans fought for our freedom from Britain two centuries ago. I just don't see how anyone can stand by and not *help* them." And without another word he dashed into the intersection, interweaving with traffic, getting honked at and cursed at and almost struck down, until he was standing toe-to-toe with the Transylvanian demonstrators, who seemed no little alarmed by the appearance of this sweaty, panting young man in a six-hundred-and-fifty-dollar suit.

Nearest to him was an elderly woman in an old floral print dress, an ancient shawl, and white Sperry Topsiders, carrying a sign that said something in Romanian he couldn't read. He reached out, grabbed her placard, and said, "Let me carry your burden, Little Mother," not realizing until he said it how completely absurd it would sound.

Unfortunately, Little Mother wasn't at all eager to give up her burden, and he had to wrestle it from her, eventually prying her fleshy fingers off the handle and darting away with his prize to the perimeter of the circle. Once he'd done so, he realized that the demonstrators were now looking at him with not only suspicion, but with growing hostility—and he noticed for the first time that Ivan the Adorable was chief among those glaring at him, with eyes as shamelessly blue as the tiles in a North Shore swimming pool.

Several passersby had stopped in their tracks and were watching him; they sensed a scene in the making. Unwilling to disappoint them—and keenly aware that Tracy must be watching as well—he lifted the placard high, and, in a reedy, embarrassing voice, cried out, "Freedom for Transylvania?" as if he were asking them if they thought this might be a good thing.

By this time, most of the demonstrators had become aware of the disturbance he was causing, and had broken ranks to crowd around him and stare at him in suspicion and bewilderment. The only one who had anything to say was Little Mother, who had now worked herself into a fit of pique over the theft of her placard and was loudly commanding a younger activist—presumably her son—to go and retrieve it for her.

Panicking, Lionel swelled his chest and cried out again, this time pridefully and manfully, *"Freedom for Transylvania!"* The sound of his voice surprised even him. He'd made the banal slogan sound like an imperative from Almighty God.

Some of the demonstrators yelled something that he couldn't understand but chose to interpret as support. Little Mother was nagging anyone who would listen to retrieve her placard, and a moment later two demonstrators in the rear got into a shoving match while trying to see Lionel. The march was dissolving into chaos, all because of Lionel— and Ivan, his broad neck bulging with power and authority, was trying to shout everyone back into order.

But before that could happen, a sharp voice sailed over Lionel's head and pierced the pandemonium. "If this isn't just *typical,*" it said.

Lionel turned and found himself facing an extremely thin, appallingly aged man in dirty Birkenstock sandals and a ratty white cardigan sweater with yellow armpit stains down to its waist, who was carrying a tattered plastic grocery bag which he was apparently in the process of filling with discarded aluminum cans. *"Typical,"* he repeated, almost barking it in Lionel's face. He rocked back on his heels—Lionel thought he was going to fall over—and regarded the Transylvanians. "This is how it ends, the Great Experiment, the Revolution. Not with a glorious class war, but with a rabble of fragmented and disunited splinter states racing to become as bourgeois as the West, in the process reviving the petty bickerings and divisions that Comrade Lenin purged from the Soviet sphere. Serb turns on Croat, Armenian on Azerbaijani, Transylvanian on Romanian." The demonstrators were again climbing all over each other to view this latest confrontation, and the onlookers in the street had begun to block traffic. Horns blared; the demonstrators had become a mob, and Lionel was being berated by a demented and smelly socialist. He was beginning to wish he'd just introduced Toné to Tracy.

The old man waved his grocery bag at Lionel and the cans clinked together ominously. "And now you clamor like animals on a city street, howling for what you want handed to you on a silver platter! In the foppish vestments of imperialism, you shamelessly crowd this place like a herd of cattle and *dare* to demand freedom, freedom that socialism could have given you, had you not allowed it to be subverted and *destroyed.*"

The Transylvanians now started some seriously ugly murmuring. Lionel, who was a little put off by the old man's vehemence—he wasn't used to this kind of passion in his own daily exchanges—tried to get him to leave. "Listen, pal," he said, "back off, okay? No one here wants to make a big stink about this with you."

"Of course not," he said, sneering. "Argument and debate are devalued things in your materialistic world." A little pearl of saliva leapt out of his mouth and fell on Lionel's shoe; Lionel grimaced in distaste and wondered how he could get it off without touching it. "What you *want* is what you *want,*" the old man continued, less eloquently now, "you *creatures* of appetite—you *monsters* of free will—you *abortions* that lived to eat your mothers! You have undone us! You have thrown us into a new Dark Age. Were Comrade Lenin to see wh—"

Suddenly he was struck down. From behind Lionel, a placard had come down hard on the old man's head, knocking him to his knees. Lionel whirled and saw Ivan at the other end of it, a look of such hatred on his face that Lionel almost didn't recognize the big fuzzy bear of his masturbatory fantasies. "Shall I show you how socialism saved my *niece,* you black rogue?" Ivan howled. "Dead at the age of two. Shall I show you what that feels like?" Lionel didn't see how Ivan *could* show a ninety-year-old what it felt like to die at the age of two, but no doubt Ivan wasn't at his most rational right now.

The old man rubbed his bruised head, glared at Ivan, and said, "The same fate should have been *yours.*"

And then all hell broke loose. The old man had apparently underestimated the effect that an invocation of the old regime would have on a bunch of post-Communist Eastern Europeans—especially post-Communist Eastern Europeans who were extremely pissed off to begin with. From what Lionel could tell, the word *socialism* had the approximate effect on Romanians that *motherfucker* had on a surly American crowd. In a flash, six or seven Transylvanians had piled on top of the Leninist curmudgeon and were beating him with their placards (or at least trying to; the signs had a distressing tendency to butt together well above the victim's head).

As for Lionel, he got a good kick in the backside from Little Mother, who, it seems, hadn't been fooled a bit by his rhetorical eruption; and the kick sent him flying square into the center of the violence, which by now had been joined by a couple of football-player types who had taken it upon themselves to help the old commie coot.

Lionel was trying to crawl backward out of the melee when someone stepped on his head, and as the heel of his oppressor's shoe ground into his ear, he wondered how he could even begin to explain to Julius Deming how it was possible for someone to have stepped on his head during an ordinary lunch hour. Because he was certain that, by now, he'd been scuffed up enough to be more or less unpresentable at the office for the remainder of the day.

Not that returning to the office even remained an option for much longer. By the time he got to his knees and was shaking the stars out of his head, he was able to untangle the whine of a siren from the other shrieks and screams that surrounded him. He was then peremptorily lifted to his feet by someone he couldn't see—but since whoever it was tossed him into the back of a paddy wagon, he made an educated guess that it was a police officer.

He tumbled to the back of the vehicle, reeling a little from the effects of violence and confusion, and when he punch-drunkenly turned his head and looked outside, he saw, just before the doors slammed shut, a sight that gave him no small measure of relief.

For across Michigan Avenue, among the many amazed persons who had stopped to watch the riot, he saw Tracy and Toné, both of whom were in turn staring at him, their eyes wide and their jaws firmly lodged on their chests. But they were several yards from each other, and separated by a phalanx of bodies at least eight persons wide. They had not seen each other; they had not met.

chapter

■ ■ ■ ■ ■ ■ ■ ■ ■ ■ ■ ■ ■ ■ ■ ■ ■ ■

nine

At the police station, which was located on the near South Side in what looked like one of the more interesting neighborhoods in Beirut, Lionel was placed in a holding cell with the seven Transylvanians who had ended up sharing the paddy wagon with him—one of whom was Ivan, whose Disney-blue eyes were now fixed on him with a glowering intensity.

As the matronly detective closed the cell door, Lionel pressed his face against the bars and said, "Listen—this is a mistake! You've got to understand, I don't *belong* here!" The detective twisted the key in the lock and then slipped it out and onto her belt, ignoring Lionel's plea with a time-sharpened obliviousness. As she made her way down the corridor, Lionel called after her, *"Goddamn it, I don't have a drop of Slavic blood in my body!"*

"What makes you think *we* do?" said one of the demonstrators directly behind him, and by the half-husky, half-honeyed sound of that voice, Lionel had no doubt which one of them it was.

Sheepishly, he turned, and sure enough there was Ivan standing right at his elbow, so close that he could feel his breath on his face. In spite of himself, he felt a major erection coming on.

"Well," Lionel said, his voice wavery with anxiety, "you're Romanians—Transylvanians—whatever. Aren't you?" He stepped back a few paces, but Ivan stepped forward to keep the gap between them a small one.

"We are Romanians by nationality," he said. "And Transylvanians by ethnicity. That's just the point. We *aren't Slavs*! This is a common misconception, because we were for so long a Soviet client state. But Romania is not a Slavic country, Romanian is not a Slavic language. It is a Romance language, and we are Europeans."

Lionel had to admit that Ivan's accent sounded more Italian than Slavic. "Sorry," he said. "I didn't know." He was acutely aware that all the other Transylvanians in the cell were watching him, hanging on his every word. He tried hard not to stare too longingly into Ivan's well-deep eyes, or to think about what it would be like to lick chocolate syrup out of the cleft in his chin.

Ivan stretched out one of his superbly muscled arms and propped it against the wall of the cell, effectively cutting off Lionel's only avenue of escape—not that there was any place to escape to. "You know so little about us," he said, his eyes narrowing, "and yet you disrupted our demonstration and, it seems, took up our cause. Why? Was this some sophisticated American form of mockery?"

"No—*God,* no," Lionel said, throwing up his hands in alarm. "Of *course* not. I *meant* it. It's just that—I—well, I guess I was sort of overcome by your, I guess you'd call it your *persistence.*" He loosened his tie with his finger and unbuttoned his collar; he was beginning to sweat. "I've seen you out there, every day, for—three, four weeks, however long it's been. I guess you just finally—you know—*got* to me." Yeah, he was thinking; oh, *yeah,* Ivan, you really got to me, but *good.* He folded his hands before him to try to hide the swelling in his crotch.

Ivan stared at him a little while longer. Then his body seemed to relax a bit; the tension in his posture eased. "If that's so," he said, "then you are a very unusual man. It's been difficult to get anyone to take us seriously."

Lionel shrugged. "I'm really sorry about that."

Suddenly Ivan pushed himself away from the wall, stood upright, and extended his hand for Lionel to shake. (Lionel, who for a moment thought that Ivan was preparing to hit him, responded by jumping back a full eight inches in alarm.)

"I'm pleased to make your acquaintance," he said with a dazzling smile. "My name is Emil Apostal."

Relief flooded over Lionel. "Please to meet *you*; I'm Lionel Frank," he said. Then he took the large, hairy hand that had been offered to him, and made an effort to give it his manliest shake.

Too manly, apparently. Emil gave a little yelp and snatched his hand away.

He held it before him as if it were a wounded animal, and said, "Mr. Frank, you are a *vigorous* man."

"Oh, Christ, I'm *sorry*," Lionel blurted, reaching out to touch him on the shoulder, and only stopping himself at the last moment. "Jesus, I didn't mean to be such an *ape*. I just wanted to make a good impression."

"You've made a fine impression." He slapped Lionel on the back with his good hand, and Lionel felt something snap in his chest; was this really a gesture of forgiveness, or was Emil just getting revenge? "You are a friend of Transylvania," Emil continued, "and therefore a friend of ours."

Lionel looked at the other demonstrators, who smiled and nodded reservedly; apparently they didn't share Emil's largeness of spirit. (Nor, he thought with a touch of scorn, did they share his Marlboro Man good looks. One of them uncannily resembled Miss Jane Hathaway from *The Beverly Hillbillies*, only with facial hair.) Still, if being Emil's friend meant being Transylvania's friend, then Lionel was all for Transylvania, and he said as much.

Emil nodded in grave appreciation. "Perhaps you don't know it, but Transylvania *was* independent once," he said a bit condescendingly, as if explaining the facts of life to a fourth-grader. "Many centuries ago, to be sure, and for only a brief period, but it proved that we *can* be a nation. Still, we have spent so many years since being passed around by imperialist states like Turkey, Germany, Austria, Hungary, and finally Romania, that the world considers us nothing but a territory. We believe this must *change*, Mr. Frank. For

a time, after the fall of Ceausescu, we believed that freedom
for all Romanians would follow, but this hasn't happened.
Romania has no Lech Walesa, no Vaçlav Havel; there is no
great man to lead us into a new, free society. So in Romania
today, it has ended up that we have Ceausescuism without
Ceausescu. That is why we Transylvanians have said, Enough!
Let Romania founder. Transylvania will go her *own* way, we
will build our *own* state, and we will astonish the world!"
Emil's eyes lit up as he warmed to his subject, and Lionel,
whose erection was now at full mast, was so stirred by this
handsome patriot that he would have thrown himself in
front of a lit cannon if it meant guaranteeing Transylvanian
sovereignty.

Just then the detective reappeared. "You joes are in
luck," she said as she fumbled with her keys. "The old guy
you beat on decided not to press charges. Matter of fact,
he seems to have slipped out of the station when we
weren't looking, and no one's got any idea where he went."

Emil leaned close to Lionel and whispered, "He's probably a fugitive from justice himself, the filthy Marxist."

"So," the detective continued, swinging open the cell
door, "there's just the little matter of disturbing the peace.
If you've got bail bond cards, or if you post a cash bail, you
can go, and we'll notify you about your hearing date later."

The Transylvanians started filing out of the cell, most of
them digging into their pockets to fetch their wallets. Only
Emil stood still, a look of terror on his face.

"What's wrong, Emil?"

"I have no bail bond card, I have no cash."

Lionel, who had already gotten out his checkbook, nodded in the direction of the other demonstrators. "Your pals
can pitch in to make cash bail for you. It can't be all that
much."

Emil shook his head. "It's a matter of pride, Mr. Frank. I
couldn't ask them. I am the newest of them—I've only been
in the country for a year. I couldn't possibly disgrace myself
by—by—" He gulped down the rest of the sentence. Lionel
thought he might cry.

He looked at Emil's pursed lips and high cheekbones, and
he thought, The things I do for love! "Well," he said flipping
open his checkbook and taking his pen from his jacket

pocket, "you don't have to worry about disgracing yourself to *me,* so why not let me lend you what you need?" Lend, schmend, he thought; I'll never see this money again.

Emil looked at him, his face registering an almost volcanic mixture of astonishment and emotion. Then he did in fact burst into tears, reaching over and enfolding Lionel in a great big bear hug and sobbing on his shoulder.

Worth it! thought Lionel. Even if the bail is a hundred thousand dollars, it's worth it, worth it, *worth* it!

chapter

■■■■■■■■■■■■■■■■■■■

ten

Lionel was so enraptured by the turn of events that he felt he had to tell someone about it or burst. So after taking a cab to the Loop and retrieving his car, he drove to Live Long and Prosper, the science-fiction bookstore where Yolanda worked as a sort of clerk-cum-archivist.

When he entered the store, passing beneath a dangling mobile of papier-mâché starships that never failed to bean him in the head any time he dared walk in, he found that Yolanda had left the counter and stepped into the far-right aisle. There, she was busy relating the merits of a certain paperback offering to a huge, gray-skinned customer who was carrying a bulging briefcase, wearing a highly unseasonable parka, and who appeared to be having trouble breathing (all in all, thought Lionel, a typical science-fiction fan).

"This is not the next entry in the Attiveldan Tetralogy," Yolanda was saying as she passed the book to the customer, who opened it to a random page and practically touched his face to it as he skimmed down the lines of text. "That does not come out until December. But this is a collection of short stories that all take place in the Attiveldan Universe, and they feature some of the same characters, in adventures that take place before the Tetralogy begins."

The customer turned his thick head toward her, slowly, like one of the animal kingdom's larger beasts of burden. His hair was so greasy that despite its length it refused to fall into the book and stuck to his skull, resembling nothing so much as a shiny brown bathing cap. "What about Grand Duke Giron?" he asked in a voice like the bleat of a sheep. "Is he in here?"

"Yes, he has a small part in one of the first stories." She tried to take the book from him, to show him the story in question, but he snatched it away from her.

"How about Barbeeta?" he yelped. "Is *she* in here?"

"Well, no, she is not," Yolanda answered as politely as possible. "Remember, she was not born until the second book of the Tetralogy, and these stories take place *before.* There is, however, a story about Barbeeta's *mother,* which also reveals who her father was—whether he was human or, as has been speculated, whether he was in fact one of the Presences of Yeryar."

The customer frowned. "Well? Which was he?"

Yolanda shook her head. "I must not tell. It would spoil one of the other surprises in the book."

The customer snorted, then looked again at the paper- back he held in his grime-encrusted hands. (Lionel certainly hoped he bought it, for who else would after he'd left his mark on it?) He turned for one last question. "And what about the Qi? Are *they* in here?"

Yolanda was unfazed. "Oh, yes, indeed," she said, and Lionel rolled his eyes. When on earth did she find time to *read* all this junk? "The concluding story, as a matter of fact, is set entirely in the Qi Dominion, and it tells why that race first decided to attempt the colonization of Attivelda space."

The customer sighed and shut the book. "Okay. I'll take it."

Yolanda turned to lead him to the counter, and it was then that she caught sight of Lionel. She mouthed the words *One moment,* then slipped behind the cash register.

She located the book's price with her fingernail. "Six- fourteen, please," she said sweetly, and as she inserted the book into a paper bag and taped it shut for him, he reached into one of his parka's deep pockets and pulled out four crumpled dollar bills, one at a time, and presented them to her. Then he proceeded to pull out the balance of the amount due in the form of loose change, retrieving at the same time crumbs of food, bits of lint, and used Band-Aids.

Lionel, who was standing at the magazine rack holding an open copy of *Mondo* and pretending he understood even the first thing about it, watched in amusement as Yolanda regarded the heap of money sitting on the counter with a stricken look on her face. She didn't even dare to count it. She just handed the package to the customer and said, "Thank you! Come again!"

The customer grunted and headed out the door.

Lionel instantly dropped the magazine back onto the rack and trotted over to Yolanda, who was with some perplexity regarding the oily mess of pocket change her customer had left her.

"Don't touch it," he advised her. "You're sure to get a skin disease."

Sensing that she was being mocked, she grimaced at him, then bravely swept the change into her open palm and deposited it (rather eagerly, thought Lionel) into the top drawer of the cash register. Then, wiping her hands on her Levis, she said, "Hello, Lionel. What is new?"

"What's *new*?" he repeated gleefully. "Well, let's see: so far today, I've done time in jail and fallen in love."

"Oh," she said coolly, stepping from behind the counter and sailing past him to the middle aisle, where she began moving copies of a book called *Wormwitch's Prophecy* from a cardboard box to a special display stand that had been set up. Lionel wondered if she knew what she was doing; the cover of that book would've been enough to scare any normal reader away, with a big snake's head on a green woman's body, complete with enormous scaly breasts that looked like Gucci watermelons. "My night here has been quieter than that," she added dismissively.

He could see now that she was preoccupied. "Yolanda," he said, "I'm not kidding. I really *was* in jail. I really *am* in love."

She turned toward him, brows knit, and swept a strand of hair from her face. *"Oh,"* she said. "I—do not know what to say. Are you okay, Lionel?"

"Okay! I'm *terrific*!"

"You were not raped in prison, then?"

"I should've been so lucky!"

She put her hands to her face and started to cry, astonishing him.

His spirits plummeted. They'd been perched rather precariously at their dizzying height to begin with, and Yolanda's sobbing was more than enough to upset them. He reached over and took one of her hands away from her face. She lowered her head so that he wouldn't see her tears. "Hey," he said, "Yolanda. What is it?"

She shook her head and dried her eyes. "You will think I am silly."

He released his grip on her. "Not any more than usual, no."

She snorted a laugh; his teasing had taken her by surprise. Smiling now, she reached her hand into the pocket of her jeans—which were so tight that when her hand reappeared, he saw that her fingers had turned purple—and fished out a fraying tissue, on which she now blew her nose. "It is Bob," she said, daubing her nostrils with the balled-up wad of paper.

Lionel felt a kind of stillness, as though his blood had suddenly stopped flowing. It was partly due to his anxiety for his friend's distress, partly due to anticipation of some *really* good dirt. "What is it?" he asked, his voice hushed. "Another woman?"

"Oh, no!" she said wildly, stuffing the tissue back into her pocket. "That I could handle. No, I am losing him to other *men.*"

Lionel felt like he'd just hit the Mother Lode of dirt. "I *knew* it," he said, slitting his eyes and shaking his head. "Goddamn, I just *knew* it."

She sniffled and looked at him strangely. "Do not be ridiculous, Lionel. You could not possibly have foreseen this."

He leaned against the display case, rather proud of himself. "I've got greater powers of observation than you know, kid," he said loftily.

"Then why did you not *warn* him?"

"Wa—*warn* him?" he said, a little flustered. "I don't follow you."

"I am so afraid of what they will *do* to him," she cried,

a little catch in her voice. "What if they make him sit around a campfire naked and do his private business in the bushes? I know they will! They will make him put warpaint on his face, and he becomes *suicidal* when his skin breaks out!" She clutched her forehead in dismay. "And what will they make him *eat*? He cannot digest any cut of meat that is not saturated with Bernaise sauce!" She went back to the counter, sat on the stool and buried her head in her hands. "I am so worried about him, I am losing sleep!"

Lionel knit his brows. "Maybe we'd better make it real clear what we're talking about here," he said, a little embarrassed at his previous assumption.

She sighed, tossed her hair back, and swiveled around to face him. "I thought you said you knew. Never mind. His boss at the insurance company has invited four of the junior executives to accompany him on a 'male retreat' based on the writings of a musician named Nathan Beatty. The retreat is called 'Resurrecting Your Inner Chieftain.' That is Beatty's word for what modern men have lost—the chieftaincy of their destinies. And the only way they can find it again is to subject themselves to the wisdom of their 'tribal elders.' Lionel, it sounds like something you would find in one of the books we sell *here.*" She pushed her hair out of her face and looked at him plaintively. "Bob is *terrified* of going. Yet if he does not go, he will not be promoted from his current position."

"His boss *told* him that?" Lionel asked incredulously.

She shook her head. "No, no, but it was made clear without saying so. It was—it was—" She picked up a tiny rubber dragon and unconsciously started twisting its neck. "What is the word, Lionel?"

"Implicit?" he offered.

"Thank you, yes, implicit," she said, and all at once the dragon's head snapped off. She reached under the counter and deposited it in a wastepaper basket. "His boss has already been on one retreat, last year, and Bob said it changed him utterly. Now he has made it *implicit* that only those who are his tribal 'brothers' can continue up the ladder in the company. My poor darling Bob. He is not *like* other men. That is why I got so upset when you made a joke about rape in prison. It could *happen* to him."

Lionel hopped up onto the counter and sat there, letting his legs dangle. He folded his hands and looked at his thumbs, entwined together like chubby pink hatchlings in a nest, and he did his best to keep a straight face. The truth was, he couldn't take this problem of Yolanda's even a fraction as seriously as she was, because he found it so perversely funny. He cleared his throat to prevent any levity from sneaking into his voice, and said, "Yolanda, I've read about these 'retreats.' The men who sign up for them mainly go off together to fart and belch like they used to at summer camp. Then they come back and feel like they have some control over their lives, because they've spent a week peeing in the sink and not having to answer for it. It's harmless. Bob doesn't need to be afraid to go. You should tell him."

"Oh," she said, shaking her head emphatically, "I could *not*. He does not *admit* that he is afraid. He says that he thinks it will be a 'hoot.' He says that these retreats are all the rage, that they have been written about in all the magazines. But I know that deep down he is terrified. Last night I was helping him pack, and I went into his bathroom and found him standing at his sink with his Louis Vuitton cosmetics bag open, trying to decide which of his ointments and gels he should take with him. He said he was trying to pare it down to 'absolute necessities,' and asked me if I thought his Clinique Scruffing Lotion was a nonessential, or should he pack it just in case? You should have seen the look on his face when I said he would probably only be allowed a bar of Irish Spring and a comb."

Lionel felt the need to clear his throat again. He examined his cuticles, trying *very* hard not to let Yolanda get a good look at his face lest she see the malicious glee in it. He said, "Let me play devil's advocate, Yolanda. How do you know this retreat won't do him some good? I mean, it could end up making him more assertive and—I don't know—direct. I'm not saying he needs it or anything, but if he's willing to go through with it, well, we should give it the benefit of the doubt. And if it butches him up a little, well, is that so bad? I mean, we all love Bob, but come on, if rediscovering the tribal savage in him means he doesn't go around ironing his socks anymore, can it be such a bad thing?"

He turned away from his cuticles and met Yolanda's eyes. He saw at once that her nostrils were flaring, a sure indication of her rage. "Lionel," she said in a low voice, "sometimes I think you understand nothing at all."

It was as fierce an admonition as she'd ever given him, and he was chastened by it. He winced a little, hopped off the counter, and immediately started backpedaling. "Aw, gee, I'm *sorry*, Yolanda. I was just trying to cheer you up." He stuck his hands in his pockets and stared at his shoes. "You're right, it's *awful*. I guess I'm just so sky-high myself right now, I can't imagine anyone else's life not being wonderful, too."

She shook her head; and as her long coils of hair beat her face, they must have knocked the anger out of her as well, for when she stopped and looked at him again, her nostrils were no longer billowing like a pair of hyperactive blowfish. "I forgot about that," she said, actually smiling at him. "Forgive me for whining so much about my own problems. You say you were in jail? No, wait—first tell me about this new love of yours." She leaned across the counter and a glow of rosy expectation lit her face.

"Well," said Lionel, "his name is Emil, and he's a medical student from Romania who's been in America for about a year, and he's also a political activist who's trying to get the United States to help Transylvania become independent of Romania."

Yolanda's smile grew a little forced, but, being a loyal friend, she nodded happily. "He sounds very interesting," she said with beguiling understatement. "Where did you meet him?"

"As a matter of fact, I met him in jail."

She furrowed her brow. "I see. Well, that brings us back to my first question. What were you *doing* there, Lionel?"

He took a deep breath. "I guess I kind of got involved in a riot in front of the Romanian Consulate building, and got arrested for it."

She met this news with no expression at all. "I understand," she said, clearly not having understood at all.

"But that's not important, *honest* it isn't," he said. "The important thing is, I met Emil, he's absolutely wonderful, he's invited me to dinner next weekend at his uncle's house, which is where he's living, and I think he might even be gay."

She stood bolt upright. "You *think*?" she cried. "Lionel, you let yourself fall in *love* with someone for the first time since I have known you, and you are not even certain whether he is *gay*?"

"I couldn't help it," he protested. "And besides, I'm reasonably sure he is. He told me he'd been to *five* AIDS rallies since he got here. *Five*, Yolanda. *I'm* gay and I've only been to one."

"How on earth did *that* come up?" she asked.

He shrugged. "Well, we shared a cab back downtown when we left the police station, so, you know, I had to talk with him about *something* besides how horny he was making me. So I asked him what he did for a living, and he said he was a medical student and I said, What made you choose medicine, and he said it was AIDS. He said nothing in his life was more important than defeating AIDS."

She shook her head. "Lionel, forgive me, but the fact that someone is concerned about AIDS does not make him gay. I should not have to remind you of this, but AIDS is not a gay disease."

"Oh, the hell with that—it's gay enough," he snapped. "Come on, Yolanda, how many of *your* straight friends have had it?"

"That is beside the poin—"

At that moment, just when the tension between them was threatening to turn into outright hostility, Bob Smartt threw open the door and swept grandly into the store, somehow contriving not to bang his head on the starship mobile. He was carrying a paper shopping bag and wearing a sparkling white collarless trench coat that Lionel thought made him look like an unusually hip lab technician at the Centers for Disease Control in Atlanta. "Hello, hello, *hello*," he sang, and then he leaned over the counter (extending his left leg behind him) and gave Yolanda a big smooch. "*Great* blouse," he said as he appraised her outfit. "*Love* the apricot piping!"

Then he turned to Lionel, raised his eyebrows as if surprised at the sight of him, and stuck out his impeccably manicured hand for Lionel to shake. "*Lionel,*" he said in an exact imitation of real pleasure.

Lionel shook his hand with some distaste.

"I just stopped at the Century Mall on my way here," Bob said in a bright, chirpy voice. "I suddenly figured that maybe since I was going on this 'manly man's' retreat—" He turned to Lionel. "She tell you about that?"

"Uh-huh," said Lionel.

He rolled his eyes, as if to say, Can you *believe* what they're making me go through? Then he continued, "Anyway, I was on my way here and I thought, maybe since I'll be at a campsite all weekend, I ought to get new underwear, you know? 'Cause all I have are silk briefs and, let's face it, those are just *not* gonna cut it in the Great Outdoors. *So,*" he said, opening his shopping bag with the practiced flair of someone accustomed to showing off his purchases, "I stopped by the Century and got some boxer shorts. These oughtta do it, huh?" He pulled out several pairs of tartan plaid flannel boxers that must have set him back forty-five dollars each. Yolanda cooed in enthusiastic agreement while Lionel just smiled and nodded and thought to himself, They're going to eat him alive.

"So, anyway," Bob said, slipping the boxers back into the bag, "what do you say you close up this flytrap and join me for dinner, honey? Thought we could hop on down to Oo-la-la for a quick plate of butternut-squash ravioli." He placed the bag underneath his arm. "I could use a glass of Pouilly Fuissé, too, let me tell ya. Been a *bitch* of a day."

Yolanda, as usual, dribbled out some insipid agreement and began closing up, even though it was only seven-fifty and the store officially didn't close until eight. Lionel knew that the owner had adopted a hands-off attitude toward his staff—after all, the business depended on a core group of regular customers who wouldn't abandon it for anything—but this seemed a little irresponsible, even so.

They left the store (Lionel again knocking his head on the fleet of starships). While Yolanda was busy locking the door, Bob finished retying the belt of his trench coat, then turned to Lionel and said, "Hey, care to join us?" with such theatrical falseness that the invitation practically demanded to be turned down even as it was being made. Lionel toyed with the idea of saying "Sure, Bob, I'd love to," and then watching with pleasure as disbelief and annoyance trickled across Bob's long, unlined face, but he decided against it, for Yolanda's sake. It was her last night with Bob for a week, and she'd want to be alone with him.

So he graciously declined. And as he stood in front of Live Long and Prosper, watching Bob stride down the street, his gait long-legged and swift, while poor, petite Yolanda scurried along a few paces behind him like the lonely little wife of a Muslim, Lionel wondered why on earth she allowed herself to be so completely a slave to the whims and tyrannies of so flaky a cake as Bob Smartt, to the point of actually making herself ill worrying about him camping out in the woods with a bunch of other middle-class middle-managers in bandanas and hunting socks.

And it wasn't until he was in his car and halfway home that he realized that maybe Yolanda loved Bob *because* of his effeminacy, not in spite of it. After all, boyfriends who love football are a dime a dozen, but boyfriends who love Donna Karan are as rare as ermine.

chapter

■■■■■■■■■■■■■■■■■■■
eleven

The next morning, before Lionel could even slip off his suit jacket, Julius Deming stepped into his office and shut the door behind him. He was so flushed—apparently with anger—that he didn't so much resemble a cueball as a six-ball.

"Lionel, can I have a word with you?" he said tersely.

Lionel was about to say, I don't know, Julie, can you?—but he decided better of it and instead said, "Sure."

At this invitation, Deming hauled his great bulk over to Lionel's desk and lowered himself into a chair with the kind of grunting deliberation that would've made an observer bet cash money he'd never be able to get himself back out again. Once he was settled, he pursed his lips and drummed his fingers on the desktop.

Lionel tried to act as though he weren't at all anxious or concerned about his boss's demeanor, so he took his own chair, propped his briefcase on his lap and opened it, then began casually flipping through the papers inside. "What's on your mind?" he asked, taking a folder from the briefcase and tossing it onto his blotter.

Deming shifted in his chair a little; Lionel thought the armrest would surely give way and send him sprawling.

"Certain kinds of behavior are no excuse for skipping out on work, Lionel," he said in clipped, precise tones. "We give our executives a lot of latitude, because, after all, they *are* executives. But we have to draw the line somewhere."

Lionel felt the blood creep into his face like a horde of spiders up a wall. Well, he thought, I should've expected something like this. "I see," he said, and he snapped shut his briefcase.

"Two years ago, I had to reprimand Harlan Spiegleman. I had to say, Harlan, the fact that your neighbor's cat got stuck up a tree is no excuse for an assistant creative director to miss an entire morning of work."

"Right," said Lionel meekly. He put his briefcase on the floor.

"More recently, I had to reprimand Dave Burbey. I had to say, Dave, I don't care how beautiful the girl you met at that printer's luncheon was, it's inexcusable for a production manager to leave his department unattended while he runs off to a motel room in the middle of the workday."

Lionel folded his hands and examined them as if he'd never seen them before. "Uh-huh."

"And now I have to reprimand you." He leaned across the desktop. "All-Pro is our biggest biller, and you're solely responsible for keeping them happy. Now, I don't care what weird principles you may espouse on your own time. The fact remains, leaping into battle alongside Transylvanian freedom fighters is no excuse for missing a budget meeting."

Lionel released a deep sigh. "I know, Julie. You're right." He shrugged and lifted his palms in the air. "What can I say? Something came over me. It won't happen again. Word of honor."

Deming propelled a little burst of air through his nostrils, then nodded his head and said, "Okay, I guess that's what I needed to hear." With a great effort he managed to extricate himself from the grip of the chair (Lionel fought the impulse to reach over and pull his fragile desk lamp out of harm's way), then stood, slightly panting, and said, "We'll forget this ever happened, Lionel. Tracy tells me you were arrested. I presume that whatever you have to do to deal with the police isn't going to interfere with you doing your job."

"Oh, *no,* Julie, *Christ*—not at *all,*" he said emphatically. "That's all taken care of. I mean, I'll have to go get a slap on the wrist and pay a fine, but—" He shrugged, as if to say, No problem.

Deming had his hand on the doorknob and was looking at his feet. "Because—I mean if there *were* a problem, if you were in some kind of trouble—well, you *could* come to me, that's all." He scuffed his right shoe across the carpet.

Lionel's mouth fell open. Imagine Julius Deming actually extending a helping hand! Of course, he waited to do so till after Lionel had told him it wasn't necessary. Still, the fact that he even cared enough to make the gesture was revealing. Had he judged his boss too harshly? Maybe he shouldn't look on all of his superiors as adversaries just because they were such strident homophobes. Maybe they really did *like* him. Maybe they wouldn't even *care* if he came out to them. Maybe . . . maybe . . .

Maybe I'm losing my marbles, he thought all at once, slightly shaking his head. He looked up at Deming and said, "Thanks, Julie. I appreciate it. I'll let you know if I need anything, but I'm sure I won't." He paused. "I mean it. I won't let you down again."

Deming nodded at the floor, then opened the door, turned to Lionel and winked at him, and plodded out into the hall.

Got to watch myself, Lionel thought, balling his fists and shaking them as though he could threaten himself into being more careful. Can't let myself get any weird ideas about being *loved* here or anything.

Suddenly Carlton Wenck stuck his head through the door, like an impish character from a bad Depression-era comedy. "Knock, knock."

"What? Oh. Hi, Carlton."

"Get balled out?" he asked, his head still protruding past the doorframe, looking disconcertingly disembodied. He obviously wasn't going to risk entering Lionel's domain until he determined whether Lionel was out of favor.

"Just a warning," Lionel replied, hating him.

At this, Carlton deemed it safe to take a few steps into the office. "So, what's this business about Transylvania? Isn't that where Dracula comes from?"

"I don't want to talk about it, Carlton." He leaned back in his chair and put his hands behind his head, enjoying the fact that his rival didn't know what to make of his behavior.

Carlton shrugged. "Okay. But, you know, if you want to talk ..."

Lionel smiled. "Thanks, guy. Maybe some other time." Say, around the turn of the millennium?

Carlton ambled out of the office, giving him a thumb's-up just before disappearing into the hallway again. And not six seconds later, Tracy scooted in, as though afraid she might be seen.

Lionel rolled his eyes. "Don't worry," he said witheringly, "no one's going to hold it against you if you're seen talking to me."

She blushed and mumbled, "Sorry, Lionel." Then she sat on his desk, exactly as she'd sat on his desk a thousand times before, only now it seemed to have meaning attached to it. That provocatively revealed thigh of hers now seemed to be thrust at him, almost like an offering. "Are you okay?" she asked sweetly. "I didn't know what to think when I saw you get arrested and taken away. I was going to call you last night, but—well—I was just ... um ..."

Unsure, Lionel thought, completing the sentence for her, and he felt a little flurry of jubilation. His foray into Eastern European politics had left Tracy less certain of him than before, less secure in her knowledge of who he was, what he felt, where he stood in the limited scheme of things that she acknowledged and recognized and understood. She couldn't know too many people who engaged in riots on Michigan Avenue, much less for ideological reasons, and the fact that he was apparently such a person had caused her to back away from him a little. Good, good. But he cautioned himself not to be too exultant; it might also have made him more mysterious and attractive to her, given him an element of danger that she might find thoroughly irresistible.

"I'm okay," he said lightly, deliberately trying to play down the unusualness of his experience. "Sometimes I get a little riled up by injustice, that's all. It happens now and then. I mean, usually I don't end up in jail, but, you know, if it happens, it happens ..."

"Really?" she said, narrowing her eyes and knitting her brows. *"Lionel!* You're going to make me worry about you!"

And with any luck, he thought, I'll also make you consider what a terrible father I'd be to our children. "Don't worry," he told her. "It doesn't happen very often. Sometimes a man's just got to take a stand, that's all." Oh, *that* was a stupid, romantic thing to say, he scolded himself as soon as he'd said it; just look at how her eyes twinkled on hearing it!

She smiled and thrust her thigh even closer to him. He rolled his chair back to make up the difference. "My big hero helping the underdog," she said with unbearable affection. Then she slipped off his desk and pulled her skirt back into place. "Gotta run now. Julie wants me to take care of some junk. See you later, hero?"

He shrugged. "Probably."

And only a moment after she'd gone, it was Gloria Gimbek's turn to crane her neck into his office and say, "Transylvania—isn't that where Dracula lives?"

And so it went, for the rest of the morning until a quarter to noon, when Alice buzzed his intercom and said, "Lionel, a Lola Frank is here to see you."

"Aunt Lola?" he said, astounded. *"Here?* Tell her I'll be right out!"

On his way to the reception area, he passed a tall, blond, extraordinarily beautiful youth turning in circles in the hallway, as if lost. He looked like Michelangelo's David with a day-old beard and baggy khakis. He tentatively raised a finger to catch Lionel's attention, then said, in a husky, bedroom voice, "Hey, man, where's Carlton Wenck's office?"

Lionel nodded his head in the appropriate direction, and the boy headed off without even offering his thanks. Lionel continued on his own way, and when he got to the reception area he whispered to Alice, "Who's the blond kid wandering around?"

She looked at him perplexedly for a moment, then whispered back, "Oh, you mean that gorgeous hunk of teenager?"

Lionel blushed and said, "I guess so, yeah."

"That's Tim Shelton," she said. "Carlton's student intern. Here for the summer. Weren't you introduced?" She put her hand to her mouth. "Oh—wait. That's right. You were *out* yesterday afternoon." She pronounced the word *out* as though it were some kind of ridiculous euphemism.

Embarrassed, Lionel mumbled his thanks, then started around her desk. Christ, he thought; that's *all* I need—a slab of U.S.D.A. prime beefcake stumbling around outside my office for the next two months. Be lucky if I get *any* work done.

On the far side of Alice's desk he found his aunt sitting reading a copy of *Advertising Age* as though she actually had any interest whatever in it. "Aunt Lola," he said, smiling brilliantly. "What a surprise!"

She got to her feet and lurched forward to give him a hug. He had to duck, because she was wearing a sun hat so big that he was sure with a little modification it could be made to pick up signals from space.

She smiled her appallingly toothy smile. "I had to come in, I had to come *in*to the city to peddle my new line of cards," she said, "so I thought I'd stop by and see if you were free for lunch."

He cocked his head as if considering his schedule, but in actuality he was wondering if he dared be seen anywhere in town accompanied by That Hat. In the end, family loyalty won out over any concern for his reputation, and he brightly said "Sure! Give me a moment to grab my jacket." And he dashed back to his office, deliberately not offering her a tour, nor giving her time to request one. It just made sense; he didn't want any of his bitchier co-workers getting a good look at Lola's astonishing headgear, nor did he want that headgear knocking any of the artworks off the walls; and most of all, he didn't want anyone mischievously mentioning the whole Transylvanian imbroglio to Aunt Lola, which was by far the likeliest danger.

Fifteen minutes later they were sitting down at the Star of Siam, which was the only restaurant in the vicinity that was open enough to accommodate the brimspan of Aunt Lola's hat, which she was proving perversely determined to keep on her head under all circumstances. They'd just ordered a satay appetizer, and Aunt Lola, who seldom left the suburbs, had just remarked for what must have been the six hundredth time how exciting it was to be in the Big City, all the while looking at the people around her as though they were exotic and alien, like visitors from China or Mars.

Suddenly she reached over and grabbed Lionel's wrist. "Lionel, honey," she said, "I have to tell, I have to *tell* you, I'm so excited about my *gay* line, and that's why I'm here in the Big City, to go to all the *gay* shops to try and get orders from them! You don't mind if I talk about that, do you?"

The satay arrived, and Lionel tucked in his napkin. "Course I don't, Aunt Lola," he said warily. Although he wouldn't have minded if she stopped putting so much emphasis on the word every time she used it.

Lola had no idea how to eat satay, and was about to spear herself in the throat with the kabob when Lionel stopped her and showed her how to remove the impaled meat with her fork and dip it in the peanut sauce. She hunched her shoulders in glee. "So exciting, so *exciting* to be in the Big City," she said, apparently awed and amazed by the wondrous foodstuffs consumed by urbanites.

Despite having permission to discuss her *gay* greeting cards, Lola chatted largely about family matters for the first part of the lunch. The colonel was an intransigent mule, as always, but Greta, who had been feeling despondent over the lack of interest in her band, was now in high spirits. Just this week the girls had managed to book their first real gig, as an opening act at an outdoor neighborhood festival in Elmhurst.

"Is it a Christian event?" Lionel asked.

"No, no, but Greta says it's, Greta *says* it's a family type of festival, so she thinks the group's Christian message will be well received. She's hoping, she's *hoping* a lot of youngsters there who are being swayed by satanic rock music will hear them and come to the Lord instead." There was a note of affectionate mockery in her voice. She raised an eyebrow at Lionel.

Lionel smiled and shook his head. "She and I don't talk much anymore."

"Well, you're not saved yet. She prays for, she *prays* for that, you know."

He lowered his head. "Aunt Lola," he said, in a don't-get-me-started tone of voice.

"I know, I know," she said good-humoredly. "Awfully proud, isn't she? Sometimes I have to, *sometimes* I have to think that if *that* girl's saved, I'm the queen of Romania." At the mention of Romania, Lionel flinched, then tried to hide it by pretending he had an itch on his cheek.

Aunt Lola lowered her head and opened her oversized purse (accidentally dipping the brim of her hat in peanut sauce, which Lionel decided not to mention to her) and took out a bound portfolio. "Here, let me show, let me *show* you my new cards, and you can tell me what you think."

"Well, if you value my opinion that much," he said, hoping that there was no special reason she was asking him above anyone else.

As if reading his mind, she said, "Well, you're the only, you're the *only* one in the family who will even *look* at them. Your father's forbidden, your father's *forbidden* me to even keep them stocked in the *house,* and your sister says I'm trading with the devil. You've always been such a rational boy. I'd just like, I'd *just* like to have your input."

He smiled at the idea of Aunt Lola using a word like "input." She set the portfolio in front of him (he had by this time shoved the peanut sauce out of the way) and opened it. The first card, tucked in a plastic sleeve on the opening page, bore a watercolor drawing of a black leather boot with a single red rose stuck through its silver buckle. Lionel gently pulled the card from the sleeve and opened it. It bore the message, *Happy Valentine's Day to my favorite slave.*

Lionel cocked an eyebrow and looked at Lola.

"You see, I did some research, I did some *research* on gay relationships," she said, "and some of them are master-and-slave relationships. I understand it's fairly common."

No, it's not, he wanted to say, but Aunt Lola was so nonjudgmental anyway that he thought there was no reason to risk his cover trying to set her straight.

He turned to the next page. In the sleeve was a card

bearing a picture of a handsome older man with his arms around an equally good-looking younger man. Lionel removed the card and opened it; it read *"Oh! Daddy, Oh! Daddy, How you can love,"* with an attribution to the Andrews Sisters, and below that the simple legend *Happy Anniversary.*

"The thing about, the *thing* about gays," Lola explained, "Is that they love old show tunes and songs from the nineteen-forties. Also, when a younger man has an older man for a boyfriend, he calls him Daddy, just like girls did back in those days. So I was really pleased with this card. It's one of my most, it's one of my *most* clever."

Lionel nodded, a weak smile on his face. Where was Aunt Lola getting her information? When a younger man has an older man for a boyfriend, he calls him Daddy? She must have done her "research" by watching TV talk shows or reading an article on gay men in *Redbook.*

The next card was equally weird. The cover bore a photo of a foil condom package. Lionel opened it and discovered that it folded out accordion style, with more and more multicolored condom packages filling the revealed panels, until the reader came to the final one, which read, *I care for you more and more each day.*

"With AIDS and everything," Aunt Lola said enthusiastically, "condoms are the one, condoms are the *one* sure way that gay men can show they really care about each other. I thought this was, I thought *this* was a good way of showing that, visually."

He slipped the card back in its sleeve, and looked at Aunt Lola's face, shining with expectancy and pride. He felt a little ashamed of himself. He knew he could have been a tremendous help to her in getting this line of cards off the ground, that he could *still* be of tremendous help to her, but he had absolutely no intention of doing so. These cards were probably all equally off-kilter; any proprietor of a shop in a gay neighborhood would recognize at once that they'd been created by someone hopelessly out of the loop. Lola would go out this afternoon, trying to peddle her wares, and would hear nothing but polite refusals (unless she also happened to get an earful of the bitchy behind-her-back whispering about her hat).

He sighed and said, "Aunt Lola, these are really good," and as he said it he felt such a welling of shame in his breast as he had never felt before, for not only was he yet again hiding his true nature from this woman who had been the only mother he'd ever really known, he was hiding, as well, the richness, the *bounty* of his experience in that identity, at a time when that bounty was exactly what she needed.

chapter

■■■■■■■■■■■■■■■■■■■

twelve

Lionel had it all figured out. He would go to dinner at the home of Emil's uncle and aunt, and these simple immigrant folk would be overcome with gratitude at his having lent Emil money to bail himself out of jail. They would welcome him with open arms, serve him hearty, basic Romanian food, and when he left they would confer on him some ancient, potent peasant blessing, after which they would tell him that they considered him part of the family. He would come back often after that, and establish a bond of affection with Emil that might some-day—perhaps very soon—become sexual. And then the old peasant couple would fade away; they wouldn't exactly *die*—he couldn't wish them death—but their bodies would shrivel and waste away while their spirits grew more radiant and full, until the former would be gone and only the latter remained. And then Lionel and Emil would be free to live as a couple, without ever having offended their good uncle and aunt's primitive notions of Christianity with a love that they could never have understood.

This was the fantasy that sustained Lionel through all of Friday and the better part of Saturday, until Saturday night, when he found himself standing at the front door of the address Emil had given him, ringing the bell and noting with increasing apprehension that while this far-north neighborhood wasn't exactly fashionable, this big A-frame house didn't exactly scream "immigrant" either.

Emil had told him very little about his uncle and aunt—not even their names—just that he was staying with the family of his mother's brother, who had fled Romania years before. Lionel had taken the liberty of filling in the blanks of Emil's sketchy account, and now he was getting a sinking feeling that maybe his conclusions were going to turn out to be wildly inaccurate. He tried to salvage them by coming up with possible explanations for the grander-than-expected condition of the house, but before he could do so, a woman answered the door, and his fantasy crashed and shattered at the sight of her. For while her face was as lined and rubbery as that of the sainted aunt of Lionel's imagination, it was also deeply suntanned, and sat beneath a cotton-candy hairdo that had been dyed a deep, almost cherry red. Her lips were even redder, and shiny beyond belief; it looked as though she'd been drinking melted red candle wax when Lionel rang.

She flicked a cigarette onto the stoop, then reached out and gave him a hug. "You must be Lionel," she said, and her accent was about as Romanian as Mary Tyler Moore's. He noticed that she was wearing a black off-the-shoulder top, skin-tight Guess jeans, and high heels. "I'm Emil's Aunt Nancy. I *insist* you just call me Nancy. Come on in, make yourself at home."

Inside, she lit a new cigarette and then waved it around as though she were directing planes down a runway, and said, "This is our humble home." She gestured past a glass cabinet filled with more Precious Moments figurines than Lionel ever dreamed existed. "Mr. Jones—you have to call him John—and I have lived here since eighty-one, so you have to excuse the mess. You know how it is, things accumulate if you stay in one place too long." She took a drag off her cigarette and then blew the smoke in a long, wide stream; Lionel thought she looked like she was spraying for bugs.

He turned and surveyed the house, which was decorated with such an excess of faux Second Empire furnishings, paintings, and objets de' not-quite-art, that its rampant kitschiness was actually sort of endearing; it gave Lionel the distinct impression of ambition that outstripped education. Very American, he would've called it, had he not known otherwise.

Likewise the name of the couple who lived here, which he had just now put together. John and Nancy Jones. Not quite the colorful, tongue-twisting names of East European peasants. And sure enough, after Nancy led Lionel to the basement "rec" room, where a wet bar was spread with chips and dips, and where Emil greeted him with a bear hug (his enormous nipples, Lionel couldn't help but notice, showing right through the two-sizes-too-small Freddy Krueger T-shirt he was wearing), Lionel met John Jones, a diminutive man in a Chicago Bears sweatshirt, pressed acid-washed jeans, and black patent-leather shoes with tassels. John shook his hand heartily and said, "You must be Lionel! John Jones at your service. Funny name for a Romanian immigrant, huh?"

Lionel laughed because he didn't know how to answer.

"Pleased to meet you, anyway, son," John said, releasing his hand and turning toward the bar. "Let me get you a drink to thank you proper for what you did for Emil. What'll it be, a whisky?" His accent, like Emil's and unlike his wife's, had the vaguely Italian cadences Lionel now associated with Romanians.

Lionel started to ask for a beer but his tongue caught on his teeth.

"Whisky it is," John said, opening a bottle of Southern Comfort and pouring Lionel a tumbler. "Emil says he hasn't told you yet, but John Jones wasn't the name I was born with. No, I was born *Ion Jonescu.* Boy, that's a mouthful, ain't it. *I-on Jo-nes-cu,* seems like a million years ago." He handed the tumbler to Lionel, who stared at it in abject horror. He hadn't had whisky since college, and hadn't been able to handle it even then.

John then motioned for Lionel and Emil to hop up on the barstools while he continued his story. Emil was sucking on a long-necked bottle of Budweiser, and Lionel stared at it in real envy. Nancy Jones excused herself and slipped back upstairs.

"When I came to America in sixty-four," John said, resuming a narrative Lionel was sure he had related many times before, "I wasn't gonna go around with a name like *Ion Jonescu*, no, sir, not on your life. So first thing I did once I got my citizen papers, I went to a judge and said, 'Charlie, I'm an American now, I want me an American name.' And he said, 'What name you want?' And I said, 'I dunno, what names you got?' And he looked at my name and he said, 'This here's pretty damn close to John Jones, and that's as American a name as anyone born under this here flag ever carried on his driver's license.' And I said, 'Okay, judge, John Jones it is.' " He grinned in pleasure.

Lionel took a sip of his straight whisky and shuddered, and wondered where John Jones had got the idea that run-on sentences were something wonderfully American. He looked out of the corner of his eye at Emil, who was, of course, perfectly gorgeous, with both elbows on the bar, tipping the neck of the beer bottle into his mouth as if he were going to fellate it.

"So here I am twenty-whatever years later," John said, standing back and raising his arms at the sheer wonder of it all. "John Jones, the Shoelace King of Chicago, and if that ain't an American success story, you can kiss my keister."

Lionel put his tumbler on the bar, determined to have no more of it. "The *Shoelace* King of Chicago?" he said, amazed that anyone would willingly adopt such a title.

John Jones looked at him with undiluted delight. "You've heard of me?" he asked, prompting Lionel to wonder how big an ego it took to allow this kind of misinterpretation. "You deserve another drink for that!" And before Lionel could protest, John had uncapped the Southern Comfort and added another couple of splashes to his not-yet-empty tumbler.

"That's what I love about America," John continued, addressing Emil, "what I keep telling you about it! Here is where you can make a *name* for yourself. You might think it's embarrassing that I'm the Shoelace King of Chicago, but look at this—your boyfriend has heard of me!"

Lionel was in the midst of taking another sip, to be polite, and at the mention of the word *boyfriend* he spat a mouthful of whisky right across the bar, spattering John's sweatshirt with a messy, rye-smelling spray.

The Shoelace King, however, was serenely unperturbed by this. He winked at Lionel, said, "Good stuff, huh?", then grabbed a bar towel and mopped his shirtfront, as though this kind of thing happened to him every day.

Lionel sat back dumbfounded, and only after a few minutes of careful consideration did he conclude that John Jones had used the old colloquial meaning of *boyfriend*— the way it was still acceptable to talk of a woman, even of advanced age, as having girlfriends. He began to relax.

"Are you okay?" Emil asked, putting his hand on Lionel's shoulder.

Lionel felt the heat from that hand as though it were a sun lamp; he thought he might burst into flame. "Yeah," he said, nodding, hoping Emil would remove his hand, and at the same time hoping he wouldn't.

"So, as I was just saying," John Jones said, apparently miffed that Emil had interrupted him, "what do you think brought me to America in the first place? You'll never guess."

Emil grimaced, got up, and headed toward a door that bore a varnished wooden sign reading HEAD.

Lionel watched him disappear behind that door; then he turned to John and shrugged. "I don't know. Freedom?"

He shook his head, smiling in satisfaction. "I knew you'd say that. Everybody says that, but freedom you could have in Romania, if you knew how, not that everybody or even most people knew how, but I did. How to slip around corners, unnoticed, if you know what I mean," he said with a wink. "No, what brought me to America was the sixty-four World's Fair. And what made me *stay* was Miss Edie Adams."

"Who's that?" Lionel asked, daring another sip of whisky. How had he ever managed to down this stuff in college?

John shook his head sadly. "I'm sorry to hear you don't know, son, because you see, Edie Adams was one of the great show biz talents of her day. I was a cobbler in Romania back in the sixties—"

"*Transylvania,*" Emil shouted from behind the closed door of the Head; "say *Transylvania,* Uncle John."

John shrugged. "Kids today and their radical ideas— whoops! Forgot you were one of 'em. Forgive an old man, okay? Anyway, I was a cobbler outside of Cluj. How's that?" he yelled at the Head.

"Better," came the reply.

"And I got sent to New York City to represent Romanian industry in the World's Fair, if you can believe that. Of course this was back before Ceausescu went really nuts and wouldn't let hardly anyone out of the country again, but anyway of course the whole World's Fair itself opened up a new world to me, but it was a kind of scary world, and I wanted to get back to Ro—to Cluj, where it was safe and quiet, and so did the rest of my group. But then one night I happened to be watching TV and there was an episode of *The Lucy Show* guest-starring Edie Adams. Well, what that girl could do—sing, dance, be funny and sexy at the same time, and she was all blonde and saucy and had on a short skirt. Lionel, I tell you, nobody in Roma—nobody back home could even *imagine* anything like Edie Adams. She just all of a sudden became the whole country of America for me, singing those great songs and cracking jokes and showing a little leg and having a good time, all glamorous and young and happy. I knew I couldn't go back, ever, not to that old gray world I came from." Suddenly his face brightened; he held up a finger and scooted over to the other side of the room, where he opened a cabinet set in the wall. Taped to the inside of the cabinet door was a large, yellowed photo of a sultry blonde in a slinky evening gown and pearls. She was holding a cigar.

"From one of her Muriel Cigar promotions," he said. "I stole it from a drug store. You're probably too young to remember the commercial. *'Hey, big spender,'*" he began singing, his voice high and throaty; "*'spennnd a little dime with me.'*"

"Edie Adams?" Lionel asked, discreetly shoving his whisky farther away from him.

"Edie Adams," John nodded, a positive leer on his face. "I defected for Edie Adams. And I've never had a regret, let me tell you. It was my dream to meet her," he said, shutting the cabinet and returning to the bar. He hopped up on the stool that Emil had vacated. "And one day I did, I *did*, Lionel, I waited outside a nightclub in Manhattan one night to see her. And when she came out I talked to her and she gave me a big kiss right on my foreh—"

"Is he talking about Edie Adams again?" said Nancy Jones

as she alighted at the bottom of the staircase and headed across the basement. She went to the bar and collected the soiled glasses, including Lionel's far-from-finished one and Emil's still ice-cold beer. Lionel sighed with relief.

"He *is,* Aunt Nancy," Emil called from the Head. "Make him stop!" The sound of a flushing toilet drowned out something he said after this.

Nancy started for the stairs again—a little precariously in her high heels—and as she negotiated the first stair she said, "Honestly, John, no one these days even knows who Edie Adams *is.*"

John turned scarlet; he stuck his neck out, like a deranged snapping turtle, and yelled, *"Star of stage and screen! That's who!"*

Emil emerged from the Head, tucking in his T-shirt; he rolled his eyes at Lionel, then took the stool next to John's and proceeded to appear utterly perplexed at the disappearance of his Budweiser.

John shook his head. "No one forgot Marilyn Monroe. No one forgot Judy Garland. What's wrong with people that they forgot Edie Adams? I tell you, Lionel, it won't last. I look at that girl, Madonna, and everyone keeps saying, oh, she steals from Marilyn Monroe, she steals from Marilyn Monroe. Well, Marilyn Monroe was never a dancer like Madonna is! Marilyn Monroe didn't have a nightclub act like Madonna does! It's obvious to me that this Madonna steals everything she does from Edie Adams, and someday she's going to admit it. She *has* to. And *then* won't there be a change of tune around this house!"

Nancy appeared at the bottom of the stairs again. She gave Lionel a compassionate look and said, "One of his friends from the old country is exactly the same way about Mitzi Gaynor. They only ever had one discussion about it. That was six years ago, and they haven't spoken since."

John actually stamped his foot. *"Darn it,* Nancy! I told you *never* to compare Edie Adams to Mitzi Gaynor!"

She went over to him and rubbed his neck affectionately. "And after Edie Adams kissed him on the forehead outside that nightclub," she said, picking up John's story, "you know what he did? He went on to meet his wonderful American wife, with whom he had two daughters, who are both out on dates tonight, or they'd be here telling him to shut up about Edie Adams, too. And then he lived happily ever after, the end." She turned her head and pursed her lips; John tried to resist, but she pushed his head toward hers and they kissed.

Then she mussed his hair and released him, and he appeared a little embarrassed and ill at ease. He searched for something to say, eventually settling on, "Well, it was happily ever after, until it got even happier when my sister Nadia's boy wrote and asked if he could come stay with us while he studied medicine in America." And here he opened his arms and displayed Emil like he was unveiling next year's Mercedes at a car show. "And since his uncle is the Shoelace King of Chicago, I can afford to send him to Northwestern University and train him to be a great doctor so he can go back to Romania and fight disease!"

"Transylvania," Emil corrected him. "It will be Transylvania by then."

Go back to Transylvania? thought Lionel, stunned. He hadn't known that Emil had any intention of going *back*. He felt suddenly heartsick, watching the classically beautiful, adorably gauche Transylvanian patriot standing between his aunt and uncle, scratching his crotch with complete unselfconsciousness.

"Dinner's ready," said Nancy, her smile huge and wide and red, like she had a length of ribbon hung from ear to ear. "Come on up and eat with us, Lionel, and you can tell us about *your* life." She smiled and started up the stairs. "We're having Emil's favorite dish tonight!"

Lionel bravely tried to hide that he was suffering from dashed hopes. He slipped off the stool and followed the family up the stairs. "I've never had Romanian food before," he said as brightly as he could. "I'm really looking forward to it."

"Romanian, schmomanian," said John. "We're *Americans* in this house. We eat good, wholesome *American* food."

"Oh," muttered Lionel, accepting the demise of the final element of his treasured fantasy. "Well, then, what *are* we having?"

"Chop suey," said Nancy as she reached the top of the stairs; Lionel came up behind her and saw that the kitchen table was now covered with a dozen white take-out boxes. She winked at him. "I slaved over a hot telephone for this meal."

Emil laughed long and hard at the joke. John, who had perhaps heard it before, was already digging in.

chapter

■■■■■■■■■■■■■■■■■

thirteen

Dinner was over by eight-thirty and Lionel was at his front door by nine. When he entered, he found Yolanda slumped over in his reclining chair, an open paperback book on her lap and Spencer on her shoulder. At the sight of him, the bird hissed in hatred and flew down the corridor, presumably back to his cage.

Lionel dropped his jacket on the sofa, then crouched before Yolanda and gently shook her awake. She stirred prettily, and when she yawned, several locks of her hair fell lazily into her face, as though they were still asleep. "Lionel," she said. "Oh, my." She looked at her watch. "Back so early?"

"It was an early dinner. How long've you been asleep? Looks like Spencer's shit on your shoulder about twelve times."

She examined the hardening bloblets of bird crap on her blouse and scowled at them. "Damn," she said without passion. "Well, they will wash out easily enough." She stretched her arms languorously, then straightened her legs and ran her hands from her thighs to her ankles. "I suppose I have been dozing for a few hours. I started reading this book at six-thirty, but I do not seem to have gotten very far."

Lionel took the barely opened paperback from her lap. Its title was *Feudalia,* written by a certain Edward St. Onge, and its cover copy read "Can a planet mired in medieval misery defeat an invasion of star-spanning socialists?" The colorful cover scene depicted a heavily weaponed starship warrior appearing in a flash of light before a throne room filled with astonished courtiers, all of whom had Prince Valiant haircuts and wore tights and pointed shoes. The throne itself was occupied by a defiant queen who looked like a cross between Elizabeth I and Barbi Benton.

He tossed it back into her lap. "Looks riveting," he said. "No wonder you fell asleep."

She smiled, took the paperback, and stuffed it into her purse, which was at the side of the chair. "Where did Spencer go?" she asked, stifling a yawn. "Do not tell me you brought him back to his cage yourself!"

He shook his head. "Little beast took off like a rocket soon as I walked in the door."

She curled her legs beneath her. "Poor Spencer," she sighed.

"Poor *Lionel,*" he corrected her. "It was a *disaster,* Yolanda." He slipped off his shoes and sat cross-legged on the floor; then, getting a whiff of his feet, he decided he'd better follow Yolanda's lead and tuck his legs underneath him.

She cocked her head and pouted. "Oh, no. Tell me what happened."

Spencer began singing from down the corridor. Instead of flying to his cage, he had apparently flown to the kitchen, to serenade his reflection in Lionel's Alessi teapot.

Lionel raised his voice so that it would carry above his parrot's. "Well," he said, "I was *totally* wrong about the uncle and aunt. They weren't peasants—the aunt wasn't even Romanian. She was a Milwaukee lounge singer back in the seventies—that's how Emil's uncle met her. He was in Milwaukee for a shoe convention. He's the Shoelace King of Chicago, you know."

Yolanda suppressed a smile. "I did not know that, no."

"Anyway, they weren't so bad—a little overbearing, and vulgar like you wouldn't believe. They have six Franklin Mint shadow boxes on their walls, with all sorts of instant collections of the most hideous stuff—porcelain thimbles showing the fifty state flags, limited-edition saucers that each feature the likeness of a pope, that sort of thing. But *that* I could handle. *That's* not the reason it was a disaster." He shuddered and put his head in his hands. "They casually mentioned that Emil's only in this country till he gets out of med school. Then he's going back to Romania. Or Transylvania, as he'd insist on calling it."

Yolanda gave him a look of unbearable pity, then slipped out of the reclining chair and curled up beside him on the floor. She put her arm around his shoulder, taking care not to wipe any of Spencer's droppings on him. "There, there," she said, rubbing his back. "Did you talk to Emil about this?"

In the kitchen, Spencer had just reached a dazzlingly operatic crescendo, which was followed by a metallic bang and a series of horrified shrieks. He'd apparently knocked the teapot off the stove.

"I didn't have a chance to say anything to him," Lionel said. "The Shoelace King talked a blue streak the entire time I was there. He managed to tell his entire life story, some parts of it two or three times. He even told me most of *Edie Adams's* life story."

"Who is Edie Adams?" Yolanda asked.

"A star of stage and screen," he said dismissively. "It's not important. Anyway, I asked Emil to have dinner with me tomorrow so we could talk. He gave me a great big bear hug, but, Yolanda, he doesn't seem very—I don't know—very *interested.* Maybe you were right about him not being gay."

She put her head on his shoulder. "Maybe I was, but maybe I was not. Poor Lionel, always rushing in with his big dreams."

"I know I'm an idiot," he said. "It just would've been so *perfect.*"

Spencer appeared. The bird had walked down the corridor and was now peeking around the corner at them.

"He wants me to go pick up his teapot," said Yolanda, getting up from the floor. "I will be right back."

"No, for Christ's sake, stay," he said, holding her by the neck so that she couldn't rise (and in the process getting two of his fingers gooey with bird shit). "You spoil him enough as it is." He turned toward Spencer and said, *"My* turn with Yolanda. You had her long enough. Go play in traffic or something."

Spencer lowered his head, turned, and walked back down the corridor.

Lionel released Yolanda's neck and wiped his fingers on the carpeting. "Something's wrong with you, too, isn't it?" he said, noticing the dullness of her eyes. "You're as depressed as I am. What's wrong?"

"Oh," she said, toying with her bracelet, "I heard from Bob today."

"I thought he was supposed to be *incommunicado*."

"He was. But when everyone was in the sweat lodge this afternoon, he pretended he ha—"

"The *sweat lodge?*"

She nodded. "That is a tent in which they smolder herbs and incense, which then fills the tent with heat that purges and purifies the body. It is a Native American tradition, Bob told me. Anyway, he had been in there for about a half hour and everyone was howling like animals, and he could not stand it. He thought the only way they would let him out was if he pretended he had to throw up, and he was right— they practically *kicked* him out. But instead of going back to his barracks, he snuck through the window of the camp's office and called me on what he says is the only telephone in the whole place."

"They won't let him *call?*" Lionel said, aghast.

"He agreed not to call. He agreed not to use any form of technology the entire weekend—not watches, telephones, cameras, electric razors—even pills. Remember, most of the men who are attending this retreat are doing so voluntarily. They do not need to be prevented from using such things. It is part of the reason they want to go, to get back to their 'primal selves,' as Bob put it."

It was his turn to rub *her* back. "And how's old Bob holding up?"

From the kitchen, they heard Spencer begin a new song. He must have decided to simply continue his teapot serenade on the floor.

"Not well. The first thing the men had to do was pick a new name, an animal name to signify their wildness. Well, Bob arrived late, and by the time he got there all the good names had been taken. He said he thought of Wolverine, then Cougar, then Badger, and every time the admittance elder would say, Taken, try again, until Bob got nervous and blurted out, *Gander*! So that is his wild name."

Before he could stop himself, Lionel snorted a laugh. *"Gander?"* he yelped. "Oh, *Jesus.* Not a very auspicious start!" His stomach quivered; he knew he mustn't let her see how hilarious he found this.

Yet as she shook her head in agreement with him, he thought he could detect the most minute, almost microscopic trace of a smile on her face. "No," she said, "not a very auspicious start. And it has been mostly miserable for him ever since. The men are not allowed to *shower,* Lionel, not even after the sweat lodge. Bob says there *are* no showers. They can swim in the stream next to the camp grounds, if they want to, but Bob says the water is never warmer than fifty degrees, and if he jumped in he would surely suffer cardiac arrest. And besides which, all the men are talking about how 'empowering' it is for them to be able to *smell* themselves. Bob says it is as though they are having a contest: whoever smells the worst is the manliest. And they have only been there two days! Think of how they will be after a whole *week* of the sweat lodge."

"Ugh," said Lionel, meaning it.

"And the activities!" she continued. "Bob said that last night everyone had to bang drums and dance themselves into a frenzy, then sit and spew forth all the resentment they had stored up against the world, and whenever one man would stop, they would dance and bang drums again, until everyone had had a turn spewing."

"Really? What did Bob spew about?"

She shifted her weight. "I think that is what is disturbing me. He said he was the last one to go, and we laughed about that. But he would not tell me what he said. He claims that before the rite began—that is what he called it, a 'rite'—all the men were forced to take an oath never to tell the details of what happened inside. And Lionel, he sounded a little *proud* of that."

"This is all so Spin-and-Martyish," Lionel said, shaking his head. "I can't believe we're talking about grown men here."

"Do you think Bob spewed out any resentments against

me?" she asked all at once, her voice as high-pitched as a train whistle.

He looked at her, appalled. "In that pit of smelly school-boys? He'd better not have. But what would he say, anyway? You're perfect!"

She averted her eyes from him. "You once told me that he would someday resent me for not being a blonde debu-tante named Phoebe."

He sat up again and gave her a hug. "I was drunk at the time. I'm sure he said nothing whatsoever about you, Yolanda. I'm *sure.*"

"Well," she said, her voice still reedy, "I suppose not, or he would not risk calling me." She pushed herself away from him now, as if to force him to take her seriously and not coddle her. In the kitchen, Spencer's song had descended into a throaty growl. "I am silly for worrying so much."

"Yes, you are."

She stared into space and bit her thumbnail, then turned and said, "Can I be honest with you? What worries me most is that I think in some small way he is *not* as miserable as I had expected. That in some small way he is *enjoying* himself. He has never kept a secret from me before, Lionel."

"Well, come *on,* Yolanda. He swore an *oath.*"

She lowered her head and glared at him, as if disap-pointed in him. "Men swear oaths all the time, Lionel. It means nothing. You *know* it means nothing."

Does it? he wondered. Do I?

He felt a flurry of fear. At some basic and profound level, Yolanda understood men better than he did. He might be one, but maybe that was just the problem; maybe it was impossible to have an objective opinion of masculine virtues and vices when they were built into your chromosomes. And being gay couldn't help; he'd spent most of his adult life in a state of dizzied confusion about his gender. When Yolanda accused men of being essentially faithless, incapable of honoring their word, why did it make him tremble? Be-cause he recognized that trait in himself—or because he *didn't* recognize that trait in himself? Because it placed him on a level with Bob Smartt—or because it pointed up the crucial way that he and Bob Smartt were *different*? And worst of all, how could he ever know the answer to any of this, since almost all his energy since puberty had been employed in playing a role? What was beneath the mask he wore? Was there anything *left* beneath the mask he wore?

Yolanda's simple assertion had flung him into a swamp of unanswerable, almost imponderable questions, and she must have seen the stricken look that crossed his face, the lost look, the eyes that wouldn't focus, the lower lip that hung open, trembling, the skin that paled visibly. She touched his hand and said, "Lionel, have I upset you?"

He shook briefly and almost convulsively; it was a small paroxysm of terror, brought on by his realization that he was a complete stranger to himself. When he turned to answer Yolanda, he realized he had tears on his face. "Yolanda, I don't know what came over me," he said, his voice eerily weightless, as though it might disperse in the air before reaching his ears. "Something you said just really freaked me ou—"

He was interrupted by a series of enraged shrieks from the kitchen. Startled, Yolanda leapt to her feet. "Oh, dear," she said, pulling down the legs of her jeans from where they had gathered around her crotch. "This always happens if you leave Spencer alone too long with his reflection. First he loves himself, then he changes his mind and tries to attack himself."

"I know how he feels," Lionel said thinly.

"I will take care of it and be right back."

She scooted down the hall to the kitchen, leaving him on his knees in the living room, totally and terribly alone.

chapter
■■■■■■■■■■■■■■■■■■■
fourteen

"Well of *course* I'm going back to Transylvania," Emil said lightly. He picked a kernel of white cheddar cheese popcorn from the bag he was carrying, tossed it into the air, and tried to catch it in his mouth. It bounced off his teeth and fell to the ground, and was immediately stepped on by a passerby.

Lionel walked beside him, his hands in his pockets and his eyes on his Weejuns. "You never mentioned it before, that's all," he said wanly. Now that he'd heard the worst from Emil's own lips, he felt the final ebbing away of his last hopes—his delirious, ridiculous hopes that Emil had for some reason been lying to his Uncle John and Aunt Nancy about going back—and with the waning of those hopes came an overwhelming exhaustion. His nervous passion for Emil had drained away all his energy, and now he was left with nothing to restore him. He dragged his feet along the sidewalk as though each weighed as much as a Lincoln Town Car.

"Well, you didn't think I came to America to *stay*, did you?" Emil said merrily. He tossed up another kernel of popcorn, which hit him square in the eye and rolled off his face. He ignored it and said, "Why would I fight so hard for

Transylvanian sovereignty if I never intended to go back to Transylvania?"

Lionel, feeling foolish and hurt, shrugged his shoulders. "I guess I thought it was just the *principle* of the thing," he said. They rounded the sharp corner at Diversey and Clark and, distracted by dismay, Lionel accidentally hit his thigh on a newspaper vending machine that jutted into the sidewalk. He snarled at it and gave it a good, swift kick.

Emil dug into the bag of popcorn again. "I wouldn't fight for a principle I couldn't put into practice, Lionel. I am, above all, a *practical* man." He tossed another kernel into the air. This one actually hit his lips, but ended up falling down his shirtfront.

Lionel exhaled deeply and resigned himself to the eventual departure of his One True Love. "I guess I can understand that," he said. "You want to go back and make sure democracy takes hold. Who wouldn't?"

"Democracy?" Emil muttered caustically. He plunged his hand beneath his collar and scoured the area between his chest and shirt for the stray kernel. "Who said anything about *democracy*?"

Lionel was caught by surprise. "What do you mean? You still believe in communism?"

"I *never* believed in communism." He discovered the kernel in the approximate region of his navel, retrieved it, and tossed it high in the air again, determined to catch it this time. It fell on his head and got entangled in his hair.

"Well, what else *is* there?" Lionel asked, Emil's carefree attitude irritating him.

Emil raised an eyebrow. "What else *is* there? Are you *serious*?" He shook his head and dislodged the popcorn from his jet-black locks. "I thought you had more imagination than that, Lionel." Abruptly, he stopped to tie his shoe.

Lionel lurched to a halt. "I don't," he said with a frown, looking down admiringly on the muscular expanse of Emil's back. "Not about that. Tell me."

Emil stood up again, scooped another kernel from the bag, tossed it in the air, and caught it neatly between his teeth. "A-*ha*!" he cried. "You see, Lionel? I *knew* I could do that!" With a flick of his tongue, he swept the kernel into his mouth and swallowed it, then resumed walking.

Lionel followed suit. Ahead of him, he espied a woman walking two bull terriers; their leashes kept getting intertwined and he could hear her cursing at the dogs. "Sons of *bitches*!" she screamed. He didn't know what offended him more: the fact that she was abusing her pets, or the fact that she was too stupid to realize that she was in fact calling a spade a spade. He felt nothing but contempt for her, nothing but contempt for everyone. Emil was going to leave him someday, and he didn't seem to care. He'd never see Lionel again, and all he could do was play silly games with popcorn.

Lionel turned to the beefy, beautiful Transylvanian. "So what's the answer? You don't want communism, you don't want democracy. What else is left?"

"There is anarchism, my friend," Emil said gleefully, content now to transfer the popcorn to his mouth manually. He stuffed a handful into his face and chewed.

Lionel shook his head. "Everyone running around crazy, like chickens with their heads cut off? Everything going to hell? I can't believe you mean that." Please, God, make him crazy, thought Lionel; at least then medical science might be able to cure him. And a boyfriend in a straitjacket is better than no boyfriend at all.

Emil swallowed hard and said, "Lionel, you confuse anarchy with chaos. Chaos is the absence of order; anarchy is the absense of a *central* order, of a *system*. Why must a country have a system? Because there are men who seek power, Lionel, and a system is the only way they can attain it. Anarchism prevents that. Anarchism is the rule of a *million* systems, a *billion* systems. All of them interrelating, like cells in a body. It's a beautiful concept, Lionel. And what's more, it is the natural state of human affairs. Look at attempts to regulate trade: failures! Every country has a black market. I tell you, Lionel, I *love* the sheer enormity of production, of trade, that no governmental system can contain it. It's mankind's highest calling." He pointed to a storefront with a grimy window painted with the name LYLE'S NOVELTIES. "Even when I enter a shop such as that, I feel as though I have entered a holy place. I have such a *reverence* for trade, because it is the earliest invented means of social survival—it is uniquely *human*. Of *course* it overwhelms any system that tries to regulate it. It's like the urge to mate." He stuffed another fistful of popcorn into his mouth, then made little noises that told Lionel to wait until he swallowed because he had more to say. Eventually he gulped and said, "You know who I admire? Prostitutes. More than anyone else, they exemplify the anarchist rule that regulation is against human nature. You can find whores in every country on the face of the earth, even the most repressive. Whores, all by themselves, show that both trade and love cannot be regulated or controlled. They are the high priestesses of anarchism."

"That's the kind of society you want in Transylvania?" Lionel said, wanting to splash Emil's face with a dose of good, cold common sense. Anything to change his mind. "A bunch of whores running around? A pimp on every street corner? That's what you want?"

"Oh, yes," Emil said. "That kind of vitality, that kind of freedom—that is *exactly* what I want for Transylvania." He picked at a popcorn shell that had gotten caught between his tooth and gum. "But no pimps. I think whores should represent themselves. Whores should unionize." He freed the shell from his gum and flicked it onto the concrete. "I think *everyone* should unionize. Unions should be the means by which all trades co-relate. I suppose at base I'm more of a syndicalist than an anarchist."

Lionel looked at his reflection in a store window and could see how deeply he was scowling. Emil was becoming more and more foreign to him—and he was finding that foreignness less and less attractive. His exoticism had been alluring when it had been remote and unknowable, when he had been a musk-smelling peasant with a billboard-wide chest, Day-Glo blue eyes, and a paint-splattered placard bearing a slogan that even the most literate American couldn't decipher. But now that Emil had revealed his exoticism to be not merely physical but intellectual—now that he had revealed that the realm of ideas held him more surely than the realm of the flesh—Lionel found him vastly irritating.

He turned and said, "I don't suppose it ever occurred to you that that kind of wide open system would just give a lot of people license to be corrupt and to steal and to damage other people's lives."

Emil squinted into the sun and grimaced. "Which *never* happens in a democracy. Is that what you're saying? *Honestly,* Lionel." He tipped the nearly empty bag of popcorn into his mouth, and the remainder of its contents slid down his throat. Then he crumpled the bag and tossed it into a garbage can without breaking his stride. He munched the dregs and swallowed them, then shook his head and said, "Have you never read Emma Goldman, Lionel?"

He wrinkled his brow. "Didn't she used to be on *Dynasty?*"

Emil pursed his lips and wiped his crumb-encrusted hands on his pants. "She is a great thinker who lived and wrote in this country, Lionel—*this* one. *Your* country. You would do well to listen to her. Before Ceausescu took over the presses, my father bought a copy of her book *Anarchism and Other Essays,* in English. I first learned to speak this tongue by reading Emma Goldman. To me, the English language and the tenets of anarchism are inextricably bound together. It astonishes me that here, in America, it is so discredited an ideology. Perhaps because of the violence espoused by so many of its adherents. But Americans are a violent people; if they can celebrate Bonnie and Clyde or Bugsy Siegel at the movies, if they can celebrate violence in pursuit of greed, why do they so revile violence in pursuit of social change?"

"Because it's useless. There's no utopia, Emil."

"No, there is no utopia, Lionel, nor can there be. But we can at least strive for better ways to live. And there *is* better than this. What is democracy but mob rule? As John Stuart Mill said, 'Democracy leads to the tyranny of the majority.' Let me ask you: who are the disenfranchised in this country? Minorities, that's who. Ethnic, racial, and sexual minorities. Defend that, Lionel. Defend the disenfranchisement of minorities by the majority. Defend democracy."

At the mention of sexual minorities, Lionel's heart quickened. As long as they'd come to The Big Question, he might as well have an answer. Maybe in the process he'd lose Emil forever, but Emil was going to leave him sooner or later anyway. And if the answer to The Big Question turned out to be affirmative, he and Emil might at least have a few good rolls in the hay by the time that happened. In the absence of a lifetime love affair, he'd settle for a few cheap thrills.

His fingers, still thrust deep in his pockets, nervously rattled his keys and pocket change. Then, looking Emil straight in the eye, he said, "Well, I can't defend that, Emil. Being a sexual minority myself, I can't."

Emil stopped dead in his tracks, forcing Lionel to do the same. The flow of people on the sidewalk was thus forced to move around them, like a stream of water around an outcropping of rock. "You, Lionel?" he asked, his forefinger extended, his eyes as wide as Susan B. Anthony dollars. "*You* are homosexual?"

"Yes. What of it?" His heartbeat drowned out the clang and thrum of urban life around him. He felt oddly light, as though gravity were slowly dissipating.

"Well, *well.*" Emil stood back and looked at him with a sly grin—the type of grin he'd have worn had he caught Lionel naked or with a sign on his back that said KICK ME. "I wouldn't have guessed," he said amusedly. He turned and, with a little wink of appreciation, said, "You hide it very well." Then he started walking again, a little spring in his step.

Lionel paused for a moment, then scooted up to him and fell into pace with him. Nothing was said for a few moments, but at least Emil was still grinning. This sufficiently emboldened Lionel to say, "I thought *you* might be, too."

Emil once again stopped dead. "*Me?*" he hooted. "Oh, *no,* Lionel. *No.* Not *me.*" He chuckled. "I couldn't ever—well, not to insult you or anything—but the very *idea* of—" He shuddered involuntarily. "No, *no.*" He cocked his head. "What on *Earth* made you presume that?"

Wishful thinking, he almost blurted, but he caught himself and instead said, "Well, you told me you'd been to a bunch of AIDS rallies here in Chicago. It seemed like a logical conclusion."

All at once, Emil's face darkened and he started walking again, very swiftly this time. Lionel jogged to keep up with him, oblivious to anything but his friend's mood, which was suddenly so heavy and impenetrable. He felt a flurry of fear; he'd said something wrong, something terrible. Emil might not be gay, Emil might never be his lover, Emil might someday go away and never return, but above all, Emil was still Emil, and Lionel couldn't bear the thought that he was responsible for his friend's glowering expression at this moment.

Emil said nothing, then nothing, and then more nothing, and Lionel didn't dare to interrupt the terrible silence, until he found himself beneath the awning that bore the name CHEVEUX D'AMOUR, and had to say, "This is it, Emil. This is where I have my appointment."

Emil turned and nodded. His hands were balled into fists. Both his knuckles and his lips were milky white. Even his hair looked clenched.

"Thanks for having dinner," Lionel continued with ridiculous cheerfulness. "Sorry I couldn't hang out all night. But, like I said, I made this appointment weeks ago and—hell. You know how it is." He dribbled out some nervous laughter, then lightly hit Emil on the shoulder. "Take care, okay?" He felt as though he were an actor in a play, and that no one else had read the script.

"Three years ago my niece Mircea died," Emil said all at once.

Lionel felt a jolt of alarm. Emil's voice sounded half-deranged—quiet and even, but with something wild in it, something flapping above the calm like a lone flag in a gale. What had he let loose here?

"She was two years old," he continued. "My brother Vasile's daughter. I loved her very deeply, Lionel. Very, very deeply. But under Ceausescu there were such limited funds for hospitals that hypodermic needles were used again and again and again. This resulted in an epidemic of pediatric AIDS. Mircea was born a perfect, healthy, beautiful infant. But before she was a week old she had been exposed to the AIDS virus." He took a long, thin breath. "That was when I began my medical training. That was when I became a radical. I helped kill the system that killed her, and I will help kill the virus that killed her, too. I will help kill the virus that killed my heart."

Lionel, stunned, moistened his lips with his tongue and said, "Oh, God, Emil. Forgive me. I never—I *never*—*God*. I'm so terribly—well, sorry doesn't begin to cover it."

Emil shook his head, as if to say, Never mind, then turned away and headed across the street, mindless of traffic. A bus started honking at him and he gave it such a glare of hatred that it actually stopped. Then, when he had passed, it pulled ahead and obscured him from view. Lionel watched the bus go by and felt his heart bleeding all over the sidewalk. When his view of the street was clear again, Emil was nowhere to be seen.

I wish I could cease to exist right here, he thought, and he meant it. I wish I could just disappear, right off the face of the earth. Dissolve into vapor. I don't deserve any better.

He staggered into the salon and was greeted in the reception area by Toné, who was wearing a silk chemise and leather pants, and whose ponytail was braided and hung over his left shoulder, curling at the end like the tail of a rhesus monkey. *"Mon brave!"* he cried. "You're a tad *en rétard,* you dear tease, you. One thought that perhaps you had forgot. Tomorrow is the *grande affaire,* is it not? Come, sit; time escapes us!"

Lionel turned, and he must have looked at Toné with too naked an expression of despair, because the hairdresser's hands flew to his face. (Since two of his fingers were inserted in a pair of scissors, this came close to resulting in the loss of an eye.)

"But, *cher ami,"* he trilled, "what *horreurs* have you been suffering?"

Lionel grunted in agony. "Forget it," he said, his voice nearly breaking. He walked past Toné and into the crowded salon, where he climbed into the chair at Toné's station. "Just cut my hair."

The hairdresser followed, and made a little tch-tch-tch noise as he swept a full-length, peach-colored vinyl bib around Lionel's neck and fastened it behind his head. Then he put both his hands on his customer's shoulders and said, *"N'importe,* dear lad, *n'importe.* There is *rien* in this world that is so bad as to cause such a *visage* as this." And, grabbing Lionel's cheeks, he turned his head so that he could see himself in a mirror.

"I really don't want to talk about it," Lionel said after Toné had released his face.

Toné said, "Come, one must shampoo you." He then started sashaying across the salon at a pace so leisurely that a fashion model on a runway would've seemed an Olympic sprinter by comparison. Lionel lumbered after him, trying not to meet the gaze of any of the other stylists or customers in the shop. He wasn't in the mood for any style-conscious queens today.

When he and Toné finally reached the sink, Lionel at once slid into the reclining chair, stuck his head back toward the faucet, and sighed. From this vantage point, he was able to watch as Toné lifted his hands to the level of his ears, wiggled his fingers, and looked around perplexedly. "Now, if you were one, where would you have left that shampoo?" Toné asked.

Lionel could see the bottle of viscous, emerald liquid at the hairdresser's left elbow. "It's right there," he said testily, pointing to it with his nose.

Toné looked and said, "Oh, no, *ce n'est pas la.* One meant the *amber* shampoo that one uses on *thinning* hair."

"My hair is not thinning," snapped Lionel, resting his head again.

There was a slight pause. Toné put his hands on his hips and stared at Lionel with one eyebrow arched. After a moment's contemplation, he reached out and grabbed the green shampoo. Then he turned on the water (perhaps it was only Lionel's imagination that it was quite a bit hotter than usual), pumped a glob of the shampoo into his palm, and started massaging Lionel's head. "One gets the feeling one mustn't cross you today. Well, *ça ne fait rien.* One's mood is so light and pleasant that even the most uncivil humors cannot affect it." He ran the scalding hose over Lionel's head; Lionel gasped and lurched forward, but Toné pushed him back down again. "Stay still, *mon brave. La reine le veut.* Anyway, one suspects that the occasion of your date with that *jeune fille* is to blame. When is the gala affair? *Demain?* One thought so. And are you perhaps now, at the eleventh hour, finding yourself reluctant to squire a member of the opposite sex to an evening of music and merriment? *Quelle surprise!*"

He turned away, and Lionel took the opportunity to reach from beneath the vinyl sheeting and feel for his head. It was still there; his scalp hadn't been flayed away. "I'm perfectly comfortable about my date tomorrow, Toné," he said in what he hoped was his most acid-tongued manner. "I really wish you'd butt out of my personal life and just cut my hair."

When Toné turned around again, he was holding a large white towel and his lips were pursed. "Or perhaps one is wrong," he said, and he began toweling Lionel's head with the kind of manic fervor that might have resulted in lifelong paralysis had Lionel tried even slightly to resist. "Perhaps your disagreeable mood is caused by *quelque chose d'autre.* A flat tire, perhaps. Or a large credit card bill in today's mail. Or a recent arrest for participating in a Transylvanian riot on *le rue Michigan.* It could be any one of those things. But one would never be so rude as to inquire." He lifted the towel away from Lionel's head, and Lionel watched the world spin for a moment. "If *mon cher ami* wishes to be rude to one and to treat one like a simple service provider and to keep secrets from one, then one will by all means acknowledge his right to do so." He dropped the towel into a basket and said, "Come back to one's chair now, and one will see what one can do to make you look worthy of the *grand monde* among whom you will be seen *demain.*"

Lionel shut his eyes and cursed his stupidity. He'd forgotten that Toné had witnessed the whole embarrassing incident in front of the Romanian consulate. Of *course* he'd be expecting a complete recounting of the events leading up to it. And instead, Lionel had come in and treated him—his sole gay friend!—like an insect, not even mentioning the arrest. First Emil, now Toné. How many more of the people he cared about could he manage to hurt today? He hated to think.

As he resettled himself in Toné's chair, he made up his mind to come clean. After all, if he persisted in keeping the stylist in the dark, there was no telling what kind of haircut he'd end up with. He'd go to the Trippy Awards looking like Emo Phillips or Larry Fine. And so, while Toné began to clip and snip and spray, he let the whole sordid story gush forth: how he'd been walking down the street with Tracy, seen Toné coming at them from the other direction, and leapt into the Transylvanian demonstration as a means of avoiding having to introduce them. Then his arrest and the subsequent notoriety at the office. He left out any refer-ence to having fallen in love with Emil. It was a little too painful at present.

Toné was silent throughout, until, when it was clear that Lionel had finished, he lifted his scissors and comb from Lionel's head and stood in front of the mirror where Lionel could see him. "One thanks you for your honesty and can-dor," the hairdresser said. "But one is rather hurt that you considered one so socially irresponsible that you thought one would have revealed you to that *jeune fille.* What kind of barbaric savage do you think one is, Lionel? Hasn't one earned your friendship and trust by one's behavior over the years? Hasn't one always acted in accordance with your wishes, even when one considered those wishes misguided?"

"You have, you have," Lionel said, wiping the stray hairs off his nose. "Listen, what can I say? I'm sorry. I wasn't thinking. I got scared, I panicked, I paid for it. It'll never happen again. You're a good friend, Toné. Good friends for-give. So forgive me?"

Toné took an atomizer and spritzed the top of his head. "One might consent to forgive you if you admit to one that your hair is thinning."

"It *isn't,* Toné. My hair is *not* thinning."

Toné sighed. *"D'accord, d'accord.* One forgives you anyway."

Lionel smiled and let his shoulders relax. "Thanks, Toné. It means a lot to me."

"Well," he said, plugging in the hairdryer, "one is only being so lenient because, as one said earlier, one's spirits are so light and pleasant today. One is actually feeling quite *laissez-aller,* as a matter of fact—one might almost say *gamin.* And can you guess why?"

"Why else?" said Lionel, resettling his buttocks in the seat (he'd slid several more inches during the haircut). "Same reason as always. You're in love."

"Ah, but this time, it is real, Lionel!" He switched on the hairdryer and then, to Lionel's mortification, continued his narrative by shouting above the roar of the dryer's motor. "HIS NAME IS GUILLAUME," he cried, "AND HE IS FRENCH! AS YOU KNOW, IT HAS ALWAYS BEEN ONE'S *DREAM* TO

BE FRENCH, BUT AS ONE WAS BORN HALF-JAPANESE, HALF-IRAQI—SUCH A BURDEN!—ONE HAS HAD TO RE-SIGN ONE'S SELF TO GOING THROUGH LIFE OTHER-WISE." He fluffed up the sides of Lionel's head, aimed the dryer at his ears, and raised his voice even higher. "BUT IF ONE CANNOT *BE* A FRENCHMAN, IS NOT THE NEXT BEST THING TO *ROMANCE* A FRENCHMAN, TO HAVE HIM AS YOUR *LOVER*?" He turned off the hairdryer, grabbed a razor, and said, "Well, actually he's Belgian, but it's nearly as good." Then he straightened out the edge of one of Lionel's sideburns.

Lionel had by this time slid a few inches down in his seat again. He had come close to expiring of embarrassment during Toné's shrieking declaration of love for his Belgian boyfriend. Certainly everyone else in the salon had heard him—and probably a good many on the street outside. Thank God it was over!

But it wasn't over. Parts of his hair were still wet, so Toné flipped on the hairdryer again and continued. "GUILLAUME HASN'T GOT HIS GREEN CARD YET, SO HE'S BEEN UN-ABLE TO FIND A JOB," he yelled as he aimed the dryer up and down the back of Lionel's head. "HE WAS WORKING AS A WAITER AT CHEZ DEIRDRE UNTIL IMMIGRATION GOT WIND OF IT. HE WAS NEARLY APPREHENDED! THAT WOULD HAVE KILLED ONE'S HEART." He turned off the dryer and said, "Look up." Lionel obeyed and hoped that Toné was now going to slit his throat, because then he wouldn't have to get up and walk past everyone in the salon after this appalling scene. But Toné merely took a razor and scraped a tiny patch of beard from his throat, then resumed both the hairdrying and his blaring narrative. "AND YET, LIONEL," he cried, "ONE MUST CONFESS, IT TRIES ONE'S PATIENCE TO HAVE ONE'S LOVER ACTUALLY *LIVING* WITH ONE. IT HAS ONLY BEEN A WEEK, AND ONE FEELS IT HAS BEEN CLOSE TO A CENTURY." He moved to the right side of the chair and continued drying around Lionel's temple. "HE CAME HOME AT TWO IN THE MORNING ON THURSDAY AND ONE COULD *SMELL* THAT HE HAD HAD SEX. WHAT COULD ONE DO BUT ACCUSE HIM? OH, THE FIGHT WE HAD! ONE THREW A *CHAIR* AT HIM, LIONEL! ONE WAS REDUCED TO THAT! AND NOT JUST A CHAIR,

BUT A *FAVORED* CHAIR—A LOUIS *QUINZE*! THAT ONE
PURCHASED FOR *BEAUCOUP D'ARGENT* AT THE ESTATE
SALE OF ONE OF ONE'S UNFORTUNATELY DECEASED CLI-
ENTS!" By now Toné had ceased his labors, and was stand-
ing pointing the still-running hairdryer aimlessly into the
air, caught up in his impassioned narrative and eager to get
Lionel to share his indignation. "AND WHAT DO YOU
THINK GUILLAUME DID? HE HAD THE DEPRAVITY TO
COME AT ONE WITH A *KNIFE*, LIONEL—A *KNIFE*! THE
SAME KNIFE THAT ONE HAD ONLY JUST USED TO CUT
ONE'S BELOVED'S PORK CHOPS FOR HIM! LOOK!" He
turned off the hairdryer at last and rolled up his left sleeve,
then extended his arm to show Lionel a fresh red wound,
about an inch long, on his outer biceps that was only just
beginning to heal. "Note well, *mon brave*," Toné said,
"the extremities to which love drives one. Seldom does
such satisfaction as one has found with Guillaume come
without great attendant cost." He turned on the hairdryer
again and gave Lionel one last going over. "OF COURSE,"
he shouted, "AFTERWARDS, OUR LOVEMAKING WAS
MAGNIFIQUE."

And then it was finished. Lionel was relieved of his vinyl
sheeting, dusted off, and sent on his way with a cheery *"A
bientôt!"* On the two occasions he dared to lift his eyes
from his shoes, he saw that he was being scrutinized as he
departed the salon, stared at by smiling young men with
billowing blond hair in Italian clothes who, he was sure,
had probably brawled with and brutalized each of *their* succession of one-week lovers, and would probably gladly perform the same function for him, if he cared to ask.

Outside the night air was cool, and when it met his face
he could feel how hot his skin had become. He gulped a
breath and began making his way home. He felt the sweat
that saturated his shirt become cold and uncomfortable.

Was that what he had longed for with Emil? Savage jealousy, sexual voraciousness, flying furniture—*knife fights*?
With, no doubt, an embittered separation not more than a
few days later? It was a narrow escape; too narrow. Emil's
being straight was without a doubt the luckiest thing that
had ever happened to him.

No such sick, perverted relationships for him. He'd descended into the pit and been plucked out, at the last moment, by the merest whim of fate—by the object of his homosexual lust turning out to be resolutely straight. Well, if he could somehow make himself love Tracy, *she* would be able to reciprocate, and she'd rescue him from the kind of disgusting life Toné was leading. He owed it to himself to try for that kind of life, to give himself the chance to escape from this whirlwind of savage lust and self-disgust.

His breathing became steadier with the thought of Tracy and tomorrow night. Tomorrow night! Just twenty-four small hours away. It was so short a time to have to wait for salvation!

chapter

■■■■■■■■■■■■■■■■■■■■

fifteen

Lionel's armpits were *killing* him. He had somehow managed to convince himself that heterosexual desire might come if only he were *clean* enough, and had accordingly scrubbed himself almost raw. And so, when he applied his environmentally incorrect aerosol deodorant, it had settled on his tender flesh with the approximate virulence of nuclear fallout.

He stood at the door to Tracy's apartment building with his sharp new haircut, bedecked in his rather dashing rented tuxedo and holding a bouquet of ripe, red roses. And yet the air of easy sophistication and worldly charm he desired to give off was more than a little undone by the fact that he found it excruciatingly painful to lower his arms to his sides. He had to swivel his entire torso to ring Tracy's bell, then stand with his shoulders hunched awaiting a response, looking something like a gentrified scarecrow, or Michael Jackson in a mid-dance move.

The speaker above the doorbells crackled to life. "Who is it?" said an electrically distorted voice that was still recognizable as Tracy's.

"Lionel and Abner," he called out. "Wait a minute— ABNER! COME BACK HERE! LEAVE THAT GELATO

VENDOR ALONE! ABNER!" A pause. "Make that just
Lionel."

He couldn't hear whether she was laughing or not, but
a moment later the door buzzed and he was allowed to
enter the building.

Try to relax your arms, he commanded himself as he
mounted the stairs. He let his shoulders drop a little and
instantly suffered the kind of sharp, shooting pain he
might've felt had he tied twenty-five-pound weights to his
armpit hairs.

He found Tracy's apartment, 2-B, and knocked. There was
a flurry of whispers and then footsteps behind the door,
before a strange woman opened it—a chunky, rather plain
brunette wearing a T-shirt that said PARTY NAKED. She said,
"Hi—Lionel?" He nodded and she continued, "I'm Ronnie,
Tracy's friend? I was just leaving?" She gave him a quick
once-over, then called behind the door, "TRACE, I'M LEAV-
ING? HAVE A GOOD TIME? CALL ME?" Then she scooted
past him and down the stairs.

A little put off, he tried to step through the door she'd
left open, but before he could do so two more women
appeared, one with stringy blond hair and a sweater with
baby chicks around the collar, the other with too much
lipstick and mascara and wearing a leather skirt. They gave
him a quick appraisal, too, as though they believed if they
did it swiftly enough, he might not figure out that they'd
been waiting around to get a look at him. "Hi," the masca-
raed one said, "we're friends of Tracy. We're just leaving.
I'm Connie."

"I'm Maria," said the blond. "Bye." And they slipped past
him and down the stairs. He heard giggling on the landing,
then it receded; eventually he heard the front door fall shut.

He felt a little silly now about making that joke about
Abner over the intercom. Abner was for Tracy's ears only;
the others must have thought him some kind of raging
geekoid.

He grimaced and stepped into Tracy's apartment, then
closed the door behind him. He looked around; a pretty
place—the kind of standard good taste a girl without much
money could assemble from pieces purchased all at once at
places like Crate & Barrel and Pier One Imports. On an

etagere sat a collection of photographs in teak frames: an older couple, presumably her parents; a gaggle of girls in sorority T-shirts hugging each other and holding plastic cups of beer; a Siamese cat rolled up like a croissant, fast asleep on a sofa. There was also an open spot among the photos, too wide to have been a simple aesthetic miscalculation. He knew intuitively that this is where Guy's picture had been. He went over to the etagere and looked at the glass shelf. Sure enough, there was a little film of dust across it, except for a clear strip where the hypothetical frame would have sat. Too bad, Lionel thought; he'd been curious to see whether Guy was cute or not.

But, no, no, he told himself; no more succumbing to *that.* Tonight, with any luck, his life as a fully initiated heterosexual would begin.

"LIONEL?" It was Tracy's voice, calling out from what he presumed must be her bedroom, down a hallway to the right. "YOU THERE?"

"HOLD ON," he called back, "LET ME CHECK." A long pause. "YES, I'M HERE."

He could hear her laugh. Then she called, "BE WITH YOU IN A SECOND."

"A METAPHORICAL SECOND OR A MATHEMATICAL ONE?" he asked. No laughter. Why was he babbling like this? Was he *that* nervous? He walked across the apartment to the kitchen and it felt like he was floating—or rather, that his body was dangling from his head. He *must* be nervous. Everything was suddenly dreamlike and indistinct, scarily unreal.

In the kitchen, he put the roses on the counter. "DO YOU HAVE A VASE ANYWHERE?" he called out. "SOMEONE BROUGHT YOU A DOZEN ROSES. I THINK IT MUST'VE BEEN CONNIE."

Again, he heard her laugh, and he thought, Why am I doing this? Why can't I stop being a joker? Maybe, he thought, because he'd been a joker with her all along, and it had gotten him this far. Maybe it was because laughter really *was* an aphrodisiac, and he needed all the help he could get. Or maybe it was just a nervous reaction.

He decided not to worry about it. He was having too much trouble breathing at the moment to worry about anything else. He reached up and opened one of her kitchen cabinets. No vase here; just an array of drinking glasses, all tinted green. He lowered his arm, careful not to lower it too far.

A flicker of movement at the corner of his eye caused him to turn; there was Tracy, standing at the end of the hallway. She looked—astonishing. Transformed. Her girlishness, her kid-sisterishness, had been streamlined and tucked away. She wore a black strapless cocktail dress that flared at the waist and erupted into layers of diaphanous webbing. It wasn't quite see-through, but it gave that impression. She also wore incredibly tiny shoes with diamond-sharp heels, and a pair of earrings that looked like dangling black Lego blocks. Her hair was pulled back from her face and her cheekbones had been accented by some arcane cosmetic or other. Tracy, he realized, was in fact a great beauty. He appreciated her beauty; he admired her beauty; he was even moved by her beauty. He was forced to admit, however, that he was not yet aroused by her beauty—not even slightly.

"JUST LOOKING FOR A VASE," he shouted at her.

She jumped back an inch and put her hand to her nearly naked chest. "For God's sake, Lionel, why are you *yelling?*"

"WE'VE BEEN YELLING FOR FIVE MINUTES," he cried. "YOU STARTED IT."

She laughed, but through gritted teeth; he could tell that he was frustrating her. She'd obviously imagined this moment differently.

Chastened by her reaction, he picked up the roses and came out of the kitchen. "Seriously," he said, "these are for you. I only wish they looked half as good as you do."

She visibly melted. She gathered the roses in her arms and sniffed them, then took them back to the kitchen and put them in a pitcher filled with water. Then she returned to the living room.

"They're lovely," she said, looking at him from beneath half-lowered eyelids.

"Thank you," he said, touched by her, loving her, but not wanting her. Dear God, he thought; I'm *really* going to have to knock back the drinks if I'm ever going to pull this off!

"No, thank *you,*" she said, and she leaned over to him and parted her lips. He kissed her, and before he could stop himself he thought of the kiss he'd wanted so desperately from Emil—big, hairy, vulgar Emil, so different from this slight, fair young woman—and when their lips touched he felt the flash of that fantasy for a split second, but that was apparently long enough. Because when Tracy drew away, he could see that she had felt it, too, and it had been real for her. Her lips were still parted, and her eyes were gazing into his, without even a trace of embarrassment.

He swallowed hard and said, "Shall we go?"

She nodded, her eyes still locked on his.

"I'll race you," he said. "You take the elevator, I'll take the fire escape. Last one down pays for parking."

She grimaced, but there was affection in it. "Do you *ever* stop clowning?" she asked gently.

"When I'm shaving," he said. "Not 'cause I want to. I just bleed less that way."

She rolled her eyes and smiled, then went over to the coffee table and picked up her purse. Lionel headed for the door.

"Why are you walking that way?" she said, catching up with him.

"What way?" he asked. He stopped and turned to face her.

"*That* way," she said, nodding at his chest. "With your arms stuck out like that. You look like a bad mime or something."

"Oh," he said sheepishly. "Well—this is true, I swear it— I scrubbed my armpits too hard, and when I put on my deodorant spray it just stung like high holy hell. Feel like I've got third-degree burns under there." He shrugged. "Kind of stupid of me, I know."

She regarded him for a moment, as if uncertain whether to believe him. Then she shook her head and said, "My great big goofball." She carefully slipped her arm through his. "What am I going to do with you?"

"Beat me, whip me, whatever you want," he said airily as they started for the door. "Do your worst. My laundry detergent gets out most stains."

chapter

■ ■ ■ ■ ■ ■ ■ ■ ■ ■ ■ ■ ■ ■ ■ ■ ■ ■ ■ ■

sixteen

Peg Deming, the rotund and florid wife of Julius Deming, swept into the ballroom of the Ritz-Carlton Hotel and, leading her husband by a good fifteen paces, found their table. Lionel and Tracy had the misfortune to arrive there at exactly the moment she did.

"Oh! Lionel, it's you. Peg Deming, remember?" She dropped her purse into the nearest chair and turned her cheek to him.

"Course I do, Peg," he said, dutifully kissing it. "How are you? I'm sure you know Tracy."

"Don't be silly, how could I not?" She opened her arms, grabbed Tracy by the shoulder, and air-kissed her. "Good to see you, dear," she said. Then she turned to the table and, making her way around its perimeter, plucked each place card from its corresponding plate.

Julius Deming finally reached the table, his face scarlet and his breathing labored. "Peg, I wish you wouldn't do that," he said.

"You should've *seen* the way they had us situated," she said, resetting the place cards in an entirely different order. "Husbands and wives all next to each other. I'm glad I in-

sisted we arrive early enough to change that. Say hello to
your employees, darling."

"Hi, Lionel, hi, Tracy," he said, barely nodding. Then he
turned back to his wife and said, "Maybe some of the husbands and wives *want* to sit next to each other. And what
about these two, here?" He tossed his broad, shiny head in
Lionel and Tracy's direction. "Christ. It's their first date!"

Peg stood erect and pursed her lips at her husband; her
nostrils flared for a moment, and then she said, "Honestly,
Julie, I don't know why I bother doing any of this. No one
appreciates it, least of all you. As for these two," and here
she nodded her head in Lionel and Tracy's direction, "from
everything you've told me, they've been sweet on each
other for years without doing a thing about it. They can
stand to sit apart from each other for one more evening."
She picked up her purse. "Now, if you'll excuse me, I've
got to go powder my nose." She looked at Tracy and said,
"While I'm gone, honey, maybe you could rearrange the
centerpiece. It's too symmetrical as is. Wildflowers should
look *wild.*" And then she bustled away.

When she was out of earshot, her husband shrugged and
said, "Sorry, kids. She's been on far too many cruise ships."

At that moment Hackett Perlman and his wife Becky arrived, Perlman rubbing his hands gleefully, as if anxious to
get his grip on the gold Trippy plaque.

They exchanged hellos with the rest of the group, and
Lionel could see that Becky was already excited about the
possibilities for scorn and derision that were presenting
themselves this night. She was a woman Lionel deeply and
devoutly feared. She might've been handsome, had her face
not pinched itself into an aspect of unconditional hatred,
had her eyes not receded behind slits so that they resembled beady little Christmas-tree lights. Lionel remembered
thinking her attractive on their first meeting, at a previous
awards banquet, during which he had been seated next to
her at the table. But then she'd spent the entire four hours
spewing vilifications and indemnifications into his ear, with
no lessening of passion when she switched from discussing
personal acquaintances to entire ethnic groups. It was only
after the evening had ended and she had shaken his hand
and, with a brilliant smile, thanked him for being such an

enjoyable dinner partner that he realized she'd been having the time of her life. That's when he knew that Becky Perlman's hobby was hatred, and that, like the folkloric countess who kept herself young by bathing in the blood of virgins, she drew a rejuvenating kind of pleasure from verbally skewering the entire world.

"Do you know Perlman's wife?" Lionel whispered to Tracy.

"Believe it or not, I've never met her," Tracy whispered back. "She nice?"

"No," was all he had time to say before the Perlmans were upon them. Hackett was already sipping at a Manhattan, which increased his air of malignancy. He looked at Lionel as though preparing to spit on him, and said, "You're not drinking, Lionel," with the precise cadences he would've employed to say, You don't sleep with women, Lionel.

"No, I haven't made it to the bar yet," he replied. "Get you something, Trace?"

"Sloe gin fizz, thanks," she said with a pretty smile.

"You'll probably have to explain to Gunga Din how to make it," said Becky of the dark-skinned bartender, her lips curling into a sneer. "Swear to God he just got off the boat. Asked him for a brandy Alexander and he looked at me like I was speaking pig Latin or something. I tried to get through to him but it was like talking to a brain-damaged houseplant. Ended up settling for a white wine. Goddamn *nerve* of the caterer, giving us a Muslim for a bartender. Those people don't even *drink*, for Christ's sake." She tossed back a gulp of wine and smiled at Lionel, deliriously happy with the evening already.

Lionel smiled weakly at her in return, then slunk away to the bar. On the way there, he ran into Peg Deming, who was on her way back. She craned her neck over the thickening crowd, and said, "Honey, your girlfriend didn't get to the flowers!"

"Sorry, Peg, I wouldn't let her. I was afraid her dress would fall off her if she reached that far." He leaned closer to her. "No straps," he murmured, "and no bra."

She shook her head and said, "Why a woman would wear a dress that doesn't let her *do* anything is beyond me. You're heading toward the bar?"

"Uh-huh."

"Get me a martooni, would you, dear? I've got to see to those flowers before the Magellans get here."

In Becky Perlman's defense, Lionel had to admit that the bartender *was* rather obtuse, and that the long wait in line to get to the bar was nothing compared to the wait he had once he'd ordered his drinks. But eventually they were produced for him, and, his hands filled with his own drink, Tracy's, and Peg's, he turned just in time to be almost broadsided by the Babcock Magellans, who swept past him like the SST. He followed them silently.

Peg Deming, who was kneeling on the table trying to figure out what to do with one last sprig of sunflower, nearly toppled off at the sight of her husband's powerful client. Lionel raced around the side of the table and set down the drinks, then helped the heavyset Peg to the floor again. Flushed and embarrassed, she picked up her martini and whispered to Lionel, "No one appreciates it. I don't suppose anyone will even look twice. I don't know why I do it, I honestly don't." Then she downed half the drink in one gulp and went to meet the Magellans.

Lionel gave Tracy her drink and she gave him a big, beautiful grin, and he felt something in his loins twinge; he didn't know what it was, but he convinced himself that it must be sexual desire. Thrilled, he put his hand on Tracy's waist and led her over to the Magellans.

Dolores Magellan was already drunk, but of course she was an alcoholic, so what else could you expect? No one could remember a time when she wasn't at least sloppy, and usually she was a mess. But Babcock Magellan was a million-dollar client, so everyone had grown accustomed to suddenly having to tie a shoelace or fall prey to a coughing fit every time blowsy, wavering Dolores accidentally dumped a full gin and tonic down her cleavage, or told someone who got in her way to "Eat my pussy, peon, my husband could buy and sell you!" Tracy had worked at the agency too long not to know the stories, but even so, Lionel caught her staring too fixedly at Dolores, whose blond wig tonight was sitting on her head at approximately a twelve-degree angle from the position it should've. Lionel nudged her and, when her eyes met his, he frowned and shook his head seriously.

She swallowed a giggle and put her drink to her lips; she couldn't stop smiling.

For several minutes, Babcock Magellan prattled on about how proud he was of his agency and how excited he was about winning the award, and at every syllable that might somehow be construed as wit, everyone (save his wife) laughed aloud and slapped their thighs, and then said, "Seriously, Babcock, you make it all possible," and "Babcock, we'd be nothing without you," and other such expressions of their honest, genuine feelings. Then the Magellans headed for the hors d'oeuvres table, and the rest of the group followed, en masse.

Tracy grabbed Lionel's arm. "Let's not go with them," she said; "I've got an idea." Her eyes were twinkling.

"What? I'm hungry!" he protested, but she just laughed and pulled him back to the table. There, before his horrified eyes, she picked up their place cards and rearranged the table so that they would be sitting together.

"Are you out of your *mind*?" he stage-whispered. "Peg is going to go *nuclear* when she sees this."

"No, she won't," she replied, amused by his fear. "She wouldn't *dare*—not in front of Magellan."

"Oh, God, oh, God," he said, suddenly panicking. He picked up a napkin and wiped his forehead with it before he could realize that it wasn't even his. "Oh, Christ. Get me a fresh napkin. Oh, God! We're gonna get fired."

She slipped around the table and poked him in the stomach. "You're such a *wimp*, Lionel," she said. "*I'm* not gonna get fired for this, and neither are *you.*" And just as these words were beginning to reassure him, she followed them with, "And so what if we do?"

He moaned and put his hands to his face, and she laughed gaily. "Come on. Let's sit down so Peg can't change everything back while we're at the buffet."

Lionel felt faint, but did as he was told. And, sure enough, Peg Deming was the first to arrive back at the table, her plate heaped with cauliflower and broccoli and other such foods which, she was always assuring anyone who would listen, did a remarkable job of cleansing the colon. She looked at Lionel and Tracy and smiled maternally, then suddenly realized that they were sitting together. She froze; her smile disappeared, and she stared at them with nothing less than stupefied disbelief, as if no one in the world had ever before crossed her in so fiendish a manner as this. Lionel felt her stare as though it were a deadly beam from a laser cannon.

Just when she had recovered enough to open her mouth and berate them, Babcock and Dolores Magellan arrived back at the table, with Perlman and Deming dancing attendance on them like medieval fools, except that Babcock was the one making the jokes and they were the ones laughing. Babcock had a plate filled with tiny beef sandwiches, and Dolores had filled hers with about thirty or forty black olives, which, when she had careened into her chair and steadied herself against its armrests, she proceeded to eat, one after the other, with no expression of pleasure at all.

Magellan looked at Peg Deming, who was still standing, and said, "I can't sit till you do, Peg." It probably didn't help Julius Deming's marriage that, from behind Magellan, he flappped his hands at his wife and mouthed, *Sit down! Sit down!*

Peg made her way around the table, saying with artificial sweetness, "I was *planning* on sitting down, Babcock, dear, but someone seems to have *moved* the place cards and now I really don't even know where I'm suppo— Ah, *here* I am."

Impishly, Tracy had put Peg's place card directly next to Lionel's. And as Peg lowered herself into her seat, Lionel could feel a cold front rise up between them that no conversation could cross. Suddenly he realized that Tracy had planned this so that she'd have him all to herself.

And then he began to relax. The worst had happened— Peg Deming was mortally offended, and there was nothing he could do about it now. But, strangely, the anticipation of that offense was worse than the reality of it; and he surprised himself by finding the whole thing increasingly funny. He turned and looked at Tracy, whose eyes were alive with girlish merriment, and he actually felt his penis stiffen for a moment. The sensation elated him. He could do it! What did Peg Deming matter if he could become Tracy's lover?

Becky Perlman, needing only hate to feed her, had taken nothing more than a few token cheese wedges for her plate, and was now ignoring them. Instead, she was feasting on the rich repast of the Leo Burnett table. "Did you see how they sit right up front, by the podium?" she sneered. "Think they're God's gift. Three years ago when Hacky won an award for that Foto-Finisher's campaign, I snuck up to take a snapshot with my Polaroid, and oh my *God,* I made the unfor*giv*able mistake of resting my purse against a Leo Burnett snob's chair. Thought he was gonna take my *head* off. I see him here this year, too. Looks like he gained weight, the big pig. Some people are too goddamned self-important for their own good. Probably a junior copywriter, how much you want to bet? Well, what goes round, comes round, that's what I say. I pointed him out to Hacky and said, He ever comes to you for a job, you know what to say." She nodded twice, then leaned back in her chair and patted her stomach, as if she'd just consumed a whole joint of beef.

Underneath the table, Tracy kicked Lionel's ankle, as if to say, Can you even *believe* this? And Lionel, who had for years been completely obsequious in the presence of his employers and their wives, now allowed himself to snicker at their expense—not only this once, but often over the course of the half-hour that followed. It was Tracy's presence—joyful, untainted, anarchic, and wild—that freed him so. It was Tracy who liberated him; Tracy who lifted him so high; Tracy who—could it be?—aroused him. As yet, his erection was an unremarkable one, like a stick of butter after just a few minutes in the refrigerator—still soft, but with the beginnings of solidity. By the time the night was over, who knew what it would be like?

And Lionel allowed his imagination to drift for a moment, into a rosy, television-commercial heterosexual future. He and Tracy, rolling around in a field of leaves in autumn; he and Tracy, making angels in the snow in winter; he and Tracy, twining magnolia blossoms through each other's hair in spring; he and Tracy, bronzing their bodies while stretched out on a single jumbo beach towel in summer. A future of picture-postcard moments, of breeder bliss; it was all before him now. The wheels were in motion. Tracy was right: so what if he did get fired? He'd found something more important—something he'd thought forever denied him.

When Hackett Perlman interrupted his reverie by groaning, "Oh, no. Oh, no," he didn't at first realize that Perlman, who sounded as always like a Greek chorus heralding disaster, could in fact be doing exactly that. After all, what disaster could befall him here? And whatever it was that was upsetting Perlman, how could it have anything to do with Lionel?

But when Perlman explained himself by saying, "It's Jennifer Jerrold, and she's headed this way," Lionel felt his stomach drop, and he knew that doom was at hand, indeed. And sure enough, when he turned to see the forbidding Ms. Jerrold make her approach, he discovered that she was accompanied by her handsome young husband, Kyle.

God, do not let this happen, Lionel prayed. I will give half my earnings to the church. I will eat only crumbs and wear only rags. I will work with lepers. *Do not let this happen.*

"Who's Jennifer Jerrold?" Tracy whispered in Lionel's ear.

"Talent agent," he whispered back. "She represents Jack Fahey, the guy we've been using in all the Bennet's Bridal radio spots. The Bennet's people are crazy about him, so that means we're stuck with *her.*"

And then she was there by his side, and she placed one of her taloned hands on his shoulder, the other on Peg Deming's shoulder. (For a second Lionel thought Peg was going to bite it.) Jennifer was treading water somewhere in her late fifties, pretending to all that even *she* wasn't sure of her exact age after too many decades of lying. But if her chronology was murky, her presence was not. She always dressed in black, and tonight was wearing a floor-length vest that draped itself over a roomy black jumpsuit, making her look something like a cross between Orson Welles and Lily Munster.

"Well, if it isn't one of my *favorite* agencies," she intoned as if it were the first line of a particularly portentous Shakespeare tragedy. "Are you here to collect some delicious prize or other?" Little scotch-scented breaths tumbled from her mouth and drifted past Lionel's nose.

Perlman, Deming, and Magellan all got to their feet; Lionel tried to, but Jennifer's clamp kept him down. He gave up the effort immediately, vastly preferring to sit in his chair and stare at his plate.

"Evening, Jennifer," said Deming, extending his hand for the talent agent to shake. "Don't believe you know Babcock Magellan, head of All-Pro Power Tools."

Jennifer lifted her hand from Lionel's shoulder and shook Deming's hand, then turned to Magellan and shook his. "What extraordinary good luck," she said with embarrassing sincerity. "The pleasure is entirely mine."

"Not at all," said Magellan, trying to free his hand from her viselike grip. He was grinning too much; apparently he, and probably the rest of the table, had by now figured out that Jennifer was drunk.

"May I present my husband, Kyle?" she said, and she stepped away from Lionel's chair.

Oh, God, Lionel thought. Oh, Lord King Heavenly Father.

The fortyish, sandy-blond, Arrow-shirt-modelish Kyle made his way around the table to shake hands with the three other men. Kyle's teeth were too white, his manner too precise, his walk too mincing. None of them could help making assumptions about the *real* nature of the Kyle-and-Jennifer marriage.

And then Kyle turned in Lionel's direction, and his eyes lit up. "Hey—Lionel, right?" he said. "Haven't seen you in— God, when *was* that?"

Lionel shut his eyes for a second and felt the floor fall away. When he opened them, however, he was still faced with Kyle's sculpted good looks. He blurted out a laugh that sounded like a cat being drowned. "Can't remember," he said. "Good to see you again—Kyle, was it?" He rose out of his chair and shook his hand.

Kyle put one hand on his hip and said, "Haven't aged a *day,* you horrible old thing. What's your secret? Some dreadfully boring New Age diet?"

"Just having a job I love," Lionel said, unable to stop giggling nervously.

Kyle rolled his eyes theatrically. "How *terribly* Protestant-work-ethic," he exclaimed. "I suppose you're to be commended."

"Well, thanks." He sat down again.

Jennifer leaned over the table and said, in a voice just loud enough to carry to the Eastern Seaboard, "Kyle, you stop that. We're here to network, not flirt." Lionel reeled as if he'd been hit, then squeezed his knees together to prevent himself from urinating all over the chair and floor. "For what masterwork are you to be lauded tonight?" Jennifer continued, in a more hushed tone. "If it's for Bennet's Bridal, I may have to scold you for being so secretive."

Hacket Perlman put his hand on Magellan's shoulder, as if to protect him from Jennifer, and said, "Actually, it's for our All-Pro work. A chainsaw spot. Maybe you saw it."

"Maybe I did," said Jennifer, straightening unsteadily and furrowing her brow. "I'll have to think about it and let you know." Then she swept the left panel of her vest over her arm and stepped back. "Well, congratulations all around. If you have any new projects coming up this year, remember us, won't you? We always like to see of bervice." She furrowed her brow again, aware that something was wrong with what she'd just said.

Kyle appeared at her side and said, "C'mon, Jen, let's move along."

"Dear Kyle," she said, patting his cheek while letting him guide her away. "Such a treasure. Such a help. How long has it been since I raised your allowance?"

When the couple had moved out of earshot, everyone at the table burst into little grunts of laughter.

"Drunk as a *skunk*," said Becky Perlman, leaning over her plate. The entire scene had been, for her, the equivalent of an all-expenses-paid romp in select European hot spots. "Did you smell her *breath*?" she gasped. "It's amazing that woman can still *stand.* I guess that's what happens when party girls get old. And," she said, turning to Peg Deming, who she knew would appreciate this insight, "they *always* get old."

"She's been doing that as long as I can remember," said Deming to Magellan, worried that Jennifer might have offended his client. "She's really pretty harmless. And a shrewd businesswoman, too."

"Who said I drunk?" sneered Dolores Magellan, only half in tune with the conversation. She tried to adjust her wig, but it had gotten hooked on her left ear; the more she pushed, the greater the pain she inflicted on that ear, until she yelped in agony, gave up, and tossed back another swig of her Manhattan.

"And how about that *husband*?" Becky continued, a look

of almost beatific delight on her face. "That guy a Tinkerbell, or *what?*"

Lionel felt the color leap to his face, and was just beginning to worry about seeming too affected by Becky's remark when Tracy astonished him by saying, "What a terrible thing to say. You ought to be ashamed of yourself!"

Becky looked crestfallen, as though someone had just yanked her hand away from a sand castle she'd only half built. "It's *not* a terrible thing to say," she protested, with all the indignation of someone who believes herself truly innocent. "It's the truth!"

"It *is* the truth," said Perlman, coming to his wife's aid. "Everyone in the business knows it. Jennifer Jerrold married a fag ten years younger than her."

"You're just as bad," Tracy said, balling up her napkin and throwing it on the table. "So what if he's gay? You act like he's some kind of *freak* or something. And so what if she was drunk? Why is that so bad? I've seen you guys at *least* as drunk as that, *lots* of times. But she's a woman, isn't she? Women aren't supposed to get drunk. And women aren't supposed to marry men who like men. That's it, right? You lay down all the rules for everyone else in the world, and the rules are simple—everyone just has to be exactly like you."

"If you're going to talk about men who like men, I can't sit here and listen," Peg Deming said, pushing her chair away from the table. "It makes my brain itch. Ugh! I'm going to go and empty these ashtrays till you can think of something decent to talk about again." She grabbed the two butt-filled trays from the table and trotted away.

Becky, offended by Tracy having spoken to her in such a tone, was now sitting with her hands folded and her lips pursed, looking very determinedly in the opposite direction.

Lionel could see that Babcock Magellan's face was growing red; he was obviously uncomfortable with the turn this conversation had taken. What's more, Deming and Perlman could see it, too, and were eager to trivialize Tracy's anger to the point at which they could chuckle at it and move on. Unfortunately for Lionel, they chose *him* to be their ally in this.

"And what's with you and Kyle?" Perlman said, winking at him. "Seemed to know you pretty well."

Lionel felt panic start to well in him—it was like a thousand electrified cockroaches crawling up his spine—but he forced himself to be calm, to think his way through this. Any attempt to lie about how he knew Kyle would undoubtedly be labored and overwrought, and would doubtless raise more questions than it answered. Falling back on his tried-and-true technique for these situations, he took refuge in the truth—but truth conveyed in a manner in which no one would recognize it. He took a breath and said, in what he considered his queeniest voice, "Kyle and I? We slept together a few times. Didn't I ever mention it?"

Deming, Perlman, and Magellan all laughed uproariously, out of relief at the lessening of the tension as much as out of appreciation for Lionel's joke. But Tracy regarded Lionel with a look of astonished betrayal, as if to say, You, too? After which she slid her chair from the table and left the ballroom, without having bothered to excuse herself.

Lionel couldn't afford to worry about her just now. He waited until the laughter died and then said, "Seriously, it's a long story and not that interesting. He's a friend of a friend of a friend, he called me and took me to lunch a few times 'cause he wanted to get into advertising and wanted my advice, blah, blah, blah." He moved to pick up his vodka-and-tonic, but noticed at the last second how seriously his hand was trembling. He withdrew it and put it in his lap.

"That must be when he married Jennifer Jerrold," said Deming. "Got *into* advertising then, didn't he?" Some scattered laughter at this.

"Bet he didn't," said Magellan, and at this witticism Deming, Perlman, and Lionel all burst into fulsome hysteria, as though it were the greatest joke ever told. Even Becky forgot her wounded pride enough to be able to grin at it.

Dolores Magellan regarded her laughing dinner companions for a few moments, then leaned over to her husband and said, without even lowering her voice, "Just because they're kishing your ash doesn't mean you have to *like* it sho much." Magellan's face darkened and Lionel thought, *In vino veritas.*

Peg Deming came back with ashtrays so clean they looked newly minted. She put them on the table, resumed her seat, and said, "Are we on to pleasanter topics now?" When no one answered her, she inferred that the tension had only worsened since she'd left, and quietly pretended to be busy with her carrot sticks.

Lionel saw a chance to cut the tension when a familiar figure passed the table. "Look," he said in a low voice, "there goes Franklin Potter. The ceremony must be about to begin."

"Speaking of fags," said Perlman, craning his neck to see the actor make his way across the ballroom.

Lionel snapped his head toward him in alarm. "No!" he exclaimed. "Not Franklin *Potter!*"

Perlman lowered his head at him, as if to say, Come *on,* Lionel.

"But my Aunt Lola says he's dating Helena Clement," he protested.

Perlman said, "Your Aunt Lola hears what his P.R. guy *wants* everyone to hear. Truth is, the guy flames more than a Burger King char-broiler."

Lionel sat back in his chair, genuinely surprised—and more than a little titillated. "No *shit.*"

"No shit," Perlman said, turning back to the table. Franklin Potter had disappeared into the men's room. "Got this straight from my director friend Gary in L.A. He directed an episode of *Breadside Manor* two years ago, and said that during a five-day shoot Potter showed up with *three* different guys, one of whom Gary is pretty sure he *paid* for."

This started Becky off on a blistering tirade against voracious male homosexuals, which in turn led to a blistering tirade against AIDS activists, which in turn led to a blistering tirade against Jesse Jackson (Lionel wasn't sure how she'd made the connection, but knew that *most* of Becky's blistering tirades ended up being about Jesse Jackson). When she finally ran out of breath and out of vitriol, her spirits had been so restored that she was actually able to cheerfully get up and go back for a second helping of cheese, which inspired Magellan and the Demings to go with her. The tension had been broken.

Lionel had listened to her with only half an ear, because most of his concentration was fixed on the men's room. He had not yet seen Franklin Potter come out. Now it was five minutes to eight; the actual Trippy Award ceremony, which Franklin Potter would be hosting, was set to begin at eight.

If he was ever going to get a good, up-close look at Franklin Potter, now was the time. And he definitely wanted an up-close look at Franklin Potter. It was something in his nature: any celebrity whom he discovered to be gay immediately became much, much more alluring to him, and Franklin Potter, with his quirky grin and bright-blue eyes, was heart-throb enough to make even Lionel forget his heterosexual fantasies of only ten minutes before—although he told himself that he *wasn't* forgetting them, he was just pushing them aside for a moment. He was perfectly confident that he could give in to this compulsion to see Franklin Potter in the men's room, then come back and continue his hetero-sexual romance with Tracy.

It was then that he realized that Tracy had been gone for even longer than Franklin Potter, and that gave him the excuse he needed. He put his napkin on the table, slid his chair back, and said to Perlman and Dolores Magellan (who gave a very good imitation of listening), "I'd better go see what's keeping Tracy."

Perlman nodded. "She's probably waiting for you to find her and apologize. Take my advice—do it."

Lionel nodded and left the table, and as he made his way across the ballroom he felt his heart pound and his knees weaken. He wasn't starstruck, but a gay star—a *cute* gay star—was something entirely different. He felt a little metal-lic taste in his mouth, as if he might vomit. It was really ridiculous, getting this excited over the prospect of being a celebrity voyeur. He probably wouldn't even *see* anything. Potter was probably holed up in a stall with the door closed. If he were lucky, he'd get a good glimpse of his shoes. But this was a compulsion, not a rational desire; he had to follow it through to the finish.

He swung open the men's room door and looked around the tiled interior. There were two men present, both for-mally dressed, one at the sink, washing his face, the other at a urinal, leaning into it with one arm against the wall.

The man at the sink suddenly lifted his head and his eyes met Lionel's in the mirror. It was a middle-aged pink-faced bozo—definitely *not* Franklin Potter. Lionel looked at the man at the urinal, and suddenly recognized the billowing brown hair. *Definitely* Franklin Potter.

He casually walked over to the urinal directly to the left of Potter's, the first in the row, right next to the toilet stalls. He unzipped himself and pulled his penis through the fly, and managed to urinate loudly enough to allay any suspicions the man at the sink might have about his motive.

And then he waited for that unwanted third party to leave. After an eternity of primping and preening in the mirror, he eventually did so, leaving Lionel and Franklin Potter alone together in the men's room, at exactly adjacent urinals. It was too exciting to be believed.

Lionel took a deep breath and then slowly turned his head. And before he could see Franklin Potter's face, he smelled Franklin Potter's breath, which was like a distillery. A very *busy* distillery. And when his eyes finally settled on Franklin Potter's face, he was amazed to find that the actor was asleep; his eyes were shut, his cheek puffing out with each breath. Franklin Potter was so smashed that he had fallen asleep while standing at a urinal!

Lionel looked at his watch. It was two minutes to eight. At any moment, someone would come in here looking for Franklin Potter. This was a once-in-a-lifetime opportunity and he only had seconds to grab it. He had been given, by a benevolent God, the perfect opportunity to stare with impunity at the unveiled splendor of Franklin Potter's cock.

He leaned a little to the right; he could see the actor's arm reaching into the interior space of the urinal, but he couldn't see the hand, nor could he see what that hand was presumably still holding. So he leaned a little further—he could make out the golden tones of Franklin Potter's wrist; a little further—and he could just make out that telling pinkness—that glorious expanse of skin—if only he could lean just a *little* further—

And that's when Franklin Potter began to topple. Lionel had pressed himself into the actor's shoulder, upsetting his balance. His arm slid down the wall and back to his side, and the weight of that arm started to pull him away from the urinal and toward the floor. Lionel yelled and grabbed him, and pulled him up again and toward him.

Which was a big mistake. Because now, instead of slumping to the floor, all one-hundred-and-seventy pounds of Franklin Potter's dead weight was falling on Lionel. Lionel tried to push him up again, but the tiled floor was slippery, and he lost his footing. Trying to regain it, he stumbled back and into the stall, where he finally fell and hit his head against the base of the toilet. He barked in pain, then shook the stars from his eyes, caught his breath, and sat up to find Franklin Potter lying on top of him, with his face right next to Lionel's exposed penis.

Lionel panicked; Lionel yelled.

The yelling had two effects: the first was to partially revive Franklin Potter, who began to stir; the second was to summon into the men's room four or five men who had overheard him and come to help. Among these, as fate would have it, was Hackett Perlman, who was carrying a plate of Vienna sausages rolled in pastry shells, which, at the sight of Lionel and Franklin Potter lying together in a toilet stall with both of their penises hanging out, appeared to become less appetizing to him. He put the plate on the sink and forgot it.

"Lionel," he said—and he was the only one of the five men gathered who was able to find his voice—"what the *hell* is going on here? I thought you went to look for Tracy!"

And Lionel opened his mouth to explain, but no sound emerged. He was facing a final and bitter defeat. And even worse, he had brought this exposure on himself, all for the sake of a petty voyeuristic act that wasn't even a *real* sexual experience. The autumn leaves with Tracy began to go up in smoke.

chapter

■■■■■■■■■■■■■■■■■■■

seventeen

Lionel found Tracy sulking in the hotel lobby. She was sitting with her arms folded and her lips pursed, the delicate webbing of her dress pressed beneath her carelessly, as if she'd thrown herself into the chair; that dress would certainly not look right again the rest of the evening. She had her right knee crossed over her left, and her right foot was bouncing in the air, as if waiting to kick anyone who passed too hear.

He sat opposite her. She couldn't help but know he was there, but she refused to look at him.

"You're not going to believe what just happened to me," he said.

She arched an eyebrow; she hadn't anticipated *this* as an opening gambit. But still she said nothing.

"I went to the men's room to take a leak, and ended up standing at the urinal right next to the one *Franklin Potter* was using."

A hint of interest; the foot stopped bouncing momentarily.

He rubbed the back of his neck. "And, get this, the guy is so blotto, so smashed, that he's standing there *asleep.*"

She finally looked at him, but it was a do-you-take-me-for-a-moron look.

"I'm not kidding! He had one arm against the wall like this," and here he demonstrated, bringing on a fresh squall of pain in his armpit, "so he had himself propped up. Anyway, it was, like, two minutes to eight, and I knew he was supposed to emcee the awards banquet at eight, so, right in the middle of my wizz, I kind of, well, tapped him on the shoulder, and said, 'Hey. Hey, *Potter.*' "

Tracy's foot stopped bouncing entirely. She couldn't resist him any longer. "And?" she asked.

"You'll never guess."

"I'm not going to try. What'd he do?"

"He *fell* on me."

Her hands leapt to her mouth. *"What?"*

"He tipped over, right on *top* of me. Knocks me right into a stall, and I hit my head on a toilet and almost pass out. So I yell, right? And then who should come in to see what's wrong but *Perlman.*" He could see her eyes widen with alarm and delight; he warmed to his story. "And there I am, lying on the floor with Franklin Potter, our schlongs hanging out of our zippers."

"Oh—my—God," she said, putting her hand on her heart. "You must've *died.*"

"Well, Perlman was looking at me like—like I don't even *know* what—and when I tried to explain he looked at me even *weirder.* But fortunately, right then Potter's manager comes in and gets all upset and apologizes, and he tells us that this is something the guy does all the time—gets smashed at parties and goes to sleep it off at the urinals. Because apparently the only time people leave him alone is when he's taking a piss, so he's learned how to crash that way." He shrugged. "So I'm vindicated. Although I don't think Perlman's *ever* going to stop ribbing me about this."

The clouds disappeared from her face and she laughed sunnily. "Serves you right for being such a homophobe," she said, picking up her purse and starting back into the ballroom. *"God* was punishing you for what you said."

Maybe not for what I said, Lionel thought with a sudden and alarming realization; maybe God was punishing me for what I *thought.*

More determined than ever to become a heterosexual, Lionel took the Almighty's warning to heart, and for the rest of the evening was as attentive and charming to Tracy as he knew how to be.

For his part, Franklin Potter demonstrated that amazing ability many celebrities possess of being able to perform exceedingly well while exceedingly wasted. During the entire awards ceremony he was witty, polished, and well-paced, and no one in the ballroom who hadn't seen him lying on the floor of the men's room immediately beforehand, with both tongue and phallus hanging limp, would've guessed that he was anything but stone-cold sober.

A Gold Trippy was in due course awarded to Deming, Stark & Williams, and Hackett Perlman went up to claim it. Becky applauded energetically, deliriously happy for her husband. That happiness was doubled by the way the Leo Burnett table kept committing what she considered blunders of etiquette serious enough to warrant her running condemnation. ("Look at them *now*," she kept sneering to Tracy, whom, in the face of a greater evil, she had quite forgiven for her earlier outburst.)

While Perlman was at the dais, shaking the presenter's hand and (as was customary at these local events) wordlessly accepting the agency's award, Babcock Magellan got to his feet and gave him a standing ovation. Lionel, in spite of himself, got a little lump in his throat; didn't they all work hard, and wasn't it somehow moving to have their work lauded not only by their peers, but at the same time by their client, in whose cause they toiled? Following Magellan's lead, everyone at the table got to his or her feet as well, and continued applauding, applauding, until Perlman came back to the table flushed with success, his suntanned forehead slick with sweat. He shook Magellan's hand and, grinning like cats, they all sat again (except for Dolores Magellan, who happily stayed on her feet applauding until her husband rather brusquely pulled her down again—which brusqueness was, oddly enough, sufficient to shift her wig into its correct position, so that she found herself suddenly comfortable and accordingly raised no objection).

Lionel, who perhaps with justification regarded the award with no small measure of propriety, looked at Tracy, who in turn looked at him, and when their eyes met they couldn't help but giggle a little. Ridiculous their bosses might be, but it was a grand night, and he was proud of them—they were proud of each other. He reached under the table and took Tracy's hand, squeezed it. She squeezed back, and they held each other that way for several longish moments until Lionel got embarrassed and took his hand back, pretending to have to adjust his cummerbund.

Several other awards were presented after that, but for the Deming, Stark & Williams table the evening was essentially over. After another round of drinks, during which client and agency toasted each other with palpable cheer, the conversation broke up like clay and each couple at the table found itself making eye signals at each other, which at any social event portends their imminent departure.

Had the Magellans been the first to go, the agency people might have taken the opportunity to linger and discuss the evening's triumph more freely than they'd been able to in his presence. But after waiting what they all considered sufficient time for him to take his leave, he remained in place, ordering black coffee after black coffee for his wife, on whom the megadoses of caffeine were having no discernible effect. (Lionel knew it was hopeless when a waiter two tables away let a few dishes drop and shatter, causing Dolores to burst into sobs because it was "all such a waste, such a *waste.*") Finally, the Demings got up, showered their tablemates with extravagant good-byes, and departed. Then, once Becky had had a final opportunity to cast aspersions on the parentage of the waitstaff, the Perlmans got up and followed them. That left Lionel and Tracy alone with the Magellans, which was clearly a danger—Dolores's tongue may have been swollen, but it might still prove too sharp for polite company, and Tracy's love of mischief might inspire her to make things worse.

But now, when push had come to shove—or would, shortly, if they followed tonight's romantic agenda—Lionel felt himself completely disinclined to leave the table, no matter what Dolores might say or Tracy do. The very idea of leaving this hotel and taking Tracy home—and of confronting what came after that—made Lionel go as flaccid as a deflated balloon. Fear and inertia kept him in his seat, and he could feel Tracy's eyes on him, could almost see her quizzical expression as he and Babcock Magellan exchanged an occasional word about some triviality that could easily be discussed during the week. Eventually it became apparent that even Magellan wanted them to go, so that he could stay and deal with his sodden wife without risk of further embarrassment.

Lionel got up and stood behind Tracy's chair (he resisted the urge to say "We who are about to die salute you"), and went through the motions of helping her with it. Then he and Tracy said goodbye to Magellan, who again thanked Lionel for all the good work, and as they exited the ballroom they could hear Dolores behind them muttering "Son of a bitch" to something her husband had said to her.

Exhausted of conversation and sated by their meals, Lionel and Tracy were silent on the elevator to the parking garage, and exchanged only a few words in the car, largely to do with the best route to take home at this late hour. But there was a tension between them—the tension of not being sure of What Happens Next. Lionel drove up Lake Shore Drive and tried to resist the urge to swing into the path of oncoming headlights, because however much doubt there might be about What Happens Next, he was growing increasingly certain of What Wouldn't Happen Ever. Tracy was enchanting, she was a soulmate, and he was fairly certain that she regarded him as nothing less than Mr. Right. But Lionel's shrunken loins assured him that, whatever fleeting waves of desire he might have felt tonight, he was definitely the wrong Mr. Right. He recalled the incident with Franklin Potter and thought, maybe it *wasn't* God's punishment—maybe it was God's *warning*. Accept yourself, He might have been telling Lionel; take this as proof that you cannot change.

I *can't* change, he admitted to himself as he glided onto the Belmont Avenue exit ramp. Tracy rolled down her window and looked at the sailboats napping in drydock. She rested her arms on the window ledge and sighed. Contented creature, natural creature; woman, through and through. What had she hooked up with? *Accept* himself? Could the Almighty really ask him to do anything so loathsome? To accept that he preferred a hairy Romanian anarchist who scratched himself in public to an ethereal blonde *gamine* in a strapless cocktail dress?

His head was spinning, and, becoming a fatalist, he actually ran a yellow light to get Tracy home all the sooner. He no longer cared to delay the inevitable. He wanted to get it over, as quickly as possible, over and done with, and then he would do whatever he could to repair the damage.

He pulled up in front of Tracy's building, shifted into park, but pointedly did not turn off the engine. He turned to her—his seatbelt still tight around his waist—and said, "What a wonderful evening. Thanks for coming with me."

She giggled, as though he were putting on an act for her, suddenly becoming coy to amuse her. Although she was seemingly calm, he noticed that she'd used the thumbnail of her left hand to scrape all the nail polish off the thumbnail of the right. She must be as nervous as he was, and that didn't help at all. Better that she didn't care, better that her ego weren't so vulnerable to his every move. Because his every move was now dedicated to escaping her.

A little chasm of silence opened up between them, and a moment later she shrugged her shoulders, gave her thumbnail another scratch, and said, "Would you like to come up for a drink?"

"Oh, I don't drink," he said at once. "Liquor is poison. It kills millions every year."

She rolled her eyes and laughed a little. She couldn't help but be amused, but she was fighting it. His wit was the last thing she wanted from him now.

"Then come up and have an *Ovaltine,*" she said. "I'll even nuke it for you."

"Oh, I *couldn't,*" he said with faux earnestness. "Microwaves release radiation that can kill you. Millions die from it every year."

She put her hand to her forehead and shook her head.

"It's a *fact,*" he said insistently. "I read it in the *Enquirer.* Right next to that story about the colony they found on the dark side of the moon that's inhabited entirely by clones of Princess Grace."

She scrunched up her face and turned away from him. She didn't want him to see that she was laughing, but her shoulders shook, giving her away. Then, when she regained control of her voice, she said, "Get out of the car and come upstairs."

It was as close to a command as she could make it. Lionel's heart gallumphed. "I *couldn't,*" he said in desperation. "I might accidentally trip over the curb and smash my face on the cement! Millions die from it every—" She whirled and looked at him with an expression of almost maniacal frustration. He paused, swallowed, and said "I couldn't and remain a gentleman."

The engine was idling high, causing the car to vibrate a little. "For God's sake, Lionel, no one's *asking* you to be a gentleman," she said, a little edge of exasperation in her voice. "Come on up for a drink. For God's *sake.*" She reached over and unlatched the passenger door, which fell open a few inches. Exhaust fumes started seeping into the car.

She turned and looked at him, and saw that he wasn't following. "*Li*onel," she said, now fully irritated. "This isn't *funny.* What's wrong?"

He gulped, and felt like a boa constrictor swallowing an ostrich egg. "*I'm* wrong," he said. "Don't ask why."

"Why?"

He rolled his eyes and sat back. "I told you not to ask."

"I don't take orders very well." She shut the door again. "Lionel. *Look* at me." He obeyed. "What's the matter?"

"*I'm* the matter."

"Oh, for—" She reached over and put her hand behind his head, pulled him close to her, and kissed him on the mouth.

He let himself be kissed, but didn't reciprocate. She let him go with a gasp of anger, then looked at him with a look of naked hurt on her face. It broke his heart to see her this way.

"You're not going to come up, are you?" she asked, her voice cracking.

He shook his head, mortified, ashamed, hurting. "No."

"Just come upstairs," she said, almost pleading. "It'll be all right." She put her hand back on the door handle, and Lionel noticed the thumbnail again, bare of polish except for a few remnant flecks. The sight of it caused him so much pain. That must be what he was doing to her heart, just scraping away at it.

"I can't come upstairs, Tracy. I mean, I *can,* but it

wouldn't do any good. I'm—I'm—" He ran his finger along the cool vinyl of the steering wheel, staring at it as he felt its contours and textures. "I'm actually from the planet Krypton, you see—"

The passenger door opened with a *ca-thunk*, and Lionel, still staring at the steering wheel, heard the rustle of fabric as she slipped out of his car. He ran his finger up the opposite side of the steering wheel, and when it had reached the twelve o'clock position the passenger door slammed shut with such force that it knocked his finger off the wheel and onto the steering column. His heart did a quick game of hopscotch and then settled into a steady Gatling gun rhythm.

He dared a look. Tracy was walking up the sidewalk to her building. Her heels were making sounds like gunshots. Her fists were balled. He realized that as much as he dreaded her crying, he would have dreaded this anger more, had he ever been able to anticipate it.

And then she turned for one last inquiring, murderous look. Their eyes met, and Tracy's were black like a raccoon's, streaming with squid-ink tears. But her jaw was set; she wasn't about to spare him any more tears. He realized that she'd already accepted his rejection of her, and had begun to convince herself that it was his fault, not hers. She was well on her way to sacrificing their friendship to rescue her self-esteem. And there was nothing he could do about it—nothing except follow her upstairs, which was impossible, impossible.

She whirled, flung open the door to her building, and stormed inside. The door threw itself back a moment later.
Gone.

He realized that he was trembling, and that it wasn't the motor idling that was causing him to shake so—or at least not that alone. He lifted his hand and looked at it, and it quivered and twitched, like a just-caught fish lying dying on a rock.

chapter

■■■■■■■■■■■■■■■■■■■

eighteen

L ionel remembered nothing of the drive home. His mind was so fogged by his mortification that nothing could stick to it. Sights, sounds, smells, all dissipated as soon as he had experienced them. He likewise remembered nothing of parking the car, or of getting out of it and locking it, or of letting himself into his building and climbing the stairs. And then Emil's face appeared before him, and it took a solid eight seconds for him to realize that this really was Emil in the flesh and not some manifestation of his shame.

"Emil," he said, the mists parting. *"Hi."*

Emil had his hand on the rail and each of his feet was on a different step. Apparently he had been coming down the stairs while Lionel had been coming up. Now they stood, facing each other, having taken each other by surprise.

"Home at last," Emil said. "I've been waiting for you for hours; I only just now gave up. What a coincidence!" He laughed nervously.

Lionel's head had cleared enough for him to begin speculating why Emil was here. A change of heart? An attack of romantic love? A homosexual epiphany? His heart began beating; and all he could think was, Not tonight, for God's sake. Tracy's scorn was still ringing in his ears.

He shrugged and said, "Here I am."

Emil nodded at his tuxedo and said, with endearing obviousness, "You've been out."

Lionel shifted his weight to his other foot. "Yeah. An awards ceremony. For advertising work." He paused. "I forgot to tell you about it."

An uncomfortable pause settled over them. Emil grinned, and Lionel attempted a smile. The only sounds were the creaks and moans of the building settling.

Emil finally broke down and said, "I came to apologize, Lionel. I'm afraid I upset you yesterday."

"No, no," Lionel insisted, shifting his weight again.

Emil took a step closer. "I did," he said. "You mustn't deny it, Lionel. But you mustn't think that I meant to hurt you, either. I wasn't angry, although I must have seemed so. It was just that you made me recall Mircea, and—those memories—they're very painful to me."

Lionel backed away. "I understand," he said. "I never thought you w—"

"You've been such a good and true friend," Emil interrupted. "I am not well-liked among my fellow Transylvanians here, first because I'm an anarchist and not afraid to say so, but also, even more damningly, because I'm studying to be a doctor, and most of them are laborers of some sort. They don't trust that I am one of them. I find myself always having to prove myself to them. I must always weigh my words, take care not to say anything that will provoke their jealousy. Aside from my uncle and aunt, you are the only friend I have in America to whom I can speak freely and without fear."

Lionel shook his head. "I'm flattered, Emil. You don't have to worry, though. I know you weren't angry, or—well, there's just no need to explain, that's all."

Emil reached forward and grabbed Lionel, then quickly drew him toward him in a smothering, musk-smelling embrace. Lionel felt his penis come to life. *Where were you earlier?* he felt like screaming at it.

He'd lost his footing on the stairs, so when Emil released him he stumbled a little and had to grab the railing. He made a little noise on the staircase as he did so—a grunt of effort.

The door just off the landing above them opened and someone peeked out. Lionel recognized the eyes—it was Yolanda. Until now, he hadn't even realized how far up the stairs he'd come.

"Sorry," she said, and she closed the door again.

"No," Lionel called out. "Yolanda! Wait. Come back."

She opened the door again, wider this time, to reveal her entire visage. At the sight of her, Emil smiled broadly.

"I thought I heard your voice," she said, looking at Lionel but taking an occasional sidelong glance at Emil. "It sounded like there might be a fight."

"No fight," Emil said jovially, "just my insistent pleading that my friend forgive me."

"Come and meet Emil," Lionel said, eager for a third party to join them and dispel the upsetting intensity of their encounter.

Yolanda opened the door a bit wider and stepped out. She was wearing hound's-tooth flannel pajamas, about three sizes too big for her. They could only be Bob's. She was carrying her copy of *Feudalia* with her index finger inserted in it to mark her page. Her feet were bare and her toenails were painted lavender.

"Yolanda, Emil," Lionel said. "Emil, Yolanda." And as the two shook hands he breathed easier. They were concentrating on each other now, and wouldn't expect too much from him. Mortification was, he found, a draining exercise. He had nothing left to offer them.

"I'm glad to meet you," said Emil, releasing Yolanda's hand a second later than he should have. Lionel detected her giving it a little tug just before he gave way.

"Thank you, I feel the same," she replied, and she backed away a little. She turned to Lionel and said, "Did you have a good time? Is Tracy with you?"

"No, and no again," he said. He wondered if Emil would find it strange that Yolanda had asked him if he had brought a woman home, but Emil was busy staring at Yolanda's paperback.

"That's a St. Onge novel, isn't it?" he asked.

She looked a little surprised at this. "Yes. Have you read him?"

"A little. My uncle sent me some copies of his books when I was a teenager. Miraculously, they made it through customs."

"Emil grew up in Romania," Lionel stage-whispered.

"Transylvania," he clarified. "I didn't like St. Onge at all. Too much of a primitivist. All his stories were about the benefits of feudalism."

"This one is the same," Yolanda said, displaying the cover to him, careful not to let her finger slip and lose her place. "It is about a planet where three monarchs must battle an invasion of a vastly superior socialist invasion force."

"Feudalism and socialism," sneered Emil. "As if those were the only choices. A science-fiction writer has a duty, I think, to be *progressive.* He should be seeking to invent *new* systems, not glorifying old ones that have become archaic."

Yolanda shrugged and looked at her feet. "I would have said that his only obligation is to stimulate thought," she said. "To inspire the reader to consider existing realities in new ways."

Lionel took two steps up the staircase. "Well, I'm glad you two could finally meet," he said drearily. "But I think it's time we called it a night." He was dying to be in his apartment, alone.

"I don't know how you can say that," Emil said, rather more forcefully than the situation warranted. "That's such a subjectivist, *modernist* view of science fiction. That definition extends the boundaries of the genre so far that they serve no *purpose.* It allows works of no moral weight to be called science fiction simply because they're *clever.* Because they set a pretty *stage.*"

"I mean, it's practically midnight," Lionel said, displaying his watch to them. Neither one looked at it.

Yolanda straightened her back, but inched closer to her door. "I hear talk of this kind more often than I can say," she said heatedly. "It makes me so tired—all this expert advice on science fiction from those who have no stake in its future. You, for example, would keep it in a ghetto. *Other* forms of fiction are free to experiment—why must *science* fiction hold back?"

"Because fiction should *not* experiment," Emil said. "It should be *didactic.* It's the autobiography of our culture, and if it's rootless, if our fiction meanders and wanders and fixes on nothing but itself, if it loses its moral point of reference—if it loses sight of *us*—then it predetermines our cultural decline. Our fiction—our science fiction especially—is a self-fulfilling prophecy! We must be vigilant as to the state of that art."

"Tomorrow's a workday, remember," Lionel said, more loudly.

"What would you do?" asked Yolanda, coloring, shaking *Feudalia* at him. "Burn books like this one?"

He grimaced. "I wouldn't burn books, not ever. I think you mean to insult me. I *would,* however, encourage more open debate about the purposes and obligations of fiction such as this."

"I have to put my bird to bed," Lionel said, breaking past them at last and starting up the stairs. "G'night."

Yolanda ignored him and said to Emil, "This does not feel like a debate to me. It feels like a brow-beating."

Emil folded his arms. "That is a personal attack and is outside the acceptable limits of debate, as well as being, if I may say so, predictably womanish."

Yolanda narrowed her eyes. "Good night, Mr. Emil," she said, and she slipped into her apartment and slammed the door.

"MR. APOSTAL," Emil cried, oblivious to Lionel, who was by now almost a full flight above him anyway. "EMIL IS MY CHRISTIAN NAME!" Then he pounded down the stairs. Lionel heard the vestibule door slam.

He locked the door behind him, slipped off his jacket and hung it over a chair, and went into the kitchen, where, at the sight of him, Spencer raised his crest high and emitted a shriek that could've shattered the Crystal Palace.

"I've heard enough of that for one night," Lionel scolded him. He picked up the battered beach towel he used as Spencer's blanket and tossed it over the cage. "I don't know whether it's worse to be screeched *at* or screeched *around,* but you're not going to be the one to help me make up my mind." He walked out of the kitchen, dousing the light behind him as he went. He could hear the parrot rustling around in his cage, grumbling and clucking angrily.

Lionel entered his bedroom, threw himself on the bed,

and buried his head in his pillow, where he allowed himself the luxury of a brief breakdown. He could only cry into a pillow, where even *he* couldn't be a witness to his tears; a likely predicament for someone so accustomed to hiding from himself.

After he'd recovered, he lifted his head and sniffled, then paused for a moment to conduct a small but intense war between his better and baser natures, which the baser nature had more than enough stamina to win.

He reached over, picked up the telephone, and dialed 1-900-HOT-GUYZ. When he'd reached the operator who provided special assistance, he asked, in a voice still quivering with unleashed emotion, "Do you have someone who can do a really *good* imitation of Franklin Potter?"

chapter

■■■■■■■■■■■■■■■■■■■■

nineteen

He awoke late, still in his dinner clothes. He refused to hurry himself, but undressed, showered, put on clean clothes, ate breakfast, and drove to work with steady deliberation. When he got to the office, at a quarter to ten, Alice didn't return his greeting, nor did any of the other secretaries in the office as much as make eye contact with him. His bosses were jubilant at having so successfully schmoozed Magellan the night before, and congratulated him many times on his part in it. But for the clerical staff it was as if he had ceased to exist. There were at least two moments when he rounded a corner only to have his sudden appearance instantly kill a hushed conversation.

Tracy, he learned, had called in sick. He couldn't help wondering what else she had called in.

His curiosity was satisfied a little while later when Donna stuck her head into his office, interrupting him in the middle of putting together a budget. She grinned wickedly and said, "Heard you chickened out last night. What a surprise." Then she winked and disappeared.

If the office's only deaf employee had managed to hear the news, then it must have reached everyone.

Even worse was Carlton Wenck's reaction. Lionel spent most of the morning dreading the moment when Carlton would stick his head into his office, chirp "Knock, knock," and then slip in and ask for every steamy detail about the night before. What could Lionel possibly say? He fretted about it for hours until, heading down the hall to make a photocopy, he ran into Carlton coming from the other direction. This is it, thought Lionel. But Carlton merely nodded at him and kept going.

Lionel felt a bad, cold kind of fear. Had Carlton heard that there were no details to inquire after? Did the entire office know the score, or what?

There was nothing left to do but harden his heart and go back to his fall budget.

And so he spent the rest of the day hunched over his calculator, pencil between his teeth, crunching numbers like an automaton. And before he knew it, Chelsea Motormouth was sticking her head in the door to say goodnight—Chelsea being, of course, the only secretary on staff incapable of adhering to a conversational boycott of *anyone.*

"I suppose you know it's late," she said accusingly, as though her inability to resist speaking to Lionel might be absolved if what she said were only nasty enough. "I suppose you know I have to lock up since we just changed the security code and only *I* know it because only *I* had the brains to write it down the day Leona gave it to us before she had to go into the hospital to have her ovaries removed. I suppose you *know* that."

He looked up and discovered that the sky had darkened. It was almost eight o'clock.

He dragged himself home and up the stairs, and when he shoved open the door to his apartment the draft from the hallway sent a sheet of paper flying down the corridor. He trotted over to it and caught it, and, ignoring Spencer's unwelcoming screams, read it. It said, *See me when you get home, please,* and it was signed by Yolanda.

He let his jacket slip off his shoulders and fall onto his briefcase, then left the apartment and descended the flight of stairs to Yolanda's door. He was about to knock when he heard a voice from within—a male voice. He halted and listened to it, but by its speed and confidence (there were no pauses for responses from another party) he determined that it must be coming from the television. He knocked.

The voice ceased instantly. It was followed by sounds of stirring in the apartment, and then by the door opening wide. Yolanda stood there, barefoot, her hair in her face, wearing only a Doctor Who T-shirt (extra-large, it hung to just below her kneecaps). "Madonna, you are home late, Lionel," she said, opening the door to admit him. "I almost forgot I left that note for you."

"I don't have to come in if you're getting ready for bed."

"No, no, come in, I have something I want to show you."

"Must be pretty good to get you to leave a note," he said, stepping into her apartment, which looked, if possible, even more strewn with books than he remembered from his last visit.

She affectionately grabbed one of his love handles as she scooted past him, causing him to double over and yelp. "I left the note for another reason," she said, motioning him to follow her to the TV room just off the corridor. "Your friend Emil Apostal stopped by earlier to see you. I told him you were at work and he said, 'Of course, how stupid of me not to remember,' and I said 'Yes, that was stupid.' " She sat cross-legged in a large Naugahyde chair and picked up the remote control device for the VCR. "He asked me if I would leave a message for you and then he followed me around the house until I found a pen and paper. And then when I was ready, he grinned like a fool and said, 'Just have him call me.' And I said, 'I would not have had to write that down.' And he said he was sorry and just *stood* there. I had to ask him to leave." She fondled the buttons of the remote and stared at the TV screen, which was blank. "He is a strange man, Lionel," she continued. "You are not still in love with him?"

"Only a little," he said. He sat back on the corduroy sofa on the far left wall and started to kick off his shoes, then changed his mind and kept them on. "Turns out he's not gay."

Yolanda lowered her head and her hair fell into her face, obscuring it. "Oh, he's not?" she said in a strange tone of voice.

"No," he said, cocking an eyebrow at her. "Are you surprised?"

She tossed her head up, sending her hair tumbling behind her shoulders. "No, just sad for you," she said. "But as long as you are here, I want to show you something." She pressed the REWIND key of the remote and her VCR spun into life, its LCD readout spiraling numerically backward. "It is a tape of Nathan Beatty lecturing." She pressed STOP when the digital display had reached 4478.

"Nathan Beatty? The men's movement guru?"

She nodded, tossing him a videocassette box emblazoned with the title *The Sacred Lyre.* Then she pressed PLAY. "Listen to this."

Beatty—a robust, rather overweight man—appeared on the screen, standing in a forest glen. He had slicked-back, dark auburn hair, but his long, thick beard was almost rust red. He had one long eyebrow that bridged the gap between both eyes. He wore an Edwardian ruffled shirt open at the neck, and a floral-print silk vest.

"Listen to this part," Yolanda said, staring at the screen intently.

"The condition of being a man is the condition of wielding *power,*" Beatty was saying. "But the farther the *source* of the power from the *arm* of the man, the greater the likelihood that his power will degenerate into brute force—hooliganism." Nathan Beatty turned to his left, walking past a softly babbling brook. "The spear was the first weapon of skill that men wielded, and without the *strength* of a man's arm, it was inert—it had no potential. Therefore, the spear was the expression of a man's *moral* worth; how it was used reflected on the spirit of its user. The invention of gunpowder created a weapon that depended only *partly* on the arm of man. Its potential was inherent; it existed before it entered a man's hand. If a gun can go off by accident—achieving a destructive power that has nothing to do with the man who wields it, but has everything to do with chemistry—it degrades man's responsibility for it; it gives him, to whatever small degree, deniability. And where deniability exists, lies will exist. Power becomes a murkier realm, prone to deceit and surreptitiousness."

That makes a rough kind of sense, thought Lionel. He propped himself up on his elbow and thought, Maybe some of this isn't as crazy as I thought.

"In the nineteenth century, the Japanese samurai caste,

recognizing this, gave up the gun and reverted to weapons of skill and strength. They restored themselves to individual sovereignty over their power—restored themselves to *chieftaincy*. Today, men *must* do the same. They must give up not only the modern weapons that define them, but the other implements that have removed true power from their grasp. For power resides not only in weaponry, but in words, in music, and in creative work. Men must, for example, put aside the stereo systems with which they seek to play music to seduce women, and must instead take up the sacred lyre and demonstrate their worth *as* men, as *sources* of music. In the modern world, the only certain chieftains are *musicians. Honor* them." And here he reached off-camera and produced a lyre, which he began playing, producing a good eighteen seconds of the most execrable music Lionel had ever heard before Yolanda pressed the STOP button and banished him from the screen.

"Did you hear the part about the spear?" she asked, reaching over and dropping the remote onto a coffee table littered with copies of *Elle, Vogue,* and *Isaac Asimov's Science Fiction Magazine.*

"Uh-huh," he said, yawning. "Kind of made sense to me."

She grimaced. "Well. Yes. I suppose. But, you know, it can be taken too far."

"What do you mean?"

"The reason I bought this tape was that I got another phone call from Bob two nights ago."

"Snuck into H.Q. again, did he? Downright *ballsy* of him."

"You do not know the *half* of it, Lionel. He told me that the elder chieftains at the camp—he mentioned Chieftains Mongoose and Stork by name—had shown the younger men how to make their own spears so that they could achieve chieftaincy as well."

"Oh, for heaven's sake," Lionel cried, a laugh in his voice. "Can you imagine Bob Smartt *smelting metal?*"

"The spears are made of stone," she said mirthlessly. "Bob sculpted the head from a nugget of flint, affixed it to a handle, and made himself a spear, which he now calls his 'closest companion.'"

"Yolanda, if you're pulling my leg, I'm going to bite you. This whole business about Chieftains Moose and Squirrel—"

"Mongoose and Stork," she corrected him.

"—and making spears, it sounds like a bad TV movie. You're not putting me on?"

She shook her head. "I wish I were. What is more, to demonstrate the moral responsibility each man assumes with his spear, they were made to write a poem about it."

Lionel was dumbstruck for a moment. "A *poem?*" he said.

"Yes. To the Japanese samurai, making poems was as crucial a skill as making war. Bob's new friends are very big on the Japanese samurai." She took an envelope from the coffee table and tossed it at him. The Naugahyde hissed and sighed as she leaned forward and then back again. "Bob sent me his poem. It arrived today."

Lionel took the sheet of paper from the envelope, unfolded it, and read it.

Ode to My Spear
by Gander

Bright as platinum, lightning-bright,
Sharper than a serpent's tooth,
Oh! How you do rend the dawn
When by chance I heft you skyward.
Heart-piercer! Your awesome power
Is to me more terrible than your beauty
Which is finer than silk, richer than port wine,
More distinguished than Queen Elizabeth's tiara.

"Bit of the old Bob showing through here," Lionel paused to comment.

"Keep reading," she commanded him.

With thee I feel such stirrings
Of potency and promise
That were I to lose you, be of you bereft
My sweet maleness would be forfeit,
My honor a passing thing, my glory perished,
My spine not at all straight, my hair limp and flat,
And I would be a miserable thing to behold
Dazzling to the eye, perhaps,
But pitiful in the sight of the soul.

He put down the paper and raised his head; his eyebrow was cocked.

"Do not laugh," she said. "If you laugh, Lionel, I will bite *you*."

"I wasn't going to," he lied.

"He is bringing home a spear. He is under the impression that Nathan Beatty recommends that men from all walks of life carry a spear. That is when I thought I should perhaps get a tape of this Nathan Beatty and see for myself."

"Well, I think he's over-interpreted the spear thing."

"Thank you," she said, and she fell back in the chair, clearly frustrated and exhausted. The Naugahyde cushion sighed as loudly as she did. "This men's group that he has fallen in with, I think they are some kind of zealots. I am sure that he will not be home long before he realizes that he cannot carry a spear with him to visit his clients or to his favorite French café for lunch. And then he will discard it. But what about the things he brings home that are in his head? The things that convenience alone will not make him discard?"

Lionel, having no answer to this, could only shrug. "Wish I could tell you," he said, his voice low. "But I can't predict, I can't speculate. I've given up on the future." He stopped himself from adding, Just like it's given up on me.

part

2

chapter

■■■■■■■■■■■■■■■■■■■■■■

twenty

Summer was on the wane, and
Lionel was on the prowl.
It had taken some time for
him to descend to this. Terrible anxieties had gripped him
for weeks after the Trippy Awards, anxieties that had shut-
tered up his penis like a telescope. After Tracy had spread
what must have been her scorching account of his rejection
of her, he was certain that the secretaries were just a
thought shy of figuring him out, and if they figured him out,
there'd be no keeping it from his bosses. And then Lionel's
days as the All-Pro Power Tools wonder boy would be
numbered.

Fortunately, Donna was the only member of the staff who
could supply the vital information the secretaries needed to
fill out their theories of Lionel's depravity, and as yet there
were no exchanges of confidence between the clerical staff
and the intimidating lesbian art director. (God forbid! Imagine the damage that would result from just a five-minute
chat between Donna and Chelsea Motormouth!) And before
any such exchange could be initiated, two things happened
that rescued Lionel from discovery.

The first was that Guy, devastated by Tracy's abandonment of him, came crawling back to her, begging forgive-

ness and brandishing a diamond engagement ring. Tracy, newly affianced, would certainly be less inclined to waste her time heaping infamy on a bad one-time date. And the secretaries, cooing over her ring like pigeons over their reflections, began to think of Lionel's cruel treatment of her as ancient history, an anomaly in the happy history of her life.

And if, by chance, there existed any lingering curiosity about the motive behind that cruelty, it was drowned forever by the second event: the discovery, two weeks after the Trippy Awards, that Carlton Wenck had been having a torrid office romance with Gloria Gimbek, who also happened to have a husband at home. (As she hadn't yet been married quite a year, it had been the habit of the secretaries to consider her still a newlywed, which made the scandal all the greater.)

This electrifying news came to the office's attention one unforgettable day when Gloria's husband called and asked for Carlton. Alice the receptionist (already suspicious at this) put him through to Carlton's office, but it was Carlton's student intern, Tim, who picked up the phone, Carlton being in a client meeting and not to be interrupted.

Gloria's husband, not knowing that the man on the other end of the line was not the one who was cuckolding him, immediately launched into a series of threats, culminating in the promise to "rearrange your face with a razor if you don't stay away from my wife." Tim, thoroughly confused and even more thoroughly upset, rushed out to the secretarial pool to tell them that a lunatic was after him and to ask their advice. The fragment of time it took Chelsea Motormouth to determine what had really happened cannot be measured by manmade instruments; call it a trillisecond. The time it took her to *relate* her conclusion was something else again; suffice it to say that within an hour (or two), the entire office, from the top of the hierarchy on down, knew all about Carlton and Gloria's affair.

When he heard the news, Lionel had three initial reactions. The first was relief that his bad behavior toward Tracy would now no longer be subject to dangerous speculation. An office scandal of immediate presence and far greater magnitude had cast his peccadillo into deepest shadow. His

second reaction was to realize suddenly why Carlton had
not, as he'd said he would, cornered him for details about
Tracy's sexual habits the day after the Trippys; by the time
the ceremony rolled around, Lionel now understood, Carlton's sex drive had been driven elsewhere. His third reaction was simple joy that Carlton had disgraced himself in
this way. Carrying on in secret with another member of the
staff would carry heavy punishments, he was sure; and in
the glare of Carlton's disgrace, Lionel would look more
golden than ever.

Unfortunately, this proved not to be the case. While officially taking a stern view of the romance and of the wild
disruption it had caused in the daily workings of the office,
Julius Deming was clearly tickled by Carlton's high jinks
and couldn't seem to refer to them without letting a sly
grin tiptoe onto his face. The same was true of the other
male members of the staff, who could be heard whispering
things like "Way to *go*" to Carlton whenever they thought
no women were listening.

Gloria Gimbek was fired.

The scandal was so overwhelming that it drew almost
the entire office into something resembling a feeding frenzy.
Every day, up and down the hallways, co-workers exchanged bits of minutiae about the forbidden romance with
the speed of electrical impulses traveling along brain syn-
apses. Lionel found himself completely forgiven by the secretarial staff, if only because he would agree to stand still
and listen to their passionate recitals of the latest Carlton-
and-Gloria gossip. At the height of the scandal, even Tracy
was so overcome by a piece of news that she stopped by
Lionel's office and delivered it to him with crazed, excited
eyes. But once the scandal was over, she made no further
attempt to renew their friendship.

Feeling utterly safe now—as if the black smudge on his
reputation had been washed away by a tidal wave of
bleach—Lionel began to feel the urge toward sex again. It
was an urge he had successfully quelled during the period
when he feared himself under suspicion, but he had now
reached the point at which sex with men was just about all
he could think about.

Yet for all the time he spent standing against the walls

of ever seedier bars along the Halsted Street strip, working up the courage to make smoldering eye contact with other men along other walls wanting equally strongly from him what he wanted from them, Lionel found himself unable to follow through. In his early twenties, he'd managed this mating ritual without undue anxiety, but that was long ago. In the interim, he'd suffered a failed love affair, flung himself into a career, and virtually sublimated not only his sex drive but his social skills—until they worked about as well for him as a bicycle he'd left to rust in a garage for six years.

And each failure of nerve only made him hornier and crazier, so that each time he went out, much more seemed to depend on each wanton exchange of glances. The enormity of it inevitably scared him into a retreat. And so the cycle continued, until he found himself sexually wound up like a spring, suffering agonies of desire over the most impossible objects.

Even Bob Smartt was starting to look good to him, which was possibly the most alarming symptom of all. But it wasn't just Lionel's long-neglected desires that were to blame. Bob had returned from his "manly man's" seminar looking, well, just a little bit *wild.* The spear that he had insisted on carrying everywhere when he first returned was abandoned after only a few days (after an unfortunate incident in a rather snug taxicab on a particularly bumpy road; Yolanda was still angry about her dress, and the driver needed eleven stitches behind his ear). Without the spear to provide a focus for his ridicule, Lionel had taken his first hard look at the new Bob Smartt over drinks at Yolanda's one night, and thought, Oh my God—*hot.*

Bob was still Bob, of course—on this occasion, reclining on one of Yolanda's beanbag chairs attired in a muslin chemise, Beltrami trousers and a pair of buff-colored Italian shoes that he boasted had cost just a tad less than his rent— but there was something subtly *different* about him. His face, for one thing, didn't look quite so pinched. And his hair had been breezily blown dry and left to fend for itself— no gel, no mousse, no dizzying feats of gymnastic combing. A few strands fell into his face, and he was entirely content to let them stay there, as if he didn't even *care* about them! What's more, he had actually *rolled up the sleeves* of the muslin chemise, revealing an attractive spiral of strawberry blond hair encircling his forearms and collecting at his wrists. It occurred to Lionel that he had never actually seen Bob's naked wrists before.

Bob looked leaner beneath his clothes as well, wirier. His garments had used to drape him like a drop-cloth over a Thanksgiving turkey, but he'd lost his milk-fed, pampered roundness during the seminar and hadn't yet gotten it back. Now his clothes draped him provocatively, like silk over marble.

His attitude, too, was altered, if only barely. He still tended to chirp and bray, but the florid adjectives and adverbs had fallen out of his speech, as completely as if they'd been surgically removed. After a recent restaurant jaunt, he'd finished with a tiramisú that he had not gone on to describe, as the old Bob would have, as "too *strikingly* decadent for words; it gives new meaning to the word *evil.*" Instead, he'd simply rolled his eyes suggestively and in a low, erotic growl said, "The tiramisú was ... *artful.*" Lionel had felt his legs twitch at this.

Faced with the full horror of being attracted to Bob Smartt, Lionel retreated from his friendship with Yolanda and into his fixation on his job. But even there, he found himself beleaguered by his libido. Even Carlton Wenck, for God's sake, was looking good to him these days, and, as if that weren't enough, there was the devastating news Carlton delivered one night in his infuriatingly off-handed manner.

He and Lionel were sharing an elevator at the end of the day, descending to the building's lobby at a rate just a hair short of a plummet, when Carlton, still audaciously unrepentant of his role in Gloria's fate, turned and said, "Guess I'm free now."

Lionel couldn't believe his insensitivity. He straightened his back and, looking straight ahead, icily said, "I guess you are."

"No more eyes watching every move I make," Carlton chuckled.

Lionel felt like puking. "No, I suppose not." He stared at the rows of numbers, following the illumination of each descending button: 21, 20, 19 ...

"Good kid, though," Carlton continued, leaning back against the far wall of the elevator and yawning.

Good *kid*? This was unbelievable! Lionel took a step away

from him. Carlton had ruined poor Gloria's life with his attentions, and now he was dismissing her as a *good kid.*

"Kind of made me a little anxious, though," Carlton said out of the corner of his mouth, as though this were a dirty secret. "Wanted to get in my pants, if you ask me." He snickered.

Lionel turned and looked at him with narrowed eyes. "Are you actually trying to make me believe she *didn't?*"

Carlton knitted his eyebrows. *"She?"* he said. "Whoa. Crossed signals. Who are we talking about?"

"Who are *you* talking about?" Lionel responded, suddenly wary. If Carlton *hadn't* been referring to Gloria, *he* certainly didn't want to bring up her name.

Carlton grimaced. "I'm talking about *Tim,*" he said. "Christ's sake, who *else?*" He bent one knee behind him. "Last day of his internship. Heads back to school tomorrow." He looked at Lionel's flabbergasted face and said, "Well, you *knew* he was a fruit, didn't you?"

"I—I—"

Carlton laughed. "Lionel, you *gotta* get out of your office more often. Whole *agency* knew Tim was a fudge packer. Jesus, gave me the *creeps* when he'd bend over my shoulder to look at one of my budgets." He shuddered. "Anyway, gone now. Nice kid, but—*you* know."

The elevator doors slid open. Carlton winked at Lionel, strode out into the building lobby, and headed for the door.

Lionel somehow found the presence of mind to follow before the doors shut on him again. But he was deeply and profoundly shaken; he felt like a starving man who'd been invited to a twelve-course feast but hadn't read the invitation until it was all over.

On his drive home, he gripped the steering wheel hard, as if trying to strangle it. It would certainly have felt good to strangle *someone.* Intellectually, he knew that even if he'd known Tim was gay, he wouldn't have dared approach him. Having a sexual relationship with someone in the office—well, if it had been a scandal for Carlton with a woman, imagine how much worse it'd be for Lionel with a man! No, no, he'd never have risked it.

But just the *idea* of that gorgeous, blond youth sauntering down the corridors, just the idea of all the eye contact

Lionel had resisted all these weeks, all the *observing* he could've done—it was enough to push him to the brink of madness.

While ascending the stairs to his apartment, he found himself, for some reason, suddenly thinking of Emil, and he wondered what had inspired him to do that. For all Emil's charms, he was older, heavier, and less smolderingly sexual than the lithe young intern who disturbed Lionel's thoughts at present. Before he could wonder at it further, he rounded a landing and heard loud music, an energetic, driving salsa number, and the farther he climbed the more certain he became that it was issuing from the apartment below his— from Yolanda's, where nothing of greater urgency than a Chopin étude ever wafted.

He stopped before her apartment and listened as the thunderous bass of the music shook the door on its hinges. He wondered if he should knock and say hi, see what she was up to on the pretext of a neighborly visit. He hesitated, aware that he'd been neglecting her in his quest to be away from Bob, and aware also that Yolanda must know this. But, hell, she wasn't one to nurse a grudge. He knocked.

No answer. The music must be *really* loud in there.

He knocked again—pounded, really.

Then he heard the familiar tak-tak-tak of Yolanda's heels, and a moment later she flung open the door and stood before him, her hair teased into its tentacled state again, her trim little body wrapped by a cherry cocktail dress so tight he could count her ribs through it.

"LIONEL," she shouted above the music, "WHAT ON *EARTH* IS THE MATTER?"

"NOTHING," he said, his face reddening. "SORRY. JUST HEARD THE MUSIC AND THOUGHT YOU WERE HAVING A PARTY."

She turned and, leaving the door open, tap-tap-tapped over to her stereo, where she gave the volume knob a swift turn. The level of the music dropped like a shoe. "I am sorry," she said, turning back to him. "Was I making too much noise? I did not mean to disturb you."

He slipped through the door and stood in her corridor. "No, no," he said, not putting his briefcase down, aware that there was a stiffness between them that had to be managed carefully. "I just—hadn't seen you in a while, an—"

"Because of Bob," she said instantly, surprising him. "I understand."

"Well, I hate to say it, but yes, because of B—"

"I know this, Lionel," she said, cutting him off. "I am not unaware of your loathing for Bob. But, you know, I am not attached to his hip. You can come and see me on my own, sometime, if you like." She smiled. There wasn't a trace of recrimination in her. He felt a flash of relief—then a feeling of rejection settled in; he'd thought she'd at least be miffed at his neglect of her. This lightness—as if she hadn't cared—hell, hadn't she *missed* him?

"Well," he said, scuffing his right foot back and forth on her floor, "I guess that's what I'm doing now." He peeked up at her. "That okay?"

"Of course it is okay," she said, and she turned the music up a little louder, then gave him a brilliant smile and tak-tak-takked over to him. "In fact," she said, "you are just in time to zip me up."

She turned her back to him and lifted her mane of hair away from her dress. He stooped to put his briefcase on the floor, then, surprising himself by being a little embarrassed at this physical intimacy (she wasn't, as he could plainly see, wearing a bra), he fumbled with her zipper until he got it to her nape. Then he released it and said, "You're set."

She dropped her hair and shook it in his face. Then she turned and said, "Thanks, Lionel. You are a honey."

She started down the corridor toward her bedroom and, unwilling to follow her, he stood rooted to the spot and called out, "YOU GOING OUT TONIGHT?"

A brief pause. "NO, I AM STAYING HOME AND GIVING THE PLACE A GOOD VACUUMING."

Sarcasm? From *Yolanda*? What was going on here?

Then he heard her erupt into gales of silvery laughter. She sounded like a Las Vegas slot machine giving forth a jackpot of nickels. He suddenly became aware of how long it had been since he'd heard her laugh like this.

"OF *COURSE* I AM GOING OUT," she called down the hall. "YOU ARE VERY SILLY TONIGHT, LIONEL." She appeared in the corridor again, fastening a big gold-link belt around her waist. "How does this look?" she said.

"Like *hell,*" he said, shaking his head. "Absolutely *not,* Yolanda."

She grimaced and removed the belt. "Come and help me pick one out, then. I hate having to yell at you out here in the hall." She disappeared into her bedroom again.

He shrugged his shoulders and followed her.

The bedroom looked like it had been hit by a cyclone. There were clothes strewn everywhere, hanging over the radiator and laid out on the bed and draped over the backs of chairs.

"Jesus," he said. "Do you go through this *every* time you go out?"

"Not usually, no," she said, picking up a white vinyl belt and fitting it around her waist. "Bob usually picks out my clothes for me. This one?"

He shook his head and she dropped the belt on the bed again. "So," he asked, "does the New Bob not do that anymore, or what?"

"Oh, he still does," she said, picking a Hermès scarf from the window sill and tying it around her waist. "But I am going out with some girlfriends tonight, not with Bob." She thrust her hip in his direction, showing off the scarf.

He made a grimace of distaste and shook his head. She pouted and removed the scarf.

"Do you always dress to kill when you're meeting girlfriends?" he asked mirthfully.

"What?" She blushed. "Well, *yes,* Lionel, most of *all* for girlfriends." She handed him the scarf, avoiding his eyes. "We are all—I suppose you would say, in *competition* with each other, you see."

He took the scarf from her. "In competition for what? Men?"

"No, no, no," she said, blushing ever more deeply. "Just for status. I suppose it amounts to showing off."

He rolled his eyes and held up the scarf. "What am I supposed to do with this?"

"I do not know. Hang it on the lampshade on the nightstand," she said, still not looking at him.

As he made his way through the sartorial debris to the

side of the bed, he said, "Honestly, Yolanda, you don't *need* a belt or sash with that dress. It's perfect the way it is."

She looked down at it. "But is it not too tight? Does it not need something to break up the lines?"

"Most women would *kill* to have your lines," he said. "If you want to score some points over your friends, show off that *waist,* for God's sake." Then he turned and draped the scarf over the lampshade. As he did so he noticed a book on the nightstand. "Hey," he exclaimed.

"What?" she said, kicking a skirt from out of her way.

He picked up the book and held it out for her. "*Anarchism and Other Essays,* by Emma Goldman," he said. "I didn't know you were reading this."

"I just started it," she said flatly. She turned quickly away and started rummaging through a drawer.

"What a wild coincidence," he said. "Someone else was mentioning this exact book to me not too long ago." He knitted his brow. "Now, who *was* that?"

Yolanda slammed the drawer shut, yanked open the next one and started foraging similarly through its contents.

"Oh, *yeah,*" Lionel said, snapping his fingers. "How could I forget? It was my friend Emil Apostal! You remember Emil, don't you?"

"A little," she said lightly, flinging nylons and panties out of the drawer and onto the floor.

"Funny—it's not the kind of book I'd expect *you* to be reading."

She slammed the second drawer shut and pulled on the knob of a third with such force that the entire drawer flew right out of the dresser and landed on the bed with a muffled *plop.*

Lionel put his hand to his mouth and grunted a laugh, but Yolanda didn't seem as amused by the incident as he was.

"Lionel, I am so sorry, but I am running a little late," she said. "Thank you for your help, but will you leave me now? Come again and visit tomorrow or the next day."

He was somewhat taken aback by this, but was of course obliged to comply. He put the book back on the nightstand, gave her a kiss on the cheek and wished her a good time, then retrieved his briefcase at the door and started up the

stairs toward his own place. The salsa music was still in full
flow, and after unlocking his door, he did a little dance
into his apartment, slid his briefcase down the length of the
corridor's hardwood floor (startling Spencer into a shrieking
fit), then twirled and shut the door with a kick.

As it flew into its frame, the door squeezed a little current
of air from the hallway into the apartment, where it hit
Lionel in the face. And within that little current was a concentrated dose of a scent that had been barely perceptible
in the still air of the hallway.

Lionel couldn't place it at first, so he opened the door
again and flapped it back and forth, sending a few more
bursts of concentrated scent into his nose, until he finally
remembered where he'd smelled it before.

And then he knew why he'd thought of Emil as soon as
he entered the building tonight.

It was the scent of Emil's aftershave.

"Weird," he muttered. Then he shrugged, shut the door,
and trotted off to the bathroom to have a pee.

chapter

■■■■■■■■■■■■■■■■■■

twenty-one

The next day Lionel received two eleventh-hour invitations.

The first came at an inopportune time. He'd been busy all morning trying to pick up on any office gossip about Tim the intern, who was now absent and could be dished freely. Since the Carlton-and-Gloria imbroglio had finally faded into history, he thought Tim was a likely next subject for the secretarial vultures. And sure enough, on his fourth trip to the coffee machine (on an average day he made only two), he caught Chelsea Motormouth and Rosa the bookkeeper loitering in the kitchen, with Chelsea at the very beginning of a typically circuitous dialogue about Tim.

"Well," she was saying, "it's such a waste of a man, if you ask me, and such an *adorable* little hunkoid, too. Because, if you ask me—what could he be, nineteen? Twenty?—twenty is no age to decide whether you like boys or girls. He should give himself at *least* until he's thirty."

"He can't help it," Rosa said, dumping a fifth packet of Equal into her cup and stirring. "It's in his genes. I read an article in a science magazine that said that some men have an extra X chromosome that makes them gay, and some men have an extra Y chromosome that makes them criminals."

"How do you explain gay criminals?" Lionel blurted out, forgetting that he was supposed to be pretending not to eavesdrop.

Rosa and Chelsea glared at him briefly. Chelsea, ignoring him, took a sip of her coffee and continued her previous thought. "It's like when *I* was twenty, I got engaged to this guy, Horace, who lived in Libertyville, and I thought he was the total end of the world because he had a black Trans Am with Bose speakers and every Stones album ever made on eight-track. But I was too young to really know who I wanted to marry, because, you know, I'd never even been to Chicago before, and I'd never got a good look at the guys here, who make Horace look like a career rest-room attendant." She paused and took another sip of coffee. "I mean, to begin with, *no one* in Chicago has eight-track tapes. You can't even *buy* them here, and who would even *want* to? I hate the way they fade out in the middle of a song and then you get this big *ka-chunk* as they change tracks, and then the song fades back up again. What were they thinking of when they did that? Also, after a while, all the tracks sort of blend in together, so no matter what track you're on you hear four songs at the same time. . . ."

She was spiraling farther and farther away from the subject of Tim, but Lionel was determined to wait until she spiraled back. He'd slowly and laboriously changed the coffee machine's filter and refilled it with water, and just as Chelsea had gotten onto the subject of her mother's recent marriage to a truly cretinous bigot, which Lionel thought might conceivably lead back to Tim, he was notified over the office intercom that he had a call.

He returned to his office in a snit at having been interrupted. But his mood changed instantly to one of consternation when he picked up the phone and was greeted by Greta, who hadn't called him since the day Killer died the year before.

"We've got a gig *tonight* in Chicago," she said breathlessly. "You have to come." There was some kind of commotion in the background of the call.

"Congratulations," he said. "What's that noise?"

"Just Pop," she said. "One of the chinchillas got loose." Lionel listened harder and could hear his father bel-

lowing, "GET BACK HERE, SCHWARZKOPF, YOU SUBVER-
SIVE LITTLE RODENT!"

"So, you're coming?" Greta asked.

"Well—uh—I don't know," he said. "When? Where? This
is pretty short notice."

"It just *happened* last night. Wanda—our lead singer—
has this friend Robin who's in this band called Don't Say
Gorgonzola, and they're playing tonight at the Metro on
Clark Street? Well, they had this opening band coming in
from Atlanta, called The House of Boris? And their van like
totally broke down in Louisville and there's like no way
they're gonna make it to the Metro tonight. So Robin says,
I know this other group called Terrible Swift Sword? Which
is, you know, *us.*"

"I know," said Lionel. "I know your band's name, Greta."

"*GOT* YOU!" howled the colonel in the background.
"*GOT* YOU, SCHWARZKOPF! HAHAHAHA!"

"So, anyway, we're like booked *tonight* as the opening
act for Don't Say Gorgonzola. Which is like an incredible
chance to bring Christ's word to a bunch of downtown
headbangers. But you've gotta *come*, Lionel. You've *gotta.*
I'm your *sister.*"

Lionel raised his eyebrows. Who'd have thought that family meant so much to Greta? Her filial appeal rather touched
Lionel. He sighed and said, "Sure, sure. I'll be there. What
time?"

"Eight," she said. "Thanks a lot, Lionel! Jesus loves you!
Jesus and I *both.* See you then!"

Just before she hung up, Lionel heard his father shriek,
"*OW!* GOD *DAMN* YOU, SCHWARZKOPF! YOU'RE DEAD,
YOU LITTLE MONSTER! *DEAD!*"

The second invitation came not half an hour later. Julius
Deming squeezed through the door of Lionel's office, his
face flushed and his expression happy.

"What've you got going on next week?" he asked.

Lionel looked up at him. "Next week? I don't know off-
hand." He flipped open his Filofax and checked his calendar.

"Nothing too urgent?"

"Nnnnno," said Lionel, running his finger down the page.
"Doesn't look like it. Special project you want me to take
on?"

"In a way. Magellan just called. Just seen his latest sales figures."

"Good?" He leaned back in his chair.

"*Sensational.* And he credits us with a large part of the success. So to say thank you, he's invited us up to his cabin in Wisconsin next week. You, me, Perlman. And wives and girlfriends, of course."

Lionel panicked. "An entire *week* in Wisconsin?" He sat bolt upright. "But—but who's going to handle things here if we're all away for an entire *week?*"

"He's got a phone and a fax up there," Deming said, beaming. "And you just said yourself you don't have anything urgent coming up."

"But—what if something urgent *does* come up, and we're all the way up there?"

"Then it's only a four-hour drive back." He winked at Lionel and said, "You gotta learn to relax, Lionel. This is one of the perks of being a big shot in advertising. Hobnobbing with the rich and powerful on their chosen playgrounds. Enjoy it." He started to waddle away. "I've got Tracy making photocopies of the map to the cabin. She'll get it to you later. You're due on Sunday night for dinner." Just before he squeezed back out the door, he turned and said, "Oh, yeah. *Do* bring a date with you. Magellan's girlfriend hates having an odd number at the dinner table."

"His *girlfriend?*"

"Yeah. Don't think he'd bring that drunken *wife* of his, do you?"

And then he was gone, leaving Lionel to sizzle with dread, not only at having to find a woman to spend a week with him at a cabin in the Wisconsin woods, but at having to spend that week with two of his bosses and his client. Was a violent death not preferable to this?

By the time he returned from lunch the entire office was abuzz with the news of the incredible favor Babcock Magellan had conferred on him. Only three of his co-workers didn't congratulate Lionel or express their envy: Carlton Wenck, who was visibly jealous and pretended not to think much of the offer; Donna, who either hadn't heard the news or was too disdainful of Lionel's sexual hypocrisy to congratulate him on anything else; and Tracy, who left the photocopy of the directions on Lionel's desk while he was out at lunch, with no note attached.

"I haven't been to Wisconsin since I was six," said Chelsea Motormouth as she scooted into the elevator with Lionel at the end of the day. (She appeared oblivious to the fact that her smiling friendliness was in direct contrast to the blatant snub she'd handed him in the office kitchen just a few hours earlier.) "But we didn't stay at a cabin, we stayed at a campground. Well, not a campground, really, a parking lot for trailers, but we didn't have a trailer, we had a station wagon and some mosquito netting. It's beautiful country up there, isn't it?" She grinned at him beatifically. "I had to sleep on the back seat next to my older brother George, who had this major acne that kept bursting at night and sliming up the vinyl."

By the time they reached the lobby, Lionel knew more about Chelsea's 1971 Wisconsin trip than any Chelsea biographer would care to. And as he tore himself away from her and fled to his car, it occurred to him what must have been going through her mind: She knew he was a workaholic, she knew he had no social life, and she'd seen that when he was forced to attend a work-related social event, he was willing to ask one of the women from the office.

Chelsea was plainly angling for an invitation to accompany him to Wisconsin as his date.

He clutched his shoulders and took a sharp breath, riding the terror until it had passed. Then he reached his car, slipped inside, and drove home very quickly.

A week in the wilds of Wisconsin with Babcock Magellan and his mistress, and Hackett Perlman and his evil wife, and Julius Deming and his anal-retentive one! It was just too horrible—like a level of hell Dante had forgotten to describe. He decided to put it out of his mind as best he could. After all, it was still four days away. A lot of things could happen in four days. A major earthquake. A civil collapse. Nuclear war. It wasn't worth worrying about Wisconsin just yet.

He met Yolanda on the stairs. She was on her way up to her apartment bearing a basket full of laundry. Her hair was tied behind her head in a careless ponytail and she wore tatty gray sweats, but her glamour survived; she resembled nothing so much as a Hollywood starlet making a bid for serious critical acclaim by appearing in a role without makeup.

"Hello, Lionel," she said dismally. Lionel remembered how deeply she loathed doing laundry. This was due only in part to the drudgery of the task itself; far greater was her distaste for the dank, ill-lit basement laundry room, which resembled a place Torquemada might have designed for torturing heretics.

He fell into step with her. "Yolanda, can you do me a favor?"

"That depends," she said, resting the basket of clean clothes on her thigh as she freed a hand to open her apartment door. "What is it?"

"Can you look after Spencer if I end up going away next week?"

She raised her eyebrows. "Oh, of course, Lionel! I would do *anything* to make it easier for you to get away and have some fun." She kicked the door open and hefted the basket inside. "You have so *little.*"

He stuck his head in after her. "Well, thanks—I appreciate it. I probably won't be having *fun,* exactly, but that's beside the point." His eyes adjusted to the dimness of her hallway, and he could make out two more heaping loads of laundry awaiting their turn in the Kenmore. He whistled in awe and said, "When was the last time you did the wash?"

"I do not recall," she said, dropping the basket outside her bedroom. "It has been a while. I have probably only done it a handful of times since you moved in. I keep thinking, if I just continue to buy more and more clothes, I will never have to do it again *at all.*"

He smiled weakly at her, until she looked at him and crossed her eyes. He realized that she had been kidding him.

She crouched to the floor and started indiscriminately flinging the just-cleaned clothes out of the basket with one hand, while with the other dumping a dirty pile of clothes in to replace them. "What are *you* doing tonight?" she asked. "Would you like to help me iron?"

"Gee, that *would* be a treat," he said impishly. "Unfortunately, I'm sure I've got a prior commitment, to read Wittgenstein, or trim my chest-hair or something." Suddenly he realized that he did, in fact, have an engagement. "Oh, *shit,* Yolanda—I'm glad you reminded me! I *do* have to be somewhere tonight!" He checked his watch. "I'd better go upstairs right now and boil dinner."

"Where are you going?" she asked, looking up at him enviously.

"My sister's rock band is playing at Cabaret Metro," he said, fumbling through his pocket for his keys. "She practically *begged* me to come."

Yolanda put her chin in her hands and looked at him with dreamy eyes. "I have not been to the Metro in five years," she said. "Bob refuses to go because he is afraid the beer on the floor will stain his shoes."

He knew her well enough to know what she was hinting at. "How soon can you be ready?" he asked.

"Just four hours. I swear. Maybe less."

"Can you make it twenty minutes?"

She grimaced. "Well, I suppose, but I do not guarantee the results."

"That's okay. You don't have to try to impress me. I only like guys, remember?"

"I remember," she said, standing up and stripping off her sweatsocks. She shook one at him and said, "You should remind *yourself* every so often."

He bounded upstairs, burst into his apartment, let Spencer out of his cage and actually gave him the Alessi teapot to keep him quiet, then began alternately flinging off his clothes and heating a pot of water in which to cook his Bag O' Ratatouille.

While putting on a clean polo shirt, he extended his arm through a sleeve too quickly, and ended up knocking the kitchen telephone receiver off the wall. As he bent down and picked it up, it occurred to him how much fun it would be to invite Emil along as well. He and Yolanda hadn't gotten along on their first meeting, but now that Lionel knew they had Emma Goldman and anarchism in common, he was sure they'd have a lot to talk about. And Lionel had to admit it—he longed to see Emil's neon blue eyes and hairy knuckles. He dialed the phone.

"Jones residence," he was greeted. "Nancy Jones speaking." There was loud, elevator-disco music playing.

"Hello, Mrs. Jo— I mean, Nancy. It's Lionel."

"Lionel! Excuse me for a moment while I turn off my exercise tape." He was about to protest, but at that same instant he heard Nancy's receiver clunk onto a table, so he waited until the music was stilled. Then he heard her distinctively awkward tip-tap, tip-tap as she returned to the phone. He had to laugh.

"I suppose you'd like to speak to Emil," she said after picking up the phone again.

"Well, yes."

There was a pause. "Excuse me, I was just lighting up," she explained, and then she exhaled in the receiver. Lionel could almost smell the smoke. "I'll get him for you, Lionel, but only if you promise to come see us again soon."

"I promise, I promise."

"We'll have a big Italian dinner next time you're over," she said. "I found a great new place that delivers in just half an hour." Once again, she put down the phone with a clunk, and he heard her call. "*EEEEE*-MIL, IT'S *LIIII*-ONEL." A moment later the music started up again.

Seconds passed before he heard the clump-clump-clump that could only mean Emil was coming down the stairs. He was enjoying this; it was so seldom these days that he called anyone who didn't have a hold button. This eavesdropping-by-permission on the Jones family's private life was kind of a kick.

"Hello," said Emil, slightly winded. "Lionel?"

"Yeah, hi," Lionel said, sitting down at the kitchen table and slipping his legs into a pair of Girbaud jeans. "Listen, before I say anything else, I have to ask you: Is your Aunt Nancy really doing her exercises wearing high heels and smoking a cigarette?"

"Yes," Emil said matter-of-factly. "Why do you ask?"

"That's such a riot," he said, quaking with laughter. He held the phone between his chin and shoulder blade, leaned back, and zipped up the pants.

"I don't see why," Emil said, nonplussed. "Aunt Nancy wears high heels and smokes cigarettes no matter *what* she does."

"ARE YOU BOYS TALKING ABOUT ME?" Lionel heard Nancy yell from somewhere in the thick of the music.

"LIONEL IS WONDERING HOW YOU CAN EXERCISE

WEARING HIGH HEELS AND SMOKING," Emil called to her.

"Emil!" Lionel yelped. "Christ!"

"TELL LIONEL HE CAN COME AND WATCH IF HE'S SO CURIOUS," she shouted back.

Lionel stood up and tucked in the back of his shirt. "*Jesus*, Emil! You didn't have t—"

"She doesn't mind. Listen, Lionel, I really cannot talk, I—"

"Oh, say you're not busy. My sister's rock band is playing at a club near Wrigley Field tonight, and I was hoping you could come see it along with Yolanda and me." He started looping his belt through the jeans.

There was a brief pause. "Did Yolanda ask you to call me?"

"Of *course* not! Yolanda can't stand you, remember? But I thought you might get along better now that I've discovered you have something in common."

"Lionel, thank you, but I'm very busy, not just tonight, but for the next week, at least. I'm studying for my first big chemistry exam and must not be distracted. I miss you, my friend, but Uncle John is paying dearly for my medical schooling, and it would be rude of me to shirk my responsibilities—especially while I'm living under his roof."

"It was just an idea," Lionel said, buckling his belt. "Let's get together after your exam, though. I miss you, too." He'd stumbled over those words; he still felt them a little too keenly for comfort.

"I assure you we will," Emil said. "Good-bye, Lionel."

Lionel hung up, slipped his feet into his Weejuns, and started for the stove. The water hadn't even begun boiling; he hadn't turned the flame high enough. Irritated, he switched it off entirely. He'd just grab a McSomething on the way to the club.

He turned to go and fetch Yolanda, but just as he did so she opened his door and came sailing into the apartment wearing a black miniskirt, black boots, and a black leather jacket over a red silk halter top. A purse hung over her arm and she was busy attaching one last earring.

"I'm glad you're here," he said. "Can you get Spencer back in his cage for me?"

"Of course," she said, heading for the kitchen. "That's why I came up. But if he scratches this leather, you owe me four hundred dollars."

He followed her, smiling. "You look like a slut."

"We are going to the Metro," she said. "I *want* to look like a slut."

"What would Bob say?"

"I cannot imagine." She climbed the footstool and patted Spencer's head, then picked him up and put him in his cage. The cockatoo cooed at her.

"I called Emil and invited him along," Lionel said. "He can't make it, though."

"I could have told you that," she muttered, backing down the footstool, bringing the teapot down with her.

He cocked his head. "What do you mean?"

For a moment, it seemed as though she looked at him with panic in her eyes. Then she swept a strand of hair from her face and shrugged. "It is such short notice, isn't it?" She pursed her lips and turned away from him. "Who *would* be able to make it?"

The clock caught his eye and he felt a jolt of alarm. "Oh, God, we'd better get going," he said, grabbing his jacket. "Parking's going to be *hell.*"

chapter
■■■■■■■■■■■■■■■■■■■■
twenty-two

As Lionel entered the lobby of Cabaret Metro, he was struck with wonder at the mysteries of the aging process. No one had ever come to him and said, "You are now too old to frequent the Metro anymore," nor had he ever *felt* himself too old to do so, and yet here he was, suddenly realizing that, like Yolanda, he hadn't been here in years, and that there was a very good reason for that.

Had he really ever been as young as the people surrounding him now? They were so eager to appear cynical and hip, having transparently contrived to wear clothes so ragged that they surely would have collapsed in a heap at their feet, had they not been held in place by huge, zipper-laden and studded leather jackets. These kids had shaved their heads into the most flagrantly affronting patterns, as though they'd spent years defying authority and flouting convention, and all the while the freshness of their skin was giving them away, letting all the world know that they were at most a year or two out of some broad-lawned, pampered collegiate womb. They leaned against the walls, encircled by cheap jewelry, smoking the cheapest cigarettes imaginable, pretending to be ever so disappointed in the entire fucking world.

No wonder Greta had begged him to come tonight. All of the women in Terrible Swift Sword were either past thirty or on the cusp. God help them when they got onstage tonight with their crow's feet and sagging breasts, to screech about Jesus to a crowd of puppy nihilists whose idea of sophistication was to denigrate everything between puffs of acrid smoke.

Lionel wished he had dressed differently; he must look ridiculous in his floppy jacket and polo shirt. Why not just tuck an ascot around his neck and be done with it? Even his shoes were recently shined. Had he been out of his mind when he put them on?

Yolanda, however, was garnering lots of stares in her "slut duds." After all, a striking woman was a striking woman, whatever her age. And despite her diminutive stature, she knew how to walk like a statuesque beauty—slowly, but not deliberately, extending each leg casually as the opposite hip swayed gently from it. And every third or fourth step, she gracefully tossed her head a little, sending her hair into an intoxicating jumble around her face. The Girl from Ipanema could not have walked more perfectly. Yolanda would probably be able to grab a crowd's attention this way when she was seventy.

They squeezed up the stairs to the mezzanine level, where, Lionel seemed to remember, they could get a better view of the stage and dance floor. The place was crowded already, even though it was a weeknight; Lionel almost said to Yolanda, "Don't these kids have *jobs*?" but it was so uncannily like something his father would say that he let it drop and went to the bar to get some beer.

He came back with two opaque plastic cups filled to the brim with a nameless tap brew. He handed one to Yolanda, who had found two chairs and propped them against a pillar so that they'd have someplace to rest their heads. Yolanda took a sip of the beer, then smiled at him with a little foam moustache. "This is very exciting," she said, licking the foam away. "It makes me feel young again, just *being* here."

Lionel nodded and looked around him. Here on the mezzanine he was comforted to see people his own age—generally sitting, of course, and drinking beer, the two favorite activities at any of the sedate parties he attended these days—and he began to feel better about the evening. Of *course* the hard-core youngsters would hang out in the lobby; they were here to be seen, more than anything else. He turned back to Yolanda and, over the raucous burble of the crowd, said, "Noisy here."

"Wait till the music starts," she said, crossing her legs. Her skirt almost disappeared beneath her jacket. Lionel got a glimpse of scarlet underwear. He surprised himself by being momentarily shocked.

He grimaced and swallowed a mouthful of beer. It was thick and moist and clingy, like pond water. He'd been spoiled, in recent years, by expensive name brands. "I'm a little worried about Greta," he said. "Funny, we're not close or anything, but this is the first chance she's had to prove herself, and I'd hate to see it go badly."

Yolanda patted him on the thigh. "She is a big girl."

"In some ways," he said. "In others, she's a big kid. She's always resisted conformity, but I don't know if that hasn't been out of fear, or—well, you know about my pop. He's a little intimidating. He intimidated my brother Eugene right out of the state."

Yolanda took another sip of beer and licked her lips. "I do not know what you mean. About Greta." She tossed her hair back again.

He shrugged. "Well, school was hard for her, I remember—she wasn't bright—and she used to bring home these terrible report cards and Pop used to blow up at her. They'd have these incredible arguments, and she'd always take the stand that grades weren't important, who cared if she flunked out, she was going to be an artist anyway."

"I still do not understand."

"What I'm wondering is, did she really think that, or was that just a defense she adopted because Pop was attacking her? A defense she started to believe after a while. God, I *hope* not."

"Yours would not be the first parent to be accused of ruining a son's or daughter's life," she said, running her finger along the outside of the cup, leaving a little trail in the condensation. "My *own* mother came close to doing that. From the time I was a young girl, she pressured me,

all the time, to become a nun. Every time she made a reference to my future it would be, 'After you have entered the
convent,' 'After you have entered the convent.' "

Lionel raised his eyebrows. "Well? What happened?"

She smiled at him wickedly and half-shut her eyes. "I
did not enter the convent," she said dismissively. Then she
downed her last mouthful of beer.

He was distracted by an extraordinarily beautiful youth
with jet-black hair and five earrings, who came and stood
in front of him while apparently scouring the mezzanine for
a friend and then moved on.

Lionel sighed, then turned back to Yolanda. "And how is
old Bob lately?"

"Old Bob? Old Bob is dead," she said. "*New* Bob, however, is too busy to see much of me."

He furrowed his brow. "Really? What's got him so busy?"

"Meeting with his chieftain friends, mostly," she said, and
she turned away from him for a moment to deposit the
empty plastic cup on the floor beside her chair. "They get
together and, I suppose, scratch themselves and wave their
arms at each other and grunt. Really, Lionel, I would rather
not talk about it."

That's a switch, Lionel thought gratefully. For a while
there, she hadn't been able to talk about anything else. He
finished his own beer and set the cup beneath his chair. "It
can't be *that* bad," he said. "I mean, Bob *was* a little flighty
before he went away. Now, at least he—"

"Before he went away, he was flighty, but he did not
know it," she said, more angrily than he had expected. "And
if you told him he was flighty, he would have been appalled.
Now, however, he *loves* to think that he is some kind of
irrational, primal man who acts on instinct. I cannot bear
it. He does not *talk* to me anymore, Lionel. I think he distrusts me." She shrugged. "Maybe he distrusts women in
general—or anyone who will not howl at the moon with
him. Or who will not at least say, 'What a good thing it is
that you howl at the moon.' "

"So, what are you saying—it's over between you?"

Before she could answer, the speakers unleashed a cas-
cade of hideous feedback, and Lionel looked down at the
stage. He could make out Greta's silhouette behind a big

guitar. "Oh, it's her, it's *her,*" he yelped. "They're getting ready to play!" He scooted to the edge of his seat.

The beautiful youth with the five earrings made his way back to the other side of the mezzanine, where he took a seat alone, turning his chair around completely and sitting astride it, his arms resting on the chairback.

Funny, thought Lionel, how every time I'm at some public event, I'm always aware of the exact whereabouts of the most gorgeous man in the crowd. Sometimes the top two or three.

The youth must have felt Lionel's eyes on him, because he turned and gave him an inquiring, rather irritated look. Lionel reddened and turned away.

Suddenly, spotlights leapt onto the stage and held fast there, like barnacles. Terrible Swift Sword were revealed in all their Ringling Brothers glory. Greta, Lionel noted with alarm, had bleached her hair and was wearing a white jumpsuit with white buccaneer boots, which made her look something like a reverse-image Emma Peel. She'd drawn a veil over her face—literally drawn it, with a make-up pencil. The lights were hot and the lines of the veil were already starting to run with her sweat.

"HELLO, CHICAGO," yelled the lead singer into the microphone. She yanked the strap of her silk teddy (which she was wearing with a pair of ancient fishing waders) over her shoulder. *"WE'RE TERRIBLE SWIFT SWORD, AND WE'RE HERE TO ROCK YOU!"*

Lionel couldn't believe she'd said anything so mind-numbingly clichéd. He'd have to have a word with Greta about the group's stage banter.

There was some polite applause, but since almost everyone in the club had come to hear Don't Say Gorgonzola, they continued their private conversations through most of the first song in the set, an incredibly loud and dissonant and ugly screed, whose lyrics, to the best of Lionel's ability to understand them, seemed to be,

> *Saaa*-tan, *Saaa*-tan, you're a *looo*-zah,
> *Saaa*-tan, you are out of *luhhhck,*
> *Saaa*-tan, *bet*-tah drop your *weap*-ons,
> *Saaa*-tan, *Saaa*-tan, how you SUHHHCK!

Greta, who was somehow managing to hit a bad chord about every six-and-a-half seconds, was clomping around the stage as though she were stamping out a series of very small fires, tossing her bleached and matted mane around like a cat-o-nine-tails. She jumped in the air dramatically and swung around, and as she did so, she caught her foot on the cord to the lead singer's microphone stand, which responded by toppling over and hitting the floor with a head-jangling crash. But the lead singer was undaunted by this. She simply threw herself to the floor, pressed her face against the supine microphone, and continued singing.

> *Saaa*-tan, *Saaa*-tan, you're pa-*theh*-tic,
> *Saaa*-tan, *bet*-tah wake up *faaast*
> *Saaa*-tan, got no *few*-chah *on* Earth,
> *Saaa*-tan, *Saaa*-tan, kiss my *AAAAASS!*

It was all fairly typical of the Christians Lionel knew; they all preferred to ignore the New Testament message of love, mercy, forgiveness, forbearance and tolerance, and instead concentrate on taking sides in a cosmic soccer match between corporealizations of Good and Evil (with the outcome conveniently foretold, thanks ever so much, Book of Revelations). He found it intellectually barren, ideologically ridiculous, and personally embarrassing. He'd known that Greta treated her Christianity with something akin to elitism—no one he knew was more "holier than thou" than she—but to hear her onstage, making a fool of herself in a getup that made her look like a heroin-addicted Man from Glad—that was different. He'd expected her, now that she'd been given the chance to be heard by so many, to have something more positive—less arcane—to say.

And yet, something strange was happening. He looked around him, and people seemed to be *enjoying* themselves. The beautiful youth sitting backward on his chair was nodding his head in time to the unimaginative beat, and *smiling*; you could see the pearly perfection of his teeth. And all across the mezzanine, and below, on the dance floor, people were swaying to the music, jumping up and down, whistling at the band.

There was only one explanation: Terrible Swift Sword

was so camp, people thought they really meant to be lame. Like Spinal Tap, or the Ruttles.

Lionel turned to Yolanda, who, he found, already had her eyes on him. He shrugged, as if to say, I didn't promise you a good time. When the song ended, she put her hand on his thigh and said, "Oh, Madonna. They are so *awful.*"

Yolanda had felt compelled to say this. Yolanda, who never said anything bad about anyone. Yolanda, who would've said of Hitler, "He painted well."

"The crowd seems to like them," he responded blankly.

"Then the crowd is mad."

And then they were flung into a new song, this one a blistering anti-abortion number called "Mommy Wants Me Dead." Lionel caught some of the crowd on the dance floor whooping in wild pleasure between chugs of beer.

"I wonder if they realize the audience is laughing at them," he said when the song had screeched to a halt.

"You must not tell them," Yolanda insisted. "Besides, who is to say that they do not *wish* to be laughed at? Many rock groups *invite* ridicule."

"Not headbangers," he said. "Not thrashers."

The lights dropped. The stage was bathed in a swirling pink miasma. The lead singer (who by this time, of course, had righted her microphone stand) cupped her hands over the mike and growled, "*Loah*-wud, my man done *left* me for a *plaaaace* called Sod-*DUMB.*"

Oh, no, thought Lionel, his heart skipping a beat. I should've expected this. I should've known.

"Whoa, *Loah*-wud," she continued, wailing like a banshee, "how could he *leeeave* me for the *arms* of anuthuh *main.*"

Lionel sat still as a redwood, listening to every appalling word, every innuendo, every hissed accusation. He could feel the eyes of the beautiful youth on him—the youth he'd been caught staring at.

And in the middle of this sweaty, grimy, interminable song about two hell-driven, sin-obsessed men who defied every known law of God and nature to commit acts of brutal carnality with each other to the sheer delight of the Devil—in the middle of this, Yolanda took Lionel's hand and shouted, "LIONEL, I THINK I HAVE A HEADACHE. I THINK I WOULD LIKE TO LEAVE NOW."

He looked at her, barely visible in the dim pink light of the club, and he knew she had nothing like a headache. This, rather, was an act of kindness, a demonstration of such sensitivity and caring and selflessness as the hate-filled members of Terrible Swift Sword would be incapable of recognizing, much less understanding.

He gripped her hand, leaned over and kissed her cheek, and then got up and headed for the door. He waited for her to catch up to him, not even caring if she saw the splatters of tears on his cheeks. If by chance she did, she wouldn't mention them.

chapter

■■■■■■■■■■■■■■■■■■

twenty-three

"You didn't *stay,*" Greta whined into the telephone. "I looked for you after the show, but you didn't *staaay.*" She sounded like a particularly interruptive school fire alarm.

Lionel swiveled around in his chair and faced away from his office door. He still hadn't come to terms with what had happened last night. In a burst of filial affection, he'd gone to his sister's concert, and before the show had actually worried openly about her doing well, only to be confronted by her performance of a song that he found deeply and personally offensive. He ought to have it out with her right now—clear the air. She was his sister, she deserved nothing less. *He* deserved nothing less.

"My friend Yolanda had a headache," he said sunnily, losing his nerve. "Nothing connected with the music, of course. I think she's just having her period. Anyway, I had to take her home."

"When? When did you leave?"

"About twenty minutes into th—"

"No, I mean, after what *song*? I want to know which *songs* you heard."

"Oh—uh—it was after the—uh—the anti-abortion one."

" 'Mommy Wants Me Dead?' Oh, *faboo.* I really like that one. I wrote some of the lyrics. I'm glad you liked it."

"I didn't say I li—"

"Wasn't the Lord *with* us last night, Lionel? Wanda thought it'd be an uphill battle, but the crowd just *opened up* to us. It was like we just *filled* them with the love of Christ."

He sighed. "Uh-huh."

" 'Course, it's the same old story—first taste of success and everyone's ego goes nuclear. Now Donna wants to like get different costumes and Heather wants to like do some of the lead vocals and Wanda wants to change our name to Stigmatarama."

"Mm-hmm," said Lionel. He picked up his pen and began doodling on his notepad. *Hang up,* he wrote in a broad, elaborate script, fraught with curlicues, *just hang up.*

"Last night after the show we were like all so *pumped* and we all had these great new *ideas*? And I don't know what went down—all of a sudden our joy just turned into like this horrible *anger.* We had a huge fight, backstage, where everyone could hear us? Everyone was probably thinking, Some *Christians.* In the end we had to calm ourselves down and pray together for a couple of minutes. But for a moment there, I thought the band was like not gonna survive."

"Oh, dear." Lionel put a big exclamation point after *Hang up*!

"Everything's okay now and we're working on getting our next gig." She paused. "But I ask you: *Stigmatarama*?"

"Greta, listen, I have to go. My boss just stuck his head into my office for the third time since you called." A complete lie, but she'd never know.

"Oh, okay. Well, thanks for coming. Stay longer next time! And bring friends?"

He uh-huhed her until she got off the line, after which he hung up himself and went back to work. An upsetting night, but not a tragic one. He'd only just begun renewing his relationship with Greta; it wasn't any big loss to dump it on the scrap-heap again. Some families just weren't meant to be close. For that matter, he hadn't heard from his brother Eugene since Christmas.

Suddenly, as if not wanting to make him *too* much of a liar, Julius Deming did indeed stick his head into Lionel's office. "You order those reprints of the sandblaster flyer?" he asked.

"I'm having Cindy do it." Cindy was the production manager.

"Make sure she doesn't fuck it up." No one in the Deming, Stark & Williams hierarchy trusted a woman with even the most simple tasks; sometimes Lionel wondered how Cindy, the only managerial-level female in the office, had even gotten hired. She must've agreed to work for a ridiculously low salary. Or shown off her legs during the interview.

"I'll check on her," Lionel said.

Deming nodded, then winked. "Just talked to a friend of mine who's got a house up near Madison. Said, this time of year, bring mosquito spray by the gallon."

"It's *autumn,* for God's sake."

He shrugged. "Just telling you what he said." He ducked out and was gone.

They were working out what to *pack* already! Lionel hadn't even come up with a date yet, and his bosses had already started putting together their checklist of necessities. He dropped his head into his hands and groaned.

"Lionel?" It was Alice's voice, over the intercom.

"Yes?"

"Bob Smartt on line three."

Bob Smartt? Calling *here*? For *him*? Alarmed and intrigued, he reached over to pick up the phone, then noticed that while half a dozen lines were in fact blinking, none was line three. He got Alice back on the intercom.

"Alice, for God's sake," he said.

"—old for a moment, please," he heard her say, then, "Lionel *what*? It's crazy up here this morning!"

"You said Bob Smartt is on line three for me. Line three isn't even blinking. What line is he on?"

"Oh, *shit,*" she snarled. Then she murmured, "He's—uh—he's—oh! Wait!" A pause. "He's here to see you!"

He shook his head, switched off the intercom, and went out to the reception area, where a red-faced Alice averted her eyes from him while muttering the agency name to an

incoming call. Bob was standing nearby in an olive Armani
suit, an cubist-pattern tie, and black opera slippers. He was
slightly hunched over, his cheeks puffed out and his lips
pursed. Clearly, he was holding in a burst of laughter that
would erupt as soon as they were out of Alice's earshot.

And so it did, and all the way back to his office Lionel
had to listen while Bob repeated Alice's embarrassing mistake and hooted with laughter over it. So many people
looked out into the hall in astonishment as he passed that
once he was ensconced inside Lionel's office, Lionel shut
the door to keep the curious from peeking in at him.

Bob fell into the chair in front of Lionel's desk and
clutched his stomach, helpless with giddy laughter. *"Oh—
wait—he's—here—to—see—you,"* he gasped, then broke
out laughing again. Lionel nodded, smiling weakly. Eventually, Bob took out his handkerchief and dabbed at the corners of his eyes.

Then they sat staring at each other, grinning courteously.
Lionel, whose previous night salivating into his receiver during a call to 1-900-HOT-GUYZ had done nothing to quell
the still unreleased sexual frenzy in him, began to feel a
hint of arousal now that Bob was in repose before him,
no longer braying and looking at least *serviceably* cute. He
couldn't help but notice the long lock of blond hair that
curled under Bob's ear and brushed his collar; why did he
find that so powerfully erotic?

He had to snap himself out of this; it was appalling.

He shrugged his shoulders and said, "So, Bob."

"So, *Lionel.*"

He raised an eyebrow. "Been a long time."

"Too long. We gotta get together more often. You an'
me an' Yolanda."

Something in his voice alarmed Lionel. If he hadn't
known better, he'd almost have thought Bob *meant* that.

"Well, you know, busy schedules and all," he said with
a wave of his hand.

Bob rolled his eyes and groaned theatrically, implying
that no one could tell him a *thing* about busy schedules.

Being careful to phrase it in as friendly a manner as possible, Lionel said, "So Bob, what brings you my way?"

Bob shrugged and pursed his lips. There was a long silence, and Lionel noted with alarm that his eyes were misting.

"To be perfectly honest, Lionel," he said at last, "I've got a problem."

No way am I involved in this conversation, thought Lionel. Wait till Yolanda hears!

"What problem?" he asked cautiously.

"Yolanda," Bob answered glumly. "I'm pretty sure she's seeing another man."

Lionel's heart dropped into his stomach, and he thought, Maybe Yolanda better *not* hear this.

"Bob, I'm sure you're wrong about that. I live right *above* her, remember."

"I know," he said. His voice cracked pathetically. "That's why I came to see you. You haven't spotted her with anyone else, have you?"

"No, of course not. And odds are I'd have picked up at least a *few* clues if she'd been seeing anyone else." He chuckled and thought, hell, she'd have *told* me if she'd been seeing anyone else.

"And you haven't?" His tone was desperate. He was virtually pleading for reassurance.

"No," Lionel said, half-laughing. "Swear to God!"

Bob ran his hand through his hair and sighed. He snatched a snow globe from Lionel's desk (it was an old All-Pro giveaway; inside it was a tiny model of a snow-blower) and shook it. The white plastic granules whirled around the perimeter of the globe. "I wish that made me feel better," he said.

"It *should* make you feel better."

"I know it should." He held the snow globe upside down and watched the flakes drift down and collect at the top of the dome. "But, Goddarn it, it doesn't! I haven't seen her in *days,* Lionel. Every time I call, she's got some elaborate excuse why she can't see me. She's either going to meet an old friend who's got a layover at O'Hare, or going to a one-night-only booksellers' seminar, or going out with a bunch of her girlfriends or something. It never ends."

"But she *did* go out with a bunch of her girlfriends!" Lionel exclaimed, lifting his palms high. "Bob, I know it for a *fact*! I stopped by her apartment and talked to her while she was getting ready!"

Bob squinted at him, as though not quite trusting him. "What night would that be?" he asked, in the exact tones of an expert prosecutor trying to catch a witness lying.

Lionel thought for a second. "Night before last," he said confidently. He crossed his arms and sat back.

Bob sighed in defeat, then rallied and said, "Well, what about *last* night?" He shook the snow globe again, this time so hard that the tiny snowblower came loose and went spinning around the interior of the globe along with the granules. "I called her *repeatedly,* all *night,* and she wasn't home! And she'd told me only *that morning* that she didn't have any plans." He scowled. "I was going to surprise her— just show up with roses—but she was out till all hours, doing *God* knows what with *God* knows whom."

Lionel shook his head, uncrossed his arms, and leaned forward. "Bob, *relax.* She was out with *me* last night."

"You?" he asked, looking at Lionel's unfashionable suit and wrinkling his nose at the idea.

"Yes, *me.* I ran into her on the stairs. She was buried under a pile of laundry, so I invited her to come with me to see my sister's rock band play at Cabaret Metro. She jumped at the chance." He shook his finger at Bob. "And you *didn't* keep calling her all night, because I had her back home by ten. You just gave up too soon."

He pursed his lips again. "You sure she didn't just turn around and go out again after that?"

"Oh, for Christ's *sake,* Bob."

He returned the ruined snow globe to Lionel's desk and began wringing his hands. "I suppose I'm being paranoid. But, Lionel, I don't know if I could *control* myself if I found out she was two-timing me. It'd be just too much to handle, having that happen to me *twice.*" This was one of the only times Lionel had heard Bob refer even glancingly to his faithless ex-wife. "I'd go off the deep end, I really would. I'd do something crazy and *drastic.*"

Lionel suddenly conjured up a picture of Bob bursting in on Yolanda and her alleged new boyfriend, then leaping at his rival, scratching wildly, his head turned and his eyes shut. A laugh burbled out of his mouth; he quickly turned it into a cough.

"And I'm not *imagining* Yolanda's behavior," Bob continued. "She's *different* lately. Cold. Stand-offish."

Lionel shrugged. "Maybe *you're* the one who's different."
He bristled. "What's that supposed to mean?"

"Well, not to tell tales out of school or anything, but I
know Yolanda was feeling a little jealous of your buddies
from your—whatever you want to call it—your 'manly
man's' retreat. She says you see quite a lot of them now."

"Not 'quite a lot'! Oh, that *witch*!" He balled his fists and
gave his thighs a pair of swift punches. "I've *begged* her to
try to understand, but *oh* no . . ."

Now I've gone and done it, Lionel thought. Time for
some damage control. "Maybe I misheard her," he said
quickly. "Anyway, the thing is, she probably thinks *you're*
the one neglecting *her*." I can't believe I'm playing Cupid
for Yolanda and this jerk, he thought.

Bob's nostrils were flaring. "You didn't misunderstand
her. She said what she meant, and she meant what she said."

Lionel plucked a stray paper-clip from his desktop and
started unbending it, trying to focus his nervous energy on
the task. This whole scene was becoming awkward and
difficult.

"All we guys *do* is get together and *drum*," Bob said.
"That's all. Maybe once a week, *tops*."

"You *drum*?" asked Lionel, not quite sure he'd heard *that*
correctly.

"Yes. You know. Make noise. Bang on things." He
grinned. "It's a very masculine kind of therapy. You mean
to say you never *drum*, Lionel?"

"Not since I was four and drove my Aunt Lola crazy
pretending to be Ringo Starr."

Bob threw up his arms. "Oh, what an opportunity! Let's
do it now!"

Lionel's heart froze. "What? *Here*? Are you *crazy*?"

"Yes, yes I *am*! That's just the *point*! Yolanda's got me
crazy, so I need to do some drumming to help me calm
down. It's a natural response—a natural release for the pain
of being a man!"

"The *pain* of being a man?" Lionel asked, raising an
eyebrow.

"Yes, yes, *yes*. The pain of being misunderstood, the pain
of not being able to express ourselves, the pain of knowing
we disappointed our fathers, the pain of knowing how our
fathers disappointed *us*."

Lionel cocked his head. "*My* dad wanted me to go into the army when I got out of high school, which I let him know I thought was the stupidest idea since quadrophonic stereos. I'm sure we disappointed each other there, but I have to tell you, Bob, I'm not in *pain* about it."

"You have pain you don't even *know* about," he snapped, his face turning crimson. "Don't *analyze* it, don't think about it in *rational* terms—that's a trap! Reason is *confining.* Just let it loose—let the pain *loose.* Come *on,* Lionel!" He started slapping the top of the desk with the palms of his hands. "Join in! It's the most *basic* form of communication between men. It predates speech! You'd be surprised at how much you can release when you do this!" Slap, slap, slap-slap-slap. Slap, slap, slap-slap-slap.

There was no stopping him. I'll just do it for a little while, thought Lionel, just for thirty seconds, and then he'll be satisfied and go.

He gave the desk a couple of haphazard whacks.

"Get into a *rhythm,*" Bob squealed. "You need to *feel* the beats." Slap, slap, slap-slap-slap. Slap, slap, slap-slap-slap. "Me, I like to pretend I'm drumming to 'The Lady Is a Tramp.'"

How very primal, thought Lionel. But he gave up and started beating the desk to match Bob.

His heart started racing. He was alarmed by the noise they were making, by the look of blissed-out contentment on Bob's face, and by the fact that after thirty seconds they had not only not stopped, but appeared to be just warming up.

And what alarmed him most of all was that he was finding all this kind of *hot.*

It was embarrassing; he was embarrassed for himself. He hoped desperately that this would at least make a good story at a cocktail party somewhere down the line. But before he could convince himself of that, the door to his office swung open.

Hackett Perlman stood in the doorway, popeyed with amazement. "Lionel, what the *hell* is with the racket in here?"

"We were just drumming," he said, trying not to let his mortification show. "It's a kind of male therapy." He nodded at Bob. "This is my fr—this is Bob Smartt. Bob, Hackett Perlman, our creative director."

"Hi!" chirped Bob.

Perlman drew his head back. "*Drumming,* you said?"

Lionel shifted in his chair. "It's kind of a Nathan Beatty thing. You know Nathan Beatty?"

Perlman shook his head. He looked at his shoes, then up again. "You're weird lately, Lionel." He sighed. "Anyway, keep it down, all right? Sounded like the fucking roof was being knocked in."

He left, shutting the door behind him. As soon as he'd gone, Bob clasped a hand over his mouth and turned to Lionel. "*Whoops,*" he said through his fingers. "Hope you're not in trouble now!"

"Course not," he said, hoping he was right. "But, listen, I *do* have to get back to work." He rose from his chair. "I don't want to kick you out or anything, but—"

"Say no more! I understand!" Bob sprang out of his chair and brushed the wrinkles out of his pants. "I didn't mean to keep you this long, honest." He rounded the desk and extended his hand. "Lionel, I want to thank you for taking the time to hear me out."

"No problem," he said, taking his hand and shaking it. "It's the least I can do*oof!*" He found himself pulled into Bob's embrace, and was now cheek to cheek with him, being hugged and patted on the back like an infant with gas.

When Bob released him, he reeled a little. Bob smiled and said, "Men shouldn't be ashamed to hold each other. We're *brothers,* Lionel. We've *drummed* together."

"To 'The Lady Is a Tramp,' " he said dazedly.

Bob laughed uproariously, then winked at him and headed for the door. "It's okay, I'll show myself out," he said, then slipped away and was gone.

chapter

■■■■■■■■■■■■■■■■■■■

twenty-four

That night, Lionel was on a step-ladder in the kitchen, a hammer in his hand and his lips wrapped around a clutch of nails, when someone knocked on his door.

"CUH IH," he called out.

The door opened and Yolanda crept through it. "Lionel?" she called into the half-darkened apartment, her hand still on the doorknob.

"IH HEAH," he called down the hallway to her. Then he took the hammer and banged it against the nail he'd positioned against the top of the doorframe. From the corner of his eye, he saw Yolanda jump at the noise.

She swept a strand of hair from her face and came down the hall to the kitchen. "What are you doing?" she asked.

He put down the hammer, took the nails from his mouth, and said, "I got home from work today and found the trim on this lintel just *hanging* off. I'm trying to nail it back up again." He waved a hand at it in disgust. "Fucking building's falling to pieces. The heat, the water—even the ventilation's gone sour now. I can still smell Emil's cheap cologne out on the staircase, and he hasn't been here in *weeks.*"

She approached the ladder. "Could you come down here for a moment?" she said. "I need to talk to you."

"Sure!" he said happily. He tucked the nails into his pocket and descended, then brushed himself off and stood before her, smiling. "What's up?"

She furrowed her brow, grimaced, and cuffed him on the jaw.

"*Hey!*" he said, flinching. "What's *that* for?"

She struck him again, and again, and then again. Spencer, who was perched atop his cage, cheered her on with a couple of deafening screeches.

Lionel stumbled backward, holding his arms before his face. "Yolanda, for Christ's sake, what's got *into*—"

"I thought you were my *friend,*" she blurted, her voice raspy with anger.

"*Jesus*—I thought so, *too.*"

Spencer, eager to see the violence continue, had spread his wings and was swaying from side to side, growling, as if to say, Come *on,* come *on.*

"You say that, and yet you went and told Bob all the things I'd told you in confidence! About how I disliked his men's-movement friends and was—and was *jealous* of them, when that's not even *true.*"

Oh, brother. He should've expected this. "Look," he said, lowering his arms a little, "he came to my office and took me by surprise. He was all upset because he thought you were seeing another man. I told him you weren't, because if you were I'd have found out about it."

"Oh, of *course,* I am such an open book, you know everything about m—"

"*Listen,* will you?" He paused to catch his breath; he was upset, nearly panting. "He wasn't convinced. He said you'd changed, you weren't the same woman anymore. All I did was say that maybe *he* was the one who'd changed. And then I may have mentioned that I thought you were a little ticked off by all the time he was spending with Colonel Beaver and Captain Aardvark, and *that* whole crowd."

She was still breathing fire, but had unclenched her fists. "You should not have interfered."

He dropped his arms. "Well, *he* shouldn't have come to see me. Unannounced, like that. He caught me off-guard.

I'm sorry, Yolanda, I didn't have time to call and ask you how to handle it. I used my own judgment. If I was wrong, I apologize."

She rolled her eyes, then turned and went to the kitchen table, where she took a seat and crossed her legs. Some of the charge went out of the air. Lionel breathed a little easier.

Spencer, however, screamed in disappointment at the end of the fisticuffs. He retired to the interior of his cage, where he sulked in a corner.

"He just called me a few minutes ago," Yolanda said. She took a piece of junk mail from the table and started ripping it into confetti, letting the pieces drift down to the floor. "He said he could no longer trust me because I was telling *you* my feelings and not *him.* Then he accused me of seeing another man behind his back. He called me a floozy. I do not even know what that means, but it sounds *awful.*" She sighed and ripped a long strip off the envelope, then flicked it to the ground. The bisected head of Ed McMahon looked up at her mournfully.

Lionel took the chair opposite hers. As he lowered himself into it, the nails in his pocket bit into his thigh. He winced, removed them, and spilled them onto the table. "What did *you* say?" he asked, dropping into the chair.

"I told him that if I *were* seeing another man, it would not be any of his business. I told him that we are not married, not even engaged, and that he should not presume that he owns me." She finished tearing apart the envelope and lifted her hands; the remaining shreds of paper dropped aimlessly, like dandruff. "Well, that made him even angrier. He said that we had an *understanding*—can you *believe* that?—and that if he ever learned that I was seeing someone else, he would not be responsible for his actions."

Lionel lowered his head. "I'm sorry, Yolanda. I didn't mean to cause all this trouble."

She sighed and folded her hands on the table. "You did not cause it. It has been a long time coming. Ever since he returned from his retreat, carrying that ridiculous spear. Bob is easily influenced—anyone who pretends to have discovered the next big fad can lead him anywhere by the nose—but this 'inner-chieftain' nonsense is somehow worse. It has affected his *behavior.* He has been so aggressive since his

return—*proudly* aggressive! He never listened to me much
before, but since his return it is almost as though he cannot
even bother to *hear* my opinions before dismissing them.
And he became so *indignant* at the idea that I might have
a life of my own beyond him. And the way he spoke to me
tonight!" She shook her head. "He said nothing outright,
Lionel, but I felt myself threatened. I only wish I knew how
to *avoid* him for the next few days."

"You think he'll calm down by then?"

She shrugged. "I hope so." She looked him in the eye.
"Then I will be able to break up with him without fearing
that he will hit me."

He let loose a long, low whistle. "*Wow,* Yolanda. I wish
I could be here to help you through all this."

"Do not be silly. Go to Wisconsin and have fun. This is
not your problem."

"Listen, if it'd help, you can stay here, at my place. I
mean, you're taking care of Spencer for me anyway, so why
not just move in? That way, you can avoid his phone calls,
and if he ever comes over, you won't be home, an—"

"No good," she said, shaking her head. "He knows I am
to take care of Spencer for you. He would look for me
here."

Lionel rubbed his forehead. "I can't believe we're sitting
here trembling in fear of a man who has every Josephine
Baker movie ever made on videocassette!" Suddenly he remembered how terrified she'd been of keeping Bob waiting
while she searched for her missing earring several weeks
before. He clasped his hands together and looked up at her.
"Listen, I really think I should stay. You *need* me. To look
after you. I don't want to go to Wisconsin, anyway. I mean,"
he laughed, "I'm supposed to be leaving the day after tomorrow, and I still haven't managed to find a date. And if I show
up without one, it'll be sheer disaster. So, hell, I might as
well stay home and let it be a disaster here, instead."

Yolanda clicked her tongue at him. "Really, Lionel! I cannot believe that women have not been *jumping* at the
chance to go with you to a log cabin in the woods of Wisconsin. It sounds so romantic!"

"That's just the problem," he said, flinging his hands up
in exasperation. "I have to find a woman who's willing to

go with me on a romantic week-long holiday *without* getting any romantic *expectations* along the way. Such a woman is a bit hard to find." He sighed. "And it's not like I know loads and loads of women to begin with." He started rocking on the back legs of the chair. "In fact, I'd pretty much given up, I was just going to go stag and let the chips fall where they may. But now I think I should stay here instead and help you keep Bob off your scent."

She shook her head. "Absolutely not. Whether it is a disaster for you I cannot know, but all the same I will not allow you to miss your holiday because of me."

They sat in silence for a spell, the only sound being the creaking of Lionel's chair as he rocked back and forth, back and forth. The air hung heavy over them, like a wet shroud.

After a few minutes, Yolanda suddenly looked at him and said, "Lionel, we are such imbeciles."

"We are?" He stopped rocking.

"The solution to *both* our problems is right in front of us." She smiled brilliantly. "And it is so amazingly *obvious*!"

chapter

■ ■ ■ ■ ■ ■ ■ ■ ■ ■ ■ ■ ■ ■ ■ ■ ■ ■ ■ ■

twenty-five

It was Yolanda's turn to drive, so after Lionel had pumped and paid for a new tankful of gas he handed her the keys and slid into the passenger seat. As she pulled back onto the interstate and picked up speed, he rolled down the window and let the flow of warm autumn air splash him in the face. This was going to be a *perfect* week. He was enjoying it so much already—just getting away, shirking the burden of the everyday and slipping into a strange new setting. It made him feel almost weightless.

Yolanda had one hand on the wheel and one hand on the radio dial. She was trying to find a decent station, but here in the middle of nowhere it was next to impossible. She ran through the FM spectrum, getting nothing but varying degrees of static (or an occasional burst of the same gassy Michael Bolton song, which couldn't exactly be counted as an improvement).

She cursed in Spanish. Lionel laughed; she sounded like Ricky Ricardo.

He twisted his torso, dug into the bag he'd thrown on the back seat, and retrieved the box of animal crackers he'd bought at the convenience store they'd stopped at two hours before. Something about being on the road always made him crave foods he hadn't had since childhood.

Yolanda gave up, switched off the radio, and vented her anger on the pokey Ford Taurus in front of her. She careened into the opposite lane, sped ahead of it, and then swerved back, cutting into its path with frightening precision and causing its driver to honk and flip her the bird.

Lionel bit the head off a zebra. "You *daredevil,* you," he said, chewing.

"How am I supposed to drive without music?" she asked in irritation. He recognized it as rhetorical and didn't reply.

The road ahead of them was free and clear now. The sun was low, red, and in their faces, but Yolanda had borrowed Lionel's Vuarnets and looked, with her billowing hair and mirrored lenses, like the hell-bent heroine of some violent road movie.

He sighed in pleasure and nibbled at the rump of an elephant.

They rode in silence for a few minutes, each looking out at the countryside—flat, seemingly infinite, splotched here and there with a thicket of browning trees, swelling at intervals into a range of unambitious hills. Not a prepossessing sight; it was a landscape that couldn't make up its mind. He hoped for better at the end of the road, in the highly touted acres of Wild Rose, Wisconsin.

"I do hope Spencer will be all right," Yolanda said, trying to break the monotony of the view with the monotony of trivial conversation. She was sticking her hand out the window, letting the air burble through her fingers.

"He'll be fine," Lionel assured her.

"This Toné, he is a reliable person?"

He shrugged. "Not terribly, no."

She snapped her head toward him, her mouth agape. "But—Lionel! If you think he is not reliable, why did you ask him to take care of Spencer? What if he does not feed him, or accidentally leaves a door open and lets him fly away?"

He picked a giraffe's leg from between his teeth. "Gee, that'd be too bad."

She shook her head. "You are teasing me." She turned her attention back to the road. "I know you love that bird. I *know* it."

"I'd love him better basted over a bed of wild rice."

"Stop it, Lionel. You don't fool me. I *know* you love him."

"Oh, *do* you, now?"

"Yes, I do." She grimaced. "If you did not love him, why would you have bought him?"

He curled one leg underneath him and stared at her. The question surprised him. "Actually, he was a gift," he said. "From Kevin. My ex."

"Your ex-what?" she asked.

"Ex-lover. What did you think?"

She almost swerved into a ditch. "Lionel! You never told me!"

He readjusted his knee and sat back. "It was a long time ago," he said. "Didn't last more than—gee, five months. Six at most."

"What happened?"

"Well, I moved in with him and a month later we were at each other's throats."

"Why? How could that happen?" She was so concerned, she was barely watching the road.

He shrugged. "The pressure of being secretive was too much for us. Everyone in the building started to clue in to what was going on between us, and we couldn't han—" He stopped himself. "*I* couldn't handle it. I kept inventing excuses for not going out and being seen together. He was pretty closeted, but next to *me* he was a goddamned exhibitionist." He shrugged. "So in the end he kicked me out. Which wasn't such a big deal, 'cause I'd never really unpacked my bags in the first place."

"Is that when you moved in above me?"

He nodded. "And took Spencer with me. Kevin *loved* that bird, but since the horrible thing was technically a birthday present for me, I decided to exercise my right of ownership and, not coincidentally, hurt Kevin at the same time." He shook his head. "Backfired on me, didn't it? Spencer's been after my blood ever since. He only ever really bonded with Kevin." He paused. "And, of course, you."

She shook her head. "Lionel, Lionel, Lionel. You are a very mixed-up man."

He chuckled, tossed the box of crackers back into the bag, then settled into the seat and folded his hands over his stomach. In a matter of moments, his eyes fell shut. With the garbled hiss of the radio now stilled, he felt a sense of peace settle over him like a fresh cotton sheet. The steady bass hum of the motor, the giddy effect of the barreling momentum they'd attained, the constant caresses of the air on his face, and now Yolanda's quiet whistling, all conspired to put him in as close to a state of grace as he'd ever encountered. Noise did not exist; strife did not exist; inertia did not exist. In his contentment, he fell into a thin sleep— still aware of his surroundings, but watching dream scenarios play out in his mind the way he might watch a movie on television.

Yolanda's whistling threaded into and out of his dreams like a leitmotif from a 1940s tearjerker. He was dimly aware that he recognized the tune, but couldn't concentrate long enough to place it. Sometimes she would stop whistling for a moment, the better to concentrate on changing lanes or making a turn. But then she would start again, and the tune would once more insinuate itself into Lionel's half-consciousness.

Then she stopped whistling and actually sang a verse.

"Hey, big spender," she warbled in a small, sexy voice, "spennnnd a little dime with me."

Dime, not *time.* Funny, he'd heard it sung like that not too long ago. Who had done that? He shifted in his seat, settled his cheek against the acrylic-nap upholstery, and gave a little yawn. It had been Emil's Uncle John, hadn't it? He'd sung it that way because that's how Edie Adams sang it in an old 1960s commercial. Imagine Yolanda remembering a commercial from thirty years ago!

At this, something pricked at his brain like a burr under a saddle. Yolanda, he remembered, was only twenty-five! He inhaled sharply and opened his eyes.

And it all rushed in at him. Yolanda having the Emma Goldman book on her nightstand. The scent of Emil's aftershave hanging perpetually over the staircase. Bob's near certainty that Yolanda was seeing another man. And now, Yolanda singing a lyric she could *only* have heard from Emil's uncle.

He turned his head toward her and said, "You *slut.* You're *sleeping* with Emil Apostal."

She almost lost control of the car. "What?" she exclaimed, grabbing the steering wheel and wrestling it back into place. "Lionel, have you been dreaming?"

"Don't even try to deny it," he said, sitting up and wiping the sleep from his eyes. "How long has it been going on?"

"How dare you call me a slut? Apologize at once!"

"Don't change the subject. That night I stopped by and you said you were getting ready to go out with your girl-friends—you were *really* getting ready to go out with *Emil,* weren't you?"

She looked straight ahead and tapped her fingernails on the steering wheel. "I have not yet had my apology."

"And two days ago," he said, growing excited at being able to fit all the pieces together, "when you came up with the idea of being my date up at the cabin, it didn't hurt that Emil was going to be too busy studying for his exam to pay any attention to you for a week. Am I right?"

"I am *waaaiti*ng," she said.

"I'm not going to apologize, Yolanda. Far from it! *Slut, slut, slut,*" he yapped at her. "What *else* do you call a woman who sneaks her boyfriend in and out of her apart-ment so that no one can see him?"

"Not 'no one'—just you."

"Oh, just *me.* Oh, *thank you,* Yolanda. I feel so much *better* now."

Tears were collecting at the corners of her eyes. "You are being horrible."

"I have a ways to go to catch up with *you!*"

She gave the wheel a good swift yank to the right, and the car careened off to the side of the road, spitting gravel everywhere. They just missed hitting a Day-Glo orange sign advertising sweet corn for sale at a dollar a bushel. When the car had ground to a halt, she knocked the gearshift into park and turned to confront him.

"Lionel, I did not want you to know," she said. "You were in *love* with him. How could I let you find out that he was now with *me* instead of *you?*"

"It wasn't any kinder to *hide* it from me," he said. Despite his tone, he was alarmed to discover that he wasn't nearly as hurt as he was pretending to be. It made him feel a little ashamed at putting her through this.

She swept her hair behind her shoulders. "I thought it might not last," she said, "and then there would be no reason for you to ever know. I thought it might just be a physical attraction that would soon fade."

"But it didn't."

She shook her head. "No, it did not. And I do not think it will."

He took a deep breath, sat back in his seat, and looked at the roof of the car. He felt inferior before feelings such as these; he felt like a child. He had to rise above his inadequacy. What was left but the heroic effort to meet a love such as Yolanda's with what little love he could muster himself? He balled his fists and made the effort.

"Well," he said, the word sticking in his throat, "congratulations."

He'd taken her by surprise. She cocked her head and said, "What did you say?"

"*Congratulations.* I'm happy for you. For *both* of you." He saw the way she was staring at him—as though he'd suddenly grown an extra head—and added, "I *mean* it."

"You do?"

"Course I do! I wish you hadn't kept it from me, that's all. Yolanda, I love Emil, and I love you. I'm *thrilled* about this." And saying so was almost enough to make it true.

Her shoulders slumped and she fell back into her seat. "Well, then, *you* had better drive, because I am too upset to continue."

chapter

■■■■■■■■■■■■■■■■■■■

twenty-six

Five minutes later they were en route to Wild Rose again, Yolanda in the passenger seat, unraveling the hem of her right pants leg as she filled in the blanks for him.

"I always felt flattered by Bob's attention," she said. "He always seemed to care about how I looked and what I wore and what other people thought about me. But that also made me feel so dependent on him and so terribly afraid of his scorn. Still, I thought that he was such a wonderful man because he put me on a pedestal."

"Department store mannequins get put on pedestals all the time," Lionel said, shifting the overhead visor until it was actually grazing the left side of his head. The sun was more unbearably red than ever. It hung just above the horizon, like a coin about to drop into a jukebox.

"I know, I know," she said mournfully. "I did not understand how little Bob actually cared to know me until I first met Emil, on the landing outside my apartment—you were there, remember? At first I thought he was so inconsiderate, the way he spoke to me. It was only later that I realized he was speaking to me as an *equal*. That he may have said rude things, but he could not have said those things except in response to things *I* said *first*. Lionel, it was such a shock to realize that a man had actually *listened* to me."

He drove into the shade of a high hill, and peered over the top of his Vuarnets at the suddenly darkened road. "Yolanda, I think you must be some kind of pre-feminist anachronism," he said in amazement.

"Why?" She stopped toying with her frayed hem. "Oh— because I am flattered that a man listened to me?" She crossed her arms and legs and thought for a moment. "No, no, Lionel. I would be just as flattered if a *woman* listened to me. If *anybody* listened to me. So few people ever bother to pay attention to what anyone else says these days."

"*I* listen to you," he protested.

She patted his thigh. "I know, and that is why you are my friend. That is why I love you. People such as you are so rare."

They passed the hill and were back in the realm of the wicked sun again. The blazing disk had slipped partly past the horizon, but was still there, playing a blinding game of peek-a-boo with Lionel.

"What impressed me most about Emil was that he spoke so passionately about science fiction," she said. "Bob often made fun of me for reading S.F., and because he was so sophisticated and successful I let myself think that maybe he was right, maybe it was an embarrassing, juvenile trait of mine, and I should be grateful that he could overlook it. But Emil—who is even more confident and self-assured than Bob—Emil is like me!" She paused. "S.F. is my inner life, Lionel. I try not to talk about it too much, because so few people understand. But what Emil said, about S.F. being the literature of hope, about how it should serve as our culture's self-fulfilling prophecy—that is what *I* have always felt, but not been able to put into words." She hunched her shoulders and hugged herself. "Lionel, Emil *stirs* me."

He felt a peculiar catch in his throat, as though an angel and a devil were sitting on either shoulder, playing a tug of war with his ears, one advising, "Be happy for dear Yolanda," the other, "Hate her for stealing your boyfriend."

Ultimately, the seraphic side won. He puckered his lips and said, "Well, fine. But if the two of you head for one of those silly conventions dressed as Darth Vader and Princess Leia, don't stop by and ask *me* to take your picture."

She punched him in the arm. "Lionel! I am baring my *soul* to you!"

"Which is the very least you can do, considering how you've been sneaking around behind my back. So what happened next?" He noticed a police car ahead, parked on the side of the road, and began coasting to a lower speed. He'd been going almost seventy.

She shrugged. "Emil came by a day or so later, pretending that he wanted to see you, but of course he must have known that you were at work. And when I told him I would give you a message, he had no message to give. Do you remember me telling you this? I knew then that he had come to see me, not you. He tried to talk to me some more about S.F. and anarchism and about how they relate, but I was too upset at the time because I had bought the Nathan Beatty tape and had just started to watch it."

Lionel remembered that afternoon. He must've been blind not to notice Yolanda's revealing body language when she was relating Emil's visit. He shook his head, and as he did so he glided past the cop car at exactly fifty-four miles an hour. He gave a sigh of relief.

"Well," Yolanda continued, oblivious to their narrow escape, "I was so upset that I called Emil later. He had left his number with me, 'In case Lionel does not have it,' he said, but I knew he really wanted *me* to have it. I told myself that I was calling him because he was so smart and he could help me figure out what I should feel about Nathan Beatty. But his aunt answered the phone and when I asked to speak to Emil she said, 'Are you that Spanish girl he cannot stop talking about?' And she was just about finished inviting me to dinner when Emil must have grabbed the phone from her, because suddenly it was him, and not her, and all at once it was very awkward. So I started jabbering about Nathan Beatty and he started jabbering back that Nathan Beatty was a primitivist and a nativist and so on, and in the background his aunt kept saying 'Invite her to dinner. Invite her to dinner.' So he invited me to dinner."

The sun had finally gone from the world. Suddenly the sky looked rubbed with wet charcoal. Lionel turned on his headlights. "So," he said, "your first date was at Uncle John and Aunt Nancy's house, with you and Emil looking at each other sideways and blushing while Uncle John told you all about Edie Adams and shoelaces and Aunt Nancy scooped lots of moo shoo pork onto your plate."

"Actually, we had pizza," she said, rolling up her window against the suddenly cool night air. "But otherwise, yes, it was just as you say."

He laughed. "Yolanda, you *have* to marry Emil now, That story's too goddamned *cute* to waste on a failed relationship. You can tell it at your fiftieth anniversary party."

She sighed and curled her feet beneath her. "It certainly seems that it may come to that. I have seen him nearly every night since. He calls me his *guivaer frumos,* which is Romanian for 'beautiful jewel.'" Suddenly she became self-conscious and placed a hand on Lionel's thigh. "I am so sorry I did not tell you all of this before," she said. "I was so afraid you would be devastated that *I* was seeing the man *you* loved." She cocked her head. "Of course, I am very relieved that you are taking it so well. But even so, I have to say I am surprised."

"Why?" he asked. A car passed him going the opposite direction, and then the road ahead of him was empty and long. He switched to his high-beams. "I'm not a child, you know, Yolanda. I can take disappointment. I can roll with the punches."

"But you loved him, Lionel. You *loved* him."

And when she said this he felt a spectacular emptiness inside him, next to which the emptiness of the road was nothing. He didn't speak for a long time. The roar of the motor and the hissing of the cold wind filled up the silence until he found his voice again.

"Maybe I didn't love him," he said, his voice low, as though he were afraid someone else might overhear. "I thought I did, but—well, if you're so amazed that I got over him so quickly, then maybe I didn't. Maybe the truth is that I just *don't know* what it's like to really love someone." And before he could stop himself, he thought, Maybe I never will.

chapter

■ ■

twenty-seven

They reached Wild Rose without realizing it. Yolanda, who was scrutinizing the map by starlight (occasionally allowing her nose to plunge into Madison, Wisconsin), looked up suddenly after Lionel announced their arrival at a certain rural intersection, and cried, "We are here!" Lionel was too tired to make a joke of that.

Even in the darkness, the town charmed them. Despite the accelerating race to find ever more unspoiled and remote places to hide out, Wild Rose had as yet escaped the notice of too many city dwellers. The commercial part of town, such as it was, hadn't yet been paved or prettified or invaded by shops selling stationery, notions, handicrafts, or aerobic clothing. Boards warped, paint peeled, shop windows were decorated with construction paper cut-outs and Scotch tape, and Lionel found it all completely enchanting. He couldn't wait to come back in broad daylight.

They passed a dinky airport, several Quonset huts, and then managed to lose themselves for a good twenty-five minutes on increasingly narrow roadways hemmed in by increasingly menacing trees. "We're going to be late for dinner at this rate," Lionel fretted, checking his watch every twenty-three seconds. But just as he was getting ready to

really panic they stumbled onto the very road they were
seeking, and so turned and made their way up a pebbly
incline, past rows of knobby, eccentric-looking cabins on
either side.

They located Magellan's cabin by its address—possible
only because the entire house was lit up like a Christmas
tree. They pulled into the driveway next to Deming's Saab
and Perlman's Beemer. Lionel stilled the engine. They got
out and stretched their limbs. Music was wafting from the
cabin's open windows—Mel Tormé singing "Straighten Up
and Fly Right."

They raised their eyebrows at each other and smiled.
Yolanda stifled a yawn. Lionel popped open the trunk and
they grabbed their duffel bags. When he slammed it shut,
someone from inside the cabin hollered, "THAT YOU,
LIONEL?"

"YEAH," he called back, and a moment later Babcock
Magellan greeted them at the door, his hands dripping wet.
It was the first time Lionel had ever seen him out of a suit.
He was wearing a red polo shirt, plaid shorts, and red deck
shoes. "I can't shake, I'm a mess," he said when introduced
to Yolanda, and he displayed his hands to her. He was smiling ear to ear, and as he held the door for them to enter he
said, "You're just in time—we've only just started preparing
dinner. Chaos in here. I forgot how tiny the kitchen is. You
two can go out back and shuck corn. Be by yourself. You
know how to shuck corn?"

"*Course* I know how to shuck corn," said Lionel, dropping his duffel bag at his feet now that he was inside. Yolanda followed suit.

"Well, we got plenty of it," Magellan said. He slammed
the door shut with his rump. "Found a place on the way
up here selling it for only a dollar a bushel!"

From around the corner there appeared a trim, perfectly
coiffed woman wearing acid-washed jeans, pink Reebok
sneakers, a plastic head-band, and a T-shirt bearing a cartoon
of an anguished woman (the balloon read OH NO! I CAN'T
BELIEVE I FORGOT TO HAVE CHILDREN!). She appeared to be in
her mid-thirties. She smiled and said, "Maybe you should
show them their room first and let them freshen up," and
each syllable was as crisp as a newly minted dollar bill. She

trotted over to them and extended her hand. "Hi, I'm Wilma Tripp. Like the Trippy Awards, only not as prestigious."

"Your hostess for the week," Magellan said while giving her a one-armed hug—as though he didn't trust Lionel to infer the nature of their relationship from her presence alone. (Did he think his bosses hadn't *told* him about her?)

Wilma frowned at the wet spot Magellan's hand had left on her shoulder, then quickly smiled again as Lionel and Yolanda took turns shaking her hand. Lionel found it cold, like a corpse's.

"Your room's this way," she said, leading them with a crooked finger. While Mel Tormé launched into "Lullabye of Birdland," she took them halfway across a large sitting room with a low, oak-beamed ceiling and a fireplace, then paused long enough to turn and say, "Baba, back to work! There are still potatoes to peel."

Baba! Lionel thought, astonished and alarmed. She calls Babcock Magellan, president of All-Pro Power Tools, *Baba*! He wondered how she managed to do this and live.

"This is your inner sanctum for the next week," Wilma said, and she flicked on a light in a tiny, cramped little closet of a room with a dinky twin bed shoved against the wall and a rickety nightstand propped at its side. "No one would dream of bothering you here." She entered and took a turn around the room as if seeing it for the first time herself. Lionel and Yolanda followed and dropped their duffel bags on the floor. "Sorry you can't have a bigger bed," Wilma continued with an almost rehearsed bonhomie; "Baba says you're the junior exec of the bunch, so you get last choice."

"It's okay," Lionel said, trying not to appear mortified. He turned to Yolanda and mouthed the words, I'll sleep on the floor. He zipped open his bag, revealing a pair of patterned boxer shorts; embarrassed, he zipped it shut again.

"Take as much freshening-up time as you like," Wilma said insistently. She'd backed into the doorway, as if wanting to show her awareness that she was now trespassing on private territory. "But the sooner you join us, the sooner you can get the corn shucked, and the sooner we all eat." She smiled to punctuate this happy thought, and left them scurrying to the adjoining bathroom, to slap water onto their faces as quickly as they could.

"Lionel?" Yolanda said as she ran a brush through her hair.

"What?" He was toweling dry his forehead.

"I do not think I am going to like Wilma Tripp."

Lionel detected the first hint of a disaster in the making. And he didn't have long to wait for the second hint, for when he and Yolanda found their way to the kitchen, they were met in the doorway by Deming and Perlman, each of whom was wearing the dopey, schoolboy smile that still stretched across Magellan's face. Behind them, Lionel saw Peg Deming pursing her lips, Becky Perlman whispering something acid, and Wilma Tripp wearing a smile that could've refrozen the polar ice cap.

Instinctively, he knew what had happened. Magellan had rushed to the kitchen and told everyone about Lionel's hot Latin girlfriend, causing the other guys to get giddy with excitement about meeting her, which in turn made her an object of instant detestation for the wives.

Sure enough, Deming and Perlman practically knocked each other over in their efforts to be first through the door to greet her. Beneath their plaid Bermuda shorts, their lumpy red knees actually got hooked together and threatened to trip them before they disentangled themselves and lurched forward. Yolanda made the mistake of giggling at this, causing Becky to hiss something into Peg's ear.

Perlman reached Yolanda first. "Hi, Yolanda—Hackett Perlman," he said, shaking her hand with both of his. "Hacky to my friends. Which I hope you're gonna be one of. Isn't this a great house? Big lake out back. Lake Gilbert. You bring a swimsuit?"

Deming edged him out of the way and took her hand for himself. "Julius Deming—just Julie to you," he said, shaking her whole forearm as though trying to dislocate it from her shoulder. "I'm Lionel's boss at the agency, so you better be nice to me or I'll take my disappointment out on *him.*" He laughed—a little too loudly—and Lionel thought he might die of embarrassment. Yolanda, however, had gone all girlish from the flattery.

She was then introduced to the two wives, who each grazed her fingertips with their own for approximately a nanosecond and said "How do you do?" in the exact tones the Queen of England would use on a foreign dignitary who smelled bad. Then they all turned back to their work—Becky hacking apart lettuce as though it had somehow offended her, Peg slicing vegetables with mathematical precision, Wilma preparing a vinaigrette dressing in a bowl, Magellan peeling russet potatoes, and Deming and Perlman teaming up to dismember a family of chicken carcasses, a pair of beer bottles at their sides.

"Lionel, dear," said Becky with a sweetness he had never heard her use before, "the bag of sweet corn is sitting right by the refrigerator. Would you take it out on the back deck and shuck it, please?"

"Sure," he said, stepping into the kitchen and grabbing the bag. "Yolanda can help."

"Unless," Yolanda said, as though suddenly aware of the need to win over her female cohorts, "there is something I can do here instead?"

"Oh, no, *no*, dear," said Wilma as she dropped a dollop of Dijon mustard into her dressing and began stirring. "We wouldn't *think* of asking you to help, not with those lovely nails of yours. What a shame it'd be if you *broke* one!"

"I do not mind risking that," Yolanda said, looking at her hands as if they had somehow betrayed her.

"Be that as it may, we have everything covered here," said Wilma, still smiling like someone waiting entirely too long for a photographer to snap her picture. "So by all means do go out back and shuck with Lionel."

"Lucky *Lionel,*" Perlman muttered, and Deming almost spit out a mouthful of beer. Wilma looked at them with a face as red as a Bing cherry. The edges of her mouth wilted, but she was still attempting to smile—she looked like she was holding an invisible knife between her teeth. She turned back to her salad dressing. Deming, Perlman, and Magellan all lowered their heads and giggled.

Lionel and Yolanda went out to the back deck, and just as Lionel was closing the glass door behind him, Perlman caught his eye and winked, and gave him a thumb's up.

Lionel nodded in response, then turned to join Yolanda, who was already seated at the edge of the deck, dangling her legs over the side, stripping the canvaslike leaves off the sweet corn. The cornsilk fibers stuck to her fingers and she looked perfectly miserable.

He sat beside her and took up an ear. It was indescribably quiet out here; all they could hear were crickets, and the occasional lapping of Lake Gilbert against the shore. The darkness was near-absolute; the deck was floodlit, but the lake—which, by the sound of it, was just a dozen or so yards away—was invisible.

"What have I gotten you into?" Lionel said as he peeled away his first corn leaf.

"Oh, Lionel," she said with a sigh, "we will be fine. We will go off by ourselves a lot."

"I'm sorry," he said. "I couldn't know that everyone was going to get so *weird* about you."

"Never mind. No one could have known." She wiped some fibers on her jeans.

"Maybe they'll get nicer as they get to know you."

She shrugged, then smiled and said, "Anyway, I am out of Bob's way, and you have a girlfriend to impress your bosses, so everything is the way we wanted it."

"But those women—"

"They do not hire or fire you, Lionel. And their *men* like me. So you should be happy. You brought me here for just that reason."

"But I nev—"

"Are you ever going to finish shucking that ear?" she said, interrupting him in a mock-scolding tone. "I have already finished four."

He rolled his eyes and sighed, but in relief, and the two of them worked in silence for a few minutes.

Then Babcock Magellan surprised them by sliding open the glass door and sticking his head out. "Gonna get eaten alive out here without this," he said, and he tossed them a can of bug repellent. Lionel caught it. "Spray it all over yourselves. I'm not kidding—*all* over. This place is like Insect Disneyland."

"Thanks," said Lionel, offering the can to Yolanda to use first.

"Oh, and Yolanda," he said, "don't mind the she-devils in the kitchen. They're just jealous, that's all. And if they don't warm up to you, I promise the guys and I will beat them till they scream."

She turned her head coquettishly. "They have been very nice so far," she said with convincing ingenuousness. "I do not know what you mean."

"Like hell you don't. Anyway, my son David's coming up tomorrow, too, so if the Bitch Patrol is still giving you grief, you two can at least hang out with him. He's around your own age."

"I didn't know you had a son," said Lionel. He swatted a jumbo-size mosquito just as it landed on his arm. "You never mentioned him."

"Well, he leads—he *led* a kind of reclusive life," Magellan said haltingly. "We didn't see him very—uh—hell, it's no secret. He used to be a priest. Now he's left the Jesuits and he's all torn up about that. Wants to come to the cabin to be by himself and think things over. I told him I'd have Wilma here, and he didn't seem to care. Here's a kid who never even wanted to speak Wilma's *name* before. Go figure *that.* Anyway, he'll be here tomorrow and—actually, I was kind of hoping you two *would* try to cheer him up a little." His eyes brightened and he winked at Yolanda. "Figure *you'd* brighten up just about *anybody's* day."

She smiled. "How sweet. Thank you."

He grinned from ear to ear. He appeared to be absolutely smitten with her. Without another word, he pulled his head back in, slid the door shut, and left Lionel and Yolanda to their shucking.

"That's all we need is a holy roller in spiritual distress waiting for us to hold his hand," Lionel said. "But he's my millionaire client's son, so I guess I'll have to do it."

"Do not jump to conclusions about someone you have yet to meet," said Yolanda. "He may be very different from what you expect."

chapter

■ ■ ■ ■ ■ ■ ■ ■ ■ ■ ■ ■ ■ ■ ■ ■ ■ ■ ■ ■

twenty-eight

Magellan lifted his wine glass and said, "To a week of fun and friendship. And to Deming, Stark and Williams for a hell of a job this year!"

"To Deming, Stark and Williams," echoed the rest of the table, and all downed a mouthful of the wonderfully woody Pinot Grigio. Mel Tormé had moved on to "Mountain Greenery," and platters of food began making their way around the table.

Magellan was sitting to Yolanda's left, and insisted on scooping her a heaping pile of potato salad.

"Oh, Mr. Magellan," she protested, trying to cover her plate with her hands, "thank you, but I will never eat all this!"

"Call me Babcock, and don't be silly," he said. "I made it myself! You wouldn't want to hurt my feelings, would you?"

She seemed to be considering that option, so Lionel gave her a little kick under the table and she yelped, "*No*! No, of course not. I will eat what I can."

"Isn't it horrible how we girls have to starve ourselves to stay so thin and beautiful?" Wilma said, a completely unsympathetic smile on her face. "And for what? So men can paw and drool over us like we're cheap floozies? I wonder why any of us put up with it!" She tried to smile but it looked for all the world like she was baring a set of fangs.

Yolanda merely smiled back and took a bite of the potato salad. "Oh, it is *very* good!" she said. "There is *garlic* in it!"

Magellan seemed overwhelmed with pride. "Yes, yes there *is*!" he said breathily. "I chopped up the garlic myself! Do you really like it?"

She was chewing now, and so resorted to nodding her head enthusiastically.

"Well, *I* can't eat it, then," Becky Perlman said, pushing away the platter of potatoes. "When I was pregnant with my second, Hacky's sister and her godawful brood came to stay for a week and she *insisted* on cooking for us. Well, everything she made had about fifty cloves of garlic in it. And it was the dog days of summer, so of course the next day everyone would start in sweating and at high noon I swear to God you'd think we had the entire Third World in for a visit."

"Becky," Perlman said in a warning tone.

"What?" She pressed her hand to her breast. "Am I lying? Is any of this anything but the truth?" She turned away from him. "At the time, I was having morning sickness, too, so ever since, whenever I smell garlic, I turn *green.* Can't *touch* the stuff."

"It's very good for you though," said Peg Deming, making up for Becky's abstinence by taking a double portion. "Garlic, that is. Helps you live longer. Good for the blood. Unclots your arteries. Gives you good skin tone."

"Yolanda doesn't need it, then," said her husband with an almost juvenile leer on his face. "Her skin's just about as perfect as I've seen."

Yolanda blushed and said, "How sweet. Thank you." Then, a bit self-consciously, she lifted a forkful of her green salad, turned to Wilma and said, "What delicious dressing, too!"

Wilma was far too sophisticated to fall prey to this transparent ploy to win her favor. "Oh," she said, "but it's oil-based, and has lots of cheese shavings and bacon bits in it— all things I'm sure you've crossed off *your* diet, or you wouldn't look so fetchingly *trim,* dear."

Lionel felt his face flush. He'd begun to take offense at the way Wilma kept picking on Yolanda. "Nonsense," he said heartily. "Yolanda practically *lives* on red meat and butter! If she goes a day without a steak, she goes through goddamn *withdrawal.*"

Yolanda looked at him as though he'd gone crazy.

"A girl after my own heart!" Magellan said, and he dared to place a hand on her shoulder. "I'll have to grill us up some big, juicy, fat ones later in the week, okay?" He caught sight of Wilma's laser-cannon stare and quickly removed his hand.

Hackett Perlman was staring at Yolanda now, spinning the stem of his wine glass between his thumb and forefinger. Suddenly one of his eyebrows arched. "You look familiar," he said, his perpetual air of menace reasserting itself for the first time since meeting Yolanda. "I'm certain we've met. What is it you do, Yolanda?"

"I work in a science-fiction bookstore," she said, a little hesitantly.

"Why, we have an entrepreneur at our table!" said Wilma, deliberately misunderstanding her. She clapped her hands. "Oh, I find that *fascinating.* Tell us, is it difficult to get a small business started these days?"

Yolanda shook her head. "I don't *own* the store, I just work there."

She pretended to be surprised. "Oh, silly of me! I must have misheard you. You're a clerk, then? Very interesting, I'm *sure.*"

"Oh, yes it is," Yolanda said with disarming sincerity. "I know it is such a cliché for merchants to say that their stores attract interesting people, but you have no *idea* the kind of customers we get. Some of them are actually quite brilliant, but in a very intense, even *paranoid* kind of way. Some even *scare* me a little."

"Lunatics, is what I'd call them," said Becky. She gave up shoving her chicken leg around her plate and began to feast on a much more appetizing morsel. "My hairdresser, Doris?" she said, almost salivating. "Her boy Eric got involved in this sci-fi thing. He used to go to a friend's house and play this game, Viziers and Vampires I think it was called, where he'd spend hours—hours!—pretending he was a sci-fi character and that this game board everybody played on was an actual real *place* and whatever happened on it, happened to him. Used to get so worked up he didn't know *what* real life was all about anymore. One night he came home upset—told Doris some other player had put a 'curse' on his character. And then he went upstairs and blew his brains out. Doris went a little nuts; she was out *six weeks.* And even after she came back, on two occasions she singed my temple with a curling iron, which, need I say, *never* happened before."

There was an awkward pause after this. Peg Deming cleared her throat and said, "Too much imagination is unhealthy. People like that ought to get more *fresh air.*" She wiped the corners of her mouth and then refolded the napkin into a perfect triangle and centered it exactly in her lap.

"I could *swear* I know you from somewhere," Hackett Perlman said again, like a Nazi SS officer about to pierce the identity of an Allied spy. He turned his head and squinted at her, as though that might help him place her. "Never worked in advertising?"

"No," she said.

"For a film editor? A recording studio?"

"No, no," she said, laughing nervously. "Someone who looks like me, perhaps."

"Looks like you?" he said, scoffing. "*Two* of you, in the same universe? That'd be enough to make *me* believe in God."

Becky shot him a glance that almost physically toppled him.

"I read a lot of science fiction when I was a kid," said Magellan. "You know Issac Asimov? Arthur C. Clarke? Ray Bradbury?"

"Oh, very well indeed," she said, and they began spouting the arcana of their chosen genre, leaving the others no point of entry, until tempers had somewhat cooled.

After the meal, Magellan and Wilma began clearing away the dishes, and despite their commands that everyone else remain seated, Peg, who couldn't stand to witness a cleanup operation in which she had no part, leapt to her feet and began helping them, which of course obliged Becky to grudgingly do the same. Yolanda excused herself and went to the bathroom.

Lionel, Perlman, and Deming stayed seated at the table, finishing the last of the wine and placing their hands over their bulging bellies. After a few moments of listening to the commotion in the kitchen, which completely drowned out Mel Tormé, Deming said, "Lionel, long as we've got a moment alone here, Hack and I would like to have a word with you."

Lionel's heart quickened. "Oh yeah?"

Deming nodded. "You've been with the agency for a couple of years now, and you've done a great job. Maybe you've had some reverses that weren't your fault—I mean, no one blames you for Romeo Springs—and maybe you haven't brought any new clients on board, but All-Pro's still our biggest client, and I know for a *fact,* Lionel, that other agencies have tried to woo them away from us."

Lionel licked his lips nervously. He had no idea where this was leading. "I'd heard rumors," he said.

Deming and Perlman both nodded. Then Deming continued, "But you've kept Magellan happy through it all. Not just happy, but—hell, *look* at us, here. The guy treats us like we're part of his fuckin' *fami—*"

"Get the salad bowl, will you, dear?" said Wilma to Peg as the two women reappeared at the table. Wilma picked up the heavy wooden cutting board that had held the chicken, then started back to the kitchen with it. "Just be careful," she said as she and Peg rounded the corner. "That bowl has a lot of sentimental value. It's the first thing Baba and I bought together when we got this place, just after we met, and it's the first thing we ever picked out togeth—" A shattering crash ended her reverie.

A long pause. Then, "Never mind, dear, it wasn't *terribly* expensive."

Deming rolled his eyes and turned back to Lionel. "Anyway, what we're saying is, we're considering you for partnership."

Lionel's heart almost exploded out of his chest. "You're kidding."

Perlman shook his suntanned head and, for once, seemed virtually *benevolent.* "Gary Stark's dead," he said, "Don Williams is dead, and Julie and I are the only partners left. And, I mean, we're not *old,* certainly, but we want to ensure the future of the agency. And you're the only one who cares enough to keep the place going."

"So it's just *me*?" he said, dumbfounded. "What about Wenck?"

"Carlton?" Deming wrinkled his nose and shook his head. "Too much of a hotshot. No *loyalty*. Someone comes along tomorrow and offers him a ten-thousand dollar raise, he's *gone*. You think we don't know that? Plus, he's just not partnership material. That whole business with Gloria— now, I don't hold it against him, not really—not as an employer, anyway—but can you imagine a *partner* acting like that?"

"Not to mention," said Perlman, leaning forward, "the guy risked his reputation for a fling with *Gloria Gimbek*." He shook his head in disbelief. "I mean, come *on*. I'm gonna screw around with a married co-worker, she'd better at least be a *primo* piece of ass."

"That's another thing," said Deming with a smirk. "Your taste in women is *way* better than his. First Tracy, now this hot little Yolanda ..."

As if on cue, Yolanda came back from the bathroom looking radiant and happy. "Did I miss anything?" she asked, resuming her seat.

Lionel stared at her with mouth open, unable to speak. Then Wilma reappeared with Peg and Becky in tow, each of them with dishtowels in their hands. She looked straight at Yolanda and cheerfully said, "Is the noise in the kitchen too loud? None of us wants to disturb your conversation out here."

Yolanda shot Lionel an amused glance, then got up and said, "You really must let me help."

"No, no," said Wilma at once, then an instant later, adding, "Well, if you *insist*."

chapter

■ ■ ■ ■ ■ ■ ■ ■ ■ ■ ■ ■ ■ ■ ■ ■ ■

twenty-nine

"Not a goddamn thing to buy in this town," Becky Perlman snarled into Peg Deming's ear. She looked back at Lionel, who was a few paces behind her. Lionel looked in a window and pretended to have heard nothing. Satisfied, she continued: "All these barns filled with crap any decent person would've thrown out in nineteen-thirty. Is *this* what we have to look forward to all week?"

"Of course, it's all very *tidy*," Peg said, trying to give the town the benefit of the doubt. It was a warm day, and her face was more florid than usual. She shifted her Volkswagen-size purse to her other arm. "But we haven't passed any-place decent to *eat* yet. I'm beginning to think people in these parts don't touch anything that hasn't been glazed or fried in lard."

They were on the outskirts of Wild Rose, along a rural route dotted with old farmhouses chock-filled with antiques for sale. At Wilma's urging, they'd parked at one such place, an enormous barn with a door barely hanging by its hinges; it was filled with rickety furniture, ancient dolls, tin advertising signs, yellowing china, and an entire wall of brittle player-piano rolls. The accumulation of so much useless history made Lionel's head ache. He told Yolanda he'd wait outside.

Peg and Becky, whose *nouveau riche* sensibilities wouldn't allow them to purchase anything that hadn't been manufactured in the past year and subsequently sold at full retail, were completely disenchanted with this outing. The only reason they'd agreed to it was that their husbands had refused to lend them their cars, effectively stranding them at the cabin. So when Lionel and Yolanda had decided to drive into town on an exploratory mission, the women—Wilma included—put aside their dislike of Yolanda and jumped at the chance to escape. They'd squeezed themselves into Lionel's not extraordinarily spacious Celica, and left Magellan, Perlman, and Deming to fish in peace off the pier.

At first, Lionel had thought he'd made a mistake, agreeing to squire the women around town when he should be staying at the cabin with the menfolk, on whose good opinion his future depended. But before he could change his mind, Magellan took him aside, winked at him, and said, "Thanks for getting the magpies out of our hair, Lionel. I know you and Yolanda must've wanted to be alone, but trust me, we'll make it up to you later." He paused. "Listen, long as you're in town, you mind picking up my son David at the bus stop at twelve-twenty? You'll recognize him—looks like me. A real hunk." He laughed. "Only blond, green eyes. Probably carrying a big suitcase with a Notre Dame sticker on it."

Lionel had agreed. What else could he do? He checked his watch now; it was close to noon. He turned with impatience toward the entrance to the barn, just in time to see Yolanda and Wilma exit from opposite sides. Yolanda was carrying a mottled, decrepit rocking chair, and Wilma had her arms around an enormous wooden picture frame. He dashed over to them.

"Oh, *my*," Wilma was saying to Yolanda when he reached them. "Have you bought that, dear?"

"Yes," Yolanda answered, lowering the chair to the ground and wiping her dusty hands on her cut-offs. "I thought I could strip it and refinish it and put it in my living room."

"So clever of you," cooed Wilma. "But, what a *pickle* that

puts us in. You see, *I* just bought this *frame*, and I very
much doubt that Lionel's trunk will hold *both* our little
finds."

Yolanda looked at Wilma blankly, as if unable to comprehend what she was getting at.

"I'll tell you what," Wilma continued, patting the frame,
"I'll just take this back and ask the shopkeeper to hold it
for me until I can come back and get it. I'm sure I can
convince Baba to drive me back here during the week. And
if not—well, I'm sure I'll think of *something*."

"*No,*" Lionel cried. He grabbed the chair from Yolanda, who
for a moment resisted letting him have it. "We've already
planned to come back here during the week ourselves, Wilma,
so I'll just have the shopkeeper hold on to Yolanda's chair,
instead." He looked at Yolanda, imploring her to understand.
"We can pick it up tomorrow or the next day."

"We are coming back?" she asked.

"Yes. Remember? I *told* you." Come on, Yolanda, get with
the program!

All at once her face lit up. "*Oh,*" she said. "*Yes.* When
we come *back.* Of course, yes. We can get my rocking chair
then."

"You're sure?" said Wilma with an uncanny impression
of sincerity. "I wouldn't want to put you out."

"I am quite sure," said Yolanda, nodding.

"Well, then, thank you, dear," she said, smiling coldly.
She headed toward Lionel's car.

Lionel rushed the chair back into the barn. The geriatric
proprietor took about six full minutes to prepare a label for
it. He had Lionel spell out Yolanda's name letter by letter
as he inscribed the tag, and yet when he affixed it to the
chair Lionel saw that it read HOLD FOR ROLAND A. REYNOSO.
He didn't even bother to correct him, but raced back to the
car and found the four women waiting in varying degrees of
impatience. He unlocked the door and they piled in.

"Guess we should head back to town now," he said. "See
if we can grab a bite to eat somewhere, and wait for David
Magellan's bus."

"Oh, we're picking up David, as well?" Wilma said,
feigning delight. "Baba didn't tell me that! He must've
wanted it to be a surprise."

Lionel started the car. "He asked me to do it before we left the cabin."

"Well," said Wilma with a clattering, phony laugh, "what a good thing all us girls are so slender! I'm sure we wouldn't have much room for the dear boy otherwise."

Becky Perlman was so upset by this news that she wouldn't even speak. She clutched her purse in her lap and looked out the car window, her head rigid and her lips white. Peg Deming, seated in the middle with her elbows pressed into her sides, was going through her purse with great difficulty. "That greasy breakfast is really talking back to me," she said, shaking her head. "And these bumpy roads don't help, I tell you—*ah*!" She pulled out a package of Aspergum and popped a piece into her mouth.

Lionel shifted into drive, steered the unhealthily heavy Celica onto the road, and made for the center of town. The cool of the morning had begun to ebb, and the pavement was giving off waves of heat. He could feel his T-shirt sticking to his back.

A short while later he was following the women up the quaint streets of the business district, with Wilma pointing out the various dining spots and judging them on the basis of the shade of green Peg turned when she described each menu. Lionel took the opportunity to survey the other people on the street. Many were immediately recognizable as seasonal visitors; their clothes were too cute, their sunglasses too expensive, their attitudes too happy-go-lucky. The town natives seemed to regard them begrudgingly, as a necessary evil. He wondered what they thought when they got an eyeful of *his* group: three middle-aged *Town & Country* wanna-be's, a young Latin beauty with a music-video saunter, and a hapless male wandering behind them wearing a Lloyd Llewellyn T-shirt.

Eventually they found a little diner whose menu boasted both leek soup and assorted sherberts, which Peg decided wouldn't be so horrible, so they entered and requested a table. Lionel, aware of the time, tried to hurry them through ordering so that they could meet David at the appointed hour, but Wilma, who was apparently miffed that she hadn't been consulted about picking up her lover's son, made a point of reading through the entire menu aloud and commenting on how good each item sounded before consenting to choose one. As a result, Lionel's patty melt and fries had only just arrived when the minute hand of his watch slipped into alignment with the faux brass VI on the perimeter.

"Jesus," he muttered in frustration, and wished that Wilma might choke on her tuna salad. He wolfed down half the patty melt, gulped at his Diet Coke, and dumped his fries into a napkin, which he carried out with him. "Gotta run across town to get David Magellan," he said as he rose from his chair. "Take your time with lunch; I should be back in ten minutes or so." He lowered his head and whispered to Yolanda, "Take care of my share, okay? I'll pay you back."

She nodded, but her wide-eyed expression said, Don't leave me alone with these three harpies!

The bus stop was both near enough and far enough to cause him to stop and consider whether to walk or drive. Hell with it, he thought; I'll walk. It'll take longer, but let Wilma sit and stew for awhile. Do her some good.

He'd only glanced at the bus stop on his way into town and so got lost twice trying to relocate it, but he refused to panic. He'd just finished his fries and deposited the greasy napkin in a trash can when he spotted a tall, blond stranger walking this way, past the Post Office, carrying a suitcase with a Notre Dame sticker on it.

Well, that could only be one person. And when Lionel took a closer look at him, he felt his stomach spin like a top.

David Magellan was *beautiful.*

Hair the color and texture of flax; eyes as startlingly green as a suburban lawn during a rainstorm; a chin with a cleft deep enough to hold a bookmark. Lionel reeled; he had to warn himself to be careful. This was, unexpectedly, the figure of his most venerable fantasy: the sexy seminarian—the gorgeous Jesuit. He hadn't entertained any fantasies until now because he'd naturally assumed David would look like his father.

His father! That was the danger. This was his client's son. And even if he weren't, he probably wouldn't relish being the object of someone's homosexual crush.

As all of this was gushing through Lionel's head, David's

approach narrowed, and he appeared to be perplexed by the way this stranger was staring at him. Lionel had to shake himself out of his stupor before he could pass and say, "David Magellan?"

David turned; the veins in his neck made him look ascetic and irresistible. "Yes?" he said. Ah—a high-pitched voice. He wasn't *perfect,* then. Lionel was almost relieved.

He extended his hand. "I'm Lionel Frank. One of your father's guests this week. I'm in town with some of the others and he asked you to pick me up." He shook his head. "I mean, he asked *me* to pick *you* up." He giggled nervously.

"Oh," said David. He looked at his shoes and sighed, as if he'd expected something like this. Lionel realized that this man was in the midst of a personal crisis, and had probably been hoping to have a few minutes alone with his father before getting to the house. But instead, his father had sent Lionel. He looked up again. "You're kind of late," he said. "I thought maybe Dad had forgotten me. I was walking into town to see if I could get a cab."

"Oh, I've got my car," said Lionel a little too eagerly.

David hefted his suitcase into his other hand and said, "Great." He looked around a little bewilderedly. "Where is it?"

Lionel winced. "Well—fact is, I walked here from the restaurant where we were all having lunch. It's a hike." David rolled his eyes and Lionel blurted, "See, I saw the bus stop on the way in and I guess because I was driving I didn't realize how far it was from the center of town. Here," he said, reaching out for the suitcase, "let me carry that."

"That's okay," said David as he resumed his walk.

"No, seriously, it's the least I can do." He ran after him, reaching for the suitcase.

David ignored him and kept going. Lionel gave up and just walked beside him, his head hanging low.

It was blisteringly hot by now, and that, added to Lionel's acute embarrassment, was enough to shift his sweat glands into overdrive. As he walked beside the searingly handsome David in awful silence, he kept wiping his forehead with his arm, then wiping his arm on his shirt, till he looked down and noticed that he'd made an appalling damp smudge over his stomach.

David stopped at a corner next to a gas station. "Where do I go from here?" he asked.

"Left," Lionel said, grateful to have the silence broken. As they rounded the corner, he said, "You've never been here before?"

David shook his head. "Been invited plenty of times, but it's really Dad and Wilma's place, and I'm kind of loyal to my mom. She doesn't even know I'm here now. It'd really hurt her, and she's been hurt enough."

Lionel didn't know what to say to this, so he put his hands in his pockets and said nothing.

"I'm sure my dad's told you that I've just left the priesthood," David said, almost accusingly.

Lionel wasn't about to reveal his million-dollar client's indiscretion to his son, no matter how beautiful he was, so he chuckled nervously and looked away.

"It's okay," David said, shifting his suitcase again. "I didn't ask him to keep it a secret. Not that he would've if I had."

"Hey, it's your business," Lionel said.

"That's right, it's my business." As soon as he'd said this, a guilty look flickered across his face, and he added, "Sorry, this has nothing to do with you. I shouldn't treat you like you're some kind of adversary. I don't even know you."

"Well," said Lionel with absurd joviality, "you will soon!" When David looked mystified and somewhat alarmed by this, he explained, "Pretty close quarters up at the cabin, and all."

"Great," said David. Lionel never knew so much sarcasm could drip from a single syllable.

If only I could stop *looking* at him! Lionel thought. But those *cheekbones*! How did a simian thug like Babcock Magellan ever produce anything as sublime as *this*?

They walked another block until Lionel couldn't bear the silence any longer, and was about to comment uselessly on how close the restaurant now was, when they rounded yet another corner and ended up directly in the path of someone carrying an ice-cream cone.

"Sorry," said Lionel, and as he stepped aside he looked up for a split-second and was struck by a thunderbolt of recognition. *"Kevin?"* he exclaimed.

"Typical Lionel, always in a hurry," said this man from

his past, this former lover. Kevin had grown leaner, more muscular, his body rippling out of a tank-top, Madras shorts and royal-blue boat shoes. He licked at his strawberry ice-cream cone and said, "What the hell are *you* doing here?"

For a moment Lionel was too stunned to speak, but the intensity of David Magellan's questioning eyes on him prompted him to dribble out an answer. "I—I—I'm—here on business."

"Business? In Wild Rose, Wisconsin?" Kevin laughed, and his tongue darted out of his mouth and flicked the ice-cream residue off his mustache.

"Well, *well,* not really, not *really,*" he said, achingly aware that he was sounding a lot like Aunt Lola. "My bosses and I are up here as guests of my client who—who—who's rewarding us for the job we did this year."

Kevin chuckled derisively. "Mighty white of him." A blob of chalky pink ice-cream fell on his forearm; he wiped it up with his thumb and then stuck his thumb in his mouth.

"This, this, *this* is my client's *son,*" said Lionel, trying not to notice how the entire world was whirling around him. "Kevin Glasser, this is David Magellan, son of Babcock Magellan, *president* of All-Pro Power Tools."

David dropped his suitcase and shook Kevin's hand. "Bet you're impressed as *hell* by that," he said.

Kevin laughed, and Lionel felt a surge of panic. Not quite a minute yet, and already they were in league against him. How had reality managed to derail so completely in the last half-hour? This was stupefying!

An older man in a Forbidden Broadway T-shirt and paisley shorts joined them, carrying his own ice-cream cone, this one chocolate. Lionel was only dimly aware of him as he asked Kevin, "So why are *you* up here?"

Kevin nodded toward the older man. "Stephen has a summer house up here," he said. "Stephen Ailies, this is Lionel Frank, one of my old—or should I say one of my *ex*—"

"One of your cast of thousands, eh?" Stephen mercifully interjected. He shook Lionel's quivering hand. "Pleased to meet you, Lionel."

"And this is David—sorry, what was your last name again?"

"Magellan, David Magellan." He shook Stephen's hand.

"Stephen's my spouse," Kevin explained, just before letting his tongue lap up a wide slick of ice-cream that was threatening to spill off the cone.

The four men stood smiling for a moment until Lionel felt the ground start to give way and knew he'd better get moving before Kevin said anything else in front of David. "Listen, it was great to see you," he said, and his voice actually broke, "and good to meet *you*, Stephen, but we're running late. We left some people waiting for us at a restaurant."

Kevin and Stephen both had smears of ice cream on their lips now—one brown, one pink. They looked like a matched set: trim, handsome, mustachioed salt-and-pepper shakers. No one could look at them and not know they were a couple. Kevin and Lionel had never looked like that when *they* were together. But then, they'd never really *been* a couple. Lionel, ever fearful, hadn't let them be.

David bade them good-bye, and they'd gone about six yards when Kevin called out, "HEY, HOW'S SPENCER?"

Lionel turned his head and called back, "FINE, FINE," then waved again to signal that he was moving on.

"BE INTERESTED IN BUYING HIM FROM YOU," Kevin called.

Lionel just shook his head and smiled, then quickened his pace.

"Old roommate," he said to David the second they were out of earshot.

David grinned mischievously and said, "I gathered." And Lionel didn't at all like the way he said it.

When they reached the restaurant, they found the women waiting out front. Becky appeared to have cornered Wilma and Peg, and was relating in great detail how the waitress had cheated them on the bill. Yolanda was off to the side, in a world of her own.

When the two men reached them, Wilma gave them a pained look and said, "Hello, David. Been a few years."

"A few," he replied atonally. There was no kiss, not even a handshake. The tension in the air could've choked a small dog.

David was introduced to the others, and as soon as this was accomplished Becky pursed her lips and said, "How are we supposed to fit his suitcase in the trunk if Wilma's *frame* is already in there? I'm not having that thing sitting on *my* lap. My knees are bad enough as it is."

Lionel's eyes fell shut in dismay. He'd forgotten all about Wilma's fucking frame.

To his astonishment, Wilma herself piped up with a suggestion. "Let's just tie my frame to the roof of the car," she said. "I'm sure we can buy a length of rope somewhere in the vicinity." She peered down the street for a possible vendor.

"That's *okay* with you?" Lionel asked, with perhaps too much incredulity.

"It's only a *frame,* Lionel," she said snappishly. "I don't demand that you treat it as though it were *precious* just because it's *mine.* I'm not a *monster,* you know." Lionel couldn't help but think of Richard Nixon saying, I am not a crook.

She set off in search of some rope. And all at once he understood: she didn't dare be rude to David, or inconvenience him in any way. He was, after all, her lover's son. If push came to shove, and Magellan had to choose between them—well, Wilma, being Wilma, wasn't going to *let* push come to shove.

Yolanda approached Lionel and touched him on the shoulder, then withdrew her hand as though she'd gotten an electric shock. "Lionel, what is the *matter?*" she whispered. "You are white as a sheet, and your clothes are *drenched* in cold sweat."

He looked at her, at her beautiful, wide, wet eyes, and his throat closed up with exhausted emotion. All he could manage to croak was, "Later."

■ ■ ■ ■ ■ ■ ■ ■ ■ ■ ■ ■ ■ ■ ■ ■ ■ ■ ■

thirty

D avid's presence unsettled the air in the cabin. The way his father greeted him at the door was loud and glad and phony, with Wilma at his side, her smile at its ghastliest. It left everyone feeling uncomfortable, so while David unpacked his bags, the guests took the opportunity to slip out the door. Better to leave father, son, and mistress to complete their reunion in private.

Lionel and Yolanda found their way to the boathouse, where they sat dangling their feet in the lake and drinking Diet Coke out of cans. Lionel was trying to figure out how to begin to tell her about his powerful attraction toward David and his run-in with Kevin, and about the peril both of these developments posed him, when she beat him to the punch by saying, "Lionel, I must tell you something that will disturb you."

His heart stuttered. *Now* what? "I'm listening," he said as calmly as possible.

"You may have noticed the way Hackett Perlman has been staring at me."

"Yes," he said, suddenly alerted to the possibility of a new and provocative danger. "Last night at dinner, and just now, when he was being introduced to David. Couldn't take his eyes off you."

She moved her foot in a circle and caused a rippling in the water. "Well, it is very possible that he will remember where he has seen me before."

He shut his eyes and steeled himself. "Which is where?"

The answer was worse than he could've imagined. "He used to be a regular customer at the house where I worked." She paused. "As a call girl."

His fingers involuntarily loosened. His Diet Coke slipped out of his hand and fell into the lake, where its murky contents gushed out and clouded the water.

"Jesus *Christ*," he said. "You never told me!"

"Well, no." She took an emboldening swig out of her own can. "I suppose I was trying to put it behind me. Certainly I had no wish to share it with others."

"So Perlman was one of your—what's the word—*johns*?"

She shook her head and started circling her foot even faster, churning the water to what looked like a rapid boil. "He always asked for another one of the girls, Francine. But I was usually in the lounge when he came in. He saw me there many times, Lionel. I think it is likely he will soon remember that."

"So, let me get this straight," he said, feeling hope spill out of him the way the Diet Coke had spilled out of his can. "The man who has just offered to make me a partner in his agency because of my exemplary professional conduct, is close to discovering that I've brought a hooker to my client's summer house."

She looked pale, almost bloodless, but she met his withering stare. "This is exactly what I was afraid of," she said in a low voice. "This is why I never told you. This is why I never told Bob. Especially after your crack about me not being a blonde debutante named Phoebe. How could I risk it?"

He shook his head. "I'm sorry, Yolanda. It's not that *I* think any less of you—I mean, who am I to be judgmental? But *those* guys," he said, tossing his head in the direction of the cabin. "I mean, *Christ.* What will *they* think?"

She finished off her own can and tossed it behind her, into the boathouse. "Well, at least *you* do not think less of me," she said, and it was a full four seconds before he realized she'd meant to be sarcastic.

"Oh, come *on*, now," he said. "Don't accuse me of that! I'm not a *hypocrite.*" She gave him a heavy-lidded look and he threw up his hands. "I'm *not.* Not any more than *you* are, anyway."

"What is *that* supposed to mean?"

"Well—have you told *Emil* about this?" he said triumphantly, thinking, I've got her now.

"Not exactly," she said.

"Well, then." He grunted in satisfaction.

"I did not *tell* him. He *asked* me."

"What?"

"He *asked* me if I was a prostitute. The second time we met, when he pretended to have come to see you, and ended up in my apartment."

He clasped his hands to his head. "I don't believe any of this."

"He told me that I was beautiful and arousing, and that I would make a good prostitute, if in fact I was not one already. At first I was so offended, but then I looked into his eyes and I saw that he meant no disrespect, that he was sincere. So I told him that I was not now a prostitute, but that I had been at one time. And he smiled so grandly. He said he knew I must have been. Because he knew I was the perfect woman, and a prostitute *is* his idea of a perfect woman. He calls prostitutes 'high priestesses of anarchism.' "

"Oh, yeah. I *do* remember hearing that."

"I honestly think that if I did not have this in my past, he would be far less interested in me."

He snorted. "Well, so much for his interest in your *mind.*"

"No," she said angrily, "that, too. He is interested in me, as a *whole.* Lionel, you are being *awful.*" Her voice had a hairline fracture in it that threatened to break completely if he weren't careful. "He helped me to see that there was no shame in what I had done, that it was in fact a tribute to my integrity that I had not let false standards stop me from practicing my chosen trade."

Lionel shook his head in bewilderment. "False standards?" he said.

"Oh, the way people go on," she said furiously, "pro-claiming that a woman has a right to do what she wants with her body! What they mean is, if she wants to have an abortion. *Then* all right-thinking people will stand by her in support. But if she just wants to *sell* her body, suddenly the principle no longer applies. They shake their heads and say, 'We must stop that woman.' *That* is hypocrisy, Lionel."

He couldn't think of an answer for that, so he thought he'd better change the subject. "How did you get into that—line of work, anyway?"

She leaned back and propped herself up on her elbows. "I suppose it is my mother's fault."

"Isn't it always?" He was feeling a little sarcastic himself.

She ignored him. "I told you how she was always telling me of my future in a convent. She nearly brainwashed me into becoming a nun. So even after I finally rebelled and ran away from home, I was so accustomed to thinking of myself as a novice nun that it seemed only natural that I ended up living in a house with a group of other women." She shrugged. "The differences did not seem so profound, back then. The only major one was that, in a convent, all the women are married to a man who is not there. And in Mrs. Craven's house, the women were married to *any* man who was there."

He had to think about that for a few seconds. Then he shook his head clear and said, "When did you get out of it?"

She lifted her leg out of the water and scraped a soggy, fallen leaf from where it had settled on her calf. "Well, I was still fascinated with the life I had chosen *not* to live— the life of the convent," she said, lowering her leg back into the water. "I used to read about nuns all the time. I had books and pictures of them all around my room. Mrs. Craven encouraged it, because so many of the men found that to be a turn-on. She even bought me a nun's habit, but only one of my clients ever asked me to wear it. It was stiff and starchy, so I was glad to keep it in the closet. But another client of mine was an S.F. fan, and one day he gave me some battered copies of Frank Herbert's *Dune* books, and he said, 'You will like these, there are outer-space nuns in them.' And so I read them. And almost at once I cared less about the nuns than I did about the *ideas*—environmentalism, messianism, the manipulation of gene pools, all of that. And that started me off on my love of science fiction. Pretty soon there was nothing I wanted to do more than read S.F. So I left Mrs. Craven and got the job at Live Long and Prosper, and ever since I have been happily spending my days behind the counter reading every S.F. novel that comes out." She smiled beatifically. "I *told* you that S.F. is my inner life, Lionel. It is the only one that is important to me now. That old life—it seems like a million years ago. Like an existence in a parallel reality."

"So you have no plans to go back to it?"

"Oh, Madonna, *no,*" she said in surprise. She folded her hands in her lap and kicked at the water. "Although Emil *did* cajole me into getting out my old suitcase of, well, 'tools of the trade,' and we have been putting those to good use ever since."

This was quite a bit more than he cared to know, so he held up one hand and said, "Okay, okay. I get the picture."

They sat in silence for a moment. Lionel's mind was reeling. How had all this happened? Where on the drive to Wild Rose had he taken a wrong turn and ended up in the Twilight Zone?

Yolanda broke the silence by saying, "Now it is your turn. Tell me what happened in town today that upset you so much."

He shook his head. "Not now, Yolanda. Telling my story now would be like showing the cartoon *after* the feature film."

chapter

■■■■■■■■■■■■■■■■■■■■

thirty-one

There were four canoes in the boathouse, and just before dusk Lionel and the other men pulled them out and plopped them into the lake, then stood ankle-deep and extended their hands to help the women get on board. With each canoe brandishing a pair of champagne glasses and an ice-cold bottle of Veuve Clicquot, they paddled to the center of Lake Gilbert to watch the sun set and to toast the arrival of night.

It had been Wilma's idea: "So *romantic,* don't you think?" she'd said in a tone of voice that made it clear she didn't really want anyone else's opinion. Still, Yolanda, for her part, agreed, and told Lionel she only wished she didn't have to sit on the lake under the setting sun sipping champagne with *him.* Becky and Peg, however, appeared to have no enthusiasm for the idea at all.

When the four canoes had reached the middle of the lake (the Demings arriving far behind the rest; Julie was having no end of trouble paddling), the men popped the corks amidst bursts of shrieks and laughter, and filled everyone's glass to the rim. When they were raised high, the glasses caught eight distorted reflections of the salmon-colored setting sun. "To a breathtaking evening," said Magellan, and after he'd been appropriately echoed, everyone took a swallow and settled in to watch the sun's descent.

As the world grew more amber, the canoes drifted farther and farther apart, and the champagne assumed a more ceremonial aspect. Lionel leaned back and sighed, feeling almost primeval. Yolanda crossed her legs and smiled at him. Words were unnecessary. For a moment, they were suspended in time, safe from the uncertainties of the future. For a moment, they were alone together in a twilight world where no one could intrude.

Or *nearly* no one. From across the expanse of lake to his right, he heard Wilma say, in what she must have thought a low voice but what amounted to a stage whisper, "I don't care. He's your *son.* You've got to say *something.* I don't demand that he love me, but he could at least be *civil.*"

"You're both adults. Work it out between yourselves," Magellan replied in his normal, booming voice.

"Quiet!" she said urgently. "He'll *hear* you!"

"We're in the middle of Lake *Gilbert,* for God's sake! How's he gonna hear us all the way up at the *house?*"

Then, from across the lake to Lionel's left, Becky's voice creeped spiderlike over the water: "Of course *she's* wearing a sweater. *She* stays here every summer, so *she* knows how cold it gets on the lake at night. But does she tell *us?* Oh, *no.* So we end up sitting out here with bare arms freezing while *she* tugs her four-hundred-dollar designer angora around her and smiles like everything's just *grand.*"

Well, Lionel thought, Wilma might be miserable, but Becky was clearly having the time of her life. He chuckled, and Yolanda, who had also overheard, shook her head and rolled her eyes.

When the sun had disappeared completely behind the trees that bordered the lake, he took a deep breath, held it for a moment, and then let it seep out like the air from a punctured tire. Under a canopy of bright new stars, he looked at Yolanda.

"Blessed Madonna," she said to him with a gush of longing, "how I *wish* you were Emil!"

He extended his bare leg and rubbed it companionably against hers. "I understand," he said. "I wish you were Emil, too."

At this, she gave such a hoot of laughter that from far across the lake, Babcock Magellan cried, "HEY, WAS THAT YOLANDA?"

"WELL, WE KNOW IT WASN'T *BECKY,*" called Deming.

"LIONEL, WHATEVER YOU'RE DOING TO THAT GIRL," Magellan continued, his words slurred from too much champagne, "YOU JUST STOP IT—AT LEAST TILL WE GET THERE TO WATCH!"

"WHAT DO YOU MEAN, 'WE KNOW IT'S NOT BECKY'?" yelled Becky with an edge to her voice that could've cut glass.

Laughter bubbled up from all around the lake.

"I'M NOT KIDDING!" she nearly shrieked. "WHAT DID YOU *MEAN*?"

Sensing that the excursion had ended, Lionel took up his paddles and started heading toward shore. He could barely make out the boathouse in the inky darkness.

"HEY, I KNOW WHAT WE CAN DO," hollered Magellan. "LET'S HAVE A RACE BACK TO THE BOATHOUSE! WHOEVER LOSES HAS TO WASH DISHES TONIGHT!"

"YOU'RE ON!" cried Perlman.

Suddenly the night was alive with the slapping of paddles against the water and the high-pitched protests of the wives. Lionel, who by the merest chance had gained himself a head start, could tell from the direction of the sounds that he was in the lead.

"GO, LIONEL, GO," Yolanda urged him, clinging to the side of the canoe.

He could now discern the outline of the boathouse against the velvet glow of the night sky. He bore down, working the paddles like pistons. The wind ripped through his hair like a wild animal, the spray of the water flecked his cheeks and lips, and everything was movement, action, energy—it was so exciting to be alive, so exhilarating to be *winning.*

The black mass of the boathouse soon blotted out the sky, and moments later his canoe plowed into the sandy slope at its base.

"WE WIN!" he and Yolanda screamed. They jumped onto the shore, and then just continued jumping. *"WE WIN! WE WIN!"*

"Stop this," came the harsh, reedy voice of Wilma, closing in fast behind them. "We're going to disturb the neighbors! And someone is going to get hur—"

Magellan's canoe collided with Lionel's, resulting in a deafening thud followed by a deep, resounding splash. Lionel could make out two figures in the water. He knelt down and helped one of them to its feet. It turned out to be Babcock Magellan, who laughed aloud and spurted water from his lips as he did so.

Then, as the other canoes approached more cautiously, he knelt down to help Wilma, who had crawled up the embankment on all fours. He put his hand on her shoulder; the angora sweater was soaked and cold. It felt like a dead cat.

Wilma took his hand, got to her feet, then snapped her arm away from him and said, "I'm all right now, I don't need anyone's—*oh!*" She'd turned her ankle, and now fell backward, landing rump-first in the water again.

Magellan positively *roared,* his laughter bouncing across the water and echoing from the other side of the lake.

No one else was quite so stupid.

Wilma said nothing—not even a syllable—but merely got back to her feet and started her long, drippy trek up to the house. Lionel was glad it was too dark to see her face. The others started after her, with Lionel and Yolanda bringing up the rear. Magellan—still merry with laughter—stayed behind to lock up the boathouse for the night.

By the time Lionel and Yolanda reached the house, the others had gone in. Through the back windows, Lionel could see that Peg and the drenched, scowling Wilma were now slipping into the house's two bathrooms. He tapped Yolanda on the shoulder and said, "You go on in. All that champagne, then the excitement of the race—no *way* can I wait for those two to get out. I've got to piss like sixty."

She nodded and whispered, "Can we laugh about Wilma yet?"

"No. Maybe in a year or two."

She giggled, darted into the house, and shut the sliding glass door behind her.

Lionel grabbed his crotch and loped halfway back to the boathouse, then remembered Magellan was still down there and darted to his right, into the growth of trees that surrounded the property. He had just unzipped his zipper and yanked out his penis when he heard Magellan coming up the path behind him.

Shy about being seen urinating, he crept a few yards farther, then got to his knees and, as noiselessly as possible, let his stream of urine flow against the trunk of a tree. He felt an inestimable relief. His head cleared, his ears came unstopped. Everything in him relaxed.

And he heard voices.

Two of them, at least. He couldn't yet tell if there were more. Coming from somewhere a little farther in. He zipped himself up, got to his feet, and, ignoring the mosquitoes and horseflies that were now beginning to prey on him, he inched toward the area where he thought the voices were originating. The floodlights from the house gave him minimal visibility, but it was enough to allow him to move quietly, without snapping too many branches or twigs.

"—ill wish you hadn't come here," said a voice he now recognized as David's. "I asked you not to. I asked you to respect my decision."

"You asked it in a *letter,*" said the other voice—another man's, but more shrill, more precise. "All this time you've been planning this little adventure and you never had the guts to tell your *friends.*"

"This is exactly *why* I didn't tell you," David said. "It's *not* an adventure. This is a moral, ethical, and *personal* decision."

Lionel could see them now. David was sitting on a rock, plucking the leaves off some kind of wildflower. The other man was pacing back and forth. He was considerably older than David, wearing jeans and a windbreaker. From what he had said, Lionel guessed him to be a fellow priest. His pulse quickened at the hint of real intrigue.

"Well, *well,*" said the presumed priest. He turned and a tiny, intense red glow burned through the darkness for a second; he'd obviously just taken a drag off a cigarette. "Listen to Mother Superior!" he continued. "Better than the rest of us, is that it?"

David let loose with a deep sigh. "All I said was, I can't reconcile living an actively homosexual life with acting as an agent of an institution that condemns homosexuality."

Lionel's knees gave way and he lurched face-forward into a birch tree.

David and the priest both looked in his direction, but apparently saw nothing. The priest turned back to David, took another puff of his cigarette, and said, "None of the *rest* of us has any trouble reconciling that."

"That's fine for you, then," said David. "I can't do it."

His heart pounding, Lionel pushed himself back up and rubbed his nose where it had hit the tree. There was going to be a *hell* of a lot to tell Yolanda tonight. He still hadn't even told her about being attracted to David, or about running into Kevin in town while he was *with* David. Now, what a different emphasis he'd be able to give those stories!

"So you just run out on us," the priest said, taking another quick drag. "Your best and dearest friends in the world. One day you're right there among us, the next day your room is empty and everyone is talking about this little correspondence you've been having with the archdiocese about how unfit you are for the job."

"I *am* unfit."

"That's what you *say,* and oh, so humbly, might I add. But you don't fool me. What you're *really* playing is Sister Mary Holier-Than-Thou." He dropped his cigarette and ground it into the dirt with his shoe. "I drove four-and-a-half hours to get here because I couldn't believe it till I heard it from your own lips. But the others were right: you've passed *judgment* on us."

"I haven't done any such th—"

"My *God,* David, we're a minority as it *is*! How are we going to change the church's stand if not from *within*?"

There was a long silence. "Paul, when have you ever lifted a *finger* to 'change the church's stand'?" He laughed bitterly. "How stupid do you think I am? This life is a pretty convenient mask for you, that's all. You get to sleep around as much as you want and still stand up in front of the community like a paragon of virtue. It's hypocrisy, pure and simple. You wouldn't *dream* of trying to change the church's stand on homosexuality. Your own little set-up is too cozy to risk that."

Paul had stopped pacing. "So you *have* passed judgment. I came to hear it from your own lips, and I've heard it from your own lips. That's all. That's all I came for." He started making his way back, swatting aside branches and bushes. "Just keep this in mind, honey: it doesn't pay to divorce Jesus. He's got all the best lawyers."

"What the hell is that supposed to mean?" asked David, following him.

"Oh—I don't even know. Just go to hell, will you?"

And then they were gone from Lionel's sight.

chapter

■■■■■■■■■■■■■■■■■■■■■
thirty-two

"**D**on't you ever get tired of me?" Lionel whispered. It was past one in the morning, and he and Yolanda were sitting facing each other, cross-legged on the bed, sharing a bag of corn chips and talking in low voices to prevent anyone else hearing them through the thin cabin walls. He'd just finished telling her everything that had happened to him during the day, and a spasm of self-consciousness gripped him as he realized he'd been talking nonstop for more than an hour and a half.

"Tired of you?" she said, scraping together the last few broken chips from the bottom of the bag and popping them into her mouth. "What do you mean?" she asked, chewing.

"All the hyped-up drama in my life," he said. "All the earth-shaking news I'm always running to tell you, when we both know in the long run nothing's going to come of it. Nothing ever does."

She crumpled the bag and tossed it into the ancient green wastepaper basket beneath the nightstand by the bed. "But you never stop *thinking* things will change, Lionel," she said. "So maybe someday they will."

"No, no," he said, wiping his chip-greasy hands on his jeans. "I never stop *fearing* they'll change. Deep down, I honestly don't want them to." He stretched out his legs. "David Magellan, for instance. I get all excited about him, but I'd never actually *do* anything about it. Especially since he's my client's son. It'd be sure to ruin my career."

"It might," she said, leaning back and reclining her head on her pillow. "It might not. You cannot know for sure."

He chuckled cynically. "Oh, yes I can."

"Oh, no you *cannot.* And it is a fair bet that if you know about David, David knows about you. If he is gay, as he certainly seems to be, then he must surely have figured out the relationship between you and Kevin."

"God, I *hope* not." He peeled off his socks and tossed them in a corner. "Couldn't have been too hard, though."

"How did you feel, by the way? Seeing Kevin, I mean." She bent her arm and held up her head.

He let loose a deep, contemplative breath. "*Strange,* that's how. I hadn't seen him in years. Looks good. Looks *great,* as a matter of fact."

"No *stirrings,* though? No jealousy of his new lover?"

He shook his head insistently. "Not at all. I guess I never felt very deeply for Kevin. I was so closeted when I met him—and so was he. It was just so *convenient.* I thought, 'This has to be it, because I will never meet anyone else.' I never *wanted* to meet anyone else. At that point in my life, one man seemed as good as the next."

She sighed. "Well, you have at least come a long way since then."

"I don't even feel especially *friendly* toward him," he said. "I've always thought what a shame it was that our neuroses drove us apart, because we cared so much for each other, but seeing him today—he left me totally cold. No feelings."

"That is not natural."

This wounded him a little. She was striking rather close to what he suspected about himself—his inability to love. He decided to deflect it by making a joke of it. "Well, what do you expect? I *am* unnatural. Don't you listen to the TV preachers?"

She didn't laugh. "You think it has to be a choice, Lionel. You think you must decide to become a partner in this agency, or decide to find a man to share your life. Either-or."

"Right. It *does* have to be that way."

"Does it?" she said, running her fingers through her hair. "You can see *no* way to have both?" A pause. "Or have you never bothered *trying*?"

The look that crossed his face gave her the answer. She clutched her sides, dropped into her pillow, and began loudly moaning in exasperation.

Then they heard Julius Deming's voice through the wall. It was muffled and indistinct, but it alarmed them. When Peg's voice followed, clearly saying "One-fifteen, go back to sleep," Lionel and Yolanda were too spooked to continue their discussion. They crept out and brushed their teeth, then slipped into bed (or, rather, *Yolanda* slipped into bed—Lionel lay down on a blanket on the floor) and doused the lights.

The next morning he awakened to find her bed already made. He got up, struggled into a sweatshirt and a pair of shorts, and staggered out to the kitchen. Yolanda, Perlman, and Magellan were crammed inside the tiny space, busy frying and pouring and stirring things. Yolanda smiled when she saw him. She held up two plates, each laden with scrambled eggs and toast, and said, "I have fixed you breakfast. Grab a cup of coffee and come out on the deck."

"Okay," he said sleepily.

She trotted over to the glass door, slid it open with her foot, then shut it behind her and joined the other women at the table under the umbrella.

When she was safely outside, Magellan said, "Lionel, we have to talk." Perlman came and stood beside him. Out of nowhere Julius Deming appeared with a bottle of buttermilk in his hands, and took his place next to them.

Lionel's heart was pounding. What had they found out? "I'm listening," he said.

"Yolanda tells us you're letting her take your car to go shopping today," he said sternly.

Lionel nodded. "She wants to go to that outlet mall we passed on the way in. It's about an hour drive and *I* sure as hell don't want to go." He raised an eyebrow. "What about it?"

"Didn't you know that we agreed *not* to lend our cars to our women this week?"

"No," he said, startled. "How could I know that?"

Magellan looked at Deming. "You didn't tell him?"

Deming flushed deep red and shook his head. "Didn't think I had to. What kind of man entrusts his *car* to his *girlfriend*?"

Magellan's nostrils flared. He turned back to Lionel. "The roads around here are lousy. It's easy to get lost, and the women are *terrible* drivers. Well, Wilma is."

"Becky's an accident waiting to happen," said Perlman with a derisive chuckle.

"Actually," said Deming a little defensively, "Peg's never even gotten a ticket."

Magellan whirled on him. "But you agreed: solidarity with us on this. Didn't you, Julie? Because if *one* of us lets his woman take his car, the *others* will want to, and then the entire week they'll be taking them out every five minutes and God only *knows* the kinds of scratches and dents they'll come back with—if not worse."

"If not worse," echoed Perlman with appalling toadyism.

"You're going to make us look bad if you let Yolanda take your car," Magellan said, shaking his finger at Lionel. "You've got to put your foot down! *Drive* her to the outlet mall if you have to, but don't let her drive *herself.* And for God's sake go and tell her that before she blabs about it to the oth—"

"*Baba!*" It was Wilma, storming in from the deck. She walked right up to him, her napkin still tucked into her waistband, and poked him in the chest. "How come Lionel lets Yolanda take *his* car but you won't let *me* take *yours*?"

Magellan turned white with fury. Peg and Becky crept in, too, and stood behind Wilma, awaiting his answer.

"Lionel's car is a piece of shit," he said. He turned quickly to Lionel and said, "Sorry, but—*hell.*"

"Well, why did you *bring* your precious Jaguar if you're afraid to let me drive it?" Wilma whined. "Every other time we've ever come up here you've been perfectly content to take *my* car. But I suppose you had to show off to your friends here with your shiny ballistic import. A fine impression it makes sitting there in the driveway doing *nothing*!"

Magellan looked like he might hit her. She was certainly getting back at him for laughing at her pratfall the night before.

"And in the meantime," she continued shrilly, "we're trapped here while Yolanda can go anywhere she wants!"

Magellan sputtered for a moment, then turned his fiery gaze on Lionel.

Just when Lionel was feeling the pressure reach its limit, Yolanda came in from the deck. "Did I say something wrong?" she asked timidly. "Everyone fled from me like I—"

"Yolanda!" Lionel jumped in. He went and took her by the arm, giving her a little squeeze to tell her to play along, and said, "I was just saying how delighted you'd be to take the other girls to the outlet mall with you."

Yolanda looked stricken. "They want to come *with* me?"

"Oh, *would* you, Yolanda dear?" Wilma said, suddenly realizing that this was almost certainly her only way to escape the rustic boredom of the cabin. "I assure you, we'll be quiet as churchmice, and we'll even treat you to lunch!"

"But," Yolanda said, panicking, "I—I was—going to make another stop or two—" Lionel squeezed her arm again, to no avail. "—before going to the mall, and—"

"Oh, we don't mind!" Wilma insisted. "Honestly, we'll sit in the car and wait! Won't we, girls?"

Peg and Becky added their reassurances and entreaties, and Yolanda had to agree.

Lionel was proud of himself; he'd defused the situation admirably. The men were now happy because their cars were safe from the women, and furthermore, the women were getting out of their hair. And Lionel hadn't had to make a show of authoritarianism toward Yolanda to placate his bosses (as if she'd have stood still for it, anyway).

Only Yolanda seemed upset. She shot Lionel a murderous glance, sending a chill up his spine. She surely couldn't be *that* angry about being saddled with the three "gorgons," as she called them. She'd been left to have lunch alone with them yesterday and hadn't complained much. And they were bound to be nicer to her now that they were in her debt. Indeed, they were already treating her like a kindred spirit; she was, after all, taking them away to that most feminine of sanctuaries, the outlet mall.

After breakfast, which she ate with sullen and downcast eyes, he caught up with her as she was fetching her purse from their bedroom. "For God's sake," he said, "what's *wrong*?"

She was actually crying. "Never mind," she said, and she swung her purse strap over her arm.

"They're not *that* bad," he said, following her out to the hallway.

"I *said* never *mind,*" she snarled, and then she banged open the screen door and flew out to his car. She was halfway there when she had to stop, ball her fists, and turn back.

He opened the screen door and let the ignition key dangle between his thumb and forefinger. She snatched it away from him and stormed back to the car.

The other women now filed out past Lionel, chattering like parrots, and crowded themselves tidily into the Celica like socks into a drawer. Yolanda started the engine, lurched into gear, and tore down the gravel driveway like she was trying to break out of Earth orbit.

Something was going on with her. He'd get to the bottom of it later.

chapter

■ ■ ■ ■ ■ ■ ■ ■ ■ ■ ■ ■ ■ ■ ■ ■ ■ ■ ■

thirty-three

At eleven o'clock, the door to David's room was still shut. Lionel kept inventing reasons to walk through the house—to get a beer, to go to the bathroom, to make a phone call—so that he could check on that door. It wasn't clear why he felt a compulsion to do this—he wasn't certain he even wanted to *see* David—but the need to know exactly where he was and what he was doing was overwhelming.

When he wasn't checking on David's door, he was sitting on the dock with Magellan, Perlman, and Deming, fishing. The talk was all of the baseball playoffs, the upcoming football season, and whether mortgage rates would go down or up and even if they went up how many great properties must be available in a place like this.

Lionel, having nothing to contribute to any of this, sat silently with his pole, watching the lure bob endlessly in the water. He was bored out of his mind. Occasionally he allowed his thoughts to drift to what Yolanda had said the night before; that had really shaken him. Was it true? Had he never even *tried* to reconcile his sexuality with his career, or had he just accepted that they were mutually exclusive pursuits? And if they were, who was to say he hadn't chosen the wrong one? Here he was, sitting on a dock fishing with the men he would soon call his partners, ennui lapping at his brain like waves on a beach—when the potent, irrepressible image of David tangled up in his sheets, naked and asleep just a few yards away, kept stabbing its way through his mind.

There was a lull in the conversation; he snapped to attention. They were looking at him.

"So, Lionel," said Deming, "I believe I heard your girlfriend groaning last night."

The other two men leered at him. They were leaning forward, their fishing poles slack and forgotten, awaiting details.

"Yeah, well, she does that," he said, giving his own fishing pole a little jiggle.

"No screams, though," Deming continued. "Funny thing. Gal struck me as a screamer." He grinned.

Lionel rolled his eyes and laughed in exasperation. "You guys are fuckin' *animals.*"

"So what were you going at her with? You can tell us. Finger? Tongue? Cock?"

"Nose," he said, and they laughed nervously.

"Your puny beak isn't big enough," said Magellan, whose own proboscis was something to behold.

"It is if I tell a couple of lies first." More muted laughter; they obviously didn't get the reference.

"There's a proven correlation between nose size and cock size," said Magellan, stroking his monster sniffer.

Perlman leaned toward him threateningly. "What kind of tan lines she got?" he asked, a positively carnivorous look on his face. He'd already expressed open disappointment that Yolanda hadn't yet chosen to don her swimsuit and bask in the sun. "She shave her pubes at all?"

Lionel shook his head. "I'm not gonna tell you. For God's *sake.*"

"Oh, come *on,* Lionel. We just want to live vicariously through you. For a minute or two, anyway."

He was jiggling his pole so much that the line was vibrating like a violin string. "Sorry. I just can't bring myself to talk about her like she's some kind of whore."

Perlman knit his brows at once, and Lionel knew he'd

made a mistake. That reference couldn't fail to jog loose some kind of telling image in Perlman's rat-trap memory.

When it became clear that Lionel wasn't going to divulge any of Yolanda's sexual secrets, Magellan declared himself disgusted that they'd caught nothing all morning and suggested they take one of the canoes out to the center of the lake.

It was high noon now and Lionel had reached the end of his rope. It was one thing to have to waste his time fishing on the dock; it was another thing entirely to have to do so in a tiny, cramped canoe, cut off from the refrigerator and the bathroom and, not the least, from David's door.

"You guys go ahead," he said, reeling in his line. "Don't think I could handle any more sun—my skin's burned already."

"Yeah, but that's from *friction*," said Deming, and the others snickered.

They got up and headed down the dock, toward the boathouse. But before they reached it, Magellan stopped Lionel and put his hand on his shoulder. "Do me a favor," he said conspiratorially. "Long as you're staying behind, keep an eye on my son, will you?"

"Sure," he said. As if he needed to be asked!

"Last time I checked he was still asleep. That's a sign of depression, oversleeping. Something big is bugging him, something that drove him out of the priesthood. Can't imagine what could've done that. He was such a religious kid! See if you can befriend him. Get him to confide in you. He won't say a word to me—I think because of Wilma."

Lionel nodded. "I'll do what I can." His pulse was racing. He didn't know what to think. He only knew that his million-dollar client had asked a favor of him, and he must comply.

Deming and Perlman shouted for Magellan's help to get the canoe out of the boathouse, so he winked at Lionel and went to join them. Lionel practically leaped the entire distance to the house.

When he entered, he was shocked to find David's bedroom door wide open.

He went over to it and peeked in. The daybed that took up an entire wall of the tiny room was empty, its sheets cast into a heap. David's suitcase was lying open on the floor, and several bottles and jars sat on the small dressing table above it.

He took a tentative step into the room—just for a quick look around, just to see if he could find any instant clues into David's intriguing character. But there was nothing—only the clerical bareness he assumed all priests were trained to adopt.

Someone tapped on his shoulder.

He whirled and found himself facing David, who was standing before him dripping wet and naked but for a towel around his waist. His broad, white chest gleamed like the Holy Grail.

"Your dad asked me to check up on you," Lionel blurted. "He thought your sleeping late could be a symptom of depression." *Don't tell him that!* he admonished himself, too late.

David rolled his eyes in exasperation. "Wonder what talk show he got *that* from?" he said, slipping past Lionel. He was carrying a bottle of honey-colored shampoo, which he placed next to the other bottles on the dressing table. "Well, you can tell him my sleeping late is only a symptom of fatigue."

Lionel backed out of the room and could see through the dining room window that the canoe was making its way to the center of the lake—slowly, though, as Deming was somehow contriving to send each of his paddles in different directions.

"Your dad's out on the lake now," he said to David, who held his towel around his waist as if he were only waiting for Lionel to depart before dropping it. "Listen," he said, his heart pounding so loudly that he could hear it reverberating in his skull, "I just want to tell you, I admire your integrity."

"My *integrity?*" David said, cocking his head. Water dripped from his hair onto his ivory shoulders.

"Yes, for what you—well, it can't be easy, leaving the priesthood like you've done."

"Unless you have a good reason," he said flatly. "Which I do."

"I know."

"You *know?*"

"Well—I can guess." Who *was* this talking? Yolanda's

Frankenstein Monster? He knew he was risking everything.
But the opportunity—the seclusion—the uncanny excuse of
Magellan's entreaty to him—they were too great a combina-
tion to resist.

David smiled. "Oh, you can *guess,* can you?"

"Well, *yeah.* I mean—uh . . ." He leaned against the door-
jamb and dragged one of his feet across the floor. "Well, I
know you probably picked up what—uh—well, about Kevin
and me, and, I mean because of that, I'm kind of in *tune*
with—uh—you know, with certain . . . uh . . ."

David smiled even more widely, but his eyes betrayed
no merriment. "You mean, because you're gay, you think
you've got this radar that lets you pick out other gay men,
is that it?"

Lionel felt his brain pushing against his eyeballs. His
knees were threatening to buckle. "Yeah, that's it."

"And of course it's got nothing to do with it that you
were eavesdropping on my conversation with Paul last
night."

Lionel's blood screeched to a halt in his veins. *Busted!*

But even now, he'd come too far to let that frighten him
off. Better to forge ahead, be even bolder—to resort to *no*
lies, not even any *half*-truths. *Total* honesty, now. For once,
just this *once*—just to see how it *felt* . . .

"Yeah, that helped," he said in a small voice.

David's chest started shaking. A moment later he let out
a bubbly, irrepressible laugh. "I *saw* you, after you fell
against that tree. I don't think Paul did. He was too pissed
off to see anything."

Lionel wasn't certain whether he was being invited to
laugh along, or was being laughed *at.* In any case, he didn't
feel very merry. "I mean it, though," he said gravely, his
voice raw and trembling. "What I said about your integrity.
And your—courage. It took *courage* to leave like that. Kind
of courage I haven't got."

They were facing each other now, the three yards sepa-
rating them rapidly filling up with enough magnetic energy
to stop every clock in the house.

"Courage is only part of it," said David, his own voice
trembling now.

"What else?"

"Fear."

Lionel nodded. "I know all about that."

"Loneliness."

Lionel nodded again.

David took a step toward him.

He backed away instinctively. David stopped.

"I'm sorry, Lionel," he said. "I don't usually behave like this. It's just that I'm on such a *precipice* these days. Everything I do lately has so many enormous consequences that, paradoxically, none of the consequences seems to *count.*" He laughed nervously. His eyes brimmed with wild, angry, frustrated tears. "Does that make any sense at all to you?"

Lionel lunged forward and kissed him, then took away his towel and buried his face in what he found there.

chapter
■■■■■■■■■■■■■■■■■■■
thirty-four

The distorted square of sunlight David's window allowed into the room had now moved down the wall by almost a foot. Lying on the daybed, with David spooning him and curling his hair between his fingers, Lionel tried to determine how much time had passed. At least a half-hour. Maybe more. Maybe a month, if how he felt was any clue. He'd never had such an explosive orgasm, and if David's reaction was any indication, neither had he.

He sighed deeply and contentedly, then took David's hand in his and gently pulled it away from his head. He rolled over to kiss him and found himself facing an altogether different man: someone whose eyes sparkled, whose teeth burst through his lips with the irrepressible, unselfconscious smile of pure joy. The sullen, fidgety, feisty David he'd met only a day earlier had completely disappeared.

"We'd better get up," he said, and just as he said it he heard shouts from the lake.

He jumped up and pulled on his boxers, then peeked out of the bedroom and through the back window. He could clearly see Magellan, Perlman, and Deming making their way toward shore; Magellan was screaming at Deming, "THE

SAME DIRECTION, YOU IDIOT! PADDLE THEM IN THE SAME DIRECTION!"

His pulse quickened. He turned and saw David getting dressed, slipping into his shapeless khakis and pale blue T-shirt, hiding everything that Lionel now knew so intimately.

But David didn't don his old face along with his old clothes. He continued to beam, and every time he looked at Lionel he broke into a new toothsome grin.

This wouldn't do at all. Anyone who looked at him would know at once that something material had changed in him. They'd start guessing. They might even ask him, and what would David do then? *Tell* them? Oh, he had Yolanda to blame for this! Yolanda and her insidious, subversive encouragement. Passion spent, pleasure dissipated, he could only think now of the danger.

"THE *OTHER* WAY, FOR *CHRIST'S* SAKE," Magellan was yelling. "YOU'VE GOT THEM GOING TOGETHER, BUT IN THE *WRONG DIRECTION*!"

Lionel buckled his belt and went to the kitchen. He was feeling positively parched. He opened the refrigerator and was looking for something cold to drink when David came up behind him and put his arms around his waist.

"You're terrific, Lionel," he said, still smiling. "Just what I needed." He kissed his neck.

Magellan's voice was getting louder and louder. Lionel quelled the panic in his breast. The thing to do now was to get David out of the house until the puppy-dog look left his face.

"You know what I could go for?" he said, turning to face him. "A nice, thick milkshake. Filled with artery-clogging cholesterol and about a gallon of butterfat."

"Sounds great," said David. "Want to go into town and track one down?"

Bulls-eye! "Fine idea."

"Good," said David. He cocked his head and looked at Lionel from beneath raised eyebrows. "I'm not exactly in the mood to deal with my dad right now, if you know what I mean."

Lionel almost fainted from relief. "That makes two of us."

They headed out the door, but Lionel took one look at the driveway and stopped short. "*Shit!*" he said. "I forgot—

Yolanda took my car for her goddamn all-girl shopping
expedition!"

"I was *wondering* where everyone was," said David.
"Hey, no problem—we'll take Dad's car."

"What?" Lionel was genuinely stunned. "Are you *nuts*?"
He laughed. "He may be your client, but he's *my* old
man. Yesterday he offered me use of the car whenever I
want it. Wait here. I'll just go grab the keys from his dresser
and leave a note."

Lionel, wondering what David might write in his present
state of mind, called after him, "KEEP IT SHORT!"

A few minutes later they were sailing down the bumpy
rural roads in Babcock Magellan's flashy gold Jaguar, the
windows rolled down and the stereo up full blast. Lyle Lovett was wailing, *"Man, she's no lady, she's my wife,"* which
seemed somehow appropriate, although Lionel couldn't
have begun to say why.

David took a sharp turn at about fifty miles an hour,
sending a thin hail of gravel up onto the hood and wind-
shield. Ping! Ping! Ping! Each pebble that hit caused Lionel
a minor heart seizure. Magellan was going to have a *fit.*
"Slow down," he entreated David.

One side of David's mouth crept up into a half-smile, and
he placed his hand on Lionel's thigh. "Don't *feel* like slowing
down, babe," he said. "Life—*real* life—began again for me
today." He squeezed Lionel's knee. "No pressure, now. I
know you may not want anything long-term with me, but
I've got to tell you, what you've done for me today, it's—
well, I'll never forget it." He shook his head in amazement.
"Sex without *guilt,* Lionel. No hypocrisy in it, no hiding, no
worrying about breaking vows—it felt so *clean.* It felt like—
like—" He turned to look at Lionel. "It felt like making
love."

"My *God,* watch *out,*" Lionel cried, pointing to a large
tree limb lying in the road. The danger it posed wasn't
nearly significant enough to warrant his outburst, but David
was steering into dangerous waters, and it was the only way
he could think of to steer back out.

David, however, must have known that he'd been deliberately put off. After yanking his hand from Lionel's knee to
grapple with the steering wheel and swerve around the

limb, he didn't replace it, and when Lionel looked at him, some of the sparkle had gone out of his eyes. He'd lost his smile, too.

To make matters worse, Lyle Lovett was now singing an altogether more downbeat number.

What am I doing? Lionel thought. Up at the house, in David's room, he hadn't cared about anything. He'd wanted to join David on the edge, wanted to be with him, risking everything. And now ... all it had taken was one old spurt, was that it? He was, in the end, a typical male, just a sex pig, there for the ride and then emotionally out the door.

And yet, this man, this *man* ...

He looked at David, who didn't look back, and he felt something like an illness grip him, something like a haze of nuclear radiation searing through his bloodstream, spreading like an acid, a fiery poison. He felt his stomach constrict at the slightest remembrance of where he had touched David, and David him, and of that little sigh that David had given repeatedly, and how that excited him because it said so much about his *character*—about his willingness to reveal himself, his bravery in showing himself totally to Lionel, his fundamental *honesty*. He felt his throat close up and his ears start to ring and the skin on his arms and legs prickle up with a cold, nasty pox.

Something this deliriously, wonderfully unpleasant could only be love.

He reached over and put his own hand on David's thigh. David turned and gave him a smile that could have lit up the universe's biggest black hole.

They reached town and pulled up in front of a small ice-cream shop, then rolled up the windows and got out.

David, whose daring was something Lionel would never get used to, patted him on the tush and said, "You want to go in and order for me? I just need to run down the street and get a book of stamps."

"Sure," said Lionel, his face still red from the tush-patting.

David started down the street, then turned and called, "DON'T DITCH ME OR ANYTHING!" He laughed, as though it were a joke, but there was a touch of anxiety in his voice that told Lionel he was still a *little* insecure about him.

I won't ditch you, thought Lionel; I would never ditch you, will never ditch you.

He watched until David had gone two blocks and turned a corner, then, hating himself for doing this, he turned back to the car and examined it for pebble-damage. He knew that if there were any, Babcock Magellan would hold *him* responsible.

Then he wondered why he was bothering, because if Magellan discovered what had happened between David and him, the state of the Jaguar would be the *least* of the strikes against him.

As it turned out, the car was covered by an unappealing coat of dust but was otherwise unscathed. Lionel straightened up and checked his reflection in the window of the driver's door, then noticed another reflection in the background, a reflection he couldn't be seeing—a ghost of a past infatuation, come to mock this new, true thing he had found. It was coming down the sidewalk toward him. He turned and confronted it.

"No *way*," he said, shaking his head. "No *way* are *you* here."

Emil stopped cold. *"Lionel!"* he cried. He looked like a kid who'd been caught with his hands in a cookie jar. "Oh, *God.* You were not supposed to know I was up here."

His first reaction was anger. "Don't you and Yolanda have anything better to do with your lives than invent new secrets to keep from me?"

Emil's eyebrows shot up. "You *know* about Yolanda and me?"

"Yes. I'm the official Last Person in the World to Know, but I *do* know."

He sighed. "Well, that's a relief, anyway." He stuck his hands in his pockets. "Want to talk about it?"

"Love to." He looked down the street to where David had turned, and said, "Let's make it short, though."

"Of course," he said, and they started walking in the opposite direction. "There isn't much to tell," he explained as they crossed a dusty intersection. "Just enough for you to see me back to my car. I am staying at a motel not far from here."

Emil hadn't gotten the hang of American fashion yet. The pair of shorts he was wearing were jet black and plummeted to below his knees. He was also wearing black socks with his Keds. Yolanda would really have to take him in hand.

But even more shocking was the smell of alcohol on his breath. Lionel couldn't believe it at first, was convinced the odor was coming from another source, but as Emil talked the scent traveled along with him and grew stronger.

"Is everything okay?" Lionel asked.

"Actually," Emil said, staring straight ahead, "no. To begin with, Yolanda was supposed to join me at my motel this morning, but she never showed up."

"*Oh,*" Lionel said, suddenly realizing what he'd done. "Oh, Jesus, Emil—*my* fault. She made an excuse to leave the cabin this morning, but before she could go I saddled her with being chauffeur for the rest of the women we're staying with. She couldn't say no, not to their faces. She looked like she was going to *kill* me." ·

Emil shut his eyes and heaved a huge sigh of relief. "Well, I am glad to hear that much. I thought perhaps she was having too much fun and had decided to cancel our date without even calling."

"Well, I'm sure she tried to call. But it was probably a long time before she could get to a phone. The shopping mall she was driving to was about an hour away."

"Oh, I had grown upset and left the motel by then." He shrugged; he was breathing easier. "No matter. We will laugh about it someday."

They stopped to let a stream of school-age kids dash past. Some were riding skateboards, all were screaming noisily. Emil's skin looked ashen; he must have been devastated by Yolanda's apparent desertion of him.

When they were able to proceed, Lionel asked, "What are you *doing* here, though? Don't you have an exam this week?"

"Yes, but not till Thursday. I confess, I was panicking when I told Yolanda I couldn't see her for this entire week. I was sure I would be spending every spare minute studying. But I longed for her too much, Lionel. I underestimated my need for her. Just as I cannot give up food or sleep during my studying, neither can I give up Yolanda. When the time came to put her out of my life for a week, I found I couldn't. So I called her and begged her to see me this week. And that's when she told me she'd already agreed to be your 'date' up here at the cabin."

Lionel nodded, taking it all in. "So why didn't she just back out? I wouldn't have asked for a reason. She wouldn't have had to tell me about her relationship with you. She knows that."

"Well, she'd never *think* of backing out. She loves you, Lionel, and she still wanted to help you." They reached Emil's rented Buick. He folded his arms over the roof, apparently in no hurry to drive away. "Plus," he continued, "she also still wanted to get out of the way of that kooky ex-boyfriend of hers with his linen blazers and his spear. So we thought that the best solution all around would be for me to follow you up here and get a motel room. I could study as effectively there as I could anywhere else, and Yolanda would be able to come and see me whenever she could get away. This morning was supposed to be our first rendezvous."

"Which I spoiled for you." He shook his head. "I really owe you one, Emil. Me and my big mouth."

"It's not your fault," he said, resting his chin on his arms. "If only we could have *told* you I'd be here, it wouldn't have happened. But Yolanda insisted that you not know, because she thought you might still have feelings for me."

Lionel's jaw dropped. "She *told* you about that? That loud-mouthed, traitorous bi—"

"Lionel! Lionel! I knew already. I'm not stupid." He pushed away from the car and started fishing for his keys. "And even if I hadn't known before, you must expect that what she knows, I will know. Don't lovers tell each other everything?"

"I wouldn't know."

Emil produced his car keys, then held them limp in his hand and looked at Lionel sideways. "Of course, you feel nothing for me now—do you?"

"No, no," he said, relieved to be able to say it truthfully. "There's someone else now."

"A homosexual, this time?"

"Yes," he said, laughing. "I managed to get it right."

Emil smiled and grabbed Lionel's neck in an affectionate stranglehold. He shook him a little, then let him go and said, "I'm very happy for you, Lionel. Happy for both of us. For all *four* of us, even this man I don't know yet."

At the mention of David, Lionel checked his watch. He could very well be on his way to the ice-cream shop now, and he wouldn't find Lionel there. Well, he'd wait an extra few seconds. During the stranglehold, Emil's liquored breath had almost overpowered Lionel, and he wanted to make doubly certain that his friend was okay.

"So, anyway, that was all that was bothering you—Yolanda standing you up?" he asked.

Emil took a deep breath, and Lionel thought, Uh-oh.

"Well, there is one other thing, if you care to hear it."

Lionel grimaced. "Well, I'm pressed for time, but—"

"I promise to make it quick. It would help if I could talk to someone about it."

Lionel shrugged. David would just have to understand. "Okay. Sure."

He leaned against the car again and tossed the keys from hand to hand. "It only happened last night. I was trying to unwind after studying, so I sat down and read some works by the Marquis de Sade."

Lionel shut his eyes and shook his head in disbelief. "That's what you read to *unwind*? Emil, you are really weird."

"I know this. You keep telling me. Anyway, I was reading a translation of a tract of his, published after the French Revolution, called *Frenchmen, Yet Another Effort If You Want to Be Republicans*. In it, he says that once you have vanquished an authoritarian system by ridding it of all its guarantees of laws and ethics, then you may begin to speak anew, and since there is no order to restrain you, you must say *everything*, you must *do* everything. Sade says that in a society based on liberty there should be few, if any, acts that are considered crimes; that in a republic born of insurrection, acts such as rape, theft, and murder must be protected. He further claims that since such a state must exist in a *continual* condition of insurrection, such acts must not only be protected but *encouraged*. If not, then the rule of law is reinstituted, and with it the arm of the law—oppression, coercion, the old order restored."

Lionel looked at his watch. This was very far from what he'd expected when he asked Emil if anything else was bothering him, and he wasn't taking it well. David must certainly be at the ice-cream shop by now, wondering what had happened to him. He had to get back there as soon as possible. The thought of David doubting him for even a moment was agonizing. Was this what it was like to be in love?

Yet Emil rambled on, in terms Lionel could only barely comprehend. "Lionel, I have always believed strongly in anarchism, in the beauty of Emma Goldman's definition, 'a new social order based on liberty unrestricted by man-made law.' Yet she goes on to add that anarchism is also 'the theory that all forms of government rest on violence, and are therefore wrong and harmful, as well as unnecessary.' Now Sade has made me think, what *is* her equation of 'violence' with 'wrong' if not a man-made law itself? Violence, after all, exists in nature, outside the realm of morality. And besides, many anarchists have used violence in the furtherance of our cause. And most damning of all, if Sade is correct—and I haven't been able to fault his logic—then violence is not only necessary to the establishment of an anarchist social order, but also to its *perpetuation.*"

Lionel was growing impatient. "And the point is . . . ?" he asked, providing a segue for Emil, who he feared would never get to one on his own.

"The point is, I have lost faith. Or, if not lost it, had it so profoundly shaken that I don't know if it has survived. Lionel, for the first time in my life, I have had to say, There must be a line. A line that cannot be crossed. Where is that line? I don't know. I think I will be many years finding it. For now, though, I am drawing it very close around me, in a tight circle. I am starting with the most basic of certainties: that each of us must share his life with that person whom he loves best. And that's why I've decided not to go back to Transylvania, but to stay in America and beg Yolanda to be my wife." He took a deep breath, as if a great weight had been lifted from his shoulders. "I'd come to that conclusion last night. That's why I was so dismayed when she failed to appear this morning. Yesterday, I believed fully in only two things: anarchism and Yolanda. This morning, both seemed to have vanished into thin air. I don't mind telling you, I spent the morning drinking."

Lionel was feeling the weight that Emil had shrugged off.

David was *waiting,* yet he couldn't just *leave* Emil, not after a revelation like this. He put a hand on his friend's shoulder and said, "I'm glad about Yolanda. You'll be good together. And I know she'll say yes. What about the fight against AIDS?"

"More barriers are being broken here than in Eastern Europe. I will fight here, and I will do my best to make certain that Transylvania—that *all* of Romania—isn't overlooked when new treatments are approved for distribution. I owe that much to Mircea's memory."

Lionel shook his head. "Emil, I really have to go. Someone's waiting for me. I think you're okay, now. Am I right?"

"Of course I'm okay! Go on. Tell Yolanda to call me." He slipped his key into the car door and swung it open. Lionel hesitated to leave, so he waved him away and said, "Go *on!* Go on, my friend. And thank you for listening." He smiled sheepishly. "I love you very much."

Lionel felt his eyes itch—a presage to tears—and so he smiled at Emil, then turned and began race-walking back to the ice-cream shop. He wouldn't blame David if he were pissed off, but he was certain he could explain. He only hoped that at this moment he wasn't thinking that Lionel *had* ditched him, that's all. He ought to know better—if not because of what they'd shared together this morning, then because of Lionel's utter dependence on his father.

He stopped at a street corner to let a station wagon pass; kids and dogs were almost spilling out the back. He smiled happily at the sight, and when it was beyond him, he jogged to the other side. One more corner, and the ice-cream shop would be in full view.

Imagine Emil turning up in Wild Rose! Of course he had a perfectly logical explanation for it, but after the shock of running into Kevin again, this had almost been enough to do Lionel in. If he came across one more familiar face in this town, he'd probably keel right over.

Then, a mere half a block from the corner he needed to turn, Bob Smartt stepped out of an alley and into his path.

And as a matter of fact, Lionel *did* keel over.

Because Bob balled his fist and struck him smack in the face.

chapter

■■■■■■■■■■■■■■■■■■■■■■

thirty-five

Lionel was too stunned to think for a moment. His fall had knocked the wind out of him, and the gravel on the street was biting sharply into his face and hip. Before he could get his bearings, Bob lifted him by his armpits and started dragging him down the alley, like an oversized doll.

He shook his head to clear it, then started struggling, but Bob's stringy arms were surprisingly strong—as though they were made entirely of copper or something.

People in the street had stopped to watch. "HEY!" Lionel shouted at them as they peered down the alley. "HEY, YOU *PEOPLE! HELP* ME!" No one moved. "FOR CHRIST'S SAKE, WHAT *IS* THIS, *MANHATTAN*?"

Bob shoved him up against the wall of the nearest building, face first, then pulled his arms behind his back and slipped something cold and sharp over his wrists.

"Wha— wha— *handcuffs*?" he exclaimed, now fully alert again. "Oh, *man*, Smartt, you've gone *way* over the edge now. You're gonna pay *big* time if even *one* of my teeth needs capping because of thi—"

"*Shut* up!" Bob hissed, leaning into him and pressing him deep into the wall. "You've got some *nerve* talking like that to me after what you've done!" He grabbed the chain between the handcuffs and yanked it around Lionel's side, almost dislocating one of his arms. "See these?" he said with a sneer of contempt. "These are *Yolanda's* handcuffs. I found them under her bed—"

"Oh, breaking and entering, *too,*" muttered Lionel.

"—in a suitcase full of—well, you already know all *about* it, don't you?"

"What the *hell* are you raving about?"

"Don't play innocent, you—you—*cad.*" His breath was coming fast and hard, but there was even now something effete about him. He reminded Lionel of nothing so much as an adolescent girl betrayed by her compatriots at jump rope. Despite the stinging pain in his face and hip, he couldn't take Bob the Avenger seriously.

Especially since he didn't even know what he was *avenging.*

Bob dragged him toward a car parked at the opposite end of the alley, its back half edging into the sidewalk. Lionel recognized it as Bob's Eclipse. Bob pushed him toward it, and he stumbled out of the alley and into full view of the town again.

And there was the ice-cream shop, just across the street and three doors down. He felt a rush of optimism; sanctuary was in sight!

Bob grabbed him by the elbow and held him while he fumbled his key into the lock, and Lionel thought, All I have to do is yank myself out of his grip and haul ass over to the ice-cream shop, and David will be there, and that'll be the end of this. And just as he steeled himself to make good this escape, David appeared at the window of the shop and began scanning the street, presumably for him.

He froze, waiting for David's eyes to reach him.

And when they did, Lionel smiled, half out of relief that this nonsense would soon be over, half because he now knew that David couldn't doubt him any longer, not now, because here he *was,* here he—

The door to the Eclipse swung open and Bob shoved him into the car.

He tripped into the passenger seat, instinctively bringing his feet in after him just seconds before the door slammed shut behind him. Because of the handcuffs, it took him a moment to sit upright, and by that time Bob was sliding into the driver's seat and buckling himself in.

Lionel looked out into the street, certain that he would find David there, racing to his rescue. But instead he found him still in the window of the ice-cream shop, a look of almost horrified hurt on his face. And a cold epiphany was born in Lionel: he'd been on the *far* side of the car. David hadn't been able to *see* his handcuffs, hadn't been able to *see* Bob shoving him—in short, had only been able to see him get into a car with another man, a man who was now starting the engine, shifting into drive, and zooming away like a particularly hyperkinetic bat out of hell.

The only conclusion David could make was that he'd been jilted and abandoned.

Lionel craned his neck to try for one last fleeting moment of eye-contact with David, as if that moment might telepathically reveal all, but the ice-cream shop was a rapidly diminishing blur now. All Lionel could see with any clarity was Bob's famous spear, spread across the back seat. The sight of it chilled him; this might be worse than he thought.

Bob sped out of town, his knuckles white over the steering wheel, his nostrils flaring with each furious breath. He was wearing a pair of pleated white trousers, avocado sneakers, and a collarless, pale-green striped sailor shirt, making him probably the most absurd apparition of abduction that western civilization had ever known.

Lionel was really anxious now. Yet part of him was exhilarated, too, because he knew now that whatever lingering feelings Yolanda might have for Bob would be destroyed when she heard about this stunt.

He knit his brow and tried to sound authoritative and threatening. He wriggled his shoulder blades up the back of the seat until he was sitting bolt upright, then said, "You're in *deep* shit now, Smartt—and *don't* tell me to shut up. I won't take orders from any asinine clotheshorse playing yahoo-for-a-day."

No, no, this was wrong. He tried to calm himself. It wouldn't do to *insult* Bob. The idea was to somehow get him to listen to *reason.* And soon. Nothing was more important to Lionel than being able to get to David and explain what had happened. The idea that David might be in some kind of distress because of this was more than he could bear.

Bob was almost trembling. He wouldn't take his eyes off the road. "You'll pay," he said, shaking his head. "*Oh,* you'll pay. Did you think I wouldn't find *out*? Did you think when I figured out Yolanda had run off that I wouldn't call *you* for advice? You were my *brother,* Lionel. We *drummed* together." He turned and gave him such a look of anguished betrayal that Lionel's heart almost stopped. "We *drummed* together, damn it!" His voice actually broke.

"That doesn't oblige me to get involved with you in conspiracies against your girlfriend," Lionel said, more softly. He was, against all odds, feeling a smidgen of guilt. Over what, he couldn't exactly say.

"No," Bob scoffed, "just with *her* against *me.*" He swerved off the road and sent the Eclipse barreling across a bumpy, unlandscaped field, finally bringing it to a halt within the cover of a small copse of maple trees.

He stilled the engine and then turned toward Lionel. "Like I said, I called you for advice. But your office said you were away for a week." He reached into his pants pocket and took out a tiny bottle of eyedrops. "That's when it hit me," he said, squeezing a few droplets into his left eye. "Yolanda was away—you were away—it was *too* much of a coincidence." He blinked, then repeated the process in his right eye. "Sorry, I'm all bleary today. I haven't slept. Anyway, then I remembered all those nights Yolanda made excuses for not being able to see me, the nights I couldn't reach her, the nights I was *sure* she was out with another man. And I remembered how when I told *you* about those nights, you said you could vouch for her whereabouts on every one of them." He screwed the cap back on the bottle and slipped it back into his pocket, then turned his watery, but unbearably intense, gaze back on Lionel. "And like a fool, I was actually comforted by that, because I didn't realize it was only *half* the truth. Of *course* you could vouch for her whereabouts! It was *you* all along!"

Lionel heard the wild shrieking of blackbirds in the branches above him, felt the prickling heat of the sun on his neck as though it were a hot compress, and he thought for a moment how funny it was that his senses were so heightened to these things, just as he realized that he might indeed be in real trouble. Bob, it seemed, had come unhinged. In his derangement, he'd conceived a conspiracy theory worthy of a J.F.K.–assassination buff, and nothing Lionel said would convince him he was wrong.

Well, wait a minute: there was *one* thing. He could always tell Bob that he was gay.

But no, no, *no*—he shouldn't *have* to do that, *wouldn't* do that. This was *Bob Smartt*, for God's sake. He wasn't going to allow an embarrassing, theatrical fit of *Bob Smartt*'s to force him into compromising his secret.

"Bob," he said with quiet deliberation, "you've taken this 'to-be-male-is-to-feel-pain' thing *way* too far. Just because your feelings are hurt doesn't mean everyone else is to blame for it. In the first place, I'm *not* involved with Yolanda. In the second place, even if I *were*—hell, if Yolanda doesn't want to be with you, if she wants to be with someone else instead, it's none of your fucking *business.*"

That "fucking" may have been too pointed a grace note for this particular argument. It sounded derisive, and up till he said it, Lionel thought he might actually be getting through to Bob. But at the sound of the "F" word, Bob's eyes clouded over again, and he restarted the car.

"You're going to take me to her now," he said.

"Like hell I am," Lionel said, almost laughing. "You can't make me do that!"

He pulled onto the road again and headed back toward town. "Your office would only tell me you'd gone to a place called Wild Rose in Wisconsin. They wouldn't tell me *where* in Wild Rose, though; they wouldn't give me the address." Suddenly he whipped into the opposite, oncoming lane and started rapidly accelerating. "I searched Yolanda's place and couldn't find any hint of where she was staying, so I just drove up here last night, to the center of town, and just waited, and waited, and waited."

"You're in the wrong lane," Lionel said with no small urgency.

"And my waiting paid off," he continued, ignoring him. "I found you, and now I've got you under my thumb. And you're *going* to take me to her, aren't you?"

A car was coming at them now. "For God's sake," Lionel
cried, "do you want to get us killed?" He bent over and
tried to lift his cuffed hands to the steering wheel, but his
elbows locked and he couldn't manage to get within six
inches of it.

He sat up again. Bob was barreling toward the oncoming
car. Its horn was honking at him, but he just kept staring
ahead, steadily accelerating, as though intent on meeting it
head-on.

"I won't hurt her," he said. "I'd never hurt her. But I
want to confront her with this. I want a *reason.* You'll tell
me where she is, won't you? You'll take me to her."

Lionel could now make out that the other car was a
Jaguar. Its driver was laying on his horn without let-up.
Another quarter-second and Lionel could see that the driver
was a younger man. Another quarter-second and he could
see his wavy blond hair.

He didn't need another quarter-second to know that it
was David.

David—pissed off and swearing, driving through a haze
of hurt, having been stood up, having been played for a
fool—on the road now and determined *not* to get out of
anyone's way. Maybe he even realized it was Bob behind the
wheel of the car speeding toward him, and was therefore
determined to meet him head-on.

Lionel felt adrenaline flood his body. This was a major
disaster in the making—and just a *breath* away.

He took a split-second look at Bob for a sign that he was
preparing to relent, but his knuckles were white, his lips
whiter, his foot heavy on the gas pedal.

And Lionel could almost hear the deafening crunch of
metal and glass, the way an echo of the first chord of a song
sometimes prefaces the real thing on a cassette tape.

"I'LL TAKE YOU! I'LL TAKE YOU TO HER!" he screamed
at what he thought was surely a second-and-a-half too late.

Bob nearly yanked the wheel from the steering column,
sending the Eclipse spinning away at a seventy-five-degree
angle. It skidded off the road entirely, while the Jaguar hurtled by, its horn still blaring. And it was only when that
blare Doppler-shifted into a lower register and began to
recede that Lionel, who'd been too afraid to look, realized

that he'd somehow survived. He cracked open his eyes and saw Bob wrenching the steering wheel to get the car back on the road, and suddenly understood that he'd saved not only his own life but David's too.

But at Yolanda's expense.

They continued as though nothing had happened. The road ahead was clear. Bob was safely in the right-hand lane. Lionel could still hear blackbirds.

And then the blood left his face in a sudden gush as he contemplated what he'd just been through. He wished his hands weren't bound behind him; he felt a desperate need to clutch them over his heart.

"All right," said Bob in a near-whisper, "which way from here?"

"Give me a *minute,* for Christ's sake," he said, panting for breath. "I've got to get my fucking bearings after *that* little joyride." And he tried not to start crying from relief.

chapter

■■■■■■■■■■■■■■■■■■

thirty-six

Please, please, *please* don't let
Yolanda be back yet, Lionel
prayed as Bob pulled the
Eclipse into the driveway.

But as they cleared the bushes on either side of the drive
and came into sight of the cabin, he saw that his Celica had
indeed returned, and was parked right next to the Beemer
and the Saab—and the dusty, mud-splattered Jaguar.

Bob halted the Eclipse, looked at the row of cars, and
said, "I take it you're not alone here."

"No," snapped Lionel, "we're sharing the place with a
couple of kickboxers and martial artists."

Bob chuckled and said, *"Not,"* as if this entire expedition
were some kind of merry lark. Then he backed up the
Eclipse until it sat square in the center of the corridor of
bushes, effectively blocking the driveway.

He stilled the engine and got out of the car. Lionel
tried wildly to reach his own door handle in order to
escape before Bob had time to get around to his side, but
his handcuffs made it impossible. In fact, he slipped on
the vinyl seat and hit his temple against the door." *Shit,"*
he hissed.

As he righted himself, Bob reached through the rear window and snatched the spear from the back seat, then opened the passenger door. "Out, please," he said.

Lionel shook his head and refused to budge. "Go stick a can of styling mousse up your ass."

Bob gave him a jab in the thigh with the spear.

"*Yowtch! Jesus!*" he cried, checking his pleated shorts for a rip. "You out of your fucking *mind*?"

"Just want to ensure your cooperation," said Bob cheerfully. "You've got to realize, Lionel, you're in no position to resist."

He stumbled out of the car. "I'm going to have you arrested for this," he threatened. "It's *kidnapping,* it's *assault,* it's—*kidnapping*—"

"Oh, *button* your lip," Bob snarled, using the spear to prod him forward. Any hesitance on Lionel's part would surely result in drawn blood. "Just bring me to Yolanda."

"You think she's going to help you?" he asked as he trudged forward, the spear biting into his back every third or fourth step. "You think she won't press charges as quickly as I will? You're *nuts.*"

Bob snorted in derision. "Actually, I've never felt more clear-headed in my life," he said as he followed his captive to the door of the cabin. "Law, authority—all the things you're trying to scare me with—they can't hide the simple fact that I've been *wronged* by you—*and* by Yolanda. And there are more ancient, more honorable ways of righting that wrong than flinging a bunch of notarized papers at you." They passed through the door and into the kitchen. He looked around and said, "*Cute*! Love the curtains. Chintz?"

Lionel, who wouldn't know chintz from burlap, chose not to reply, and silently led him into the main living area. The cabin seemed empty, but he could see down the hallway that David's bedroom door was shut. He guessed that David was behind it. He was torn between the urge to call him to his rescue and the equally strong urge to protect him from Bob. In the end, he kept his mouth shut. Despite the hurt David must now be suffering, it was better to leave him to it than to expose him to the danger out here.

"Well? Where's Yolanda?" Bob said, poking him in the butt with the spear.

"God*damn* it, cut that *out,*" he snapped, whirling. "Christ, we just *got* here. I know as much as *you* do!"

In the pause that followed, they heard a wave of laughter ripple into the house from somewhere outside. Bob forced Lionel to the window, from which vantage point they could see Yolanda and the others gathered out on the dock, the men fishing, the women sunning. All the women except Yolanda wore tasteful one-piece bathing suits (Peg's even had a kind of skirt). Yolanda, of course, was spilling out of a scandalously abbreviated thong. Hackett Perlman had his eyes all over her.

"Ah-*ha,*" said Bob. He stepped back and pointed the spear at him again. "Shall we proceed?"

Lionel shut his eyes and sighed. "This gets more absurd every second," he said, trying to keep his voice down lest David should hear him. "Come on, Bob—grab the fucking reins, will you, pal? Just *grab* the fucking *reins.*"

Bob looked perplexed. "I don't know what you mean."

Lionel was astonished at the sincerity in his face and voice. "You—you—you're just gonna make a *fool* of yourself down there, is what I mean—in front of *everyone,*" he said, nearly apoplectic with fury and frustration.

Bob gave him a grim look. "Is a man a fool because he takes charge of his own destiny? Because he strikes back at those who strike against him? Because he fights for the woman he loves?"

"Nice little speech. Be sure to recite it for the police."

"Oh," he said, snapping his fingers, "thanks for reminding me." Waving the spear, he herded Lionel over to a desk, upon which sat a combination telephone and fax machine. Then he reached down, pulled the phone cord taut, and, wrapping his tongue around his cheek, managed to saw it in half with the somewhat serrated blade of the spear, after which he dropped the bisected segments to the floor. "Can't have anyone calling the authorities," he said cheerfully. Then his eyes fell on the desk itself, and he ran his hand over it. "Mmm, rosewood. What do you think—Scandinavian?"

"What?" Lionel asked, astonished. "How the hell should I know?"

"Scandinavian," he said, nodding sagely. "I'd bet all the tea in China on it." He turned to Lionel. "Any other phones in the place?"

"No," said Lionel, too eagerly not to be lying.

Bob wrinkled up his nose and smiled. "Let's just take a look and see, shall we?" he said, touching the spear to Lionel's chest. "Not that I think you'd *lie* to me or anything. You wouldn't do that. Not knowing how much it might *peeve* me." He gave Lionel a tiny, almost affectionate prick with the spear.

"All *right,*" said Lionel, his forehead growing slick with sweat. "There's one in Magellan and Wil—in the main bedroom."

"Show me."

Lionel led him down the corridor, scarcely daring to draw a breath for fear that David would hear it and come out to investigate. But they managed to pass his door without incident, and, once inside Magellan and Wilma's bedroom, Bob quickly cut the cord on the phone on the nightstand, then smiled and said, "*There,* now," and led Lionel back down the hall without incident. When they were once again before the fireplace, Lionel breathed a sigh of relief.

"Any *more* phones?" Bob asked him.

"None," he said hatefully. "Go ahead and search, if you don't believe me."

Bob smiled widely. His long, pointed face looked almost elfin, mutated by raw, chthonic energy. "Of *course* I believe you," he said with magnificent insincerity.

Looking at him, Lionel began to sense the complete amorality into which Bob had descended. The trappings of high civilization he had always embraced—expensive colognes, jewelries, textiles, cosmetics—had been the things that had preoccupied, and thus neutered, his inherent primal egoism, like glittering baubles distracting a great ape. Since his men's-movement summit, those things had meant less to him; the anguished, self-centered child at his core— the monster of ego that is bred or beaten out of most of us—had been liberated. And now the abandonment by Yolanda had turned the monster into a menace. Lionel sensed, for the first time, that Bob could do him real harm. Gone was the prancing buffoon in J. Crew regalia. Here was naked male aggression, relieved of the burden of two thousand years of ethical and moral considerations by a combination of intense primitivist schooling and his own sense of unfair loss. Bob might know chintz from burlap, but in him Lionel finally saw, for the first time, the difference between the heterosexual and homosexual man. Or thought he did. He hoped he was wrong; what he saw *frightened* him.

Bob waved the spear in his face and said, "Come *on,* let's not *dilly*-dally. Time to face the music and dance!"

chapter

■■■■■■■■■■■■■■■■■■■■■■
thirty-seven

Lionel was so profoundly upset by the epiphany he'd had during his momentary gaze into Bob's ink-black, animal eyes, that he happily allowed himself to be led out the door to the deck. Despite Bob's lethal potential, Lionel had a hunch that everything might still be all right once they reached the dock. His bosses and host would look up and see him in handcuffs, a deadly weapon at his back, and they would rise up to his rescue. Magellan and Perlman would hold Bob's arms behind his back—or maybe Deming would just opt to sit on him. Yolanda's Latin temper might turn her into an avenging spitfire. However they did it, they'd go after him. Of course they would. Of *course* they would.

But Bob wasn't going to make it easy for them. Halfway across the deck, he said to Lionel, "Just wait a minute, now," and when Lionel obeyed, he felt Bob come up behind him and then jiggle his wrists for a few seconds. Suddenly the handcuffs fell away from him and onto the teak planks with a clatter. With inexpressible relief, he drew his freed hands around to his stomach and rubbed his chafed, smarting wrists.

Bob said, "Look natural, now. Don't alarm anybody.

Smile." He hid the spear behind his back. "And don't think of running away just 'cause I'm not jabbing your backside anymore. This thing has quite a reach—it's five feet long, you know—and I'm pretty swift with it. Had a lot of practice, at camp!"

"So I've heard," said Lionel with acid sarcasm. "You swung it around in the sun until it resembled Queen Elizabeth's tiara." But despite his scorn, he decided to take him at his word and not try to flee. After all, the end result would be the same. The guys and Yolanda would be ready to take him down. He was pretty sure even Becky would want to get in a kick or two.

Peg Deming was the first one to see them coming. She sat up, adjusted the strap on her left shoulder, and said, "Oh, look—it's Lionel and a friend. Where did I put that SPF fifteen sunblock? Those boys shouldn't be out here without SPF fifteen sunblock." She started searching through her beach kit.

Lionel and Bob were on the dock now, their footfalls causing vibrations all along its length. The three men turned from their fishing, and the other three women sat up and stared.

Yolanda shielded her eyes, saw Bob, and said, "Oh, blessed Virgin. Oh, Madonna."

"What?" said Wilma, instinctively covering up her chest with her Chanel beach towel. "Does anyone know that other boy? Baba, why is Lionel bringing a strange boy here?"

"They shouldn't be out here without SPF fifteen sunblock," said Peg. "Becky, have you got the SPF fifteen sunblock?"

Becky's eyes narrowed. "I'm sure if I'd known I was going to have to meet someone *new* today I would've run a *brush* through my hair. I'm sure if I'd known there were going to be *other* people coming to the cabin I wouldn't have worn this old *suit* today. I'm so grateful to everyone for filling me in on these things."

Magellan was on his feet. "Lionel, who's your friend?" he said cautiously. "Where's David?"

"Safe and sound," said Lionel, "which is more than I can say for us."

"Careful," whispered Bob through clenched teeth.

"I recognize that guy," Hackett Perlman said, laying down his fishing rod and standing up beside Magellan. "This is your drumming pal, from that day at the office, isn't it, Lionel?"

"That's right," Lionel replied. He and Bob had now joined the others at the end of the dock. "Bob, you remember Hackett Perlman, don't you? And of course, you know Yolanda. As for everyone else," and here he nodded his head as he named them, "this is Julius Deming, our host, Babcock Magellan of All-Pro Power Tools, Julius's wife Peg, Hackett's wife Becky, and our hostess, Wilma Tripp. Guys, I'd like you to meet Bob Smartt, my kidnapper."

Magellan narrowed his eyes. "What kind of farce is this? Where's David?"

"Oh, blessed Virgin," Yolanda said, rolling over to her knees, from which position she looked prepared to spring into action—or flight.

"Baba, I really insist that you find out what this is all about," said Wilma, tucking the towel beneath her armpits. "We just can't *have* this."

"This guy came to Lionel's office a little while ago, started *drumming* with him on his desk," said Perlman into Magellan's ear, like Iago into Othello's. "Said it *meant* something. Thought there was something funny about it at the time."

"I found it!" said Peg triumphantly, producing a disfigured tube from her beach kit. "I found the SPF fifteen sunblock!"

"Pleased to meet all of you," said Bob, and he produced the spear from behind his back. Wilma shrieked, Becky Perlman cursed, Yolanda invoked the blessed mother again, and Julius Deming stumbled backward and fell into the water.

Bob looked at him splashing about in the lake, like a teenage walrus making a bid for attention, and said, "What a good idea. Everybody in!"

"Who the *fuck* do you think you are?" barked Magellan. "Coming down here like you own the goddamn place!"

"Yeah, who the *fuck* do you think you are?" echoed Perlman with lamentable toadyism.

"I'm the guy with the deadly weapon," said Bob cheerfully. "Come on, now! Everyone into the water! I *am* asking nicely."

"Baba, *stop* him," said Wilma, cringing beneath her towel. "I don't *want* to go into the water! My hair's only just back to normal from when you dumped me out of the canoe!"

"Better do as he says," Lionel said loudly. "I mean, there are *eight* of us and only *one* of him. We wouldn't stand a *chance,* now, would we?" His subtle exhortation was lost on them.

Becky Perlman dropped her towel. "Well, if *I* have to choose between getting stabbed and getting wet," she said snidely, "I choose getting wet." She got to her feet and padded over to the side of the dock. "I don't understand you people. You come up here to spend a weekend on a lake, then act all horrified when some lunatic tries to force you to actually *swim* in it. I mean, wasn't that the *point*?" She clicked her tongue at them and jumped into the water.

Perlman shrugged his shoulders at Magellan, doffed his BULLS WIN T-shirt to reveal a leathery, flabby chest with nipples the color of strawberries, and jumped in after his wife.

Magellan, his face so knotted with rage that he resembled a villain in a Kabuki drama, balled his fists and threw himself angrily off the dock. The resultant splash hit Wilma in the shoulder; she shrieked.

Peg was busily slathering herself with SPF fifteen sunblock. "Just a minute, just a minute," she said, working her way up one arm, across her chest, and then down the other. "Don't know how long we'll be out there, and it doesn't pay to be unprotected." She capped the tube, replaced it neatly in her beach kit, crawled to the side of the dock and rolled off slowly, like an inner tube or a keg of beer, landing in the water with a single *plunk.*

"What's the *matter* with all of you?" Lionel whined. "We could have *taken* him!"

Bob placed the head of the spear against Lionel's neck. "Mind your manners, Lionel," he said. "Everyone's behaving so nicely and no one's gotten hurt. You don't want to be a *troublemaker,* now, do you?" Then he turned to Wilma and said, "You next, ma'am. Sorry about your hair. But did you ever consider just *bobbing* it? You wouldn't have any of these worries, and you'd look twenty years younger!"

At this impertinence, Wilma let out a wail that in its

shrillness and duration might've been mistaken miles away
for a passing train had there been anything resembling a
railroad in the area. Mortified, she crawled to the edge of
the dock. Magellan extended a hand to help her and she
shrieked, *"Noooo! You're wet!",* then slipped daintily into
the water up to her breasts. She grabbed one of the posts
and clung to it, hiding her face. "Anyone who touches my
hair is *fired,"* she whimpered.

All around the dock, Lionel could see his bosses standing
chest-deep in Lake Gilbert and watching Yolanda for what
came next. It was like the pivotal scene from some Swedish
symbolist movie.

Yolanda was still kneeling in a crouch. She bared her
teeth at Bob and said, "Am I to go in the water as well?"

Bob grimaced and nodded at the spear. "Well, I can't
very well cover *both* of you with this."

"Then let Lionel go into the water and turn your weapon
on me." The wind blew her hair across her face. She looked
like an avenging angel; her eyes were unreadable and dreadful. Lionel couldn't believe Bob wasn't terrified of her.

"Oh, no, you don't," he said. "You have a lot to answer
for, but *Lionel* is the one who took you away from me."

Yolanda looked at him as though he were crazy. "What
are you talking about? Lionel is not the one who took me
away from you!"

"That's right," Lionel swiftly interjected, not wanting Yolanda to bring up, even now, the reason that their os-
tensible love affair was impossible. "No one *took* Yolanda
away from you. She's a free woman. She goes where she
wants."

Yolanda looked at him questioningly, and he shook his
head at her, almost imperceptibly, as if to say, No, Yolanda.
This whole silly, sorry situation might still blow over, and
he didn't want her recklessly revealing anything before it
did so. Despite his fear at Bob's sudden wildness and the
lethal potential he sensed in him, he still saw this as a rogue
event, a glancing of bitter circumstance across the clear,
unblemished surface of his life. He wouldn't *let* it ruin
everything.

"What's going on here?" asked Peg, the skirt of her swimming suit floating around her. "I'm not following anything."

Julius said, "I think this guy must be Yolanda's last boyfriend." He swatted a water bug away from his stomach.

"I don't see that that gives him the right to come here and upset everyone." She squinted and said, "Are you wearing SPF fifteen sunblock?"

"Oh, for Christ's sake, Peg!"

"You should've said something while I had the tube out. That angry boy isn't likely to let me go back up and get it—although I won't know till I ask!" She turned to Bob and said, "*Young man! Young man!* My husband is very fair-skinned, and the reflection off the water *doubles* the harmful effects of the sun, you know."

"Peg, *Jesus,*" Deming whined.

"Look, I'm sorry about your skin," Bob said to him, "but once you hear why I'm doing this, you'll be on my side anyway. Unless you *like* traitors to our sex. Unless you *like* men who steal other men's women."

Yolanda, still crouching, shifted her weight to her other foot and said, "Lionel, this is insane. We must *tell* him."

"Tell me what?" Bob snarled. He jabbed Lionel's nape with the spear. Lionel could've sworn he broke the skin, but he felt no hot flow of blood. "*What,* you miserable cuckold?"

"*Nothing,*" Lionel said desperately. "Yolanda, stop trying to fool him! He's too smart for us!"

"You are a *fool,* Lionel," she said. She removed a strand of hair that had blown into her mouth and said, "Bob, Lionel and I are not lovers. We have *never* been lovers. I was seeing someone else entirely—another man who is not here. This is the *truth.* I swear it on the blood of the Virgin!" She looked at Lionel and said, "You will thank me for this later."

Lionel's heart was pounding, but he felt a small sense of relief. Yolanda had spilled the beans, but she hadn't spilled *all* of them. He started to relax.

"Will someone please tell me what's going on?" Becky Perlman said. She was shorter than the others, and her head didn't clear the top of the planks.

"My husband is contracting skin cancer," said Peg breathlessly, "and no one will help!"

"I don't believe you," said Bob to Yolanda, his face betraying a whirlwind of doubt. "You're lying."

"I wasn't asking about your flabby *husband,*" said Becky.

"What's going on up on the *dock*?" She took a little leap out of the water. "I can't see!"

"They're just talking," said Magellan. "I can't hear what they're saying if the rest of you don't shut up."

"It is the *truth,*" Yolanda insisted. "Is it not, Lionel?" Her eyes bore into his.

"Hacky, pick me up so I can see," said Becky.

"Like *hell* I will. What do I look like, Hulk Hogan?"

She gave him a look that clearly said, You Will Pay For This Later.

"Here, Julie," said Peg, "let me rub my skin against yours—you'll at least get some of *my* sunscreen." She hopped up onto her husband, lashed her arms around his neck, and began rubbing her chest into his broad back.

"My *God*—you're *depraved,*" he screamed, trying to fight her off. "Get *away* from me! *Help! Help,* somebody! *Help me*earghllph—" He'd fallen over backward, submerging both himself and his wife.

"It's *true,*" said Lionel, using his hand to gently move the spear away from his neck. "It's true, Bob. I swear it." He didn't even care if his boss and co-workers could hear.

Which, as it happened, they couldn't. "Fine, *don't* lift me," Becky barked at her husband. "I'll get *myself* up. Just don't expect *me* to keep quiet about your Vicks Vapo-Rub fetish!" And she started jumping up and down in the water, trying to peer over the top of the dock.

Between Julius and Peg's thrashing in the lake and Becky continually jumping out of it like a porpoise, the water around the dock had started to churn like a bathtub full of four-year-olds, causing a wave to lap up against Wilma's shoulder. She hugged herself to the post and shrieked, "*STOP IT!* FOR GOD'S *SAKE*! YOU'LL GET MY HAIR WET!"

Bob snatched the spear away from Lionel's hand and put it back to his throat. "I don't believe a word you're saying," he said almost expressionlessly. He extended his leg and pointed his toe at the big Oscar de la Renta overnight bag sitting open on the dock, a towel and some tanning lotion jutting innocently out of it. "That's yours, isn't it?" he asked Yolanda. "Don't bother to deny it. Seen it a million times in your closet."

Deming emerged from beneath the waves and started

coughing up water. *"Don't—worry—about me getting—cancer,"* he hacked at his wife. *"You're gonna—kill me—before I get the chance!"*

Bob hooked his foot through the strap of Yolanda's bag and started dragging it over to him.

Yolanda leapt out of her crouch and made a lunge toward him.

Seeing this, Magellan cried, *"Whoa!"*

"What?" Becky demanded, jumping up and down even faster. *"What? What?"*

Bob immediately applied pressure to Lionel's neck. "Uh-uh," he said. "Mustn't step out of *line*, Yolanda. Not unless you want your boyfriend to get hurt." He grimaced. "In fact, I think your dip in the lake is *way* overdue. *Isn't* it, Lionel?" He applied greater pressure. Lionel began panting audibly.

"Bob!" Yolanda said, balling her fists. "This has gone too far! Stop it at *once!*"

"Why?" he said, his voice breaking, his head snapping toward her. "Why *should* I?"

"Because this will go against you!" she scolded him. "You will be arrested!"

"Why should I care what happens to me?" he asked, his throat sounding as raw as ground beef. *"You* don't care about me anymore!"

Her shoulders sagged and she cocked her head. "Oh, *Bob.* Of *course* I do, Bob."

He shuddered. "You do?"

She nodded. "Yes, I do." Then, just as Bob was lowering the spear from Lionel's smarting jaw, she sighed and said, "Just not very much."

The spear bit into Lionel's skin again, and Bob, his jaw set with new determination, said, "Tell her to go in, Lionel." Lionel mumbled something, he himself didn't know exactly what, and as he did so the tip of the spear broke the skin beneath his chin; a trickle of blood flowed down the chiseled point.

Yolanda gasped, clutched her own throat, and said, *"Jesus! Maria!* Look what you have *done!"*

"Look what *you've* done," said Bob, who grimaced at the sight of the blood, but still kept the spear at Lionel's neck.

Panicking now, Yolanda said, "Very well, I am going,"

and she jumped into the lake, sending a sheet of water into
the air that ended up completely drenching her hostess's
head. Wilma took a long, astonished breath, then broke into
magnificently shameless sobs.

Bob at last lowered the spear and, nodding at his prisoner's wound, said, "Sorry, Lionel. We'll get a Band-Aid for
that later." Then he resumed dragging Yolanda's bag over
to him with his foot. It slid across the planks until it sat
between them. Making certain to keep Lionel at the end of
his spear, he bent down and started digging through the
bag.

"Look, this has gone far enough," said Magellan through
clenched teeth. Lionel couldn't see his arms or legs, but his
neck was knotted with tension and clotted with muscle. "I
want you *off* this dock and *off* this property. I don't care
who you are or *what* Lionel's done. This is an *outrage*. I
want you *out.*"

"Yeah, a real *outrage*," Hackett Perlman added.

Bob ignored them and kept digging.

Becky Perlman, who couldn't see this, looked at Magellan
and said, "Oooh, big *tough* guy. Couldn't scare a *dog* off
the dock. He's still up there, isn't he?"

"Becky, for *Christ's* sake," her husband stage-whispered,
unable to ignore her behavior any longer. "Show some fucking *manners*! Babcock's our host!"

She sneered at him. "Were you this pathetic a brown-
nose in school, or is it something you picked up later?"

"Stand under the dock," Peg insisted, trying to shove her
husband in that direction. "It's dark under there, the sun
won't get you."

"*Cut it out*," he cried. "I'm not gonna do that! There's
stuff *growing* under there! It's all *slimy*!"

All at once, Bob exclaimed, "*Ah!*" and they all looked
toward him (except Wilma, of course, who still clung to
her post, and Becky, who vainly tried to jump high enough
to see, all the while bleating, "*What? What? What?*"). From
the bottom of the bag, Bob withdrew a tube of spermicidal
jelly. "The smoking gun!" he trilled, displaying it to the
others as though they couldn't help but find it as damning
as he did. He turned to Lionel and said, "*Still* want to tell
me you're not sleeping with her?"

312 ■ robert rodi

Lionel went white. What was *that* doing there? He looked at Yolanda, who, being even shorter than Becky, had had to grasp the end of the dock with her muscular arms and pull herself up to see what was going on. She shrugged, and mouthed the word, *Emil.*

Of *course.* She'd brought the jelly with her because she'd known she'd be meeting her boyfriend up here! And if that was the case, there was probably plenty of other incriminating evidence in the bag, as well.

As if on cue, Bob, who had gone on digging through the bag, pulled out a whopping jar of sexual lubricant.

"Oh my *God,*" said Perlman in awe, temporarily forgetting their situation. "Lionel, would you really have *used* all that?"

"What?" Becky screamed, plunging in and out of the water like a piston, *"What? What? WHAT?"*

"This is ridiculous," Yolanda said. "Lionel, we *must* tell him the whole truth."

"What whole truth?" Bob said, dumping the lube back into the bag and rising to his feet again.

Lionel shook his head; suddenly he felt faint. He and Yolanda had reached an impasse. At any moment she might—

"What the hell is going *on* down here?" A new voice.

They all turned to see David at the far end of the dock. He was standing next to his packed suitcase, his hands on his hips, his mouth hanging open. "I come to say goodbye, and *this* is what I find? Who's the loser with the spear?"

Lionel was struck dumb. His tongue grew too big for his mouth. His knees began knocking like the engine of a '48 Packard. And despite the fact that he had a spear pointed so close to his face that he had to cross his eyes to get a fix on it—despite the fact that nearly everyone who had any kind of bearing on his life was now hanging on to a dock and staring at him with varying degrees of contempt—despite the fact that his terrible secret was seeping out like vinegar from a dribble glass—despite all this, there was but one thought, one dreadful realization that seized his mind and refused to let go:

David . . . was . . . leaving!

"Now is the time," Yolanda coaxed him, her body swaying almost imperceptibly as Lake Gilbert tugged at her thighs. "While David is here, Lionel—*now* is the time for the truth!"

"Finally," said Becky Perlman as she chinned herself up over the dock, legs kicking, and hung there, like a damp Christmas stocking from a mantle, surveying the confrontation.

"The *truth,* Lionel," Yolanda repeated, but her voice had a faraway, dreamlike quality. Lionel could focus on nothing but David.

"*What* truth?" Bob demanded, and he actually stamped his foot, setting the pier shaking and causing Becky to lose her grip and slip into the water again. (Half a curse was drowned as she plummeted beneath the surface.) "I'm getting pretty sick and tired of *asking* this, you guys! Come *on*!"

"Lionel," Yolanda pleaded, "*tell* him!"

David . . . was . . . leaving!

"Why is he staring at my son like that?" Magellan asked Yolanda. "What's David got to do with this? If I find out he's mixed up in any of this, I'll beat the cra—"

"It is not that," Yolanda snapped. "Just *hush,* Babcock. Let Lionel decide to tell. Lionel!" she called to him again. "Lionel, I *know* you can hear me! Listen, it is *time*!"

David . . . was . . . leaving!

Julius and Peg Deming had managed to slip a dozen yards down the shoreline and were trying to make their way up to the house again through a dense thicket of thorns and brambles. Julie was wailing like an ambulance while Peg kept reassuring him, "Don't *worry,* I have tincture of Merthiolate in my first-aid kit."

"Lionel, *stop staring at my son,*" Magellan barked. "It's *creepy.*" He apparently didn't notice that David was just as intently staring back.

For Lionel had caught his eyes and refused to let go. It was as if he somehow held him in thrall. David knit his brow and scowled and pretended to be immune to the telepathic pleading that Lionel was sending his way, but he wasn't budging from the spot, and Lionel knew that unless he looked away, or lowered his gaze, or blinked, then David *couldn't* move; he knew it as surely as he knew his own name. If he lost David now, he could have no one to blame but himself.

Then something happened—or, rather, didn't happen. In what seemed like a moment, all the passions were swept from the dock as if by a great wave, and Lionel felt as though he and the others were suspended in time. It was his eyes, he realized; inertia seeped from his eyes like an odorless gas. It had gripped David first, but it had spread through the air and now wrapped its sinuous fingers around Magellan and Yolanda and Perlman, all of whom hung on to the dock, watching, watching, like a Greek chorus gone mute. Down the beach, Deming and Peg still lived in real time, sniping their way through the brambles. Beneath the pier, Wilma and Becky still splashed about, muttering and whining. But here, above the dock, there was a dead calm, a hypnotic lull—and a fragile one, one that begged to be broken, but that couldn't be.

Not till Lionel blinked.

The strain was beginning to tell, and Lionel thought, as he held and held and *held* onto David's surf-green eyes, I know what love is, I know it at last, and *this* is it, this eyestrain, this willingness to die rather than look away, this willingness to let my eyes dry up and fall out of their sockets before releasing him, before letting him go.

But he was only human, and the moment inevitably came.

He blinked.

A second passed glacially; no one moved.

Then David shook his head and said, "I've got a bus to catch."

"You're leaving your father at the mercy of some lunatic with a *spear*?" howled Magellan. "You ungrateful little ingrate!"

"That's redundant," said David, picking up his suitcase. "But don't worry. I'll call the police from the house."

"The lines are cut," said Bob triumphantly. "Nice try, but no one's calling *anybody*."

Something wonderful occurred to Lionel. In a perfectly modulated voice, he said, "Yolanda, where are my car keys?"

"What?" she said, astonished. "Lionel, what kind of question is that for a moment like—"

"Where are my car keys?" he repeated determinedly.

"What's got *you* in such a tizzy?" Bob said, perplexed. "Even if I *let* you get to your car, you know you couldn't get down the driveway! I'm blocking it!"

Yolanda, sensing the iron in Lionel's voice, said, "They are in our room, on the dresser."

And suddenly Lionel was half-way up the dock, running like he'd never run before. "Outta the way, honey," he gasped at David as he careened past him.

"HEY," screamed Bob, "NO FAIR! GET *BACK* HERE!"

Lionel flew into the house and down the corridor to his and Yolanda's room. He kicked open the door and looked atop the dresser. They'd only been here two days, but Yolanda had managed to cram a week's worth of debris up there—chewing gum wrappers, sunglasses, a checkbook, a paperback book with a bald woman riding an orange turtle on the cover . . .

Lionel could hear Bob clomping up the dock after him, yelling his name. He had only seconds left.

He swept Yolanda's stuff off the dresser, handful by handful, until he came across the keys. Then he darted back to the main room again and found Bob just entering from the deck, his face flushed vermillion and his teeth gnashing. "STAY PUT, DARN IT!" he commanded.

Lionel emitted a little hiccup of fear. Then, out of the corner of his eye, he detected the dull bronze shine of the fireplace implements. He reached out and plucked a poker from where it rested against the hearth, then turned on his heels and bolted in the opposite direction. He escaped through the kitchen door to the front of the cabin, then dashed around the side to the back deck just as the Demings were emerging from the underbrush, very much the worse for wear. They gaped at him as he passed, poker in hand like a javelin, and from behind him he could hear Peg say, "We *missed* something."

Then he fairly leapt across the deck, which was a good thing, because Bob was coming through the glass door after him now, swinging the spear like a Watusi warrior and howling incoherently. By the time Lionel reached the dock, everyone had climbed or been pulled out of the water and was standing with their arms around their shoulders, shivering, dripping. David hadn't budged an inch from his place beside the suitcase.

Lionel tossed him the keys. *"Use my car phone to call the police,"* he rasped. Then he tore away again, because

Bob was closing in on him. His pause to pass the keys had cost him precious seconds.

As David disappeared around the side of the house, Lionel tried to run up an incline and thus avoid the paved walkway to the dock, but after only a few yards he turned his ankle on a kotty eruption of tree root, and he fell. The poker flew from his hand and landed a good four feet away.

And almost instantly, Bob was standing over him, nostrils flaring. Then, with one wild swing of the spear, he managed to bite into Lionel's arm and tear away a piece of his flesh.

Yolanda's hands flew to her face. She screamed.

Hackett Perlman stopped shivering for a moment and looked at her. "That *scream*," he said, almost to himself.

Lionel gasped in pain and clutched his arm. Blood oozed through his fingers.

Peg Deming was nearly hopping with excitement. "I have a first-aid kit!" she said in triumph, waving her arms in the air in a frenzy of self-congratulation. "It was the first thing I packed! I have sterile bandages! I have gauze! *I have tincture of Merthiolate!*" She bolted into the cabin.

Bob's bloody blow had cost him, however. The force of it had thrown him off balance and he had hit the ground hard, landing on his back. Lionel scrambled to his feet, grabbed the poker, and, after a spasm of pain, considered kicking him in the face, but he bit his lower lip and held back. He wouldn't kick Bob, wouldn't hit him, wouldn't strike out at him—he wouldn't, in short, play by Bob's rules. The only reason he was keeping the poker was to use defensively.

"*That* was a lost opportunity," Bob said as he stood up again and retrieved his spear. "You could've had me, there."

"I didn't *want* you," Lionel said, tearing his horrified gaze from the bloody gash on his arm. "This is *your* loony scenario, not *mine.*"

Yolanda, dripping wet and incomparably beautiful, had run down the dock and was now standing as close as she dared, panting with fear and anxiety. The others followed her.

"I know you," Hackett Perlman said when he reached her, his eyes boring into her.

"Of *course* you know her," said Becky from immediately behind him. "You met her on Sunday! Leave her alone, for God's sake, and think of some way to stop this ridiculous *fighting.*"

"What do you mean, 'loony'?" Bob said, almost as though his feelings were hurt. "This is how it *had* to end! You and me, in a duel! There's nothing *loony* about that!"

"There's nothing *else* about that," Lionel snapped between gasps for breath.

"You're Tina the Screamer!" Perlman said all at once, pointing at Yolanda. "Tina the Screamer, from Mrs. Craven's house! Jesus God, how could I have *forgotten*?"

"*Please,* Mr. Perlman," said Yolanda, her tears falling freely. "Now is not the time!"

"Who's Mrs. Craven?" asked Becky.

"I *knew* that girl was a screamer," muttered Deming.

Bob picked up his spear and pointed it at Lionel.

"I won't fight you," Lionel insisted, his voice breaking. He threw down the poker. "Goddamn it, I *won't.*"

"*Who's Mrs. Craven?*" Becky asked again, her voice shrill and sharp.

"For Christ's *sake,* Becky," said Perlman.

"I *mean* it, Hacky. *Tell* me."

"Mrs. Craven is a *madam,*" cried Yolanda, losing her temper. She whirled to face them and her wet hair whipped through the air; an inch closer and it would've snapped Becky's eye out. "I *worked* for her, as a prostitute! Blessed mother, what does it *matter*? Please, *someone,* just stop them from *fighting!*"

Bob turned, stunned. He looked vacantly at Yolanda.

"And what were *you* doing at a house of prostitution?" Becky shrieked at her husband.

David reappeared, *sans* suitcase. "Police are on the way," he said smugly. "Called the motor club to come tow Tarzan's car, too." He caught sight of Lionel's wound and color bled from his face. "My God—Lionel—*Lionel*—"

"Baba, exactly what caliber of people are you bringing into our home?" Wilma demanded, a look on her face like she'd just swallowed something sour. She pulled her Chanel towel around her shoulders and shivered, half with cold and half with rage.

Magellan regarded her with mayhem in his eyes. "Oh, it's all *my* fault, is it?"

Peg Deming reappeared, her face flushed, brandishing the first-aid kit high above her head. *"I've got it! I've got it!"*

"Lionel's not ready yet," Deming whispered, extending his scratched and swollen arms. "Do me first."

Bob was as pale as a sheet. He held the spear limply at his side. "Yolanda?" he said, his voice as small and soft and throbbing as a wounded animal. He took a few steps toward her. "Is—is this true? You were—you were—"

"Yes, Bob," she snarled. "I was a prostitute. A *whore.* Sometimes I even *enjoyed* it. And I hope that hurts you!"

He shook his head. "No—*no*—it's a *lie*—it's—"

"It's the *truth,"* she said, her face filled with fury.

Peg, who had been busy unraveling gauze, looked up and said, "Lionel's girlfriend is a prostitute? Oh, dear! Has he had the AIDS test, then? I can't bandage him up until I know whether he's had the AIDS test." She waved at him. "Lionel, dear, have you had the AIDS test?"

"I still want to know what *you* were doing at a whorehouse," Becky growled at her husband. "No, wait—don't tell me. You were designing a logo for them!"

"I hope you told the police to hurry," said Wilma to David in disgust. "I want these people hauled *out* of here."

Bob and Yolanda stood facing each other, separated by several yards and a chasm of misunderstanding, their eyes locked in a battle far fiercer and more terrible than the one Bob had started with Lionel. And by the way he was shaking, it was clear that Bob was losing.

Then all at once it was over. Bob's face sagged with the full weight of the truth he had been forced to accept. He turned his bloodshot, wounded eyes on Lionel. *"You!"* he screamed, and he sounded inhumanly, almost demonically angry. *"You're responsible!"* He started after him, waving his spear wildly. *"You did this to her!"*

"Oh, God, oh, God," Lionel panted as he ran back up to the deck (past Peg, who shook gauze at him eagerly) and across it to the opposite side of the cabin.

But unbeknownst to him, Bob had doubled back and gone the other way, so that when he reached the front of the cabin Bob was already there, rushing toward him and screaming murderously.

Lionel screamed too.

"You did this to her! You turned her into this!" Bob bayed as he neared Lionel, his spear lifted high.

And Lionel Frank, who had always said he'd rather die than come out of the closet, now suddenly understood what that would entail in actual practice. For here *was* death, poised before him in pleated white pants, a pale-green striped sailor shirt, and expensive avocado sneakers. Death, he discovered, was not pretty.

And so Lionel Frank, at long last, changed his mind.

"I'm gay," he shrieked. *"I never touched her! I'm gay!"* He turned and ran in the opposite direction.

"You're not," Bob howled as he chased him, swinging the spear spastically. *"It's a lie!"*

"No, no, it's true!" He zoomed around the corner again, to where the others were still standing.

"I'm gay," he yelled as he ran between Babcock Magellan and Hackett Perlman. *"I'm gay!"*

But Bob, having succeeded with the trick once, had doubled back again and was waiting for him on the deck.

"EEEEEK!" Lionel screamed. He turned and raced again for the protective covering of the others. *"I'M GAY,"* he bellowed as he circled Becky Perlman and Julius Deming, with Bob in hot pursuit. *"I NEVER TOUCHED HER! I'M GAAAAY!"*

He broke away from the cluster of dripping onlookers and hurled himself toward the lake, screaming *"I'M GAAAY, I'M GAAAAY"* at the top of his lungs. He screamed it when he reached the shore, and screamed it again as he pounded down the length of the dock, and then, at the end of the dock, he leaped into the air, into its brilliant, light-soaked, intoxicating purity, and he screamed it one more time— *"I'M GAAAAY"*—before plunging deep into the bosom of Lake Gilbert.

And then he swam, underwater, as far as he could, feeling the cold, clear currents of the lake flow through his hair and his teeth and his wound, washing him clean, stripping him of his fear and his anxiety and his shame, making him dizzy with the fullness of himself, startling him into courage, until his lungs gave out and he had to surface. Then, with his first gasp of air, he screamed it again, screamed it so that it barreled across the vastness of the lake and resounded endlessly, so it seemed, from every side, from everywhere—*"I'M GAY! I'M GAY! I'M GAY! I'M GAAAY!"*

And when the echo had at last faded, he looked toward the dock, where everyone had gathered, friend and foe alike, to stand and stare at him in complete and stupefied silence.

Epilogue

Lionel swung open the door to his apartment. He tossed his suitcase inside, dragged his feet through the door, slammed it shut behind him, and then dropped his back against the wall. He heaved a sigh.

"Qui est la?" called Toné from the other end of the apartment.

"It's only me," he said exhaustedly.

The hairdresser appeared at the end of the hallway in an off-white cotton tunic, culottes, and canvas slippers.

"You're back *days* early!" he exclaimed, his arms akimbo. "Is something *ne pas juste*?"

Lionel shook his head in awe. "Toné, what *is* that you're wearing?"

He did a complete turn, modeling the tunic. "One couldn't very well allow Spencer to go on soiling one's *chemises* with his droppings," he explained, "so one invested in an outer garment that your darling *oiseau* might have his way with."

Lionel nodded and pursed his lips to keep from snickering. Five minutes before, he'd thought he might never feel the urge to laugh again. Good old Toné. "It's very nice," he said.

Toné tripped down the hall and pecked him on the cheek. "But you haven't answered one's question! Has something dreadful brought you back here *en avance*?"

"I'd rather not talk about it, if you don't mind," Lionel said, slipping off his shoes.

Toné clicked his tongue. "One is once again a mere service provider, is that it?"

"No, no—listen, I'm sorry." He unbuttoned his shirt and let it hang open; it was warm in the apartment. "I'm just too tired to get into it now." He ran his wrist across his brow. "Next haircut. I *promise.*"

"And one is to wait till then? Lionel! *On peux mourir* from the suspense!"

"Well, do your best to hang on," he said wanly, pushing himself away from the wall. He absent-mindedly put pressure on his wounded arm, and winced.

"What's the matter?" Toné asked, concerned.

"I hurt my arm. Pay no attention."

"Well, do come and see your bird; that will cheer you up. One has clipped his feathers a bit—he looks quite *merveillieux!*"

"Thanks," he said, noting the blinking red light on his answering machine, "but I think I'll check my messages first."

Toné sighed in defeat and returned to the kitchen while Lionel went to the couch, dropped onto a cushion and depressed the PLAYBACK button on his answering machine.

"Lionel, it's Chelsea," the first message began.

"Oh, Christ," he said. He dropped onto his back and put one foot up on the armrest.

"Is it true that you resigned? Tracy just stopped me in the hall while I was on my way to file a stack of P.O.'s for that horrible WIPT job that made Simon pull out half of his mustache in June, and she told me that Deming had just called her from Wisconsin positively *ranting* about you, saying you'd left a note in the cabin resigning because you're gay and then just *disappeared* with some prostitute you were trying to pass off as your date! Honey, all of us are *dying* to know if it's true. If it is, it's the best resignation anyone's *ever* given at this hell-hole—better even than Pixie Digby's, and *she's* the one who dumped photocopier toner fluid in Perlman's crotch! Call and let us know the details as soo— What? . . . Excuse me, Lionel. What? . . . Yes, it's Lionel . . . Okay, sure! . . . Lionel? That was Donna. She says to send you a special 'hi' from her."

"I should've just let Bob kill me," he muttered, laying his hands over his eyes. When he removed them, he saw Toné's shadow meandering into the room from the hallway.

"I know you're there, Toné," he said, as the machine sounded its between-messages beep.

"One isn't trying to *pry,*" he said affronted, stepping into the room. "One is only checking the plants."

"Let them die. This is private."

Toné harrumphed and scooted back down the hallway.

The second message was from his father. "Lionel," Colonel Frank began, "I've just received a very disturbing phone call from a co-worker of yours, a Miss Monmoth. She was seeking confirmation of an obscene story about you that is apparently gaining some currency among your office-mates. In particular, it concerns your resignation—both the reasons for and the manner thereof. If you would please do me the favor of calling me to reassure me that none of it is true, I would be grateful." A slight pause. "And if, by chance, you are *unable* to so reassure me, then I would be even more grateful if you did *not* call. Ever. I hope we understand each other." Click.

"Or maybe *I* should just kill *Motormouth,*" Lionel groaned, rolling over on his side.

"Did you hear the one from Yolanda yet?" asked Toné from the hallway.

He sat up. "Nosy fucking hairburner!" He hurled a pillow at him. "Get out of here!"

Toné darted out of the pillow's way and cackled maliciously. Lionel sat with his head in his hands, waiting for the third message.

It was, in fact, from Yolanda. "Hello, Lionel! Thank you again for dropping me off at Emil's motel. The police have just stopped here to see us, and they asked where they could reach you if they had any more to ask you about the charges you are pressing against Bob. I gave them your home number; I hope that was okay. Call me to let me know how you are. I am so sorry about the way everything turned out. I do love you so. And Emil does as well. He thanks you profoundly for protecting me from Bob. Good-bye, now, dear Lionel. *Call* me."

The fourth message began in an absurdly deep, drippingly friendly recorded voice that asked Lionel to "Please hold for some vital information regarding private mortgage insurance! Thank you!"

Lionel turned off the machine and lay back on the couch again.

Toné appeared at the bedroom door, the tunic draped over his arm. "As long as you're home now, *mon brave,* one hopes you don't mind if one departs. One can use the extra time to dash across town and meet one's *cher* Frenchman when he gets off his shift!"

"Don't tell me you're still with the *Belgian*!" Lionel said, raising his head in astonishment. "Not the one who attacked you with a knife!"

"Mais certainement," Toné said, a touch indignantly. "Did one not tell you, weeks ago, that in spite of the drama, we were *meant* for one another?"

"Well, yeah—but I've heard you say *that* before."

"One *always* believed it at the beginning, *mon cher. Always.* But this time, one was lucky enough to have it turn out to be true! There is *toujours* hope, you know, *mon ami. Toujours.*"

Lionel sighed. "I'll remember that," he said, rolling over and not looking at him. "I'm happy for you, Toné. Honest to *God* I am. And, listen, thanks for everything."

"De rien," said the hairdresser merrily. "And do forgive one for having listened to your messages. One couldn't resist it."

"One could've tried a little harder."

"Is it true about your resignation? *Quelle scandale!*"

"I said *next haircut,* Toné. Not a minute before."

He shrugged. *"D'accord, d'accord.* Well, then, *mon brave—à bientôt!*"

The next sound Lionel heard was the front door clicking shut.

Alone at last.

He lay on the couch until darkness fell, sweltering in the closeness. His stomach grumbled, but he couldn't face food. He was paralyzed by the weight of too many events, all of them demanding to be sorted through, reconsidered, analyzed, judged, and filed away for future reference. It was too daunting a task. All he wanted was to sleep, but his mind kept jolting him awake with disturbing and recurring images—of Bob, of Yolanda, of David.

Especially of David.

At eight o'clock, his phone rang.

He tried to ignore it, but it wouldn't stop. Spencer started to scream along with the rhythm of the ringing. Twenty-five times it rang; twenty-six; twenty-seven—

Infuriated, he gave in and grabbed the receiver. "Hello!" he snapped.

"Lionel, dear?" It was Aunt Lola. "Thank God, thank *God* you're home!"

"Oh—Aunt Lola." He sat up and turned on a lamp, then rubbed his eyes with his fists. "Sorry. I was kind of napping."

"I can understand—all this upset! Listen, Lionel, there's been such a tremendous, such a *tremendous* battle going on about you! And the upshot, the *upshot* of it is, Sonny and Greta don't need me anymore, they haven't for some time, and now it's come to the point, it's come to the *point* where they don't *want* me anymore."

He shook his head. "Aunt Lola, I can't take this. Not now, not on top of everything else. Can you call back later?"

"No, I *can't,* dear, I'm calling from a pay phone!"

He blinked. "Why?"

"Well, your father, your father and your *sister* are so *intransigent!* No communication with you, that's their new law. It's awful! I had to sneak out to place this call. I have to get back before they notice I'm missing. But as I said, as I *said,* they don't need me, they don't want me, and I'm not staying. Not after the things they've said. There's been such a, there's been *such* a row over you!"

"Aunt Lola, you haven't been sticking up for me, have you?"

"Well, of course I, *of course* I have, dear," she said.

"You shouldn't have! Not if it meant getting driven out of the house."

"I'm not being, I'm not being *driven.* I'm *leaving.* Their lack of gratitude is what—is what—" She ground to a halt. "Oh, Lionel," she said, her voice strangely strangulated. "Didn't you ever wonder, didn't you *ever* wonder why I never got married?"

It took him a surprisingly long time to realize what she was saying. Then the planet seemed to stop spinning. "Aunt Lola—you're *kidding*—you—you're—"

"Yes," she said. "And how I wish, how I *wish* I'd had

your guts, Lionel. Back when I was younger. Back when there was still *time.*"

"Oh, *God,* Aunt Lola—it's not too late!"

"I'm in my fifties, Lionel! Don't be so sil—"

"Aunt Lola, it is *not* too *late. Jesus.* I can't *believe* I'm having this conversation with you!"

"Well, let's drop it, then. Because what I need to know, what I *need* to know *now* is, can I come stay with you for a few days until I find a place of my own? Just a *few* days, I *promise.*" She sounded on the verge of a breakdown.

"Come stay as long as you like," he said, his throat closing up with emotion. "We're family, you and me."

"Especially," she said, "*especially* you and me."

After they'd hung up, he felt strong enough to eat—if only just a can of soup and a piece of toast—and to clean up the guest room in preparation for Lola's arrival. He even attempted a reconciliation with Spencer, who allowed him to scratch his head for a record-breaking seventeen seconds.

At nine o'clock, his phone rang again. He was in the middle of doing dishes, so he dried his hands and grabbed the kitchen extension.

It was Julius Deming. He went white as a sheet.

"Look here, Lionel," Deming said, "I understand all the emotions running rampant here, and yet—by no *means* is everything smoothed over, I think you can understand that, and by no means am I *not* angry with you, but I'm angrier about this resignation stunt than anything else. To leave a note! To not even face us!"

"Look, what's the point?" Lionel said, preparing to hang up. "I know the way you and Perlman think, I know the kind of people you want working for you—and I've *tried* to be that kind of person, that kind of *man*—"

"Lionel, just shut up for a minute! Don't make me lose my temper—I'm only a hair shy of that as it is! Now, the fact is, regardless of the complete mess of the past two days, you're still *exactly* the kind of man we want working for us. I mean, you lied to us, but I can understand the reasons, if I think about it long enough. And you brought a hooker into Magellan's house—"

"She's *not* a hooker, she hasn't been in yea—"

"Lionel, let me *finish.*" He snorted in frustration. "All

right, she's an *ex*-hooker. Fact is, neither Hacky nor myself are completely guilt-free when it comes to those kinds of associations. Guiltier than *you* are, actually—you never had *sex* with yours, I'm guessing. Now, as far as that lunatic male model who attacked you with a spear—well, you did your best to calm him down, you didn't incite him. You could have made things worse, and you didn't. So after a long, *long* talk with Hacky, we've decided not to accept your resignation."

Lionel had to sit down for this. He hopped up on the formica countertop and planted himself next to the sink. "And Magellan's okay with that?"

"Magellan *insists* on it," he said at once. Then, backpedaling, he added, "But the decision's completely ours. Lionel, we want you back at the office tomorrow. We'll probably stay an extra day or so in Wisconsin to try to smooth things over with Magellan, who's a little upset over Wilma leaving him—"

"Wilma *left* him?"

"Yeah, taking his car *and* his son. He's a little crazy over it all."

"*God.* There's got to be a story *there.*"

"Never mind that. Just get back to work. I mean it, now. No more bullshit feeling sorry for yourself. Time to put this all behind us."

Since he'd already accepted being out of work, Lionel felt he had nothing to lose by pressing a little further. "And the partnership offer?" he asked.

A long pause. "We haven't discussed that yet. Naturally, we'll have to reconsider."

"Naturally."

"I'm not saying the door is closed. That would be foolish. It's not like there's anyone *else* we were considering."

"Of course not."

"I'll call you at the office tomorrow."

"You do that." Lionel was proud of himself for not saying he'd be there. But as he hung up the phone, he knew he would be. In spite of the mortification he'd have to suffer, facing Chelsea and Donna and Tracy and Carlton and everyone else, he knew he'd go back. The place was in his blood.

He dialed Yolanda in Wild Rose and told her about Deming's remarkable offer.

"I know what happened," she said, whispering. (Emil, she'd explained, was asleep.) "Becky Perlman called me and told me everything. I think if she had not been able to tell *someone* she might have exploded. It was *David's* doing."

"It *was?*" He'd filled her in on his aborted romance with David while driving her to Emil's motel.

"Of *course.* He told his father that if you lost your job, he would never speak to him again."

"Pretty melodramatic!"

"*All* lovers are melodramatic, Lionel."

"Even so, Magellan would never accept an ultimatum like that. Not in a million years."

"Of *course* not. So David, being equally pig-headed, picked up his suitcase and hitched a ride to Chicago with Wilma—and, Becky and I both agree, good riddance to *her.* Although I would love to know what she and David talked about for four-and-a-half hours!"

"God, it does all *fit,* doesn't it," Lionel said in awe. "When David left, Magellan must have realized that the only way he could get his son back was by demanding that Deming and Perlman take *me* back." He whistled in awe.

"Of *course,*" she said. "They would not have asked you to return out of the kindness of their hearts."

"I don't know," he said guiltily. "Maybe we're being too hard on them. Maybe the kindness of their hearts had a *little* to do with it."

She sighed. "This is where my experience at Mrs. Craven's comes in handy, Lionel. I have learned the hard way to be cynical about human nature. Even science fiction has not been able to cure me completely."

"There's only one problem with the story," he said. "Why would David go out on a limb for me? When the police showed up to haul Bob away, he wasn't anywhere to be found. I looked and looked for him, before finally grabbing you and slipping away in the midst of all the confusion."

"I cannot explain that, Lionel," she said sleepily. "You must ask David yourself."

For the rest of the night, Lionel stared at the phone, thinking it inevitable that David should call him.

And of course, he did, just as Lionel was turning down his covers. "I just got a hotel room in the Loop," he said. "Wilma dropped me off. You know, she's not so bad."

"All the same, I wouldn't mention that to your mother."

"Oh, it won't matter now. Wilma's through with Dad. Thanks to you. I owe you a lot, babe."

Lionel blushed. "Well, thanks. Uh—listen, I'm sorry I missed saying good-bye to you. After I wrote my resignation, I looked all over, but I couldn't find you anywhere." He emboldened himself and dared to ask the question. "Where were you?"

A small silence. "Hiding in the boathouse, actually," he said through nervous laughter, "puking my guts out at the thought of having to finally confront my dad about the whole issue. I mean, I couldn't exactly put it off any longer. You kind of took the choice out of my hands." He chuckled, then cleared his throat. "You probably think I'm some kind of pathetic coward. I'm sure you've been out to your parents for *years.*"

Lionel winced. "Let's talk about that some other time."

Another awkward silence.

Finally, David said, "Hey, can you come over here?"

Lionel instantly felt both deliriously happy and deliriously ill. This *must* be love. "I don't know," he said, clutching the nightstand while the room whirled around him. "I—I have to be at work early."

"You're still *working?*" said David jubilantly. "That's *great!* I heard you'd resigned!"

"They wouldn't accept my resignation."

"*God,* that makes me happy!" Another unwieldy pause.

"So, anyway," Lionel said to break the silence, finding it unendurable, "I was just about to hit the sack."

"*Well,*" David said, his voice low and throaty, "*my* sack is closer to the office than *yours* is."

Within minutes Lionel was happily stuffing some clothes into the suitcase he'd only just unpacked a few hours before. Then he turned off Spencer's light, locked up his apartment, raced down the stairs, and was heading for his car when he remembered how appallingly expensive parking was in the Loop. He decided to hail a cab instead.

As luck would have it, there was one already approaching. He flagged it down, hopped into its back seat, and said, "Thanks."

"Where to, pal?" asked the driver gruffly. He was, Lionel saw at once, a big, broad tower of a man, with a surly lower lip and deep-set, unreadable black eyes. He exuded *machismo* as freely as sweat. He was exactly the type of man who had for years intimidated the hell out of Lionel.

"The Inter-Continental Hotel," Lionel told him. "On Michigan."

The driver immediately pulled into traffic again, fearlessly ignoring the oncoming cars, which, perhaps sensing what he was, made way for him. Then he lit up a foul-smelling cigar and said, puffing, "The Inter-Continental on Michigan it is."

Lionel took a deep breath, summoning up all his courage; then he leaned over the driver's seat and said, "That's where my boyfriend's staying."